The Disappearance

of Georgiana Darcy

The Disappearance of Georgiana Darcy

A Pride and Prejudice Mystery

Regina Jeffers

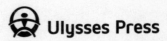 Ulysses Press

Published in the United States by
Ulysses Press
P.O. Box 3440
Berkeley, CA 94703
www.ulyssespress.com

ISBN: 978-1-61243-045-4
Library of Congress Catalog Number: 2012931427

Acquisitions Editor: Kelly Reed
Managing Editor: Claire Chun
Editor: Sunah Cherwin
Proofreader: Lauren Harrison
Production: Judith Metzener
Cover design: what!design @ whatweb.com
Cover photo: © Simon Podgorsek/istockphoto.com

Printed in Canada by Webcom

10 9 8 7 6 5 4 3 2 1

Distributed by Publishers Group West

Characters and Places Used in the Story

The Darcy Household (reside at Pemberley in Derbyshire)
  Fitzwilliam Darcy—the Master of Pemberley
  Elizabeth Bennet Darcy—the former Elizabeth Bennet;
    Darcy's wife
  Bennet Fitzwilliam George Darcy—the Pemberley heir;
    Darcy and Elizabeth's child

The Fitzwilliam Household in Scotland (reside at Alpin Hall, near Kirkconnel)
  Georgiana Darcy Fitzwilliam—Darcy's sister; is married
    to Major General Edward Fitzwilliam

The Matlock Household (reside at Matley Manor in Derbyshire)
  Major General Edward Fitzwilliam—the Darcys' cousin
    (formerly Colonel Fitzwilliam—received a promotion to
    Major General at the end of *Christmas at Pemberley*)
  Rowland Fitzwilliam—Viscount Lindale; Edward's older
    brother; resides at William's Wood in Lincolnshire
  Amelia Le Roy Fitzwilliam—Rowland's wife
  Martin Fitzwilliam—Edward's father; Earl of Matlock
  Nora Olivia Rowland Fitzwilliam—the Countess of
    Matlock; Edward's mother

The Bennet Household (reside at Longbourn in Hertfordshire)

Mr. Bennet—Elizabeth's father

Mrs. Marjory Bennet—Elizabeth's mother

Mary Bennet Grange—Elizabeth's middle sister

Robert Grange—a law apprentice in Uncle Philips's firm in Meryton; Mary's husband

Lydia Bennet Wickham—Elizabeth's youngest sister

Lieutenant George Wickham—Darcy's enemy; Lydia's husband

Catherine "Kitty" Bennet—the next to the youngest Bennet sister

The Bingley Household (reside at Marwood Manor in Cheshire)

Charles Bingley—one of Darcy's closest friends

Jane Bennet Bingley—the oldest of the Bennet sisters; married to Charles Bingley

Cassandra Elizabeth Bingley—one of the Bingley twins (approximately 18 months old at the beginning of this book)

Charles Geoffrey Bingley—one of the Bingley twins

Jackson Benjamin Bingley—another Bingley child (age 2 months at the beginning of this book)

The Joseph Household (reside in Northumberland)

Mary Joseph—Elizabeth's friend from *Christmas at Pemberley*

Matthew Joseph—a former clergyman from Stoke in Staffordshire

William Matthew Joseph—their child

Ruth Joseph—Matthew's sister; 17 years of age

Mr. Edgar Parnell—Mary Joseph's father; a powerful businessman from Northumberland

The Winkler Household (reside at Marsh Hall in Dorset)
Thorne Winkler—Kitty's intended; holds the living on Darcy's estate
Rose Winkler—Thorne's 22-year-old sister
Sir James Winkler—Thorne's father; a baronet from Dorset
Lady Camellia Winkler—Thorne's mother
Bramwell Winkler—Thorne's older brother; he'll inherit Sir James's title

The De Bourgh Household (reside at Rosings Park in Kent)
Captain Roman Southland—Edward's aide
Anne De Bourgh Southland—the Darcys' and Fitzwilliams' cousin
Lady Catherine De Bourgh—Matlock's sister; aunt to Darcy, Georgiana, Edward, and Rowland

The MacBethan Household (reside at Normanna Hall in Ayrshire)
Dolina MacBethan—the matriarch of the clan
Aulay MacBethan—the family's youngest son
Domhnall MacBethan—Laird of Normanna Hall; the eldest son; the family name is Wotherspoon
Lilias MacBethan Birrel—the lone sister of the MacBethan family; lives in Knovdart
Lord Carmichael—Lilias's husband; heir to a barony
Islav MacBethan—middle brother; lives in Crieff
Coll MacBethan—Dolina's deceased husband
Maighread MacBethan—Domhnall's first wife

Chapter 1

"YOU DECEIVE NO ONE, Mr. Darcy," his wife accused lovingly. "You worry for Georgiana's well-being."

"As do you, Mrs. Darcy," he countered as he lifted three-month-old Bennet from the boy's crib and supported the child in the crook of his arm. Whenever the child was near, Fitzwilliam Darcy felt compelled to hold his special miracle. He had his heir, at last, and he had spent countless hours just staring at Bennet Fitzwilliam George Darcy's perfect countenance. "You cannot tell me that my sister's lack of correspondence has not rubbed against your curiosity."

Elizabeth Darcy smiled knowingly. Her husband was a man of honor and of responsibility and of passion; yet, the contentment of holding his son always softened the man's usually grim expression. "Unlike you, my husband, my curiosity does not paint pictures of invading hordes. I simply wish to share in Georgiana's happiness. She and Edward deserve this time together, but I admit to being interested in how they have adjusted."

Darcy sat in a nearby chair and cradled the child. He peeled the blanket from the boy's face and traced a finger along his son's chin line. He thought he had recognized his father's features in his heir's countenance, but Elizabeth had insisted it was too early to know for certain. "I should not have allowed her to travel alone," he chastised himself.

"Georgiana is long removed from the schoolroom. Our sister is a married woman. She has a husband to protect her. It is no longer your obligation," she insisted.

Darcy's actions spoke of tenderness, but his words possessed a granite resolve. "Georgiana's safety is forever my obligation. Even Edward cannot usurp my charge."

Elizabeth moved swiftly to kneel before him. "No one can sever your bond to Georgiana, and I am not simple enough to suggest that you should ignore your responsibilities. Yet, I shall suggest that we permit Georgiana some latitude. Wellington's last push to rid the world of Napoleon robbed your sister of the wedding of which she had always dreamed. She and Edward married in a rush before your cousin returned to the battlefields. Georgiana merely wanted time to prepare the Fitzwilliam properties for Edward's return. She is still discovering what it means to be a wife."

"I, Georgiana Cassandra Anne Darcy, take thee, Edward Thomas David Fitzwilliam, to be my lawful wedded husband, to have and to hold from this day forward, for better for worse, for richer for poorer, in sickness and in health, to love, cherish, and to obey, till death us do part, according to God's holy ordinance; and thereto I give thee my troth."

His sister's eyes had sparked with the devotion she had offered their cousin. Darcy was slow to admit that Georgiana glowed when she looked upon Edward's weatherworn face. Despite the evidence of the couple's affection for each other, he had wanted to scream with the injustice of having to give his Georgiana to any man—even one as perfect as Major General Edward Fitzwilliam. She was his little sister—not old enough to be exchanging her wedding vows and leaving him behind.

"My mind knows the truth of your words, Mrs. Darcy, but my heart speaks a different language." He caressed Elizabeth's neck. "I have fretted over Georgiana for too many years to no longer give a care."

"She did send word of her safe arrival," Elizabeth insisted.

"That was some three weeks prior," he contested.

Elizabeth leaned in for a quick kiss and then stood. "Must I remind you that Edward was expected the week after our sister's arrival? Do you not suppose that the Fitzwilliams are enjoying their time together? Allowing themselves the opportunity to discover a new love, a new relationship," she argued. "Oh, my darling," Elizabeth coaxed, "you must realize that the Major General is coming to terms with the fact that the girl he protected as a child is now a woman."

She handed Darcy a wooden dowel that young Bennet preferred as a teething tool. "Christmastide thrust Edward and Georgiana together for a few days here and there, and just when they had thought to marry and create a life together, Bonaparte's escape from Elba ripped them apart. They had but three days as husband and wife before…" Elizabeth's voice trailed off. She blushed thoroughly before adding, "Do you not think that the Major General and Mrs. Fitzwilliam are claiming their shared life?"

Darcy's frown lines met. "That is not an image in which I care to indulge," he grumbled.

Elizabeth laughed lightly. "Cannot tolerate thoughts of Georgiana enjoying intimacies with her husband?" she taunted playfully.

Darcy rose to place the child on the blanket Elizabeth had arranged on the Persian carpet decorating her sitting room. "I will not entertain such thoughts," he warned. "Otherwise, I will be on horseback and riding toward Galloway to challenge my cousin to a duel."

Elizabeth good-naturedly swatted at him as he passed her. "I am just saying that your sister has other things on her mind."

"I will hear no more of such nonsense." His hand rested on the room's doorknob.

Elizabeth smiled mockingly. "Of course, my husband. To refuse to consider Georgiana's marital state is to make it nonexistent."

* * *

Elizabeth realized that her teasing had not allayed her husband's qualms. They had not assuaged her own, so she was not foolish enough to think that it might dissuade the formidable Fitzwilliam Darcy. She, too, had spent countless hours pacing the floor fretting over Georgiana's lack of correspondence. It was not typical of her husband's sister to ignore her family. Even with hopes of marital felicity for Georgiana, Elizabeth recognized how out of character this behavior had become. She had teased and taunted her husband to hide her own anxiety.

Could the major general have been delayed? Worse yet, could the couple have found little in common upon which to base their relationship? Elizabeth had recognized Georgiana's idyllic admiration for her cousin, and she now wondered if Darcy's sister had rushed into a "safe" marriage. "If that is so, Georgiana needs to discover a ground upon which to build a successful joining. I shall wait a few days more for word from Mrs. Fitzwilliam before I encourage my husband to seek an answer in Scotland."

* * *

Leaving his wife's taunts behind, Darcy closed her chamber door, but even through the thick wood he could hear her soft laughter. Elizabeth did not understand. In fact, in Darcy's opinion, no one understood. His relationship with Georgiana transcended the expected connection between brother and sister. Despite his father's last request, or possibly because of it, Darcy had devoted himself to Georgiana's happiness. He had given her the best education and the best life imaginable. Elizabeth could not comprehend the depth of his feelings for Georgiana—for the small child she was when they lost both of their parents; for the little girl who had clung to him in her grief.

His devotion to his sister had even played in his choosing of Elizabeth Bennet as his wife. Elizabeth's affectionate behavior to Jane Bennet while her sister lay ill at Netherfield had formed the basis of his early interest in the second Bennet sister. He had instantly recognized Elizabeth as the type of woman Georgiana needed in her life. His sister possessed an elegant softness, but she lacked a touch of impertinence, the very quality he had discovered in Elizabeth. And his opinions had proved correct. Under Elizabeth's tutelage, Georgiana had blossomed into the perfect balance of femininity. "I will wait one week more, and then I will to Scotland," he swore.

* * *

"I do not think this is wise," Darcy had told Georgiana when she had informed him of her desire to change the date for her joining with their cousin Edward. Darcy had hoped that the longer the couple waited, the more likely he would be proven correct: it was too early for Georgiana to wed. Many in the family thought he had delayed Georgiana's Presentation because of Elizabeth's confinements, but, in reality, he simply could not bear the idea of losing her to another man's attentions. When she finally traveled to London for her Come Out, he would pray that it would take several Seasons before Georgiana found a man she would accept. Then his cousin had returned from the American front, and everything had changed overnight. Now, she wished to speed up her eventual leaving off. The major general had arrived with other family members for the christening of Darcy's heir and had brought the news of his immediate deployment to the Belgian front. "Why can you not wait for Edward's return?" he had asked.

"What if our cousin does not return?" she had replied softly. "What if this is the last time we see him?"

Darcy's heart had lurched with dread at the possibility. Although he understood his sister's worst fear, his own need to protect her had prevailed. It was an unsubstantiated but compelling notion. "All the more reason to wait. I would not see you as a new bride in mourning."

"I would mourn our cousin even if the major general and I never marry. I would grieve for Edward for the rest of my natural days." She touched her handkerchief to her eyes. "Please, Fitzwilliam, you of all people must comprehend my agony. Do you not recall your anguish when you thought to never know Elizabeth as your wife? That is my situation with Edward. I have loved our cousin for well over two years, but unlike in your quest to earn Elizabeth's love, mine remained unspoken. I could not give voice to my desires. I have waited in the shadows, agonizing over Edward's safe return to the family. Now, I must snatch my moments with him while I may, before it is too late. Do you not see? If we do not marry before Edward leaves for the Continent, I might never know the happiness that you have found with Elizabeth. Would you deny me this, Fitzwilliam?"

Darcy slid his arm about her shoulders. He nudged her into his embrace, needing to once again hold the small girl whose world had rotated around him. Suddenly, he had realized his real objection to his sister's marriage: Georgiana's joining with Edward would mean that she would no longer require his advice. His protection. Especially with Edward as her husband. If Georgiana had chosen another, Darcy might continue to influence her, but their cousin was as a good a man as Darcy could ever hope for his sister. And, Edward had served as a joint guardian for Georgiana. Together, they had protected and guided her. And now Georgiana would prefer the major general to Darcy. He would no longer play a dominant role in his sister's life. Despite the real sense of loss choking him, Darcy's love required that he do the right thing. *This is not about my needs*, he had chastised himself. "When do you wish to marry?"

His sister clung to him, and Darcy tightened his grasp. "Thank you, Fitzwilliam," she murmured.

With his fingertips, Darcy lifted her chin and kissed the tip of her nose. "No more tears," he said softly. He had whisked her tears away with his thumbs. "What do you require of me? How may I provide what you desire?"

"The Matlocks and Rowland's family shall be at Pemberley tomorrow for Bennet's naming on Sunday. The Major General and I would marry on Monday. Mr. Winkler shall call the banns for the third time during Sunday's services. Edward rides for Hull on Thursday." A pink tint spread across her neck and face, before she added, "Might we have the dower house for privacy?"

Despite his best efforts, Darcy frowned. The idea of his sister enjoying the marriage bed bothered him more than he cared to admit. With a deep sigh, he said, "I will see to the details for the breakfast and the dower house. Send Edward to speak to Mr. Winkler." She had spontaneously hugged him, and Darcy fought the urge to keep her in his embrace forever. "Be off with you now," he said as he purposely released her. "There are many details and little time."

"You are the best brother a girl could ever have." She kissed his cheek before scurrying from the room.

Darcy had stood looking after her. "And you are the sun to my Earth," he whispered to her retreating form.

* * *

"Good morning, Father Bennet." Elizabeth's father had returned with them to Pemberley after Mary Bennet's marriage to Robert Grange in April. The couple had planned to marry in February, but Elizabeth's Uncle Philips had taken ill, and, as Mr. Grange apprenticed in Philips's law firm, the family had thought it best if they postponed the nuptials until Grange's benefactor had recovered. "You were up late."

"Good morning." The man greeted him with the smirk of amusement that Darcy had found so beguiling when Elizabeth had sported the emotion on her luscious lips. His wife certainly had inherited her father's mannerisms. "Too many books. So little time. If I could take up residence in Pemberley's library and never leave the room, I would die a well-satisfied man."

Darcy chuckled. "The Pemberley library has been the work of many generations. I cannot comprehend the neglect of a family library in such days as these." He accepted the tea the footman poured for him.

"I seriously doubt that you have ever neglected any detail of your life," Mr. Bennet observed wryly.

Darcy thought of his current neglect of Georgiana's happiness and flinched as if struck. No matter how often he told himself that there was no reason for concern, he could not shake the feeling there was something amiss. "And you, Sir, are you pleased with this propensity of mine?" Darcy roused himself to make polite conversation. "Keeping in mind, of course, that if it was not so, I would neglect your favorite daughter and the grandson bearing your name."

"Point taken, Mr. Darcy," Mr. Bennet said. They dined in silence for several minutes, each man immersed in the newspapers Darcy had delivered to Pemberley as part of the regular post. "Last evening, I was reading the biography of Earl David of Huntingdon and his rise to King David II of Scotland," Mr. Bennet mumbled as he turned the page. "Possible ancestors?"

Darcy folded over the page he read. "Probable connections rather than possible," he answered without looking up. They remained in companionable silence for several minutes before Darcy observed,

"Says here that a volcano erupted on an Indian Ocean island in April. Some scientists are concerned about the amount of ash in the air."

Mr. Bennet put down his paper. "Really? That could cause problems. I read a report which speculated on the devastation from an earlier New Zealand eruption. I cannot remember the exact source, but it spoke of widespread famine. At the time, it seemed a world away. Is it possible that the ash will reach England?"

"No one seems to know." Darcy's eyes scanned the article for the facts. "The Dutch have a colony near the eruption, but it has only been three months since the explosion. Still too early for accurate reports. Takes months to sail around the Horn. But we should be aware. Can Longbourn sustain potential losses?" he asked in honest response. Over the past few months, he and Mr. Bennet had spent countless hours discussing their estate management plans.

"I remain indeterminate. We have known some setbacks," Mr. Bennet said cautiously.

"Before Miss Bennet's wedding next week, we should develop contingencies."

Mr. Bennet nodded. "You are a God send. Should we include Mr. Bingley? He and Jane will arrive later today."

Darcy's eyes returned to the page. "That appears prudent. I will ask Bingley to join us."

"Unfortunately, we will be beset with houseguests tomorrow. My peace will come to an end. Mrs. Bennet will marry off the last of our daughters to Mr. Winkler next week, and I will become her focus. My world will collapse to a daily dose of frills and lace."

Darcy chuckled. "Maybe your future will not be so dire. You could always send the dear lady to visit with Mrs. Wickham, or to a European city..."

"Or a long stay at Pemberley," Mr. Bennet taunted.

Darcy barked out a laugh. "Although Mrs. Darcy would welcome her mother's company, how would that affect your sojourn in my estate's library?"

"Again, point taken, Mr. Darcy."

* * *

"And Mrs. Bingley has agreed to this?" Darcy asked one of his closest friends as they sat in Darcy's study.

Bingley shrugged. "It was Jane's idea. Once Kitty marries, Mrs. Bennet will be anxious to visit with her other daughters. My wife recalls all too well her mother's interference in our lives while we remained at Netherfield. With the twins and young Jackson, my dear Jane simply has no time to pacify Mother Bennet's nerves, and I will not have my wife exhausted by her propensity to please everyone. Therefore, I have pressed her to deny Mrs. Bennet's less than subtle hints for an invitation to Marwood Manor. Mrs. Bingley's solution was for us to take a holiday. If we are not in Cheshire, we cannot entertain the lady."

"Although I appreciate how Mother Bennet tended to Elizabeth's bruised soul when the Bennets visited Pemberley during Christmastide, I understand your reluctance at renewing the lady's tendency to intrude on your wife's easy nature. If our wives' mother was a bit more sensible, it would be less of an imposition." Darcy refilled Bingley's glass. "I suggested to Mr. Bennet that a journey to Carlisle might be advisable. It would seem that Mr. Wickham should share in entertaining Mother Bennet."

"God only knows that both of our wives have sent enough of their pin moneys to the couple to sustain Wickham's lifestyle," Bingley observed. "The man's debt accumulates."

Darcy did not mention how much he had settled on the Wickhams to guarantee their joining and to save the other Bennet sisters from ruin. "Then tell me of your destination." Darcy turned the subject.

"My father's brother held property between Dalry and Newton Stewart. It is a simple manor house, but more than adequate for the Bingleys of Cheshire. My uncle invested heavily in the Leswalt salt mines and in the Loch Ryan oyster beds."

Darcy sipped his drink. "If Mother Bennet insinuates herself into your lives, you could deposit the dear lady in Wickham's lap on your way north."

"There is that." Bingley's mouth curved upward.

"Will Mrs. Bingley be well enough to travel after her confinement?" Darcy inquired.

"Jane is quite hardy in that respect. And it is another sennight before we depart. We will see Kitty wed and then take our leave."

Darcy thought of the delicate-looking Jane Bingley and how she had easily delivered three children and of the robust appearance of his Elizabeth. Their joining had produced two stillbirths before finally knowing the happiness of holding Bennet in their arms. Appearances could be deceptive. "I wish you a safe journey, my friend."

* * *

"Charles and I would be pleased if you and Mr. Darcy joined us," Jane Bingley told Elizabeth as they shared tea in the Pemberley nursery.

Elizabeth smiled as the wet nurse cradled Bennet in an intimate caress. Elizabeth had liked Mrs. Prulock from the moment of their first meeting. "You plan to avoid the return of our mother's 'nerves,'" Elizabeth teased. "It is bad form, Jane."

Her sister blushed thoroughly. "Oh, do not say so, Lizzy. I have anguished over this decision. Do you truly believe it selfish of me to consider this holiday so soon after our sister's wedding?"

Elizabeth managed a smile. Her eldest sister held the kindest heart among the Bennet daughters. On more than one occasion, Elizabeth had envied her sister's goodness. It was Jane who had believed that George Wickham had married Lydia because he had held "a real regard for her." Jane had declared, "We must endeavor to forget all that has passed on either side. I hope and trust they will yet be happy. His consenting to marry her is a proof, I will believe, that he is come to a right way of thinking. Their mutual affection will steady them; and I flatter myself they will settle so quietly, and live in so rational a manner, as may in time make their past imprudence forgotten."

Of course, Jane had erred completely. The Wickhams still held in spite of everything, the hope that Darcy might yet be prevailed upon to make Mr. Wickham's fortune. It had been evident to Elizabeth, from the beginning, that such an income as Lydia and her husband possessed, under the direction of two persons so extravagant in their wants, and heedless of their future, must be very insufficient to their support. Whenever the Wickhams changed their quarters, either Jane or herself were applied to for some little assistance toward discharging the couple's bills.

"Dearest Jane," Elizabeth assured, "you have no guilt to own for our mother's care. Foremost, you have responsibilities to Mr. Bingley and your children. You spent a twelvemonth at Netherfield before removing to Marwood Manor. Our mother's disposition and that of all our Meryton relations affected even Mr. Bingley's amiable nature. Our husbands own our first loyalties." Elizabeth paused to gather her thoughts. "I no longer resent our mother's manipulations. She did what she could to place her daughters in the way of eligible young men, and despite the personal mortifications I experienced at the time, I understand her motivations. When Papa passes, Longbourn reverts to Mr. Collins's care. Our mother has done her best to see to our futures."

Jane nodded her agreement. "Other than Lydia's joining, our family has exceeded expectations."

Elizabeth smiled knowingly. "That does not mean, however, that any of us would be comfortable entertaining our mother on a permanent basis. Our parents are set in their ways. There cannot be two mistresses of the same house. Therefore, I have asked Mr. Darcy to invest in a small cottage close to Meryton, which my husband will make available to Mama upon our father's passing. She might keep Mr. and Mrs. Hill if she likes."

"That is an excellent idea. I shall speak to Charles about setting aside an annual sum for our mother's expenses. If nothing else, our mother knows how to practice economy. She has shown a real knack for entertaining with limited funds. A place of her own to live out her days with dignity and not having to depend upon Mr. Collins for her support is a true act of generosity. It is a great kindness that Mr. Darcy offers."

Elizabeth placed her teacup on a low table. "You should enjoy your time in the Scottish countryside without thought to our mother's plight. Instead, concentrate on recovering from Jackson's delivery. You, dear sister, deserve time with your family. Mayhap, we anticipate only the worst and will receive the best. I suspect it is Papa's turn to experience our mother's ministrations," Elizabeth said teasingly. "Mama is likely to badger him into taking a place in London."

Jane's eyes widened in mock horror. "Oh, poor Papa. Our mother shall invade his study and inundate his days and nights with the latest gossip!"

"Our father has neglected his wife for too long," Elizabeth observed. "But we shall face that possibility when it occurs. For now, I want to hold Cassandra and young Charles and consider all the milestones Bennet has yet to achieve."

* * *

Edward Fitzwilliam stared out over the English Channel. Finally having received his orders yesterday, he had boarded the ship some five hours earlier. Actually, he should have departed the Continent a fortnight prior, but he had refused to leave his duties until he was assured of Captain Roman Southland's recovery. His aide had suffered a severe wound to his left forearm, one that had resulted in the captain losing part of his arm.

"At least, Roman will never have to face the battlefield again," Edward told the rolling waves. Southland had sustained his injury when he had stepped between Edward and an advancing French cavalryman. Bonaparte's devotee had brought his sword down with a vengeance and had ripped away part of Southland's muscle and bone.

"How do I express my gratitude?" he had told the man as he had sat beside Southland's bed in a makeshift hospital. "You have saved my life on two different continents."

The captain rolled his eyes upward to stare at the draped bedding. "I promised Mrs. Fitzwilliam that I would see you safely returned to Derbyshire."

"And I promised my cousin Anne the same for you to Kent." Men did not speak of their fears, but Edward recognized his aide's anxiety. "Would you care to tell me what bothers you?" he said quietly.

A long silence followed before the captain's eyes caught his in a steady stare. "Will Anne think she has received the short end of our agreement? I know nothing of the aristocracy. Now, I am less than a man."

Edward swallowed hard. If not for Southland, he could have been maimed worse than his aide. Or he could be among the thousands lying in shallow graves surrounding a Belgian forest. Keeping a vigil at Southland's beside, he had wondered if Georgiana would turn from him if he had suffered the captain's injury. Somehow, he did not think it possible. His Georgiana, on first glance, appeared fragile and delicate, but he had learned otherwise. She possessed a strong will and a granite resolve that resembled her brother's. She would welcome him home with open arms. And so would Anne welcome the captain.

Edward leaned forward to press his point. "You, Sir, are more of a man—even with one arm—than a pack of foppish toffs. You are what my cousin needs. Anne requires a man who is not afraid of adversity; a man who has an honest regard for her well-being; a man who will not judge her. She carries your child, Roman. You will be a father, and your children will not care that you lost your left hand in this crazy war. They will care only that you scoop them up with your right and hold them tightly on your lap. You have given Anne a reason for hope. She has a husband and a child on the way and a better understanding with her mother. You have given Mrs. Southland a family—something she has not known since her childhood under Sir Lewis's care."

With scarcely any private fortune of which to speak, Southland had wooed a vulnerable Anne De Bourgh, but not out of malice. The captain had envisioned a connection to the De Bourgh family long before the couple had struck up an acquaintance during last December's festive days, the circles in which they moved so distinct that one would think their joining an impossibility. In fact, Edward had at one time discouraged Southland's attentions. And although Anne possessed a temper remarkably easy and indolent, upon meeting Southland, his cousin had taken it upon herself to marry, in the common phrase, to disoblige her family by fixing on a Lieutenant of the Cavalry, without education, fortune, or connections;

she did it very thoroughly by being purposely caught in a compromising kiss by her mother, Lady Catherine De Bourgh, the family's paragon of propriety. Within weeks, Edward's once-spinster cousin had become a happily married woman. Now with child, Anne had achieved her dreams when she married Captain Roman Southland.

"Do you honestly believe so, Sir? Anne is your family; you know her better than I. If you want me to bear you a debt of gratitude, tell me truly how Anne will react to my injury."

"I speak plainly, Roman. Anne has her faults, but the kindness of her heart is not among them. My cousin will not disappoint you. She will welcome you as the hero that you are."

Again a long silence stretched between them. Finally, Southland nodded his agreement. "Then I will return to Rosings Park and make my wife thankful she has chosen me."

Edward's easy smile was meant to remove any of his aide's remaining doubts. "Anne is fortunate to have such a man in her life. When next I see her, I will sing your praises." Edward leaned closer to whisper. "Go home, Roman. Take your wife to bed and show her the height of your regard. Make lots of babies and enjoy your life."

Southland's eyes danced with mischief. "And you, too, Sir. You have a beautiful wife. Join Mrs. Fitzwilliam in Derbyshire and make a few babies of your own."

"I am not certain that Mrs. Fitzwilliam is in Derbyshire. A letter found me yesterday. My wife planned to open the Fitzwilliam property outside of Galloway. We have never had our wedding trip, after all. When I received my orders, Georgiana insisted on our advancing the nuptials. We wed on Monday, and I departed on Thursday. I have known my wife less than two and seventy hours." Edward winked at the man. "When I reach England, I will first determine whether Mrs. Fitzwilliam is in Derbyshire or Scotland. Then I will seek her out immediately. I am ready to know my wife fully. I plan to have her in my bed for at least a fortnight."

Southland chuckled. "I have never heard you sound happier, Sir. More satisfied than I could imagine."

Edward looked off as if to see something his aide could not. "A dozen years, Southland. That is what I have spent in service to my country. It is all I have known. Now, I will embark on a new life, that of a country gentleman, and Georgiana will wash away the dirt and the blood buried in my soul."

"If anyone can, Sir, it is Mrs. Fitzwilliam."

* * *

"Should we be sendin' notice to the lady's family in Derbyshire?" the caretaker asked.

"Donnae see where we be havin' another choice." The house-keeper covered the furniture in the main parlor with dustsheets. "They'll not be happy, but I be tellin' the gel repeatedly that she cudnae be traipsin' about the countryside alone."

The man lifted the chair and carried it across the room to place it with the others. "Then ye'll see to it today?"

"I will tell the lady's husband that his bride be dead."

Chapter 2

"PARDON ME, MRS. DARCY." The Pemberley butler had interrupted Elizabeth and Jane's afternoon with the latest fashion plates. "There is a gentleman wishing to speak to Mr. Darcy."

Elizabeth looked up with a frown. She and Jane had spent the morning considering ways to adapt the too-frilly gown Mrs. Bennet had chosen for Kitty's joining to a more stylish affair. Poor Kitty had pleaded with them to intercede, and they had agreed upon seeing Kitty's rendering of the "odious" garment. "Mr. Darcy and Mr. Bingley shall not return for, at least, an hour." She noted the servant's unease. "Should I speak to the gentleman while he waits for Mr. Darcy?"

The butler's face relayed his approval. "I explained to the gentleman that Mr. Darcy was not available. He then asked for you, Ma'am."

Elizabeth appreciated the protective nature of Darcy's servants. "Does the gentleman have a name, Mr. Nathan?"

"A Mr. Matthew Joseph, Ma'am."

Elizabeth was out of her seat immediately. "Matthew Joseph? Conduct the gentleman to the main drawing room, Mr. Nathan. I shall be there in a brief moment."

"Yes, Ma'am."

"Matthew Joseph? The man whose child you delivered?" Her sister stared eagerly at Elizabeth.

Elizabeth turned to the door. "Come, Jane. I wish to extend your acquaintance to Mr. Joseph." Elizabeth raced through Pemberley's halls to enter the drawing room in a rush. "Matthew," she called as she extended her hands to him and ignored the obligatory curtsy. "Please tell me your visit does not bring ill news."

The young man smiled easily. "Nothing ill, Mrs. Darcy." He caught her hands and brought one of them to his lips. "Mary and young William thrive." He took a leisurely look at her. "You appear well, Mrs. Darcy. Such news will please Mrs. Joseph."

Elizabeth looked up to see Jane's entrance. "We have much of which to speak, but, first, permit me to make you known to my eldest sister. Jane, may I present my dear friend, Mr. Joseph. Matthew, my sister, Mrs. Bingley."

"It is my honor, Ma'am." Joseph bowed in greeting. "Mrs. Darcy has spoken so kindly of you that I must claim a prior acquaintance."

Jane smiled easily. "My sister has a tendency to exaggerate."

Elizabeth snorted. Her sister's "serious innocence" always brought a touch of laughter. "Just as I told you, Mr. Joseph. Mrs. Bingley speaks the truth even if she destroys my ego in the same breath." She motioned him toward a cluster of chairs. "Come join us. I would hear of young William and of Mary." Elizabeth nodded to the butler. "Mr. Nathan, please see to refreshments, and inform Mr. Darcy of Mr. Joseph's visit upon my husband's return."

The butler made an efficient exit. When they were settled, Elizabeth asked, "What brings you to Derbyshire, Matthew?"

"Mary and I are removing to Newcastle. My mother's illness tarried longer than expected, and I have given up my living in Stoke to accept a position in Mr. Parnell's firm."

Elizabeth covered her surprise. "Oh, Matthew, I am grieved to hear it. You took such pride in your calling."

The man acknowledged her words with a simple nod of his head. "My first calling is to my family. Besides Mary and William, I have two sisters who require my guidance."

"I suspect that our dear Mary has declared that God holds a different plan for you," Elizabeth said.

Joseph sighed deeply. "You understand my wife's nature: forever the romantic, completely the optimist. Personally, I cannot imagine how my writing shipping orders will impact people's lives, but Mrs. Joseph continues to say that God provides us with what we need when we need it."

"I suppose it might be what one shipped, Mr. Joseph," Jane observed. "I imagine the world could live without Oriental silks or Egyptian artifacts, but shipments of corn or coal changes how we live. Your influence may be stronger than you believe."

Joseph reluctantly agreed. "Your sister, Mrs. Darcy, should be related to my Mary. They are cut from the same cloth."

Her reply brought a ready smile to Elizabeth's face. "It is quite likely, Mr. Joseph. In hindsight, I see my immediate affinity for Mrs. Joseph's company as a desire for Mrs. Bingley's closeness."

Mr. Nathan returned with the refreshments. Joseph accepted the tea before saying, "Pemberley is certainly everything I have heard it to be." His eyes took in the room's grandeur. "Mr. Darcy has a great legacy to leave his son."

"My husband works tirelessly to secure Bennet's future," Elizabeth observed.

Joseph cleared his throat. "I have no doubt of Mr. Darcy's business aplomb. But speaking of the boy, I hope you will permit me the pleasure of young Bennet's acquaintance. If I report to Mary that I was at Pemberley and did not see Mr. Darcy's son, my wife will take me to task."

Jane gave a nod and then rose. "I shall bring Bennet down, Lizzy. Enjoy Mr. Joseph's company."

"Thank you, Jane." Elizabeth motioned a maid to the room before returning her attentions to the man. She said brightly, "I give you full reign to brag on young William. I wish to know it all."

Joseph laughed lightly. "You mistake me for Mrs. Joseph," he teased but immediately began a litany of his son's accomplishments.

"That is delightful," Elizabeth said. "I feared William would suffer from his early appearance in the world."

"Mary says he is still a bit behind for children his age, but my son has steadily gained weight and appears quite hardy."

Cradling the cup in her hands, Elizabeth sipped her tea. "And Mary is truly well?"

"She is. My wife oversees the packing. Her father has arranged the transportation of our property to my parents' home."

"Mary is in Staffordshire? Why did you not say so before? She must stop at Pemberley on her return to Newcastle. My family arrives tomorrow for my sister Kitty's wedding, and I would be so pleased to have you and Mary join us. Please permit me to send a Pemberley footman to escort her and William to Derbyshire."

Joseph informed her, "My sister Ruth travels with Mary."

"That is of no consequence. There is more than enough room at Pemberley to house your sister along with Mary and William," she assured.

Joseph smiled widely. "It would please Mrs. Joseph to have your company, Mrs. Darcy, and I do have business to conduct in Father Parnell's name with your husband."

"Who has business with me?" Darcy called as he strode into the room, his hand outstretched to Joseph. His smile said how pleased he was to entertain Matthew Joseph under Pemberley's roof.

Joseph scrambled to his feet to accept Darcy's hand. "Mr. Darcy, I apologize for not sending notice of my visit."

Darcy slipped his arm about Elizabeth's waist. "As I am certain that your appearance has brightened Mrs. Darcy's day, I hold no objection." Darcy gestured to the chairs. "Please let us sit."

"Mr. Joseph has joined Mr. Parnell's firm," Elizabeth shared. She held Darcy's gaze for but an elongated second, but their closeness allowed them to communicate without words and unmasked.

Darcy nodded his understanding. "Parnell informed me of his desire for you to join him. However, I was unaware of your acceptance."

"Mary desired that William know his grandfather, and my sisters required my assistance."

Darcy said nothing. He recognized Joseph's sense of honor. Although the man preferred to follow God's orders, Joseph would abandon his living to meet his family obligations. Darcy respected such devotion.

"I have asked Mr. Joseph to join us for several days, and I would seek your permission to send someone to escort Mary and Mr. Joseph's sister to Pemberley. Mrs. Joseph arranges their removal to Northumberland."

"Again, I have no objection. Send Jasper. He is familiar with Mrs. Joseph."

"Thank you, Fitzwilliam," she said softly.

"I do have business to discuss, Mr. Darcy. Father Parnell has entrusted me with a venture in which he would have your involvement."

Darcy's eyebrow rose in curiosity. "Really? I had thought my business with Parnell finished with our last shipment out of Hull."

"It is a new rail opportunity," Joseph shared.

Darcy noted Jane's entrance as his wife said, "Before you gentlemen sequester yourselves in Mr. Darcy's study, Mrs. Bingley has returned with Bennet. I expect you to rain praise upon the Pemberley heir's head, Mr. Joseph," she teased. Darcy sat straighter to accept his bundled son from Jane Bingley. The boy stretched and yawned as Darcy settled the child on his lap. "As one may observe, Mr. Darcy has a calming effect on Bennet's disposition." Elizabeth smiled broadly at him. "However, my husband must often compete with my father for the privilege of reading to the boy in the evening."

Joseph sported a wry smile. "If I recall, you told me you find peace in the sound of your husband's voice, Mrs. Darcy."

"So I do," she agreed.

Darcy turned the sleepy child so Mr. Joseph might admire the boy's countenance. "What color are his eyes?" Joseph asked as he lightly touched the boy's cheek with his fingertip.

"At the moment, they are still blue, but Mr. Darcy believes they shall be green," Elizabeth said softly.

Darcy's smile turned up the corners of his mouth. "More hazel than emerald. Not as pronounced a green as Mrs. Darcy's."

Joseph sat back in the chair. "Your son favors the Darcys in his facial features," the man observed. Silence filled the room for several moments as each adult admired the child's countenance. "Would you object to my offering a prayer for Bennet's well-being?" Joseph said quietly.

Elizabeth quickly said, "Certainly not."

"Eternal God," Joseph began, "to our children giveth thou mercy. Protect them from harm. Nourish their bodies. Allow them to see the strength of your hand. Grant them the truth of your words. Brighten their hearts that they may ever reflect your glory. In Jesus Christ, our Lord. Amen."

"Amen," Darcy and Elizabeth repeated together.

"Thank you, Mr. Joseph," Darcy said solemnly.

Elizabeth rose and took the child from Darcy's arms. "I shall leave you gentlemen to your business. If you will give Mr. Darcy the directions, I shall send Jasper on his way to Staffordshire." She gave both men a brief curtsy. "I shall see you at supper. I am most anxious for you to become acquainted with my father and with Mr. Bingley."

* * *

"Parnell wishes to finance the Duke of Portland's public venture?" Darcy asked as he surveyed the maps resting on a broad table near a bank of windows. "Where is Portland in these negotiations?" he continued.

"An Act of Parliament authorized the railway in 1808. It began as a fifteen-kilometer, double-track gauge, horse-drawn wagon way. It uses cast-iron plate rails with an inner flange."

"And this is the line between Kilmarnock and Troon Harbor?" With his finger, Darcy traced the route on the map.

Joseph pointed to key cities on the adjoining drawings. "Father Parnell believes we could easily connect Glasgow to Carlisle or even all the way to London."

Darcy let out a low whistle. "It would change the face of both Scotland and England, but I do not imagine it would come easily. It would take major innovations. My previous knowledge of Portland's lines says that the Duke used it purely for carrying coal from the Kilmarnock pits to Troon Harbor on the Ayrshire coast." Darcy could not remove his eyes from the geographic renderings. "What does Parnell hope to accomplish with this venture?"

"Mary's father has suggested that if the line could strictly limit the number of trader wagons it permitted to use the line, we could control the flow of supplies."

Darcy eyed Joseph carefully. The man grimaced when he explained the manipulations of his wife's father. Joseph's honest nature made him question the plan. "Parnell visualizes a monopoly?" Darcy asked cautiously. "I would have no qualms in blocking our competitors. If I have financed the line's development, I should reap the rewards. However, if Parnell plans to limit supplies to drive up prices, I will not participate. I refuse to create a legacy for my heirs earned with my cottagers' broken backs."

Joseph expelled a deep sigh. "Thank you, Mr. Darcy. You have given a voice to my qualms. I admire Edgar Parnell for his business sense, and I appreciate his creating a position for me in the firm he built from the floor up, but I question my ability to follow through on Father Parnell's vision."

Darcy purposely refused to look at Joseph. "Who says you must parrot Parnell's words? It has been my experience that people respond best to those who treat them with dignity and respect. Instead of fighting Parnell or begrudgingly executing the man's orders, why do you not take Parnell's tasks and make them your own? Likely, Mary will inherit her father's many business establishments, which means they will eventually fall to you. You must decide what face those businesses will present to the public. You can change small things, giving your name to many of the negotiations. Changing one element affects other parts of the contract."

After a long silence, Joseph said softly, "You have given me much to consider, Mr. Darcy. I will pray for guidance."

Darcy smiled knowingly; yet, he was not fooled. Contrary to first impressions, Mr. Joseph possessed an iron resolve. Joseph and Parnell were likely to butt heads often. "Just do not forget that God often answers prayers without fanfare or divine intervention. Sometimes, guidance presents itself in an unexpected manner." Darcy gestured to the drawings. "So, what role does Parnell expect me to play in this venture? I mean, besides the financial obligations."

Joseph set his shoulders to the task of answering. "Although this transaction is all speculation at the moment, Father Parnell hopes to anticipate the direction the line will take and to develop businesses to supply the rail's completion, as well as to sustain its growth."

Darcy's mouth set in a firm line. "This is not something I would take lightly. I need time to examine the documents you have brought to my attention. Plus, I would seek the counsel of my friend, Mr. Bingley. This could be a moment of great cleverness or of folly. I will not gamble away Bennet's heritage. Speculation is not a game I practice."

* * *

"I am not certain that I approve, Fitzwilliam." Elizabeth placed her long tresses in a soft plait.

"Mr. Bingley and I have discussed it. If I choose to examine the area personally, it should be now before the weather changes. Summer does not tarry in Scotland's southern uplands."

"But you would be from Pemberley for weeks," she protested.

Darcy came to sit behind her. They often held conversations in this manner: she at her dressing table, he sitting on the trunk at the end of her bed, each speaking to the other's reflection in her dressing mirror. "I would not wish to be parted from you or from Bennet for more than a few minutes, let alone days or weeks, but this is a prime investment, one which could guarantee Bennet's financial security. It would be foolish to ignore the opportunity; yet, before I invest heavily in this scheme, I wish to have answers to all my questions. My initial dealings with Parnell tell me the man can be ruthless in business matters, and I will not finance such schemes. However, I will not turn my back on an excellent opportunity."

Elizabeth looked more closely at him. "What does Mr. Joseph say?"

They sat in silence for a few moments. Finally he said, "I should have known that you would recognize the source of my reservations. Joseph and his wife's father have different approaches."

"I see," Elizabeth said slowly. "Mr. Joseph possesses some questions of his own."

"None that he has voiced," Darcy said. "However, I have listened carefully to what Mr. Joseph does not say. I have also asked Bingley to hear the man's proposal, and Charles agrees: Joseph is not completely confident in this transaction."

Elizabeth came to sit beside him. "Does Mr. Joseph fear that Mr. Parnell offers a false face, or is Matthew's objection his dislike for anything but his call to orders?"

"You have aptly summarized the situation. Matthew Joseph has admitted that he often finds Parnell's business maneuverings less than ethical. Is that Joseph's self-righteous pride speaking? We experienced the man's implacable nature first hand when we sought to bring comfort to Mrs. Joseph at Prestwick's Portal. Business dealings are never clearly black or white, and Joseph's character does not easily recognize that shades of gray are sometimes necessary." He caught Elizabeth's hand in his and brought the back of it to his lips. "Exclusive control of the rail line is possible, but does that mean that the area will suffer? Parnell and his business partners could control the price of everything shipped on the line, as well as in and out of the Scottish ports."

Elizabeth snuggled closer. "The ramifications are that huge? I had not suspected it possible."

"I am honored that Parnell has sought me out as a partner in this endeavor; yet, my caution stands tall."

Elizabeth sighed deeply. "Then it is best that you investigate. At least, you may stay with the Bingleys while away from home."

"I have spoken to Bingley about his investing in the venture as well. Your sister's husband is eager to learn more of what is planned." He stood to lead her to their shared bed. Darcy rarely slept in his own chambers. He had spent a few lonely nights there when Elizabeth first delivered Bennet, but he finally made a pallet on the floor beside her bed because he could not bear their separation. Her steady breathing as she slept brought him an unidentifiable satisfaction. "I suppose that means that you have no desire to join the Bingleys."

Elizabeth caressed his jaw line. "I would enjoy our time together, and you are aware that I shall not accept our parting with any degree of contentment. Yet, it is not likely that our houseguests will depart before you. I cannot abandon my family to Pemberley while I trail after my husband, even if I am tempted to do so." She went on tiptoes to brush her lips over his. "You will need to leave after Kitty and Mr. Winkler's ceremony."

"I was considering the day following the nuptials." He untied her wrapper's closure and slipped the silky garment from her shoulders.

"I suppose there is no alternative," she observed as she slid her arms about Darcy's waist and pulled herself closer. "However, I shall miss your warmth terribly. How shall I sleep without you, Fitzwilliam?"

Darcy kissed her temple and then allowed his lips to slide slowly across her cheek and down her neck. "I cannot fathom the emptiness," he murmured.

"At least, for the cost of a day's ride to Alpin Hall, you may visit with Georgiana and assuage your fears." She gasped as his lips sought the soft spot at the base of her neck.

"Perhaps we could finish this conversation in the morning, Elizabeth." His breathing had become shallow, and his voice was low and sensual.

She placed her hands on either side of his face. Lifting his chin so she could reach his lips, she pressed her mouth to his.

As always, his wife's passion was Darcy's undoing. He had long ago accepted his inability to resist her. When she walked into a room, Darcy had to be by her side. She was his true north. His hands tugged at the hem of her gown as his tongue teased over hers—a challenge to meet his desires.

Meanwhile, Elizabeth's fingers worked at the loose knot of his belted robe. "Fitzwilliam," she groaned when he deepened the kiss.

Darcy swept her into his arms and dropped her onto the bed. His need to feel skin upon skin controlled him. He divested himself of his clothing and then removed Elizabeth's. His mouth returned to hers. "I never want to leave you," he whispered hoarsely. "You are the breath of my life."

Arching to him, Elizabeth responded to his touch. "A clarion bell," she said as her hand slid down his back. "I cannot resist your call."

"I love you, Lizzy. More than life. You and Bennet are my world."

* * *

Elizabeth looked up to see Mr. Winkler strolling along Pemberley's entrance lane. She had brought Bennet out for some air. She held her young son in her lap and playfully teased the child with a colorful rattle. Bennet cooed and actually smiled at her. Elizabeth's heart sighed in contentment. "Mr. Winkler," she called, regretting having to share this moment with any other soul besides the boy. "Have your parents arrived safely, Sir?"

The man reached where she sat comfortably in the shade. "They have, Mrs. Darcy." He bowed politely. "I left them my gig for their use and begged a ride with Mr. Foxmour. He came to fetch Mavis, Nell, and Tavia from the school."

"How go the studies?" she asked, looking up into the sun and shadowing her eyes with her cupped hand.

Winkler leaned over to play with Bennet. "We have eight to ten students each day. Not always the same children, but I am pleased with our progress."

"You are a bit early," she teased good-naturedly. "My Hertfordshire family has not yet arrived."

Winkler blushed. "I hope my presence is not an encumbrance." He straightened as Elizabeth gathered the child to her and stood.

"Of course not." She laughed lightly. "I fear that Mr. Darcy, Mr. Bingley, and Mr. Joseph are sequestered in my husband's study and are dissecting some detestable business matter; however, Mrs. Bingley and my father are in the library. I am certain they shall welcome your company." She started toward the house. "Come along. We can wait for Kitty's return together."

In silence, they strolled leisurely across the carefully groomed path. Finally, Winkler said, "I am too transparent."

"Absolutely not," she declared. "You are simply a man in love. As the object of your affection is my younger sister, I am delighted by the news."

Winkler confessed, "I have missed Miss Bennet desperately."

As she shifted the child in her arms, Elizabeth smiled up at the man. "I had not considered that Kitty was the last of us to be called 'Miss Bennet.' As Jane and I shared our wedding date, I was only Miss Bennet for a few brief moments. And Lydia married before Jane and never knew that title. Mary has abdicated it. Now it is Kitty's."

"Only until Monday," Winkler observed.

"Yes. Yes. Then our Kitty shall be the new Mrs. Winker," she taunted. "Shall you be satisfied when that occurs?"

Winkler sighed deeply. "I have waited for our joining for nearly two years. I feel quite foolish when I consider how long I have planned to claim Miss Catherine."

"We are all fools in love."

* * *

Within the hour, the Bennet traveling coach came to rest in the circle before Pemberley. The Darcy household waited on the entrance steps to greet the travelers. "Although they have only been away since Twelfth Night, I am pleased to see my family again," Elizabeth whispered as Darcy placed her hand on his arm.

"Let us see if you have the same opinion by this time next week," he murmured. "Your dear family will all want to hold Bennet. Your private time with our son has just disappeared."

Elizabeth feigned shock in this revelation. "Then you must send them all away immediately, Mr. Darcy," she exclaimed. "I refuse to share my child with anyone but his father."

Darcy caught her free hand to his side. "I knew you to be a sensible creature, my dear." His smile widened.

"Too late," Elizabeth shuttered her words. "The footman has let down the step."

"Do not say I did not warn you," he murmured into her hair.

"Mrs. Bennet." Elizabeth's father supported his wife's step on the coach's ladder. "I am pleased you have arrived safely."

"Thank you, Mr. Bennet. It is good to be at Pemberley again. When I was last in Derbyshire, the grounds were covered in ice and snow. It is pleasant to see it at its best."

"Later, we will tour Mr. Darcy's gardens, if you did not find your journey too exhausting."

"That would be enjoyable." The woman turned to her waiting family. "Ah, Jane," she gushed. "I have so longed to see Jackson." She held her oldest close. "And Mr. Bingley," she said in welcome. "It is delightful to see you, Sir."

"You look well, Mother Bennet." Bingley embraced the woman.

As if overheated, she fanned her face with her handkerchief. "I shall be complete, Mr. Bingley, when our Kitty becomes Mrs. Winkler. A mother's task is to see to her daughters' futures."

"And you have excelled in your endeavors," Bingley said good-naturedly.

"Mama." Elizabeth had waited patiently. She and her mother had rarely found congress, but they had spent an enjoyable Christmas-tide together, and this had given Elizabeth hope that now that she too was a mother, they would develop a deeper understanding.

"Ah, Lizzy. Your father writes often of your Bennet." Elizabeth received a lukewarm hug, very different from the one Jane had experienced only moments earlier, and over her mother's shoulder, Elizabeth saw the corners of Darcy's mouth dip downward.

She maneuvered her mother in Mr. Darcy's direction; her husband bowed over her mother's hand. "I am pleased by your return to Pemberley, Mrs. Bennet." He handed her off to Bingley. "I am certain that Mr. Bingley will show you into the drawing room. Mr. Nathan has arranged for refreshments." Mrs. Bennet curtsied and then allowed Bingley to escort her to the house. "No words of thanks," he grumbled under his breath.

"My mother is likely exhausted from the details of first Mary's, and now Kitty's wedding," Elizabeth said beside him.

"Mrs. Bennet found enough energy to greet your sister with enthusiasm," Darcy countered. "I will not have you snubbed, Lizzy, even by your mother."

Elizabeth shrugged in exasperation. "I shall have Papa speak to her." Then with a renewed smile, she greeted her sisters.

"Mary." She caught the girl in a hearty embrace. "Permit me to look upon you. How does married life treat you?"

"Mr. Grange is quite kind," Mary said softly.

"I am pleased to hear it."

Darcy shook the young lawyer's hand. "Pemberley welcomes you, Mr. Grange."

"Mrs. Grange and I thank you for receiving us." He placed Mary on his arm and followed Jane Bingley into the main foyer.

Elizabeth turned to see Winkler lifting Kitty to the ground. His hands rested on her sister's waist for a few extra seconds, and their gaze intensified. Elizabeth diverted her eyes and shared a knowing smile with Darcy.

"Miss Bennet, I have waited for this moment for weeks," Winkler rasped.

Kitty blushed, but she managed to say, "As have I, Mr. Winkler."

Darcy cleared his throat. "Then may we take this homecoming inside?"

Winkler laughed self-consciously. "Of course, Mr. Darcy."

Kitty caught Elizabeth about the waist as they walked toward the open door. "Has Georgiana already departed for Scotland?"

"I am afraid so. Mrs. Fitzwilliam regretted missing your wedding, but the Major General was due a fortnight ago. Georgiana wanted the house open and waiting for her husband. She left a personal note and a wedding gift in your room."

"I appreciate both, but I shall grieve with Mrs. Fitzwilliam's absence," Kitty declared.

"As shall we all," Elizabeth assured.

Chapter 3

MY DEAREST GEORGIANA,

I cannot tell you how much I ache to hold you in my arms. I did not think it possible to give myself over so completely to anyone, but with you, I have been made whole.

I have arrived in Dover. I had hoped to take port somewhere north of Hull so I might speed my return to you, but as my departure from the Continent was delayed, I accepted what passage I could find to once more know English soil. As I intend to take half pay and to devote my life to loving my incredible new bride, my superiors assure me that it will take a few days to process my paperwork. Therefore, I will tarry in Kent until I am released from my immediate duties.

Meanwhile, I will call on our aunt at Rosings Park. Captain Southland has suffered a grievous injury in our last days of fighting Napoleon's forces. In fact, it is the gentleman's recovery which has delayed my return. The good captain has lost part of his arm, and although he will mend, I think it best if I speak to Anne prior to Southland's return to Rosings. I will preface the man's needs. Our cousin's reaction to her husband's injury could set the tone for their marriage, and I wish to counsel her regarding Southland's fear of her rejection. These matters will delay my departure for the North until, at soonest, Monday.

I pray this letter reaches you before your departure for the Fitzwilliam estate. I would not wish you to be alone in Scotland for many days. Our purpose in going to the family holdings is to

celebrate our joining and our commitment to each other. I will send
a like message to Alpin Hall to assure you receive news of my delay.
    I am counting the days until I can feast once more on your
beauty.

Your loving husband,
E.

"If you will see that these letters are placed in the post, I would
appreciate it," Edward said as he handed his temporary aide several
personal messages.

The man, Lieutenant Conrad, glanced at the directions on the
letters. "Three to Derbyshire?" he remarked curiously.

"My home shire," Edward's attention had returned to the stacks
of paperwork and reports littering the desk. "My parents and my
wife. Her brother also. My brother is the one in Lincolnshire."

Conrad blushed. "I was unaware of your marriage, Sir. The file I
received regarding this post contained no notation of your joining,"
the man confessed.

Edward paused in his paper shuffle. He could easily imagine
Georgiana's countenance. After all, he had known her from her first
breath. And with a critical masculine eye, one that had been exposed to some of the most beautiful women in the world, Edward
could gladly say that he considered her as the handsomest woman
of his acquaintance. "I married only days after receiving my orders
to join Wellington's forces. Mrs. Fitzwilliam refused to allow me
to leave England a bachelor." He laughed lightly. "The lady is quite
remarkable, and my new wife was correct. Her insistence upon advancing the date of our joining served as an impetus for my surviving Waterloo's nightmare. I refused to make the lady a widow. In
many ways, Mrs. Fitzwilliam has saved my life, and I mean to share
my gratitude as soon as possible."

"Then England should celebrate the lady's foresight. I am told that you served the Duke well during the battle," the lieutenant said.

Edward, uncomfortable with the praise, nodded curtly. "Mrs. Fitzwilliam should be celebrated for her intelligence, her beauty, and her talent. Choosing me as her husband is likely her most calamitous decision."

* * *

"Father, Mother, Rose: Permit me to present my fiancée, Catherine Bennet. Miss Bennet, my parents, Sir James and Lady Winkler, and my sister, Miss Winkler."

Kitty curtsied before saying, "It is my honor, Sir James, Lady Winkler, Miss Winkler. Your son has told me so much about you that I am pleased to finally claim the acquaintance."

Camellia Winkler gushed, "She is as beautiful as you led us to believe, Thorne." Lady Winkler caressed Kitty's cheek.

Winkler's smile widened. "Miss Bennet is certainly that."

Kitty blushed thoroughly. "Sir James, permit me to extend your acquaintance to our hosts, my sister and her husband, Mr. and Mrs. Darcy."

The couples exchanged courtesies; then Elizabeth directed Mr. Winkler's family to the main drawing room. "I fear you are about to be beset with a number of Bennets, Lady Winkler. Kitty is one of five daughters."

"Yes, my son has written to that effect," Lady Winkler assured.

Thirty minutes later, Mr. Nathan announced, "Dinner is served, Mr. Darcy."

Lady Winkler declared as she entered the dining room on Darcy's arm, "My! Such a collation, and prepared with abundance and elegance."

"Thank you, Ma'am. Mrs. Darcy is known for her hospitality." He seated the baronet's wife to his right.

When everyone had settled at the table, Mrs. Bennet declared, "This is very pleasant, having family about the table. Do you not concur, Lady Winkler?"

"It is, Mrs. Bennet," the lady agreed, "although I do so wish Thorne's older brother could have joined us for this momentous occasion. Bram is overseeing renovations on the estate. We had a disastrous spring storm with wind and lightning damage."

Mrs. Bennet accepted the fish course from Darcy's footman before saying, "I am sorry to hear it, Ma'am. The care never ceases on a working estate, does it? I am certain Mr. Winkler would prefer to have his brother in attendance, just as Kitty would prefer that Mrs. Wickham, our dearest Lydia, could see our Kitty married."

Kitty grimaced. Her mother had returned to her favorite subject of late: Lydia's absence from the family gatherings. Over the past month, her mother had harangued her daughter as to why Kitty had not insisted that Mr. Darcy send his carriage for the Wickhams. Mrs. Bennet had always preferred her youngest child, to the others' neglect. Kitty did not regret Lydia's absence as her mother did. She felt that she had risen above the insensibility she now recognized in Lydia's actions.

She recalled quite clearly how Lydia had abandoned her for Mrs. Forster, the wife of the colonel of the regiment once stationed at Meryton. When the army transferred the unit to Brighton, both she and Lydia had bemoaned the loss of the men's company, but Mrs. Forster had invited Lydia to accompany her to the resort. Mrs. Forster had become Lydia's invaluable friend. A resemblance in good humor and good spirits had recommended the woman and Lydia to each other, and out of their three months' acquaintance they had been an intimate two—leaving Kitty to amuse herself.

The rapture of Lydia on this occasion, her adoration of Mrs. Forster, and the delight of their mother had increased Kitty's mortifications. Wholly inattentive to her sister's feelings, Lydia had fluttered about the house in restless ecstasy, calling for everyone's congratulations, and laughing and talking with more violence than ever, while Kitty had repined her fate without respite.

"It shall be a glorious day even without Lydia's presence, Mama." Kitty nodded toward her other sisters. "I am thankful to have three of my four sisters in attendance. I suspect Mr. Wickham's service does not permit him the luxury of naming when he might secure a leave of absence."

"Nonsense, Kitty," her mother responded. "With the war at an end, Mr. Wickham surely has reduced responsibilities."

Kitty shot a quick glance to Elizabeth, sitting at the table's end. She was not certain what had occurred between Mr. Darcy and Mr. Wickham, but Kitty was aware of the lack of goodwill between the men. She had spent enough time at Pemberley over the past two years to overhear snippets of conversations regarding Mr. Darcy's contempt for Lydia's husband, and Kitty did not believe that it had anything to do with the fact that Elizabeth had once favored Mr. Wickham over Mr. Darcy. "Well, it is not to be," she said quietly, praying that her acceptance of the fact would turn the conversation.

Elizabeth's eyebrow rose in curiosity, but she said, "Mama, why do you not tell Lady Winkler about Kitty's gown and the wedding breakfast's preparations?" After those words, the intercourse of the two families was carried on without restraint.

Kitty exhaled deeply and then mouthed the words "Thank you" to her older sister.

* * *

"Miss Bennet, would you consider a walk in the garden?" Mr. Winkler bowed to those who kept Kitty company.

She pinked, but slid her hand into his. "That would be diverting."

"Take a maid," Elizabeth whispered.

Kitty nodded and placed her hand on Winkler's proffered arm. "I hope all goes well with the school," she said as they exited through the patio door.

"It could use your sensible eye for detail, but it is a good beginning. Miss Lyndhurst manages to meet each child's needs." He directed their steps toward the lower garden. "The Foxmour girls attend upon occasion."

"I would call on the family in the next few days."

Winkler smiled happily. "They were most animated when they learned of your return. Mavis says they have additional drawings for you."

Kitty tightened her fingers about his arm. At Christmastide, she had accompanied Winkler as he attended Arthur Foxmour's terminally ill mother. Not knowing what to expect, she had entertained the Foxmour children with drawing lessons. Since that time, the three girls had given her countless examples of their artwork. "I shall be pleased to see their latest efforts."

Once away from the house, Winkler edged her closer. "I have missed you, Catherine," he whispered into her hair.

"As I have you."

Winkler led her to a rose-covered arbor. "By that, am I to assume that you still wish to become my bride? I would release you if you have any misgivings regarding our joining."

"Thorne Winkler, if you would try to withdraw, you would meet my mother's wrath." She smiled widely when his forehead's lines met. "Let us not think of anything but our happiness," she insisted.

"You have won my heart, Sir. Is that what you wish me to say?" A "tut" of annoyance followed.

Winkler caught her hand and brought it to his lips. "I cannot say that your words displease me, Catherine. I require your assurance that my dream can come true."

"Then be assured, Thorne, that I intend to know only you for the rest of my life."

Winkler glanced over his shoulder to determine the maid's presence. Assured that the young girl's attention was on the summer foliage, he slid his arm about Kitty's waist and pulled her to him.

"Thorne!" she protested, but he was gratified to have her rest her palms on his chest.

"Yes, my love," he whispered as he nibbled on Kitty's ear. "You are everything, Catherine," he rasped. "I had thought that this day would never arrive. I have waited six and twenty years to know such happiness. Now that it is in my reach, I fear that somehow God will punish me for desiring too much."

Kitty rose on her tiptoes to offer her lips. "There is nothing, Thorne Winkler, that can interfere with our joining. On Monday next, I shall be your wife unto eternity." Her lips brushed his before Thorne claimed her mouth with ardent ferocity.

"Eternity," he groaned, kissing her in earnest. "The dream where you captured my heart."

* * *

The disturbing dream had resurfaced. Once more, the light appeared in the dark room, but she did not attempt to sit up or to even see what it brought. By now, she knew: a clean chamber pot and a plate with bread and butter, as well as a flask of water. The chained manacle attached to her left wrist only permitted her limited movements. Instead of moving, she used the few moments the light remained in the room to recover her bearings. She needed to discover more of the place where her captors held her; to explore her prison, a place without sunlight, only perpetual night. If she were to survive, she needed to find a way from this room.

The light had momentarily blinded her, but she diverted her eyes from the glare and searched the shadows to find what else the room held. The cot upon which she rested was made of wood and had a thin mattress. She knew this from lying upon it for days... or was it weeks? Adjusting her eyes to the dimness, she observed a small table with one straight-backed chair. The dark-clothed figure placed the food on the three-legged stool at the bed's head and turned to leave.

"Would you bring me another blanket?" she rasped, her dry throat slurring the words.

The figure turned to look sympathetically at her. Although she could not see his countenance, she felt the man's empathy. With a slight nod of agreement, he was gone, and with him the precious light she craved.

* * *

As soon as word arrived from the gatehouse of the carriage's arrival, Elizabeth had waited impatiently at Pemberley's main entrance. Her husband and Mr. Joseph flanked her, but it was Elizabeth's excitement which painted the moment. Darcy lightly touched her arm when she began testily to tap her foot, and Elizabeth sighed in exasperation. "I know, I know," she said good-naturedly. "But it has been seven months since I have seen either Mary or baby William."

Darcy chuckled. "And your tapping foot will speed the lady's arrival?" he asked softly.

"This is not the time to be reasonable, Mr. Darcy," she said in exasperation.

"One of us must remain so, my love." Darcy winked at her when she sighed deeply.

And then Jasper was setting down the steps, and Mary Joseph appeared in the open door. The woman's face lit with an animated smile; then she scrambled down the steps to run into Elizabeth's open arms.

"You are here," Elizabeth gasped. "I am so pleased."

Mary laughed openly. "A hug is so much better than even the longest letter."

"It is," Elizabeth said contentedly. Then she turned her attention to the coach. "Where is William? I must see your son."

"Here," Mr. Joseph said as he assisted a young girl from the coach. The girl, Ruth Joseph, handed her brother the child. Her face flushed with color, and she fiddled with a heavy lace fichu that someone had, obviously, insisted that the girl wear. Her dark, chocolate-colored eyes darted to Pemberley's majestic entrance. "My," she murmured.

Darcy smiled easily. "Do not allow the exterior to intimidate you, Miss Joseph." He bowed in greeting. "I am Mr. Darcy."

Her brother teased as he returned the boy to his wife's arms, "Allow the interior to do the act instead, Ruthie."

Joseph's sister blushed again, but she managed a quick curtsy to her hosts. "Mr. Darcy. Mrs. Darcy. Thank...thank you for receiving me."

Elizabeth caught the girl's arm. "We are so pleased you have traveled from Staffordshire with Mrs. Joseph. Please, everyone. Let us find refreshments in the drawing room." Elizabeth reached for the sleeping child. "I must hold him," she said to Mary. "It feels a lifetime since William was in my arms. My, how our young man has grown."

Darcy placed Mrs. Joseph on his arm. "It is a terrible habit of children, Mrs. Darcy." He laughed as his wife rolled her eyes in annoyance. "Perhaps we should forbid Bennet from doing so."

"If we could, I would be content, my husband."

"I have asked Mr. Winkler's sister Rose to stay at Pemberley," Elizabeth explained. She held William, and Mary Joseph cradled Bennet as they enjoyed tea in the main drawing room. "Mr. Winkler has limited room at the rectory, and I thought Kitty might enjoy the company of both Miss Winkler and Miss Joseph."

"That sounds pleasant for our sisters," Jane remarked. "But is it not amusing that those same said sisters are no less in age than were we when we married?"

Mary sipped her tea. "But we have known our husbands' pleasures."

Jane pinked before saying, "Soon Kitty shall be one of us."

"But not before we celebrate the wedding of the last of the Bennet sisters. I have planned a side trip to the abbey's ruins for today, a picnic tomorrow, and a dinner for Saturday. Besides the local gentry, I have asked several of the neighborhood's young people to join us. I am certain impromptu dancing shall be necessary."

"You have always loved to dance, Lizzy," Jane observed.

"It was one of our family's favorite pastimes in Meryton. The place where we both met our future husbands."

"Although Mr. Bingley was more congenial that Mr. Darcy was," Jane taunted.

"Mr. Darcy was just warming up to my charms," Elizabeth defended her husband. "Besides, no one can see me when your beauty outshines us all."

* * *

"Are you prepared for another carriage ride so soon?" Matthew Joseph asked his wife as they waited with the others in Pemberley's main drawing room. As planned, the group would make the short journey to Depedale between Ilkeston and Derby. "I would not have you play havoc with your health. You have assumed so many duties with our removal to Newcastle."

Mary Joseph reached for her husband's hand. "But do you not see, Matthew? This shall be no trial. I am a guest. All I must do is relax in the soft squabs of our coach and enjoy the view. I have no meals to plan or details to execute. And if young William should require anything, a dozen pair of hands are available for our son's comfort. It is quite selfish, but I look forward to some private thoughts, as well as the company of Mrs. Darcy's family. Tension between you and my father does not exist at Pemberley. Besides, I wish to see the abbey's grounds through the eyes of the man I love. You cannot tell me that the prospect of exploring a thirteenth-century abbey does not pique your interest. I know you too well, my husband."

"I admit to being eager to see the arch leading to the building's east windows. It has brought about many superstitions."

Mary laughed softly. "It is as I suspected." She squeezed her husband's hand. "We shall spend the afternoon pretending we are courting again." She leaned closer to say, "I have missed you."

Before he could respond, Elizabeth joined their conversation. "We shall leave shortly. There was some issue with a broken spoke on one of the carriages, but the wheelwright has seen to its repair. Mr. Darcy is personally checking on the safety of the other coaches. He takes great pride in his carriages." The appearance of the Pemberley butler caught Elizabeth's attention. "Excuse me. Perhaps Mr. Nathan brings word of our departure."

Elizabeth made her way across the crowded room. She adored to be alone with Darcy, but she was essentially a very social person. She thrived on conversation. She had always considered good company to be that of clever, well-informed people who have a great deal of conversation. That was what had brought her and Darcy together: their verbal battles had been exhilarating exchanges of equal minds, as well as romantically stimulating. Although she had not understood it at the time, she could admit to that fact now: they had challenged each other in a primitive dance for dominance. Just the thought of those masked sexually charged exchanges brought a blush to her cheeks. "Yes, Mr. Nathan?"

"There are visitors, Ma'am, in the small drawing room," he whispered.

Elizabeth glanced about the room to the eyes following her every move. "Would you tell whomever it is that we are not receiving today?"

Mr. Nathan turned his body to mask his response from the Pemberley guests. "The lady insists on speaking to you or to Mrs. Bennet." He lowered his voice further. "And the gentleman is Mr. Wickham, Ma'am."

Elizabeth felt the blood drain from her face. "Lieutenant Wickham has dared to come to Pemberley?" she hissed. The butler nodded his response. "I shall not have it," Elizabeth declared and immediately turned toward where her youngest sister waited, but Kitty caught her arm.

"What is it, Lizzy?"

"Our sister has arrived unannounced, and she has brought her husband with her."

To Elizabeth's surprise, Kitty straightened her shoulders with determination. It pleased her to recognize her influence on Kitty. "What do you wish of me?"

"Tell Jane to keep everyone in the drawing room. Mr. Nathan has placed Lieutenant and Mrs. Wickham in the small receiving room off the main hall. I want Lieutenant Wickham out of this house before Mr. Darcy returns from the stables."

"I shall join you in a few moments," Kitty agreed.

Elizabeth left Kitty to see to the Pemberley guests while she dealt with this perfectly orchestrated chaos, which she could firmly lay at her mother's feet. Halting outside the smallest receiving room, Elizabeth straightened the seams of her day dress. Bracing herself for the confrontation that would surely follow, she slipped into the room to find only the lieutenant awaiting her. As if he coveted them, Wickham aimlessly fingered the room's decorative pieces. "Lieutenant Wickham." She offered no curtsy. "I had understood Mrs. Wickham accompanied you."

The man bowed courteously, and she remembered how his manners had once fooled even her. He was a practiced cad and womanizer. "Mrs. Wickham needed a moment to freshen her things," he explained.

Elizabeth's mouth set in a hard line. "Mr. Nathan," she said, knowing the servant waited for her to order Lieutenant Wickham's removal.

"Yes, Mrs. Darcy." The man's voice came from close behind her.

"Send a maid to Mrs. Wickham. My sister is *not* to wander through Pemberley alone, and she is to speak to no one but me. Escort her here when she is finished."

"Immediately, Ma'am." He withdrew to the door.

Elizabeth would prefer to have her conversation with Lieutenant Wickham without an audience, but she realized she might need Darcy's servants to carry out her commands, so she did not object to the door remaining ajar. "What brings you to Pemberley, Lieutenant Wickham? I thought Mr. Darcy had made it clear that you would never be welcomed here."

"We came for Kitty's wedding," Lydia Wickham declared from behind Elizabeth.

Elizabeth spun around to find her youngest sister standing in the open door, a tall footman flanking her on each side. Her sister's usually soft hazel eyes displayed the girl's irritation. Elizabeth realized, belatedly, that it had been over two years since she had last seen Lydia. At eighteen, her sister's countenance betrayed the "hardness" she faced daily as Mrs. Wickham. Yet, even with the early lines about Lydia's eyes, Elizabeth still saw the impetuous girl she loved. Lydia's fat chestnut curls framed her heart-shaped face, but at the moment, the girl's mouth brimmed artfully with a tearful pout. *Always creating drama,* Elizabeth thought, as the girl's ploy played out. The scene would be quite a burlesque. "I have no objection to your attending Kitty's nuptials, but you cannot think of staying at Pemberley."

"Why ever not?" Lydia demanded. "Am I any less a sister than is Jane or Mary? They are both staying at Pemberley, and with their families, I might add." In a snit, she flounced into the room and flopped into one of the lush chairs.

Elizabeth nodded to Mr. Nathan, and the man quietly closed the door. "Lydia," Elizabeth began, "if you think that I will permit you and Lieutenant Wickham to importune Mr. Darcy in his own house, you court disappointment." She straightened her shoulders and delivered the ultimatum. "Lieutenant Wickham, you will leave this house immediately."

Turning to his wife, the man ignored Elizabeth's instructions. "I warned you we would not be received by Darcy or by your sister. The man cannot leave behind his jealousies."

"His what?" Elizabeth stormed forward. "Why would Mr. Darcy be jealous of anything you possess, Mr. Wickham? Do you still banter about that stale lie of Mr. Darcy's father loving you more than his own son? I cannot imagine that anyone who knows my husband could think poorly of him." Yet, even as she said the words,

Elizabeth realized that she, too, had once believed Mr. Wickham's falsehoods.

"Yes—the late Mr. Darcy bequeathed me the next presentation of the best living in his gift. He was my godfather, and excessively attached to me. I cannot do justice to his kindness. He meant to provide for me amply, and thought he had done it; but when the living fell, it was given elsewhere."

"Good heavens!" cried Elizabeth. "But how could that be? How could his will be disregarded? Why did you not seek legal redress?"

"There was just such an informality in the terms of the bequest as to give me no hope from law. A man of honor could not have doubted the intention, but Mr. Darcy chose to doubt it—or to treat it as a merely conditional recommendation, and to assert that I had forfeited all claim to it by extravagance, imprudence—in short anything or nothing. Certain it is that the living became vacant two years ago, exactly as I was of an age to hold it, and that it was given to another man; and no less certain is it that I cannot accuse myself of having really done anything to deserve to lose it. I have a warm, unguarded temper, and I may have spoken my opinion of him, and to him, too freely. I can recall nothing worse. But the fact is that we are very different sorts of men, and that he hates me."

"This is quite shocking! He deserves to be publicly disgraced."

"Some time or other he will be—but it shall not be by me. Till I can forget his father, I can never defy or expose the son."

"You, Sir, have repeatedly accused Mr. Darcy of having manners that are both dictatorial and insolent." She backed the man against a tall table as she jabbed his chest with her finger. "I recall vividly how you claimed to all who would listen that Mr. Darcy's actions could be traced to pride, and that pride has often been my husband's best friend, that it has connected him nearer with virtue than any other feeling." Wickham smiled widely, but Elizabeth no longer found his pleasing countenance trustworthy.

"I beg to differ, Sister dear," he said smoothly. "I said that Darcy's pride has often led him to be liberal and generous; to give his money freely, to display hospitality, to assist his tenants, and to relieve the poor. I also said Darcy is very proud of what his father was and that he would never wish to disgrace his family, to degenerate from the popular qualities, or to lose the influence of Pemberley House. I even praised Darcy's brotherly affection for Miss Darcy."

Elizabeth knew Wickham spoke the truth. She had allowed her own prejudice to color her early opinion of Darcy, but she would not give Lieutenant Wickham's arguments sway. "Yet, you flavored the truth with carefully placed jabs, saying that pride is a powerful motive, or that Mr. Darcy acted with stronger impulses even than pride."

"Lizzy, of what do you speak?" Lydia demanded. "Mr. Wickham has done nothing but to act with honor."

The door opened and closed soundly behind Elizabeth as Kitty entered. Kitty assumed the offensive. "Where was the honor in your elopement? Neither you nor Mr. Wickham cared for your sisters' fates. Under this infatuating principle, your reckless actions could have destroyed us all. Association tainted us. I am not fool enough to believe that Mr. Darcy did not have something to say in the Bennet sisters' deliverance. Our mother may believe Uncle Gardiner posted your dowry, but our aunt and uncle have four children, and they would not ruin those children's futures to save us. How could they offer you a settlement? Even you cannot be that naïve, Lydia?"

Lydia had risen to greet Kitty, but her sister's words inflamed the youngest. "Of course Mr. Darcy was involved. He stood beside my dear Wickham at the service. And even if Mr. Darcy did intervene, he did so to earn Lizzy's affection. He bought himself a wife with any influence he offered on Lieutenant Wickham's behalf. She had to respond out of gratitude to his offer of marriage."

Elizabeth turned on her sister. "That is the most ridiculous assertion you have ever made. First, Mr. Darcy earned my regard and my respect many months prior to your foolish flight from Brighton, and when he assisted your joining, my husband did so without any hopes of our finding each other."

"But you did 'find each other,'" Lydia accused. "And now you are the mistress of this great estate, and you mean to lord it over the rest of us."

"Be careful that you do not cut off your own fingers, Lydia," Elizabeth warned. "If you object to my position, perhaps I should save my pin money for my own use."

"Come, Mrs. Wickham." Her husband reached for Lydia's hand. "As I said we would be unwelcome. Darcy has taught your sister his brand of hatred."

"And you have taught my sister manipulation and prevarication," Elizabeth charged.

Wickham caught Elizabeth's arm in anger. "I should have taught you something of respect," he growled.

Before Elizabeth could jerk her arm free, the room's door slammed open, and her husband's angry stance filled the small space. "If you wish to continue breathing, I would advise you to remove your hand from my wife's arm." The deadly coldness of his words sucked the air from the room.

"Fitzwilliam," Elizabeth gasped. She had never seen him so angry. "Lydia…Lydia and Lieutenant Wickham…were…were just leaving," she stammered.

"But I wanted to enjoy the festivities," Lydia half whined.

Kitty rasped, "It is probably best, Lydia, that you leave." She glanced at Darcy's implacable countenance.

"You would send me away?" Lydia protested. "After all we have shared?"

Kitty swallowed hard. "It is no more than what I have shared with Lizzy or Jane or Mary or even with Mrs. Fitzwilliam. After you departed for Brighton, I meant nothing to you. Mrs. Forster became your confidante, and although for a short period I clung to the girlish dream of following you to Brighton, I soon heard the rumors that your speedy marriage generated, and I knew I must find another way to earn an honorable man's affection. Mr. Winkler is that man. I am needed in Derbyshire. At Pemberley."

"What are we to do tonight? We have no funds for the inn," Lydia admitted.

Elizabeth had not removed her eyes from Darcy's hard glare. "Our father will see to your room. I shall ask him to call on you there to settle the account. Now, you must leave, Lydia. There is nothing at Pemberley for you or for Lieutenant Wickham."

Chapter 4

UNABLE TO CONTROL HIS DESIRE for her, he had come to her room again. He had left the candle in the passageway. Tonight, he simply looked upon her lovely countenance. She was the most exquisite creature he had ever encountered, and he wondered if there was any manner of trickery that he might employ to make her truly care for him. Could she forgive him for those who had died because of his inactions? Would she look upon his face and recognize a man who would honestly love her, or would she see a man who had failed in his family obligations? He spread another blanket over her small frame. He would see to her safety. She would know protection in his arms. He would move mountains to have her recognize his worth.

* * *

Edward had fallen asleep at his desk. "I cannot seem to know enough of sleep," he mumbled as he rubbed his face hard with his palms. "Too many battles. Too much blood. Too many nightmares," he repeated. "Only Georgiana can soothe my troubled soul. I must know her presence in my arms before I will recognize that my journey has finally come to an end. If I protect her from the world's evils, I hope she will find me worthy to call husband."

* * *

"It does not surprise," Wickham grumbled. He caught Lydia's elbow and turned his wife toward the still-open door. However, when he reached Darcy's rigidly standing form, he mockingly said, "Please give Miss Darcy my regards. I understand the last four years have been very good to her." With a slight nod, he took a step to depart.

However, Darcy's anger had never receded—not today, not four years prior when Wickham had staged the elopement, which would have devastated Georgiana—not through the years of falsehoods, and not when the man had purposely ruined Lydia Bennet and had crushed Darcy's hopes of claiming Elizabeth as his wife. The memory of every degrading moment seemed to course through his veins, and without considering his actions, his right arm wound up for a perfectly executed uppercut to Wickham's finely chiseled jaw. A left jab to Wickham's nose followed the right, and the man went sprawling backward to rest at Elizabeth's feet. Blood gushed from Wickham's nose upon the man's crisp uniform.

"Bloody hell, Darcy!" Wickham exclaimed as he dug in his pocket for a handkerchief. "You are bloody crazy!"

Darcy growled, "Curse in my wife's presence again, and those imprecations will be the last words that you utter."

Elizabeth stepped around Wickham's efforts at recovery and slipped into Darcy's one-armed embrace. "Tell me you are well," she whispered as she caressed his chin.

Darcy did not remove his eyes from the scuttled figure bleeding onto his Persian rug, but he tightened his hold. "As long as you are safe," he said softly.

Meanwhile, Lydia's loud protestations were added to the clamor. "Lizzy, look what you have started." She avoided her husband's bloody hands when she cuddled his head. "What kind of man have you married?" she accused.

"The best kind, Lydia." Elizabeth looked lovingly into Darcy's eyes. "A man of honor. A man of integrity." She turned in Darcy's embrace. "Mr. Nathan, would you ask Jasper and Thomas to escort Lieutenant and Mrs. Wickham safely from Pemberley's grounds?"

"Certainly, Mrs. Darcy." He snapped his fingers, and the two footmen appeared.

"I cannot believe it has come to this," Lydia lamented. "You would turn your own sister away? Your flesh and blood?"

Elizabeth's mouth turned downward. "As my marriage vows require, I would cling to my husband above all others." She shook her head in sadness. "I never wished it to come to this. In the future, should you choose to return to Pemberley, I shall welcome you with open arms, but I shall never subjugate Mr. Darcy's desire to sever relations with Lieutenant Wickham to my desire to maintain sisterly affection. If you cannot accept those terms, then we shall communicate through the post."

As she supported her husband's rise from the floor, Lydia exclaimed, "You have turned Kitty against me."

Elizabeth shot a quick glance to the downcast countenance of a sister she dearly adored, and she noted how Kitty's mouth twitched with the desire to smile. Kitty, too, found all this drama quite amusing. Miss Catherine Bennet had grown into a sage young woman. "I hope not. I would never place Kitty in a position to have to choose between us." She silently thought, *as you have just required.* "And I hope to see you regain the family and friends you have so carelessly sacrificed. The nuptials are a public gathering. You must choose whether you shall stay until Monday for the service. Yet, Pemberley is my home, and I shall determine the events we celebrate and the guests who participate."

"I see." Lydia straightened her clothing. "We shall await my parents at the Lambton inn."

Wickham staggered to his feet. "That may not be the best idea."

"Why ever not?" Lydia demanded. "There is no coach until tomorrow."

Darcy eyed Wickham carefully. The man's nervous mannerisms made him an open book. "If your husband's demeanor is any indication, Lieutenant Wickham expects to meet those in the area who still hold his markers." Everyone turned to stare at the wastrel in the King's uniform.

"I simply prefer not to importune Father Bennet for the cost of our room and return passage," Wickham said smoothly.

Darcy laughed sarcastically. "Did you hear, Mrs. Darcy? Your father's debts grow. You suggested that Mr. Bennet would assume the unexpected cost of an inn stay, but your assumption included the notion that Lieutenant Wickham had previously arranged a return journey to Carlisle. Now, we find that not to be the case. Our brother in marriage requires both passage and room, and I suspect board, as well."

Elizabeth said accusingly, "I expect the accuracy of your words, but that is my father's issue."

Kitty said softly. "Mr. Saunders is at Kympton. Perhaps Lydia and Lieutenant Wickham could share the curate's quarters for the evening. Should I speak to Mr. Winkler? I would not wish Lydia to know any public humiliation."

"You do what you consider best, Kitty." Elizabeth admired how Kitty had handled herself. Her sister had demonstrated a firm resolve, but she had also shown charity, a quality Mr. Winkler had recognized in the young Catherine Bennet—a quality he required in his wife. "Why do you not speak privately to Mr. Winkler and then ask Papa to join us here?"

"Yes, Lizzy." Kitty dropped a quick curtsy and then disappeared from the room.

"Mr. Darcy, we shall await my father in the main foyer. Mr. Nathan shall attend Lieutenant and Mrs. Wickham. We should rejoin our guests." She reached for Darcy's hand, and he came willingly.

Within seconds, they were at the foot of the main staircase and in each other's arms. "Thank you," Darcy rasped as he pulled her closer.

Elizabeth clung to him. "For what? For loving you beyond reason? I fear that my heart is fully engaged, Mr. Darcy."

"As is mine," he whispered into her ear. "I am chagrined that my previous acquaintances have tainted your family's life."

"I shall hear none of this regret, Mr. Darcy. You, Sir, are exactly the man who, in disposition and talents, most suits me. Your understanding and temper, though unlike my own, have answered all my wishes. You are as generous as the most generous of your sex."

Before she could say more, her father appeared on the landing. "Kitty tells me that you require my assistance," he said suspiciously.

Elizabeth blushed at having been caught in an intimate embrace, but she quickly explained what had transpired.

"And your mother never indicated to anyone that she had invited Lydia and Lieutenant Wickham?" His disbelief showed. "I tolerated her maneuverings with Mr. Grange at Christmastide because Grange is harmless and unassuming. No one could object to Grange, but Lieutenant Wickham is a different story." He turned to Darcy. "I swear, Mr. Darcy, that I held no prior knowledge of this situation, but I will deal with the Wickhams and with Mrs. Bennet. "

"We will escort the others to Derby while you see to your youngest child."

With a reluctant shrug, Mr. Bennet agreed. "Mrs. Bennet will miss the journey. During your absence, my wife and I will have a serious discussion."

* * *

Although the nightmare had returned, when a brace of candles floated into the room her eyes opened to devour the precious light. She pushed herself to a seated position and shoved several loose strands of hair behind her ears. She no longer possessed an idea of the number of days and nights she had spent curled up on the hard cot.

"I have brought you a warmer gown—one of wool," a female voice said. "If ye will change from yer fine cloth, I'll be seeing to the stains." The woman placed the expected food plate on the small stool. "I've brought ye a bit of cheese this time."

She watched the movements—memorizing the actions. What would it feel like to walk across the room—to stretch her cramped muscles? By twisting awkwardly, she had managed to stand beside the cot and to mark her steps in place. To give her weakened legs some much-needed relief. But to actually take a step would be glorious. However, even the slightest shift on her part allowed the manacle to cut into her wrist.

"Come," the woman said as she unlocked the metal cuff and helped her to her feet. "There. Does that not feel better?" The woman rubbed her hands with her own, and life rushed into the girl's fingertips. She searched the woman's face, but all she could discern was the woman's age. Likely her late fifties. Silver-gray hair. Very strong hands. Not dainty like those of a woman of good breeding. Her ministrations indicated that the woman did not readily retreat from hard work. Was she someone familiar? But the shadows robbed the girl of her savior's other features. "Permit me to assist ye with yer laces and yer stays."

Obediently, the girl turned her back to the woman. "My, yer skin be so smooth," her captor said. The gown slipped down her body to the floor, and she stepped from it. A cold shiver rocked her spine, but she kept her focus on her surroundings. Where was she? Could she escape? The room resembled a cell—a place for prisoners, which is exactly what she was: someone's prisoner, and she needed never to forget that fact. Breaching the stone walls was not possible. She would need another form of flight.

"This gown should be making ye more comfortable." The woman dropped the cloth over her head and began to lace the eyelets. Without her stays, she would be able to move more freely. "I've also brought ye some gloves, as well as this strip of cloth. I'll be keepin' the shackle from cuttin' into yer skin."

She turned to the woman. "Must I be returned to the cuff?" She wanted to explore her options more fully, but she permitted the woman to refasten the chain.

"I've no right to order it otherwise." Her captor's gravelly voice held sadness, but the girl wondered if the woman offered an untruth. Something did not feel right. A shiver ran down the girl's spine as she bent to accept the fastening.

"Then to whom should I plead my case?" she implored.

The woman's mouth set in a tight line. "You'll see in time." The stranger straightened the gown's line, tugging at the seams. "It be a bit tighter than I be thinkin'," the woman said as she bent to retrieve the traveling dress from the floor.

Without thinking, the girl's hand came to rest upon her abdomen. "My family shall pay whatever you ask for my release," she said softly.

"Not yer husband?" the woman accused as she strode toward the door.

"My husband is dead."

* * *

"Mrs. Bennet, I would speak to you." His wife looked up in surprise. "In private," he insisted.

"But we are about to depart," she protested. "Could this not wait until later, Mr. Bennet?"

Obviously more than a bit uncomfortable with the situation, Mr. Bennet glanced across the room at the happy gathering. Dealing with his wife was one of his least favorite activities. He had very often wished, before this period of his life, that, instead of spending his whole income, he had laid by an annual sum for the better provision of his children, and of his wife. He now wished it more than ever. Maybe, if he had, Mrs. Bennet would not be so desperate to see to their girls' futures. If he had done his duty in that respect, Lydia need not have been indebted to Mr. Darcy for whatever of honor his son in marriage had purchased for her.

When first he had married, economy was held to be perfectly useless; for, of course, they were to have a son. The son was to join in cutting off the entail, as soon as he should be of age, and the widow and younger children would by that means be provided for. Five daughters successively entered the world, but yet the son was to come; and Mrs. Bennet, for many years after Lydia's birth, had been certain that he would. This event had at last been despaired of, but it was then too late to be saving. Mrs. Bennet's grasp of economy varied greatly with the situation; and Mr. Bennet's love of independence had alone prevented their exceeding their income.

And all his indolence had led to this moment. He had never supposed that prevailing upon Wickham to marry Lydia would have been done with so little inconvenience to himself. *Time to pay the piper*, he thought. "I fear, my dear, that we have a prior engagement."

His wife started to object, but he extended his hand to her, and despite her puzzlement, Mrs. Bennet accepted his hand and stood by his side. Possessively, he wrapped her arm through his.

When they had visited Pemberley at Christmastide, they had shared several moments of understanding, the first true honesty that had occurred between them in years. Perhaps Pemberley's magic would prevail once more.

Mr. Nathan stepped into the open door. "Mr. and Mrs. Darcy request your presence before Pemberley. Your carriages await."

A buzz of activity exploded. "I shall return the twins to the nursery," the Bingleys' nurse said as she motioned a maid to follow her with Cassandra.

"Thank you, Mrs. Olson."

"Shall William be safe?" Ruth asked Mary Joseph as they reached for their gloves and bonnets.

"I trust Mrs. Darcy to protect my son. She would not employ an incompetent staff."

"Papa," Kitty whispered softly. "Mr. Winkler has asked Jarvis to report to Mr. Saunders' cottage and to secure the curate's belongings. I thought it best under the circumstances."

Mr. Bennet squeezed her hand. It amazed him how mature his fourth daughter had become under Elizabeth and Jane's guidance. Not only had Kitty managed to think of a temporary solution to the problem of Lydia and Lieutenant Wickham's housing, she had had the foresight to remove the curate's possessions from Lieutenant Wickham's temptation. "You are quite remarkable." He glanced to where Mr. Winkler waited for her. "Enjoy your day with your young man. The gentleman has shown patience in claiming your attentions. Your mother and I will be anticipating your return."

"Now, Mr. Bennet, please explain why we could not partake of a day of friendly travel. This is most disagreeable," she declared.

As he pulled a chair closer to the one to which he had directed their steps, he grumbled, "Not half as disagreeable as I expect you to find it. Your manipulations, Marjory, have placed Kitty and

Lizzy and Mr. Darcy—nay, the whole family—in an awkward situation."

"My manipulations?" she exclaimed. "What manipulations would those be, Sir? I assure you I have conducted myself modestly."

Mr. Bennet's eyebrow rose in disbelief. His wife's actions had mortified and displeased him in no common degree. "Then you would lead me to believe that you possessed no knowledge of Lydia and Lieutenant Wickham's unexpected appearance at Pemberley?"

She was on her feet immediately. "Lydia is here. Oh, where is my dearest girl? I must see her this instant."

"Then you must accompany me into Lambton."

Perplexed, she turned to him. She scrupled to point out her earlier remarks, lest it should appear ill natured. "Surely you jest, Mr. Bennet. Why would Lieutenant and Mrs. Wickham not be asked to stay at Pemberley? Lizzy opens her doors to Mr. Winkler's family, as well as to the Josephs, a couple she barely knows. Would not her own blood deserve like treatment? I cannot believe Lizzy would deny Lydia the opportunity to witness Kitty's nuptials. I suspect Mr. Darcy has something to do with it. There were all those rumors in Meryton of how Lizzy's husband had treated Mr. Wickham after old Mr. Darcy's passing."

Mr. Bennet gestured for her to resume her seat, and although she acquiesced, his wife remained agitated. "And may I ask the source of those rumors?"

"Well, I am certain that I do not care," she said with a dismissive flick of her wrist. "Everyone repeated the worst of the man. Even Lizzy," she added defensively.

"But, apparently, Lizzy has ignored the rumors to discover a man she can revere. And among our daughters, it is Elizabeth who has the brightest mind."

His wife objected. "Mr. Bennet, what a horrible thing to say of your other children. I am certain that any of our girls can speak as well as Elizabeth."

He shook his head in denial. "Each of our daughters, except perhaps Lydia, has her talents. Yet, it was Lizzy's fine mind which attracted Mr. Darcy to her. Her mind and her impertinence. I have hopes for Kitty, but she is not of the same caliber as Lizzy."

"You always preferred Elizabeth, to the others' neglect," she accused.

"As do you with Lydia," he countered. "But we will not argue for our share of blame. The issue remains: You invited our daughter and Lieutenant Wickham to Mr. Darcy's home."

"It is Lizzy's house as well."

Mr. Bennet sighed in exasperation. "I require that you listen to the truth—without interruption." He paused to assure her agreement, and then he continued. "Mr. Darcy and Lieutenant Wickham do hold a long-standing contempt for each other, but the source of the disdain is not what you suspect. Lieutenant Wickham has repeatedly employed perfidious intent. While Lizzy's husband has acted honorably in his dealings with his former associate, Lydia's husband has defamed Mr. Darcy."

"And how would you know this with any certainty?" she asked.

"Because Lieutenant Wickham had no intention of every marrying Lydia. His gambling debts drove him first from Meryton and then from Brighton; and Lydia, in her foolish naïveté, traveled with the man. Our Lydia displayed no regard for what her actions would do to her sisters."

His wife tutted her disagreement. "Everything turned for the best."

Mr. Bennet rose quickly. "Only because Mr. Darcy stepped in. It was never my Brother Gardiner who saved Lydia and our family. It was Mr. Darcy, who tracked Lydia to London, who arranged for the payment of Lieutenant Wickham's debts, who purchased the man's commission, and who dowered Lydia with a settlement high enough to tempt Mr. Wickham into matrimony. If not for Mr. Darcy, none of our daughters would be married. No respectable man can wed a woman with such low connections. Even you must realize how close this family came to disaster."

"Of course, I understand the implications, but why should I hear this now—after over two years? Am I so untrustworthy?" she demanded.

"You are not known for your discretion, Mrs. Bennet. Only moments ago, you spoke of gossip and rumors. I do not censure your *opinions*; but there certainly *is* impropriety in making them public. Besides, other than from Lizzy, Mr. Darcy has no need of the Bennet family's adulation. The man is violently in love with our daughter. So much so that he spent a small fortune to save Lydia, and, therefore, to soothe Elizabeth's worst nightmares. Might I remind you that Mr. Darcy did so with your brother's permission? Nothing was to be done that Darcy did not do himself. He and my Brother Gardiner battled it together for a long time, which was more than either the gentleman or the lady concerned in the affair deserved. Eventually, your brother wore his borrowed feathers and accepted our praise because the man respects Mr. Darcy. As Darcy is Lizzy's husband, should we not do the same?"

"Then what of Lydia's husband?" Her argument had lost its impetus.

He ignored her continued protestation. "Mr. Winkler has arranged for Lydia and Lieutenant Wickham to stay at the curate's cottage."

"Why not the inn?"

"Because the Wickhams are short of funds, and there exists the strong possibility that Lieutenant Wickham still owes several debts in the area. A more respectable, as well as more economical, habitation has been accordingly substituted. Therefore, we will be sharing a portion of your next quarter's allowance to rescue our youngest from her recklessness."

Mrs. Bennet flustered in disbelief. "You cannot mean to ask that I make additional cuts. We are at bare bones now."

"I am well aware of the Longbourn expenditures, Mrs. Bennet. As we were scarcely ten pounds a year the loser with Lydia's situation, by the hundred that was paid to Lieutenant Wickham, what with Lydia's board and pocket allowance, and the continual presents in money, which passed to Lydia through your hands, her expenses were very little within the sum. Of course, we will save significantly more by turning Mary and Kitty over to their husbands. We will persevere, and you will learn not to interfere where you should practice prudence."

"I am to be punished for wanting the best for my daughters," she accused.

"There is no *punishment* intended, Mrs. Bennet. You will apologize to Elizabeth and Kitty for creating a rift between the sisters and for tarnishing Kitty's special day. I will not accept anything less, Marjory. Now, you will gather your things, and we will call on the Wickhams at the curate's cottage to resolve this situation without bringing censure to Elizabeth, Mr. Darcy, Kitty, or Mr. Winkler."

* * *

Lydia looked around the cramped quarters. "At least, it is clean," she offered tentatively. Since Mr. Darcy's staff had ejected them from Pemberley, her husband's countenance had held nothing but his fury.

"The bastard," he growled—his words barely audible. He turned angrily on his wife. "It is your fault. Once again, Darcy has bested me, and once again, I lay the culpability at your feet," he fumed.

"How is Mr. Darcy's rejection my burden?" she protested. "If I had come to Derbyshire alone, the Darcys would have welcomed me to their home." She realized her error the instant her husband's eyes turned a forbidding onyx. "I…I did not mean… mean my words," she pleaded as she took a cautious step backwards. "Honestly…you know I…I always say things I do not truly believe." Her bottom lip trembled when she realized she could go no further.

Her husband advanced catlike, and Lydia realized the depth of his derision. "How dare you?" he threatened menacingly. "How dare you suggest that this debacle belongs to anyone but you and that nitwit of a woman you call *mother?*"

Lydia winced when he caught her wrist and turned it sharply. "Of course," she began. "Quite foolish of me." Tears bubbled in her eyes as the pain shot through her arm. "Permit…permit me to apologize."

"You will do more than apologize," he warned. "You will plead with your mother and father to intercede in our behalf with the Darcys."

Lydia shot a glance about the room. "Could we not just enjoy the cottage's privacy? We have spent no time alone since before our nuptials. Do you not remember that night on the London Road?"

"How could I forget?" He shoved her hard against the wall. "You screamed like a cut pig. The innkeeper threatened to evict us. Then you cried for your mother most of the night. It certainly lacked a romantic enticement."

"I had not known how it was between a man and a woman," she said defensively.

He snarled, "You still know nothing of desire and need. You think what you do in our bed is how it is meant to be?" He took her by the shoulders and gave her a sound shake. "A woman should do more than lie perfectly still."

Lydia bit her bottom lip to keep from calling out. "Tell me what I must do. I would please you, George."

He contemptuously chuckled. He thought his wife prodigiously stupid. "Please me." Wickham shook his head in disbelief. "You would please me? Not in this lifetime, Mrs. Wickham." He jerked her chin sharply upward. "Why else would I find my pleasure with anyone but you?"

"It could change," she said hopefully. "We could start tonight. Start over. I would do anything to make you happy." She tentatively reached for his cheek.

Wickham caught her hand again and wrenched her arm behind her back. "I do not want to start over. I do not want anything from you except your obedience. You disgust me." He shoved her hard— sending Lydia to the floor in a crumpled heap.

"If you touch my daughter again," Mr. Bennet's voice filled the small room with anger, "it will be the last thing you do, Sir."

Wickham turned angrily to where his wife's mother and father stood framed by the open door. "Mrs. Wickham belongs to me. You no longer have any say in the matter."

Mr. Bennet stepped into the room. "Maybe not legally, but morally, Lydia is my responsibility. I will not stand idly by and watch you manhandle my youngest child."

"Be careful, Mr. Bennet," his wife said softly. She had buried her gasp in a handkerchief.

Lydia struggled to her feet. "I am well, Papa." She shoved her drooping hairstyle behind her ears. "Lieutenant Wickham is upset with our treatment at Pemberley. Lizzy and Mr. Darcy were horrid to us."

Mr. Bennet stared in disbelief at his daughter. "I suspect your sister had her reasons. Now, I think it best that you join your mother in the carriage."

"I cannot leave Lieutenant Wickham, Papa."

He said as a warning to his daughter, "I insist, Lydia."

Wickham frowned. "There is no reason to insist, Mr. Bennet. My wife is welcome to stay. I will leave." He bowed briefly to the room. "I beg your indulgence, Father Bennet. Please tell my brother Darcy that I will never forget this snub." With that, Wickham strode from the room, leaving the Bennets and his wife gaping.

* * *

"Uncle?" Finding his mother's brother in her private sitting room had surprised Domhnall MacBethan. "What a pleasant encounter. I assume this is a simple social call," he said cautiously. "Otherwise, my mother should have explained that I have assumed the duties of lord of the manor." He had returned to Normanna Hall only a month prior. His father's passing had demanded that Domhnall reclaim a life he had hoped to leave behind forever.

His mother rebraided her hair as she spoke. "Me brother be aware of yer propensity to wear borrowed feathers," she said haughtily. Since his return they had had numerous confrontations. His mother was not an easy person to love—nearly impossible, in fact, but he had respected how, despite her low connections, she had proved herself a worthy wife for Coll MacBethan. That is to say, he had respected the woman who had given birth to him until he had read his father's most private papers. Now, a rift the size of one of Scotland's largest lochs lay between them.

Domhnall remained standing. He would not permit his uncle a point of dominance. When he was younger, he had been afraid of his Uncle Oliver. Some fifteen years older than his sister, Lady Wotherspoon, his uncle's rough nature and butcher's-block features had always intimated Domhnall. Although he stood some four inches taller than Oliver McCullough, Domhnall realized his uncle could hold his own in a struggle. Square chin. Broad shoulders. A waist equally as broad. A muscular chest. Anvil-sized arms, and mutton fists, which could easily slice through the toughest shank. Not an ounce of fat could be found on the man. Tough. McCullough's chosen occupation required such strength. Dull blue eyes and straight black hair worn shorter than the current style finished off what could not be called an ugly countenance. Oliver McCullough was a self-made man, and his pride in that fact made him a dangerous opponent.

Domhnall forced a congenial smile to his lips before saying, "As the law does not permit you to be named Normanna's lord, Lady Wotherspoon, my ascension to the title's realm following my father's passing cannot be called a 'borrowed' affair."

His uncle's poorly masked gesture of warning to his sister did not go unnoticed. "Yer mother saved the MacBethan name fer you," McCullough insisted.

"And I am grateful of her efforts in my behalf," Domhnall began, "but I will no longer require her assistance. A man may not remain attached to his mother's leading strings forever. He must stand tall."

"A man should not desert his family," McCullough accused.

Domhnall bit back his retort. Somehow, his uncle had weaseled his way into a welcomed position with the MacBethan household.

Domhnall wondered what his Uncle McCullough knew of his mother's "madness"—of the way she had sent them all on a ticket straight to Hell. "Tell me, Uncle," he said through gritted teeth, "when was my father's edict regarding your presence at Normanna rescinded?"

"It be no longer Coll's house," his mother interceded.

"No, it is mine, and I am my father's child," Domhnall growled. "I may be the product of my father lying early on with a bastard's daughter, but I do not need to be reminded of my lineage by my mother's equally ruined family." He had enjoyed the look of surprise on the faces of his two companions. "You see, I know the truth of your relationship," he said bitterly. He noted how the pair flinched at his words. "I know how Lars McCullough tricked my father into marrying you," he pointed a finger at Dolina MacBethan, the woman he called *Mother*. "And if I am to continue my father's quest of bringing respectability to this family name, and if I am to make an appropriate match once my mourning period has ended, entertaining the village butcher as an intimate will not further that goal."

Dolina sprung to her feet. Her hands fisted at her waist. Domhnall had expected the confrontation, and he stepped forward to dominate her with his height. "Ye have no right," she spit out the words and raised her chin in defiance.

"That is your error, Madam, for I have every right." He held her glare with a steady gaze. "Now, if you will excuse me, I have estate business." Domhnall turned for the door. Over his shoulder, he said emphatically, "I bid you good day, Uncle."

* * *

Elizabeth tilted her head back and let the sun touch her face. She closed her eyes and enjoyed the wind tugging at her bonnet. The season, the scene, the air were all favorable to tenderness and sentiment. "Thank you." Darcy's voice spoke of his continued concern.

Elizabeth smiled contentedly, but she did not open her eyes. She trusted Darcy to see to her safety. "I gladly accept your gratitude, Mr. Darcy, and shall bank it until I do something truly horrendous." She peeked at him through slitted eyes. This was followed by a short silence before Elizabeth began again. "You seemed to enjoy your drive here very much. I was glad you were so well entertained. You and Miss Winkler were laughing the whole way."

"Were we?" Darcy's eyebrow rose in amusement. "Yes, I believe we were; but I have not the least recollection at what. Oh, I believe I was relating some ridiculous stories of an old Irish groom of my uncle's. The lady loves to laugh."

"You think her more light-hearted than I?" Elizabeth accused.

"More easily amused," he replied defensively. "I could not have hoped to entertain *you* with Irish ancestors during a ten miles' drive." Darcy wondered if his wife tasted jealousy. Although he found it a ridiculous concept, he subconsciously preened under her watchful eye.

"Naturally, I believe, I am as lively as Miss Winkler, but I have more to think of now."

Darcy slid his arms about Elizabeth and pulled her closer. "You have undoubtedly—and there are situations in which very high spirits denote insensibility. Your prospects, however, are too fair to justify want of spirits. You have a very smiling scene before you. Besides, you would never do something horrendous," he said with a cautious smile.

"Of course." Elizabeth said begrudgingly. "I am a very mild-mannered female. I would dare you to prove my temper to be anything less than genteel."

"I imagine your sentiment correct. I could not imagine, for example, that you would ever say something such as, 'I had not known you a month before I felt that you were the last man in the world whom I could ever be prevailed on to marry.'"

Elizabeth cackled. "How is it that I am blessed with a husband with perfect recall?" She smiled brightly at him. "I would place into evidence, my dear Mr. Darcy, that you speak of another Elizabeth Bennet. The Elizabeth Darcy who shares this carriage's seat is not that invidious creature to whom you refer." She wound her arm through his. "I know this to be the truth because the loathsome woman once known as Elizabeth Bennet could never have earned a gentleman's goodwill, and I have just accepted your gratitude; therefore, I cannot be the woman of reference."

Darcy shook his head in amusement before kissing the tip of her nose. "You never cease to amaze me, Elizabeth. I am the most blessed of men."

"No more words of obligation, Fitzwilliam. You are my husband. The man I esteem above all others. How could you think I would ever turn from you? You are my life." She turned her head slightly to the left and inhaled deeply. "Do you smell that?"

"What?" he said hoarsely.

Elizabeth paused briefly. "Hope. It is in the air today. Kitty and Mr. Winkler's hope for a fulfilling life. The hope of the children nestled safely in the Pemberley nursery. The hope that protected Edward in what had to be the worst possible moment of his life."

"And the hope that my sister will know the type of happiness that I have found with you, Lizzy."

"Exactly. The kind of hope that says no words of thanks are necessary between a man and a woman who truly love each other."

Chapter 5

"I CANNOT STAY IN THIS COTTAGE ALONE," Lydia whined. She rested her head on her mother's shoulder. "It is all Lizzy's doing. She could have persuaded Mr. Darcy if she were not so pudding-hearted."

Mr. Bennet's expression hardened. "If you expect my assistance in this matter, Lydia, you will not speak poorly of your sister or of Mr. Darcy," he warned.

"But, Papa, Lizzy remains jealous of my good fortune. I married first, so both she and Jane had to come after me."

Mr. Bennet's tone sharpened. "You mimic your husband's words. Neither Elizabeth, nor Mr. Darcy, has reason for jealousy, and I would venture that holds true for Mr. and Mrs. Bingley as well."

His wife silenced the girl by saying, "Your father has developed a fondness for Lizzy's and Jane's husbands, as I am certain he would for Lieutenant Wickham once he has the opportunity to know your young man better."

"That is not likely, Mrs. Bennet." He sat heavily in a nearby chair. "It is time we speak with honesty. Lydia, your actions in Brighton were injurious to your sisters. Your mother was in error to encourage your acceptance of Mrs. Forster's invitation, and I should not have tolerated the constant lamentations from you two. I realized even then that you would never be easy till you exposed yourself in some public place or other, and I could not have expected you to do it with so little expense or inconvenience to me. I deeply regret my neglect, and I beg your forgiveness for my actions and lack thereof." His were eminently reasonable remarks, but he recognized their tardiness.

"Papa, it was not like that," Lydia protested.

Mr. Bennet shook off her objections. "We are both aware that in your imagination, a visit to Brighton comprised every possibility of earthly happiness. You saw it with the creative eye of fancy; the streets of that gay bathing place covered with officers and you the object of attention to scores of them. You dreamed of the pleasures of so benevolent a scheme. However, we can revisit these fancies, or we can determine what might best serve you in your marriage." His matter-of-fact attitude said that he did not expect a response. "What was begun as a matter of prudence soon grew into a matter of choice. You have made your bed, Lydia, and you must learn to lie comfortably in it. Marriage is forever." He glanced at the woman who had once fascinated him, but who now vexed his hard-earned peace of mind.

"I have tried, Papa," his daughter said softly.

"Then you will try again." He nodded to his wife. "If Lieutenant Wickham has truly returned to Carlisle without you, your mother will escort you home after Kitty's wedding. I have already promised Mr. Darcy to see to Lizzy and Bennet. The great man intends an extended business journey in the North. If Mrs. Bennet will agree, you may use my coach."

"Certainly, I shall agree," his wife assured.

"Shall I be allowed to attend my sister's nuptials?" Lydia asked contritely.

Mr. Bennet held her steady gaze. "I will speak to Lizzy's husband, but only if you promise no words of this incident nor of past grievances will be spoken by you during the festivities. Nothing is to dampen Kitty's memory of her wedding." He reached for Lydia's hand and patted the back of it. "I suspect it is best that you remain here tonight. At least, until we determine if Lieutenant Wickham intends to return. Under no circumstances will Lizzy or Mr. Darcy accept your husband at Pemberley."

"Would you prefer that I remain with you this evening?" Mrs. Bennet offered.

Lydia said childlike, "Would you, Mama? I have missed every-one so."

Mrs. Bennet tightened her hold on the girl. "No more than your absence has clouded our time at Longbourn."

* * *

"It is beautiful," Mary Joseph said as she and Elizabeth strolled arm-in-arm across the abbey's ground.

"It is one of my favorite places in Derbyshire," Elizabeth said wistfully. "Do not tell Mr. Darcy's Uncle Matlock, but I prefer this ancient woodland, with its fine beech and oak trees, to the Earl's combed lawns at Matley Manor."

Mary nodded her agreement. "Do you come here often?"

"The first time I saw the abbey, Mr. Darcy's sister arranged our trip." They leisurely traversed the well-worn path. "It was shortly after I had lost the first of our children, and Mr. Darcy had been called away for a business appointment. Up to that point in our marriage, we had never been separated for more than a few hours, and I was taking it quite hard. That is until Georgiana insisted that I accompany her on a day trip to these exquisite ruins, and here I found peace. Miss Darcy understood me better than I did myself." They walked in silence for several minutes. "Did you know an ap-pearance of the Virgin Mary to a Derby baker inspired Deepedale? She counseled the man to live in solitude and prayer."

Mary said nothing for several minutes, but then she began to giggle. Her mirth grew and soon both women laughed openly. Happy tears streamed from their eyes, and they clung to one another. Although she did notice her husband's hesitation at interrupting their exchange, Darcy's approach could not smother their jollity. She wondered if he considered her earlier snit. She had no excuse other than the emotional swings of her pregnancy. She certainly did not consider Rose Winkler a threat to her marriage. "What brings two lovely ladies such joy?" he asked with a smile.

Elizabeth wiped at her weepy eyes and attempted to remove the smile from her face. "Just the tale of a hermit carving out a home and a chapel in a sandstone cliff," she rasped between softening breaths.

Although not recognizing the source of their mirth, Darcy chuckled. "Women. How are men to understand them?"

"You are not to know the depths of our reasoning," Elizabeth said pertly.

He smiled lovingly at his wife. "Yet, what a magnificent way to be driven insane." He bowed courtly to the women. "And now, my ladies, I have been summoned to fetch you. Our carriages await."

"Must we?" Elizabeth protested weakly.

Darcy offered an arm to each woman. "If we do not, your sister may lose a future husband. Kitty is feeling quite neglected because Mr. Winkler and Mr. Joseph have engaged in a thoroughly theological debate for nearly an hour. I have proposed that our party stop at the Dove and Dale in Derby for refreshments before our return to Pemberley. I have also suggested to my future brother in marriage that if he requires an equality in his joining, that he should soothe your sister's peevishness with an extra dose of his attentions."

Elizabeth smiled widely at him. "As you have learned, Mr. Darcy?" she teased.

He edged her closer to his side with a flex of his forearm. "Why learn a valuable lesson if one cannot pass on the knowledge?" he countered.

"I shall remind Mr. Joseph of those obligations," Mary said. "My husband grieves for the opportunity to discuss his readings with other knowledgeable followers of God's word, but Matthew can sometimes lose sight of everyday situations."

Elizabeth tightened her fingers about Darcy's arm. "I was telling Mrs. Joseph of my first visit to the abbey. It seems odd to be among these structures without Mrs. Fitzwilliam."

"I pray my sister is happy with her new life, but I admit to experiencing a void in mine."

* * *

"How many be there?" The house's master asked as his mother joined him on the turret.

"Four, not countin' the woman we brought in," she said as she scanned the open fields leading to the family's main property. It was a former Scottish keep that had been repaired and added to over the years. The style was a mix of former barbarism and contemporary elegance. The woman closed her eyes and inhaled deeply. The mist rolled across the Scottish moors, and the woman beside him rose on tiptoes as if to embrace the land.

The man intoned harshly, "Be we not countin' the woman?"

"I be thinkin'. Aulay will soon be needin' a wife."

Domhnall protested, "Surely, the lady has a man. She not be needin' another to warm her bed."

His mother shook her head in denial. "The lady say he be dead, and there be more. She be with child."

He roughly grabbed her arm and turned her to him. "How came ye to this knowledge?"

"As you instructed, I brought the gel a warmer gown. Wanted to see her meself. See if'n she be worthy of Aulay. She be thin as we say before, but her waist shows signs of the growth below the lady's bosom."

"You would thrust another man's child on Aulay? My brother is barely capable of tending to his own needs. How might he protect a bairn when he remains so childlike himself?"

She returned her gaze to the rolling hills and woodlands. "Aulay will never earn another's affection," she said without rancor. "And the gel will need someone to save her reputation. Her accent say she be English. You shud know better than I how priggish be the English regarding their womenfolk. Besides, she comes from money. The child will inherit a fortune. If Aulay takes the gel to wife, we control both the woman and the bairn, and her family can do nothin' more than turn over the funds. We could leave this madness behind."

"But you designed the madness," he observed. They remained silent for several minutes as he contemplated what she suggested. "And you are certain of the lady's fortune?"

"I sent Blane to ask about the area where she be found. I be having no doubts."

His eyes narrowed in arrogance. Her smile announced how pleased she was at having bested his plans for the woman. He could not permit the girl to walk away, but not for the reasons his mother suspected. She thought only of the possible profit. He thought of the possibility of losing a woman he had yet to meet properly. "I be considering your words," he warned menacingly. He would have to discover another way of diverting the danger in which his mother had embroiled them, but for now, he would play the hand she had dealt him.

* * *

She thought of her family's letter. The news had sent her racing across the moor. Foolishly trying to outrun the pain. As she considered it now, she realized the Countess had written in haste. Without all the facts. If Edward were truly dead, she would have known immediately. Her heart would have split in halves. She would have felt the emptiness—the dark void of losing the man she dearly loved.

"Into such a conundrum you have gotten yourself," she moaned. The cot's edge cut into her side as she turned herself to lie flat on her back. "Think, Georgiana," she chastised herself. "You must think your way clear of this." The darkness filled the room, and she accepted her need to sleep. "A few hours. Dream of Edward and of Fitzwilliam and of Elizabeth. Dream of your family."

* * *

Mr. Bennet had waited patiently for the return of Pemberley's guests. A light knock on his sitting room door signaled his daughter's concern. "Come in, Lizzy," he called.

The door opened immediately, and she slipped into the room. "How did you know it was I?" she asked as she joined him before the empty hearth.

"Who else would call on an old man besides a beloved daughter?" He reached for the glass of brandy on the side table.

Elizabeth sat quietly and waited for him to finish his drink. "Did you have your evening meal?"

"Mrs. Oliver sent up a tray." He paused before adding, "I spent some time in the nursery with my grandchildren. They grow so quickly; I wanted to capture a few moments to add to my memories." His smile turned up his mouth's corners. "Your Bennet will give Jackson a rough way to go—very much as you did with Jane. You always ruled the Bennet nursery."

"One cannot forget Mr. Darcy's propensity to organize his world," Elizabeth said with her own smile of amusement. They sat in silent companionship for several minutes. "Did Lydia and Lieutenant Wickham stay at the cottage?"

He marked his place in his book with what she recognized as a poor piece of embroidery with which she had presented him when she was twelve. It pleased Elizabeth that he had kept the stiffened material as a memento of her affection for him. "Lydia has remained. Your mother has agreed to stay with your sister."

Elizabeth's tone betrayed her surprise. "Has Lieutenant Wickham departed?"

His mouth tightened into a firm line. "Mrs. Bennet and I walked in on Lieutenant Wickham's angry response to his eviction from Pemberley."

"What do you mean by *angry response?*" Elizabeth demanded.

"Your imagination is not required," he cautioned.

Elizabeth sat forward in agitation. "Lieutenant Wickham struck Lydia?"

"I do not expect it to have been the first time," he said softly. "Your sister's husband berated her with words of his many conquests." He expelled a deep sigh. "What future have I encouraged for my child?" he whispered.

"Oh, Papa." Elizabeth slumped heavily into the chair's cushions. "It was not your fault. You did what you thought necessary to protect Lydia and the family. We all required the rescue of Lydia's reputation, but none of us would ever have wished such a fate on any woman, especially not on someone as emotionally naïve as Lydia."

"I cannot lay the blame of this matter at your feet, Lizzy," he said vehemently. "You warned me of the folly of permitting Lydia to accompany the Forsters to Brighton, but I ignored your concerns.

Neither is Mr. Darcy at fault for her consciousness of misery. He attempted to convince Lydia to return to the family fold, but your mother and I had permitted your sister too much freedom. Mr. Darcy's intervention saved Lydia's reputation and permitted the rest of my daughters to make good matches. I despise the situation in which Lydia finds herself, but as much as I bemoan the Fates for setting her situation in motion, her life is the result of your sister's impetuous nature. From the time she set her sights on Lieutenant Wickham, Lydia accepted the man's control over her. I simply wish she had more of Mary's deliberate nature. I think she might have an easier road of it."

Elizabeth sighed heavily. "What shall we do, Papa?"

"Your mother will escort Lydia to Carlisle. I have promised Mr. Darcy I will remain at Pemberley with you and Bennet in your husband's absence. Besides, Lydia must learn to run a household with more economy. Your mother can assist with that transition better than I." He stared at the empty fireplace. "I am sore to deny Mrs. Bennet the pleasure of seeing the last of her daughters married by sending her on with Lydia. Yet, Mrs. Bennet grieves greatly because of the situation in which Lydia has found herself. Both of their foolish dreams of dashing men in red coats have burst. Therefore, would you ask Mr. Darcy to accept Lydia's presence at Pemberley for Kitty's sake? I have secured your sister's promise to guard her words. If it is a worry to your husband, I do not expect Lieutenant Wickham will return for her. In case I have erred in that assumption, and the gentleman chooses to seek his wife's forgiveness, I have left the carriage at the cottage for Mrs. Bennet's use."

"I shall consult with Mr. Darcy immediately."

* * *

The following morning the questions began. "Will Mother Bennet break her fast with us?" Bingley asked as he filled his plate.

Her father shot a quick glance to where Darcy sat at the table's head, and Elizabeth surmised that the two men in her life had come to an agreement. "I imagine Mrs. Bennet still dotes over our youngest. Lydia arrived unexpectedly on Pemberley's doorstep, possibly an hour or so before everyone's return from Derby last evening."

"Alone?" Bingley questioned, and after receiving a nod of affirmation from Mr. Bennet, he observed, "It was very gracious of Lieutenant Wickham to permit Lydia's attendance at Kitty's nuptials. Mrs. Wickham was unable to attend her other sisters' joinings."

When her husband had agreed to meet with her father regarding Lydia's situation, Elizabeth had wondered whether the Bingleys would also be consulted as to the story the Darcy household would tell the world of her youngest sister's untimely appearance. Evidently, her father and husband had chosen to limit those in the know. Darcy's refusal to meet her gaze said that her husband was not pleased with the outcome, but that he would tolerate Lydia's presence over the upcoming days. Elizabeth made a mental note to keep both her mother and Lydia as far from Darcy as possible. Her husband's honor and his love for her never ceased to amaze her, and she would reward his actions by circumventing Lydia's foolishness. In Elizabeth's estimation, the man who sat at the table's other end was absolutely incomparable. He had once again risen above the expected censure.

Kitty added, "Having Lydia in attendance shall make my day complete."

Having witnessed the pain displayed on Kitty's face during the previous day's confrontation with the Wickhams, Elizabeth also directed part of her admiration toward Kitty. "The five Bennet sisters under one roof," she said weakly. "It has been too long."

"It is generous of you and Mr. Darcy to open your doors to our family," Jane observed.

Elizabeth expected Darcy to respond graciously, but her husband continued to bury his nose in the morning papers. "My husband's benevolence is renowned," she said. "And I am blessed by it," she added to let him know that she understood his reticence.

Her tone must have penetrated his efforts to ignore the conversation because he lowered the paper just a bit. Unexpectedly, he winked at her, and Elizabeth breathed easier. He would not turn from her. They would survive yet another of their familial catastrophes.

"Our afternoon guests should arrive by one of the clock. I have asked Mrs. Oliver for a picnic served on the lawn at two." She stood to take her leave. "I shall check on the preparations."

"May I offer my assistance?" Kitty asked tentatively.

Elizabeth paused by Kitty's chair. "You, my dear, are assigned the arduous task of being radiantly happy." She bent to kiss the top of Kitty's head. "Create wonderful memories of these days to tell your children."

* * *

Lydia had fought against her natural propensity to seek the attention of all the gentlemen in the room; she constantly reminded herself that she would abide by her father's edict. Often, of late, she had prayed for a way to regain the friends she had so carelessly sacrificed. *At least, I am finally at Pemberley*, she thought. *I can experience the splendor of Lizzy's life first hand, rather than in finely scripted letters describing the lovely gowns of Pemberley's guests from Kitty, or in a litany of Jane's and Mary's accomplishments from Mama*, she added silently as she looked over the room. Jane had her wealthy Mr. Bingley, Lizzy her even wealthier Mr. Darcy, Mary her highly respected Mr. Grange, and now Kitty had landed the son of a baronet. The disparity between her station in life and those of her sisters was not lost on her. *Everyone content except me*, she thought.

Kitty's approach brought her musings to a close. "There you are," Kitty said as she handed Lydia a small, colorfully wrapped package. "A little something to say that I am pleased to have you join us for the wedding. It would not be the same without you, Lyddie."

Lydia's heart lurched in happiness. Kitty had not forsaken her. "How very kind," she mumbled awkwardly.

"Open it," Kitty instructed. Lydia wondered when her sister had learned such a cultured accent. She suddenly realized Kitty's voice sounded more like the polished tones often practiced by Jane and Lizzy when they were all living under the same roof. At the time, she and Kitty had made light of their older sisters' ways, but she could not escape the fact that each of the Bennet sisters, except her, had found a man of wealth or of an honored position. Was there a connection between pursuing one's studies and finding a respectable husband? It was all so confusing. Until this journey, Lydia had never analyzed her choices—had always assumed she had acted wisely—had accepted Mr. Wickham's temper as part of the marriage bargain. Now, she was not so certain. Her parents never openly expressed affection, and more than once she knew that her mother had caused her father great embarrassment, but never had he raised his hand to her, nor to his children. She had assumed she would have a husband who treated her as her father had treated her mother, but her foolish dash to the altar had denied her girlish dreams.

Lydia unwrapped the small package to find a pair of earrings that she had once coveted. "Thank...thank you," she stammered.

"You always loved them more than I," Kitty said softly. "I want you to know happiness, Lyddie. From this moment forward."

Lydia fought back the tears forming behind her lids. She looked up to take note of Mr. Winkler's approach. "Here comes the happy bridegroom," she announced.

Winkler slid his arm affectionately about Kitty's waist. "My mother would like your opinion of a fashion plate from Mrs. Fitzwilliam's catalogue," he said privately. "Would you mind seeing to her queries?"

Kitty smiled easily. "Certainly. It would be my pleasure." She glanced at Lydia. "We will speak more later."

"Go along," Winkler encouraged. "I will keep Mrs. Wickham company until it is time for the picnic to begin."

The politeness which she had been brought up to practice as a duty made it impossible for Lydia to escape; while the want of that higher species of self-command, that just consideration of others, that knowledge of her own heart, that principle of right, which had not formed any essential part of her education, made her miserable under it. At length, after a short pause, she began with, "So you are to be a clergyman, Mr. Winkler. This is rather a surprise to me. I mean, you are a baronet's son."

"Why should it surprise you? You must suppose me designed for some profession, and might perceive that I am neither a lawyer, nor a soldier, nor a sailor."

"Very true; but, in short, it had not occurred to me. And you know there is generally an uncle or a grandfather to leave a fortune to the second son," she said defensively, but immediately Lydia wondered if she had said something foolish. Her knowledge of the aristocratic ranks might be mistaken. Were sons of baronets subject to the same fortunes as those of earls or dukes?

"A very praiseworthy practice," said Winkler good-naturedly, "but not quite universal. I am one of the exceptions, and being one, must do something for myself."

"But why are you to be a clergyman? I thought that was always the lot of the youngest, where there were many to choose before him."

Winkler's gaze flickered over Lydia. "Do you think the church itself never chosen, then?"

Lydia's spirits perked up. Although the man was Kitty's intended, Mr. Winkler's attentions were a balm to her bruised ego. "*Never* is a black word. But yes, in the *never* of conversation, which means *not very often*, I do think it. For what is to be done in the church? Men love to distinguish themselves, and in either of the other lines distinction may be gained, but not in the church. A clergyman is nothing." As soon as she had said the words, she wished to own them again, but Lydia raised her chin in defiance and waited for the man's censure.

Surprisingly, Kitty's betrothed spoke with kindness and understanding. He raised neither his voice nor his hand to correct her. "The *nothing* of conversation has its gradations, I hope, as well as the *never*. A clergyman cannot be high in state or fashion. He must not head mobs, or set the *ton* in dress. But I cannot call that situation nothing which has the charge of all that is of the first importance to mankind, individually or collectively considered, temporally and eternally, which has the guardianship of religion and morals, and consequently of the manners which result from their influence. No one here can call the *office* nothing. If the man who holds it is so, it is by the neglect of his duty, by forgoing its just importance, and stepping out of his place to appear what he ought not to appear."

Lydia thought of the supercilious Mr. Collins and giggled. "You assign greater consequence to the clergyman than one has been used to hear given, or than I can quite comprehend. One does not see much of this influence and importance in society, and how can it be acquired where they are so seldom seen themselves? How can two sermons a week, even supposing them worth hearing, do all that you speak of? Govern the conduct and fashion the manners of a large congregation for the rest of the week? One scarcely sees a clergyman out of his pulpit."

"*You* are speaking of London, *I* am speaking of the nation at large," Winkler asserted.

"I suppose the metropolis, I imagine, is a pretty fair sample of the rest, but I assure you that I thought only of my cousin Mr. Collins," Lydia said.

Winkler chuckled. "I had the dubious pleasure of making Mr. Collins's acquaintance last Christmastide, and in his case, what you attribute to the clergy likely holds true. Yet, I believe, Mr. Collins is not a prime example of true men of the cloth. Nor, I should hope, of the proportion of virtue to vice throughout the kingdom. We do not look in great cities for our best morality. It is not there that respectable people of any denomination can do most good; and it certainly is not there that the influence of the clergy can be most felt. A fine preacher is followed and admired; but it is not in fine preaching only that a good clergyman will be useful in his parish and his neighborhood, where the parish and neighborhood are of a size capable of knowing his private character, and observing his general conduct, which in London can rarely be the case. The clergy are lost there in the crowds of their parishioners. They are known to the largest part only as preachers. And with regard to their influencing public manners, Mrs. Wickham, you must not misunderstand me, or suppose I mean to call them the arbiters of good breeding, the regulators of refinement and courtesy, the masters of the ceremonies of life. The *manners* I speak of might rather be called *conduct*, perhaps, the result of good principles; the effect, in short, of those doctrines which it is their duty to teach and recommend; and it will, I believe, be everywhere found, that as the clergy are, or are not what they ought to be, so are the rest of the nation."

Lydia immediately understood why Kitty had chosen this man. Mr. Winkler answered her sister's need for order and for generosity. A pang of jealousy ricocheted through her chest. "Certainly," she said with gentle earnestness. "I concede to your point and to the fact that you are the perfect mate for our Kitty. I wish you both happiness."

* * *

"Fitzwilliam." Elizabeth cornered him in one of the second-level hallways. Immediately, she backed her husband into an empty bedroom and laced her arms about his neck. Pulling his head toward hers, she went on tiptoes to claim a kiss. As she had hoped, Darcy responded fervently. When their lips parted, Elizabeth rested her cheek against the fine lawn of his shirt. "Mmm," she sighed. "Sandalwood and my husband." She inhaled deeply. "Such an intoxicating mix."

His hand slid slowly up the curve of her waist to caress the underside of her breast. "To what do I owe the pleasure of your company?" He lifted her hips to him.

"Do you mind?" she rasped as she kissed along his cravat's line.

Darcy chuckled lightly. "Do I mind being manhandled by my wife? Not at all. Use me as you will," he said softly before returning to her mouth.

Elizabeth wriggled closer and then insinuated her hand between them to unbutton his waistcoat. She could feel his heat building as she gave his shirt a small tug to free it.

"Lizzy," he groaned as his lips slid down her neck's curve. "I can never have enough of you."

Her own heat coursed through her veins. It filled her stomach and sent the familiar ache between her thighs. "I am here, William. Take what you want of me. I have no objections."

Darcy reached behind him and turned the key. He lifted her and carried her to the chaise. "As God is my witness, I love you, Elizabeth Darcy. Beyond reason."

She wound her arms about his neck. "Then show me, William, and permit me to demonstrate in return of my deepest regard for you. I do not deserve you, but I cannot breathe unless I know your love. Above all others, Fitzwilliam. Forever, I shall love you."

* * *

Fortunately, Lydia had remained quite sedate throughout the evening's gathering. To assure her sister's compliance, however, Elizabeth had placed the girl on her right to control the conversation's flow. Besides those in attendance as house guests, Elizabeth had invited another three dozen people to spend the afternoon and evening as part of the pre-wedding celebration. Aware of Mr. Winkler's position in the community, Elizabeth had invited the most influential members of the neighborhood.

"I remember that husband of yours, Mrs. Wickham," Mr. Lowell said as he finished off the fish course. "Quite a wastrel when he was younger. Kept my Jonathan busy with one scheme after another. Old Mr. Wickham was always bailing the boy out of trouble." He paused only briefly before turning his attention on Elizabeth. "Darcy and Fitzwilliam were more studious than my boy and Wickham. Old Mr. Darcy kept a tight rein on your husband, Ma'am."

"Mr. Darcy accepted his father's firm hand with pride," Elizabeth observed. "And your Jonathan has shown himself to be very adept at handling the mill."

Mr. Lowell nodded his agreement. "The boy has a right smart head on his shoulders. And the Earl's son, Fitzwilliam, he has served England most honorably."

"We are quite proud of the Major General. Mrs. Fitzwilliam has joined Edward at the family property in Scotland," Elizabeth confided.

Elizabeth noted her sister's frown. "Was Lieutenant Wickham the only failure?" Lydia mumbled.

"What was that you said, Mrs. Wickham? I fear that I do not hear as well as I should. It is terrible getting older," Lowell declared.

Perfectly aware of her sister's complaint, Elizabeth quickly responded. "Mrs. Wickham was just commenting on how pleasant it is to hear something of her husband's youth from those who knew him best. All young men attack life differently; do they not, Mr. Lowell?"

"That they do, Mrs. Darcy. I expect those horror stories my father used to tell of my escapades would seem out of place with the man I am now. Some say it is harder with boys in the house, but having had three, I can tell you that the two girls were so much more difficult," he declared.

Elizabeth smiled easily. The conversation had turned. "I imagine that my father would agree with you. Five daughters brought him several gray hairs."

Lowell laughed good-naturedly. "Well, five girls would obviously be more troublesome than two."

* * *

"What is it, Thorne?" Kitty asked as her intended unfolded a message delivered by Mr. Nathan.

With a serious mien, he scanned the paper. "Mr. Saunders has broken his leg. The surgeon will not permit him to leave his mother's house for at least a week. He cannot pronounce our vows. There is no one else in the area. We will have to postpone our nuptials."

"No," she said a bit too loudly. "There must be someone else."

"I cannot administer my own vows," he insisted. "We will have to wait."

Elizabeth appeared beside her sister. Smiling to allay the Pemberley guests' interest in the agitated conversation between their local minister and his fiancée, she asked softly, "Is there something you wish to share?"

Kitty caught her hand. "Oh, Lizzy, it is absolutely dreadful. Mr. Saunders has sustained an injury and cannot oversee our joining."

"Mr. Polland departed for London yesterday," Mr. Winkler added.

"We shall have to postpone the wedding." Kitty's words brought tears to her eyes.

Elizabeth placed her sister's hand in Mr. Winkler's. "You shall marry the man you have chosen, and the wedding shall take place on Monday as planned."

"But..." Kitty began; yet, a flick of Elizabeth's wrist cut short the protest.

Elizabeth smiled in amusement. "Did I not mention that Mr. Joseph once held a living at Stoke?"

Relief washed Winkler's countenance. "Why did I not consider that?"

"Probably because the two of you are determined to believe that anything as right as what you are feeling cannot be possible. Trust me." She turned her head to search the room for Darcy. Their eyes met and held for the briefest second. "God sometimes answers the simplest prayers. Go speak to Mr. Joseph. I am certain the man will be delighted to conduct the ceremony. He has missed his clerical duties."

"Thank you, Lizzy." Kitty gave her sister a one-armed embrace before hurrying across the room to speak to the Josephs.

"Something amiss?" Darcy said softly behind her.

"Not any longer," she said as she intertwined her arm through his. "I resolved my sister's dilemma."

Darcy smiled lovingly at her. "I would never underestimate you, Mrs. Darcy."

"I am pleased you sought me out, my husband." She fluttered her lashes at him in an exaggerated flirtation. "I am in need of a dance partner. Mary has agreed to play for everyone's entertainment."

"Probably not as effectively as Mrs. Fitzwilliam," he observed. "But I am thankful for Mrs. Grange's efforts."

"As am I," she said softly. "Although I, too, deeply miss Georgiana. Yet, with the unexpected appearance of the Wickhams, I was thankful for our sister's absence from Pemberley."

Darcy brought the back of her hand to his lips. "It is a small blessing, but I will accept God's forethought." He paused as they approached the dance floor. "Am I to assume that Lieutenant Wickham has departed the area?"

"For all any of us know," she whispered. "Lydia has heard nothing from the man since he stormed from the curate's cottage yesterday afternoon. Lieutenant Wickham threatened my father after Mr. Bennet's interference, said he would return to Carlisle, and left one of his infamous warnings for you."

Darcy pulled her into a private alcove. "What type of warning?" he demanded in a hushed tone.

Elizabeth's forehead crinkled. "Just Lieutenant Wickham's usual posturing. My sister's husband claimed our snub was beyond the pale before saying that he would never forgive our rebuff. It is nothing of which to be concerned. Typical for Lieutenant Wickham to blame others for his own shortcomings."

"The man will spin the incident to his own benefit."

"Aye, but who is to listen? If Lieutenant Wickham announces that we refused to receive him, people shall wonder what of his offense. Pemberley has opened its doors to strangers for more than five decades. Those of sense shall know his accusations as false."

"It can be no worse than Lieutenant Wickham's previous offenses," Darcy assured. "Now, my love, it is time for our dance." He escorted her to the floor's center. Leaning down to speak close to her ear, he murmured, "I will ask Mrs. Grange to play a waltz if you promise to save me a second set."

Elizabeth's mouth lifted in that devilishly wicked way that had always made his heart race. "Oh, what a punishment!" she feigned in shocked alarm. "To be held in the arms of the man I adore. How shall I endure it?'

Darcy wondered if he had ever thanked her properly for the happiness she had brought to his life. He certainly had tried, but had he succeeded? How would he ever know for certain that she understood the depth of his devotion? "You will persevere," he assured, "because you have learned to *tolerate* my presence on the dance floor."

"*Tolerance* is such a noble quality," she teased.

Darcy winked at her before turning to those in the large drawing room. "Friends," he said loudly to draw their attention. "Mrs. Darcy and I would be honored if you would join us on this makeshift dance floor. Mrs. Grange has graciously agreed to accompany our efforts."

* * *

"How long have you served the Darcys?" George Wickham asked as he played a spade to take the hand. When he had stormed from the curate's cottage, he had not considered his purse's weakened state. Therefore, he had sought Pemberley's familiarity. He had employed a small shepherd's hut off the north pasture as shelter. Having spent his childhood on the estate, Wickham knew the land nearly as well as Darcy. "Maybe better," he had told himself. After all, his father had been old Mr. Darcy's land steward, an exalted position within the Darcy household. Darcy's father had served as Wickham's godfather, and the old man's kindness had been liberally bestowed.

Not a day had gone by that he had not cursed his youthful disregard of the opportunity, which had once presented itself. The former Mr. Darcy had supported him at school and afterwards at Cambridge, but he had squandered away the completion of his gentleman's education, having been sent down from university before Mr. George Darcy could intervene in his behalf.

The elder gentleman had thought that he might accept a living at Kympton as his profession, but Wickham had had other ideas. Forsaking his vicious propensities was not part of his nature, so having resolved against taking orders, Wickham had written to Darcy and had requested a more immediate pecuniary advantage in lieu of the preferment. At the time, he had considered studying the law; yet, he soon abandoned that aspiration to the joys of idleness and dissipation. For three years, he had avoided Darcy, but with the decease of the incumbent of the living, which had been designed for him, Wickham had applied to Darcy by letter for the presentation. His circumstances, by that time, were exceedingly bad, and his creditors had been hounding him for payments.

He had tried to convince Darcy that he had had a change of heart and that he was absolutely resolved on being ordained. After all, many of the divinity students were of Mr. Collins's ilk, knowing less about religion than did those to whom they delivered God's word. However, Darcy had adamantly refused. Even when he had reminded his former friend of old Darcy's intentions, Fitzwilliam Darcy ignored Wickham's entreaty. Just the thought of those days still brought a hard fist of panic to his stomach.

"Been working fer Mr. Darcy come on four years now," the groom replied. "Me Pa worked for the master's father. They both be fine gentlemen."

Wickham had removed his uniform jacket to lessen a chance of recognition. "I knew the present Mr. Darcy when we were both youths. He was a bit starchy in those days."

"He ain't no easy man, but Mr. Darcy treat me right," the man argued. "Not a fairer master in the shire."

Wickham refused any kind thoughts of the man he had once called *friend*. He laid out his hand and reached for his winnings. He would have preferred a game with higher stakes, but he would accept these men's meager earnings. It was a convoluted way of stealing from Darcy.

"What goes on at the main house?" he asked casually. For a brief second, he wondered whether his wife had been permitted to join her family festivities. Lydia, despite her immaturity, had aligned herself with him. No one had ever shown him such loyalty. Maybe in the future, he should see to the girl's happiness. Resenting having been trapped in their marriage, he had never given Mrs. Wickham the opportunity to become a good wife. He could possibly mold her into the type of woman that he needed to advance in his military career. Lydia did have a pleasing personality, and she was adventurous. Yet, he would not consider any such move until he had exacted some form of revenge on Darcy for the slight he had suffered at the man's hands.

"Big party for Mrs. Darcy's sister and the local clergy, Mr. Winkler. Ye know the man?" the groom continued to speak for the group.

"No. I departed the neighborhood a decade since." Wickham reshuffled the cards for the next round. "Is the whole family in attendance? I recall Mr. Darcy having a cousin that was as close as a brother." He had always despised Edward Fitzwilliam. The earl's youngest son had thought himself too far above Wickham to claim a close acquaintance, and Fitzwilliam had often counseled Darcy to ignore Wickham's taunts and schemes.

"That be the Major General. He and Miss Darcy marry in March. The new Mrs. Fitzwilliam not be at tonight's celebration. She be meetin' her husband in Scotland at the family home. He be fightin' old Boney until recently."

Wickham continued his interest. "Really? I suppose that will be pleasant for them both. I mean, a man likes to have his woman beneath him." He smiled congenially at the men sitting around the makeshift table in Darcy's barn.

The groom snickered. "That he do."

Wickham thought of how he had once schemed to make Georgiana Darcy his wife. He had nearly gotten away with it, too. He had manipulated his former amour Mrs. Younge, who had secured a position as Miss Darcy's companion. The woman had been easy to seduce. Almost as easy as Darcy's little sister. He had plied the girl with reminders of his kindness to her as a child, and Georgiana's affectionate heart had retained a strong impression of those shared memories. In fact, Wickham was certain the girl had fallen in love with him.

However, Darcy had arrived before the intended elopement could take place. All his carefully executed plans had fallen through. Late in the night, he collected his belongings from where he had stashed them in a nearby copse. His resolve for revenge against the Darcys hardened against Georgiana, her aristocratic husband, and the haughty Fitzwilliam Darcy. He would have to content himself with Mrs. Darcy suffering indirectly for aligning herself with the Darcys of Pemberley. *After all*, he told himself with a wicked grin gracing his lips, *I cannot harm my wife's sister*.

Chapter 6

"LIEUTENANT? IS SOMETHING AMISS?" Having his temporary aide follow him to Rosings Park had set Edward's disaster instincts on alert. He had called on his aunt and cousin as he awaited his release from duty. Lady Catherine's devitalized state had worried him, and he had made a point of spending time alone with the lady to better ascertain what had brought on his imperious aunt's reduced presence.

"It will be important that the household not treat Southland as an invalid," he remarked as they shared tea in Her Ladyship's favorite drawing room.

His aunt smoothed an imaginary wrinkle from her gown. "I shall speak directly to Mr. Varney and Mrs. Montgomery. It shall be as you suggest."

"How goes Anne's transition to the estate's helm?" he asked nonchalantly.

Lady Catherine drew in a deep breath. "Anne has a good grasp of the ledgers, but she has no concept of the why and the wherefore of purchases and upkeep. It shall be a relief to welcome Captain Southland home."

"Then Anne and Roman have found a measure of happiness in their joining?"

She busied herself with refilling her cup. "Neither shall handle the responsibilities of Rosings without the other. They have gaping weaknesses, but together, they shall persevere."

"And you, Your Ladyship? How are you persevering?" Again he eyed his aunt suspiciously. Something was different, but Edward could not pinpoint the exact change. Lady Catherine appeared less robust, but he was unsure whether that had to do with despondency over the idea of turning her beloved Rosings over to Anne, or whether is was something more pronounced.

"What do you insinuate, Edward?" Lady Catherine said tersely. "That I lack the magnanimity to see my daughter into my position?"

Before he could respond, Mr. Varney had interrupted their conversation with news of Lieutenant Conrad's unexpected arrival. Having asked the Rosings' butler to show his aide into the room and then having made a hasty introduction, Edward had asked, "Is something amiss?"

Conrad fixed his mouth in a tight line. "I beg your indulgence, Sir. Headquarters demanded that I seek you out." He extended his hand, which held an official-looking letter.

Edward reached for the item. Despite his best efforts, his hand trembled as he accepted the message. "If Napoleon has escaped again, someone else must report to the Continent," he said pointedly. Using the knife from the tea tray, he broke the wax seal and began to read. "What the…" he growled. "How could this happen?"

A raised eyebrow said his tone had worried his aunt. "What is it, Edward?"

"Some asinine clerk at Westminster has sent my parents and Georgiana news of my demise." He was out of his chair and pacing the floor. "My God! The Earl must be devastated. And Georgiana. This mistake will destroy my wife. Lord! I apologize, Your Ladyship," he rasped. "But I must leave. I must be to Derbyshire."

She struggled to her feet with Conrad's assistance. "Of course, Edward. Tell me what I might do to settle this error. Poor Martin is likely to be apoplectic."

"Would you write to the Earl and assure him of my survival? My father will believe you above some military missive. Explain to him that I must reach Georgiana before this news becomes common knowledge. She is alone in Scotland, and I worry how she will handle such erroneous garble without family to support her."

"I shall have Mr. Varney send for your horse. Go pack your things. I shall see to the rest."

Edward caught her up in a quick embrace. "You are quite remarkable," he whispered into her hair, and then he rushed from the room.

"As are you," she murmured to his retreating form.

* * *

"You look absolutely lovely," Lydia gushed as she joined her other sisters and their mother in Kitty's suite at Pemberley.

Kitty giggled. "I feel lovely." She spun in place. "The gown is perfect."

"I preferred the one Mrs. Swift designed," Mrs. Bennet fussed over one of the seams, "but I bow to Jane's and Lizzy's knowledge of fashion. God only knows that I have no opportunity to observe the latest fashions in Hertfordshire. We are slow in the countryside to incorporate London's whims."

Lizzy gave her mother's shoulder a quick squeeze. "Mrs. Bingley and I have cheated, Mama. We borrowed Mrs. Fitzwilliam's fashion plates."

Kitty twirled again. "I do not care how it came about. This dress is exquisite. My gratitude knows no bounds."

Elizabeth's smile tugged at her mouth's corners. "I have a present for you. This is from Mr. Darcy and me." She handed Kitty a colorfully wrapped package.

"Oh, my," Kitty gasped. With trembling fingers, she pulled the paper away and lifted the lid. "Lizzy," she rasped breathily. "They are magnificent."

"At Georgiana's wedding, I noticed your wearing the tear-drop diamond. You seem never to remove it."

Kitty thought of the secret she had shared with Major General Fitzwilliam and her special reward from the Prince Regent. "It is a gift from Mr. Winkler's grandmother," she lied. She prayed that God would not strike her down for beginning her wedding day with an untruth.

"The necklace is so dainty, but so striking," Elizabeth added. "When I saw these, I thought them the perfect match."

Kitty removed the earrings from the box. They were small diamonds. As Elizabeth had said, they would highlight the diamond resting at the swell of her bosom. She rolled them across her palm. "You shall express my gratitude to Mr. Darcy?"

Elizabeth embraced her, and Kitty felt the tears prick her eyes. "I shall be pleased to have you so close to Pemberley." Her sister caressed her cheek, and Kitty fought another round of tears. "We must to the church," Elizabeth announced. "Come everyone. Our carriages await. Kitty, Papa shall be up to escort you to the services in a few minutes."

Each sister embraced her as they rushed to join the gentlemen waiting below. Soon, only her mother remained. "It hurts a woman to send her child off to the home of another." Mrs. Bennet placed a loose curl behind Kitty's ear. "You are the last of my children—the last to leave Longbourn."

"Mama, you have spent the last decade on a campaign to find us all proper husbands. You should be pleased with your success. Few mothers can claim such worthy gentlemen as family."

Her mother preened with the praise. *Just like Lydia*, Kitty thought. Until this moment, she had not considered how very similar her youngest sister's personality was to their mother's. Although she silently cringed with each of her mother's exclamations of delight, for years, Kitty had tried to fit into the family by imitating Lydia's actions. *A person cannot have it both ways*, she reminded herself.

"I would not call it a campaign," Mrs. Bennet said, "but I did my best by each of you."

"That you did, my dear," Mr. Bennet declared from the open doorway. "It is time, Mrs. Bennet. Mrs. Darcy awaits you in her coach. Everyone else has departed for the church."

"Of course, Mr. Bennet." With one last caress of Kitty's cheek, she disappeared. Loud sniffs of happiness echoed through the hall.

Her father paused before opening his arms to her, and immediately, Kitty hurried to fill them. "Oh, my precious girl," he whispered. "You have blossomed into quite the young woman."

Kitty fought the sobs gathering in her chest. "Thank you, Papa."

He cleared his throat. "We cannot tarry. Mr. Winkler must be pacing the floor in anticipation."

Kitty took a deep, satisfying breath. "I am ready," she whispered.

* * *

"Dearly beloved, we are gathered together here in the sight of God, and in the presence of these witnesses…" From the church's raised dais, Mr. Joseph's voice rang clear. "To join together this Man and this Woman in holy Matrimony; which is an honourable estate…"

Thorne's eyes remained locked on Kitty's countenance. She was the most breathtakingly beautiful sight he had ever beheld. He tried to wipe the silly grin from his lips, but it was impossible to hide his elation. Joseph's voice continued in the background, but all he knew was that Catherine Bennet would be his forever.

"I require and charge you both, that if either of you know any impediment, why you may not be lawfully joined together in Matrimony, you do now confess it. For be ye well assured, that so many as are coupled together otherwise than God's Word doth allow are not joined together by God; neither is their Matrimony lawful."

Thorne wondered what had become of Mr. Joseph's prior words. He could not recall the man's resonant voice beyond "Dearly beloved." From the moment she had entered the church, he had thought of nothing but the woman beside him. For over two years, he had watched her. When he had first laid eyes upon Catherine Bennet, she had, literally, taken his breath away. He had stumbled through a sermon that he could normally have recited backwards. And when he had first held her hand, it was like a punch to his stomach. She had captured his heart with one innocent beat of her eyelashes. He was lost to all but her. But a man must move slowly when a girl is not yet a young woman, and so he had waited. However, when she had returned to Pemberley last Christmas, Thorne had been convinced that it was time to claim her as his own.

Evidently, he had pronounced his vows at the correct time, for he heard Mr. Joseph say, "O Eternal God, Creator and Preserver of all mankind, Giver of all spiritual grace, the Author of everlasting life; send this Man this Woman, whom we bless in thy Name; that, as Isaac and Rebecca lived faithfully together, so these persons may surely perform and keep the vow and covenant betwixt them made, and may ever remain in perfect love and peace together, and live according to thy laws; through Jesus Christ our Lord. Amen."

* * *

"Mrs. Darcy," Darcy said softly as he stepped behind her. "May I speak to you privately for a moment?"

"Of course, Mr. Darcy." Elizabeth excused herself from the neighbors who had paid their respects during the wedding breakfast.

Darcy led her to a recessed alcove in the large drawing room. "I apologize for drawing you away from our guests." He kept his voice low to assure privacy. "But I needed to speak to you. Mr. Joseph has received an urgent message from his wife's father. Parnell has learned of Lord McClinton's possible interest in the Kilmarnock and Troon Railway. He wants Joseph to leave for the Ayrshire coast immediately to secure the rights. Could you see your way clear to my leaving this afternoon rather than to-morrow morning?"

"Oh, Fitzwilliam," she said as she sank against him. "I know it is foolish, but I had hoped there would be another way."

Darcy held her close, lightly stroking her back. "If it were a lesser opportunity, I would not consider it. Yet, we both under-stand that change is coming to the English countryside. We can either embrace it or be knocked over by it. It is likely to take two decades for the full impact of these decisions to be known. By then, Bennet will be coming into his inheritance. This is a slow, long-term investment that will prove profitable for our children and likely for their children."

"Then I cannot practice selfishness," she murmured as she released her hold on his waist. "You shall not tarry. Go to Scot-land, and finish your business quickly. Then come back to me and to our son."

"I will have someone pack my bags. Meet me in our rooms in thirty minutes," he whispered in her ear.

* * *

"Lizzy." Jane caught her hand. "Mr. Bingley has ordered our carriages for one of the clock. We shall return to Cheshire this afternoon."

"Shall everyone desert me in one afternoon?" she grumbled. "Must you?"

Jane glanced to where Lydia spoke to two of Darcy's neighbors. "We had originally planned to leave on the morrow, but this way we may depart for the North tomorrow."

Elizabeth followed her sister's gaze. "And you would remove Lydia from Pemberley."

"Mr. Bingley thinks it best. We shall take Lydia and Mama to Cheshire and then deposit them in Carlisle on our way north."

"Although I cannot approve of your retreat, I offer Mr. Bingley my gratitude for resolving a stinging situation."

"Papa says he shall remain at Pemberley in Mr. Darcy's absence. If we take Mama and Lydia with us, then Mary and Mr. Grange may use Papa's coach to return to Hertfordshire. It is for the best."

Elizabeth frowned deeply. "Just like foul-tasting medicine. For the best; but no one wishes to swallow it."

* * *

The heavy drapes left the bedroom in shadow. "Fitzwilliam," she whispered as she slipped into the darkened chamber. Then his lips grazed her shoulder from behind. "Fitz...Fitzwilliam." She inhaled quickly and held her breath.

A smile tugged at his lips. "Yes, my love." Irresistible yearning consumed his senses.

"I thought you meant to kiss me farewell in private." She leaned heavily against him.

"Then you thought in error. If I must leave Pemberley, I will carry the scent of you on my skin."

"You say the most delicious things, Mr. Darcy." She turned in his embrace to offer her mouth.

Darcy feasted on her, implanting the memory of his wife on his fingertips, his mouth, his body. He allowed his eyes to revel in her dimly seen perfection. Darcy's hand drifted slowly up the curve of her body to cup her chin. "Permit me to demonstrate how much I love you." He trailed his lips down her neck. Like some ethereal concoction, the taste of her drove him insane. When Elizabeth shivered, he scooped her into his arms and carried her to their bed.

"Our guests," she murmured as he spread wet kisses along her collarbone.

"Will think me the most fortunate of men to have gained your affections."

* * *

Forty minutes later, they returned to the drawing room to bid farewell to their company. Darcy refused to release her hand. He needed her touch on his arm—her heat filling him from each of her fingers. He noted Matthew Joseph's possessive posture with his wife. "Still waters," he murmured to Elizabeth when she observed Mary Joseph's flushed face.

"Or maybe not so still." Elizabeth smiled knowingly at Darcy. "I shall be happy to entertain Mrs. Joseph until your return. It shall be a small consolation."

"After tomorrow, Pemberley will seem quite empty."

"At least, Kitty shall remain in the neighborhood," Elizabeth said.

Darcy kissed the back of her hand. "Let us bid the Reverend Mr. and Mrs. Winkler farewell. They will enjoy the privacy of the dowager house for the next week."

Elizabeth teased, "You sound as if you wish it were us."

Darcy's eyes twinkled in mischief. "I would welcome the privacy, but I much prefer the familiarity of our current intimacy to those early days of uncertainty." He brought her a bit closer. "I find knowing how to please you more intoxicating than learning what pleases you," he murmured into her hair. "And I will spend my time in Scotland concocting new ways to bring the pink flush to your face."

Elizabeth blushed profusely, and Darcy chuckled. However, she managed to offer him a challenge. "As you well know, Mr. Darcy, I am not an easy woman to please."

* * *

After Kitty and Mr. Winkler's departure, the various guests bid Pemberley's hospitality farewell. Within the hour, the Bingleys' two coaches rolled toward Cheshire. Sir James and Lady Winkler had retired to their son's small house. They would leave Derbyshire for Dorset on the morrow. Rose Winkler had rejoined her parents at the ministerial lodgings, a fact which had vexed Ruth Joseph greatly. "I do not see why Miss Winkler could not remain at Pemberley for one more evening," she had protested to a less than sympathetic Mrs. Joseph. Her husband and Mr. Darcy had ridden out closer to two than to the one of the clock that Pemberley's master had preferred.

Mary sighed deeply as her husband's figure disappeared over the rolling ridge leading to the main turnpike road. With a like gesture of resignation, Elizabeth interlocked her arm with Mary's, and together they turned toward the main entrance. "We have been abandoned, Mary, for the prospect of great riches," Elizabeth said in that conspiratorial tone they had often shared. "How shall we persevere?"

Mary glanced up at Pemberley's majestic entrance. "At least, they left us a proper abode in which to while away our time."

As the tension in Mary's grip lessened, Elizabeth laughed easily. "There is that advantage to our loneliness," Pemberley's mistress declared with an easily recognized false bravado. "Perhaps, Mr.

Darcy shall return to find the house decorated in his favorite shade of pink."

Mary laughed also. They would make a go of their loneliness together. "It would well serve him if it were possible to do so."

"We shall start with the gentleman's private chambers."

* * *

It was there. She had searched the room for Darcy's letter. In her heart, she knew he would leave one for her, but when she had purposely looked for it earlier, disappointment had greeted her efforts. As she retired for the evening, she had sought one of Darcy's shirts in place of her nightgown. She knew herself foolish, but she would risk the servants' whispers to keep her husband close in his absence. *Hannah shall silence the gossip*, she had told herself as she draped Darcy's fine lawn shirt over her shoulders. Elizabeth had had a delightful afternoon and evening with Mary and Ruth. They had even created a whimsical list of all the pink items she would need if she were to redesign Darcy's sitting room and bedchamber. Now, it was time to be alone with her fears for him. "I shall never order another new night rail. Only new shirts for my husband," she had told herself.

When she had passed through Darcy's dressing room to reach her own, she found the letter propped against the mirror. On the outside, Darcy had written in his familiar scrawl, "Yes, Elizabeth, this is for you!"

"The man is too self-assured," she grumbled, but she happily snatched up the letter and returned to her bed before reading it. Carelessly, she wondered how this particular letter would rate among Darcy's previous ones. For a man of few wasted words, her husband was absolutely garrulous when he took pen in hand. She should have recognized that quality in him prior to their marriage.

She had witnessed the number of letters he had written to his sister and his cousin and his man of business when they both had stayed at Netherfield.

"How delighted Miss Darcy will be to receive such a letter." Despite her best efforts, Elizabeth could easily recall Caroline Bingley's manipulations to earn Darcy's attention. The lady, on one particular occasion, had seated herself near Darcy and had watched the progress of his letter to his sister, while Elizabeth had been sufficiently amused by what passed between Darcy and his companion. Later, she had regretted thinking poorly of the man she had come to love, but at the time, she was quite convinced of her own absolute opinions. "I should have listened to my heart. I should have realized that my anger existed because I so deeply wanted his approval," she whispered to the silent room. That particular evening, Miss Bingley had repeatedly called off his attention with messages to Georgiana. The perpetual commendations of the lady on either Darcy's handwriting, or on the evenness of his lines, or on the length of his letter, with the perfect unconcern with which Miss Bingley's praises were received, had formed a curious dialogue, and was exactly in unison with Elizabeth's opinion of each at the time.

Over the past three years, her opinion of Caroline had not altered. In fact, try as she might to feel otherwise, she disliked the woman completely. "The Americans do not deserve such an abomination," she declared. Then she thought of the man with whom Miss Bingley had eloped, and Elizabeth knew her censure unjust. The man they had known as Beaufort Manneville had proven himself quite false. "The lady should have aligned herself with someone who would curtail her wickedness, not encourage it," she decided. Elizabeth's thoughts returned to how foolishly she had misjudged Darcy. "Of course, I did not always love the man so well as I do now," she thought with a self-chastising snort of laughter. "But in such cases as these, a good memory is unpardonable. This is the last time I shall ever remember it myself."

The image of Darcy ignoring Caroline Bingley hung in Elizabeth's mind. "He was quite crotchety now that I consider his words," she mused. "Oh, my," she laughed openly. "I wonder if my dear husband realizes in hindsight how often he defended me with his every rebuff of Miss Bingley's regard. It is quite delicious now that I dwell on it."

"You write uncommonly fast," Miss Bingley had said to capture Darcy's attention.

Without looking up, Darcy had countered. "You are mistaken. I write rather slowly."

"How many letters you must have occasion to write in the course of a year! Letters of business too! How odious I should think them!"

Darcy had responded in that same voice Elizabeth now recognized as the one he used when someone annoyed him. "It is fortunate, then, that they fall to my lot instead of to yours."

Miss Bingley had ignored his tone. "Pray tell your sister that I long to see her."

"I have already told her so once, by your desire." In retrospect, Elizabeth should have recognized his censure. Instead, she had thought they spoke intimately.

"How can you contrive to write so evenly?"

He remained silent.

"Tell your sister I am delighted to hear of her improvement on the harp, and pray let her know that I am quite in raptures with her beautiful little design for a table, and I think it infinitely superior to Miss Grantley's."

"Will you give me leave to defer your raptures till I write again? At present, I have not room to do them justice."

"Oh, foolish, foolish me," Elizabeth moaned. "Why did I not see Mr. Darcy's worth prior to that volatile encounter at Hunsford? I should have acknowledged our compatibility, at least to myself, when we shared the time at Netherfield, and I should have seen how little Fitzwilliam liked Miss Bingley's flattery. Was I jealous of the woman? Even then? How humiliating is this discovery! I could not have been more wretchedly blind."

Accepting her foolish pride as her weakness, Elizabeth shrugged away her self-censure. *It cannot be undone.* Upset with herself for being so naïve, she snuggled lower into the bed linens for comfort. Turning on her side where she might lay the pages on the wool pane covering the bed, she traced Darcy's script with her fingertip. Then she sniffed the shirt's sleeve and closed her eyes to bring Darcy near. "I am humbled by your love, Mr. Darcy," she said before unfolding the page.

24 July

My dearest, darling Elizabeth,

Our separation lies heavy on my soul as I prepare for my departure to Scotland. Once our lives took divergent paths, with each of us ignoring the obvious; yet, you soon became the secret place where I no longer had to hide the true me. Now, we are two heartbeats which have become one. There is nothing to compare with the power of you and me together.

In my absence, my love, I charge you not to neglect your health in your haste to be both mother and father to our son. Bennet requires a mother who does not neglect her own needs. I also charge you to seek out the invaluable staff, which adores you, our child, and Pemberley, if you find yourself overwhelmed by the everyday pressures of managing this estate.

Elizabeth chuckled. The Master of Pemberley often gave orders when he slept. Yet, she could not find fault with the man's air of superiority. He had taken on his shoulders the responsibility for all their lives, and Fitzwilliam Darcy performed his duty well. Nothing escaped his notice.

I wish to thank you for accepting even my weakest efforts to bring you happiness. It is my wish that you know your brightest days in our combined life. Whether it is a hope or a dream or a promise, together we can change it into a reality—born from a love that is sweeter than all time.

Please know, my dearest Elizabeth, that each night I will dream of you—the woman I adore. My love for you is more than true, and my feelings are deeper than those three words so easily bandied about among those caught up in passion's first flush. When you came into my life my world tilted, but it also opened for me for the first time. My life began. You are the music of my soul. Until we are once more in one another's embrace, I remain your loving husband.

D.

Elizabeth brushed aside the tear crawling down her cheek. "The man always manages to reduce every emotion to its unique core. I shall never understand how he does it." Elizabeth read the letter twice more before blowing out her candle. She slid the message under her pillow. Eventually, it would join the others in the beribboned stack in the bottom drawer of her wardrobe, but not before she had committed it to memory, just as she had done with all the others. "Good night, my love," she whispered to Darcy's empty pillow. "Hurry home. Bennet and I shall not sleep soundly until we feel your strong arms holding us again."

* * *

The Granges departed for Hertfordshire shortly before eight. "Return the coach to Pemberley," Mr. Bennet instructed his middle daughter. "I have no knowledge of when I must send for your mother. Mrs. Bennet will likely remain a sennight or more with the Wickhams, but I may need the coach sooner."

"Yes, Papa."

"And you will check on Longbourn and send word if you find something inappropriate."

"Mary knows what to do, Papa," Elizabeth said softly from behind him. "Mama may not have seen to our education when it came to studying the masters, but she taught each of us about account books and menus and running a household. We learned first hand every facet of tending to Longbourn personally. Mary shall not fail you."

"Of course she will not fail, Lizzy. Mary is as talented as all her sisters." He squeezed Mary's hand in assurance. "I am blessed to have four daughters of good sense." He assisted Mary into the coach. "Be safe. I will see you at Longbourn soon."

As the coach pulled away, Elizabeth laced her arm through her father's. "With Mama not returning to Longbourn, Mary and Mr. Grange shall have the place to themselves. Maybe by spring, she and Kitty shall each be presenting you with additional grandchildren."

"Mayhap, you, too, Lizzy." He walked slowly toward Pemberley's entrance.

Elizabeth leaned heavily against his shoulder. "I cannot say for certain, but Mr. Darcy and I are looking at the possibility."

"Is your husband aware of this grand event?" Mr. Bennet slid his arm around his favorite daughter's waist.

Elizabeth's features glowed with happiness. "If I had told Fitzwilliam, he would never have departed for Scotland, and the opportunity for securing Bennet's future and those of any other children we may have depends on this venture. Besides, I am not absolutely certain."

"And it is important to be certain of such specifics where Mr. Darcy is concerned," Mr. Bennet said wryly.

"Oh, Papa, one does not need to spend more than a few minutes with my husband to know that your words are an understatement of gargantuan proportions."

* * *

"The morning post, Mrs. Darcy." The Pemberley butler presented a stack of letters on a silver salver.

Elizabeth accepted the items. "I assume you placed the estate mail on Mr. Darcy's desk for Mr. Marlowe's attention."

"Yes, Ma'am." The butler bowed from the room.

Elizabeth began sifting through the stack.

"Anything interesting?" Mrs. Joseph asked from her seat on Elizabeth's left.

Her friend's voice rooted Elizabeth to the present. All morning she had daydreamed of Darcy's return. "Several thank-yous for the picnic and dinner. A few invitations, which I shall ignore until Mr. Darcy's return. That is, unless you have a desire for an afternoon of visits."

"Maybe in a week or so I shall tire of your company," Mrs. Joseph teased, but for now, I find myself quite content to prevail upon your good graces."

Heart quickening, Elizabeth scanned the last two missives. Her face twisted in deep regret.

"Is something muddled headed?" Mary Joseph asked.

"Not exactly," Elizabeth murmured as she turned the posts over in her hand. "Two letters from Mr. Darcy's cousin. It is a shame that

Fitzwilliam departed before they arrived. My husband has longed for news of the Major General's return."

Mary placed jam on her dry toast. "The cousin who married Mr. Darcy's sister?"

"The very same." Elizabeth eyed the letter. "Do you suppose it inappropriate for me to read Mr. Darcy's mail? The second letter is for Mrs. Fitzwilliam. Before I forward it on to Scotland, should I not read what the Major General has conveyed to my husband? Perhaps there is important information that I should send on to Mr. Darcy. If so, it would be foolish to let the unread letter lie about and wait for Fitzwilliam's return."

"You do not have to convince me, but if you require another excuse for your own conscience, I see no reason for a man to write to his wife in Derbyshire if she awaits him in Scotland. It is your responsibility to solve this mystery."

Chapter 7

ELIZABETH BROKE THE SEAL and quickly read Edward Fitzwilliam's message. "Oh, my," she mumbled as her eyes scanned the words. "Poor Georgiana missed Kitty's wedding for nothing," Elizabeth said aloud. "The Major General only arrived in England four days ago; yet, my sister anticipated his appearance some three weeks past. Georgiana must be distraught with worry."

"What delayed Mr. Darcy's cousin?" Mary asked with concern.

Elizabeth's eyes never left the page. She scanned for details. "Major General Fitzwilliam remained in Belgium because his aide Captain Southland was injured." She paused as she continued to search the words for more information. "Oh, no." Tears misted her eyes.

"What brings you anguish, Elizabeth?"

With trembling lips, Elizabeth reported, "The captain stepped before the Major General to save Edward's life. As a result, Captain Southland lost part of his arm. That is the reason Mr. Darcy's cousin remained on the Continent. Concern for his friend. It is the second time Captain Southland has given Edward such a gift."

Mary spoke from true interest. "Is this the same gentleman from Kent who married Lady Catherine De Bourgh's daughter?"

"The very same," Elizabeth said as she returned her attention to the letter. "Evidently, as the Major General waits for his release from active duty, he has gone to see Mrs. Southland to prepare her for the shock of her husband's return. He planned to start his journey to Scotland today."

"Then all shall be well," Mary observed. "It may take the gentleman another week to reach Scotland, but Mrs. Fitzwilliam shall be thrilled with his appearance."

Elizabeth's frown lines met. "Perhaps I should send Georgiana a note. Surely a letter from Derbyshire would reach the Fitzwilliam estate before the Major General does. Even if I prevent Mrs. Fitzwilliam only four and twenty hours of worry, it would be worth the postage."

"I would imagine that Mr. Darcy's cousin has sent a like letter to his new bride in both Derbyshire and Scotland. That would explain why his post for Mr. Darcy's sister came with the one for your husband. But if your uneasiness compels you to write, I suspect Mrs. Fitzwilliam would welcome news of Mrs. Winkler's nuptials, along with your reassurance of the Major General's safe return."

Elizabeth refolded the letter. "That is sound advice. I shall follow it immediately."

* * *

"Mrs. Darcy." Hannah had found Elizabeth and Mary playing with the children in the lower garden. Having completed her letter to her satisfaction, Elizabeth had joined her friend for some quiet time. "Mr. Nathan sent me to find you. Lord Lindale has arrived unexpectedly. He asked to speak to Mr. Darcy, but Mr. Nathan informed the gentleman of the master's absence. Therefore, Viscount Lindale has asked to meet with you. Mr. Nathan has placed His Lordship in the green drawing room."

Elizabeth rose immediately. She stroked the wrinkles from her skirt. "Certainly. Would you assist Mrs. Joseph with the children?"

"With pleasure." Hannah reached for the child Elizabeth held. "Come, Master Bennet." Elizabeth's maid playfully swung the boy through the air. It touched her how much Mr. Darcy's staff cared for their son. Silently, she congratulated herself for marrying so well.

Elizabeth touched the child's dark curls. *So like his father's*, she thought as she caressed Bennet's head. "No spoiling him, Hannah."

"I shall leave that dubious task to you, Ma'am." Hannah cuddled the boy in her arms. "Only a mother spoils her children. The rest of us simply dote on them for a short while."

Elizabeth smiled lovingly at Bennet. "Oh, if that were only true." She turned to Mary. "I shall return shortly."

Moments later, she strode into the green room. "Lord Lindale." She curtsied before extending both hands to Edward's older brother. Unlike the major general, Rowland Fitzwilliam resembled the Countess of Matlock in countenance and stature. At least three inches shorter than both his younger brother and Darcy, Viscount Lindale, the future Earl of Matlock, was yet a fine-looking gentleman. Sandy blond hair. Light brown eyes. An aristocratic nose above a square chin. And an ease of movement common to men of privilege. "I am sorry that Mr. Darcy is not at Pemberley to receive you."

The gentleman took both her hands in welcome before bringing Elizabeth into his embrace. "I do not often make it this far west in Derbyshire, but that does not mean that either you or Darcy are ever far from my thoughts. Is young Bennet well?"

"The Pemberley heir thrives." She motioned to the chair he had abandoned on her entrance. "And the Viscountess and your own child? Pray say that this visit has nothing to do with their health."

"Amelia and Chase have recovered nicely from her confinement."

Elizabeth gestured to the tea tray Mr. Nathan wheeled into the room, but the viscount shook off the offer. "The Earl and Countess have spoken of little else besides the Matlock heir of late. Securing the line was very important to your father."

Lindale stiffened, and his countenance became more somber. "The Matlock line is the reason for my visit. In fact, I have traveled to Pemberley at the Earl's request. I had thought to speak to Darcy and through him to my brother's wife."

"I am afraid I do not understand the seriousness of your tone."

The viscount reached for her hand. "The Earl and the Countess have recently spent time with friends near Hull, but a missive forwarded by the Earl's secretary discovered them there, and they rushed to William's Wood. The news created a troubling episode for Father."

"Please tell me the Earl did not suffer unduly," she pleaded.

He said solemnly, "Neither Father nor Mother is likely to recover."

Elizabeth tightened her grip on the man's hand. "What could bring such grief?"

Tears misted the viscount's eyes, and he looked away to cover his weakness. "The message brought us news from Westminster of Edward's demise at Waterloo. Thus, my journey to Pemberley to speak to Georgiana. Father is adamant that Edward's wife knows the family's comfort. If she wishes, Georgiana may come to William's Wood in her time of grief. I had hoped that Darcy would encourage his sister to share time with us."

For a moment, Elizabeth's brain could not process his words. "But that is impossible," she protested, at last.

"Yes, I understand," he said with some difficulty. "We all thought Edward invincible. But as Mr. Darcy is from home, I seek your assistance in informing my cousin of this tragic event."

Elizabeth shook off his words. "Edward is not dead," she declared with assurance.

He patted the back of her hand. "None of us wishes to acknowledge this awful truth."

Elizabeth was on her feet immediately. "No," she insisted. "Mr. Darcy received a letter from his cousin only this morning. It was posted but four days prior. The Major General stays at Rosings Park with Lady Catherine and Mrs. Southland."

The viscount followed her to his feet. "Do you have this letter?" he said in a rasp. Hope laced his words.

Elizabeth turned toward the door. "Follow me." With the bewildered aristocrat trailing, she lifted her skirt and rushed through Pemberley's halls to Darcy's study. Retrieving the letter, she thrust it into the viscount's waiting hands. "Please read it. Edward was in Kent until this morning."

With trembling fingers, the viscount unfolded the two closely written pages. He walked to a nearby window for a closer inspection. "Praise the Lord," he gushed as his eyes scanned the paper.

Elizabeth watched as Darcy's cousin swayed in relief. "Georgiana is in Scotland awaiting Edward's return. According to the letter, your brother planned to depart for Scotland today to join her there."

The viscount refolded the pages. "Mother had suspected that Georgiana would anticipate Edward's return. She sent a carefully worded message to the Scotland estate. The Countess prayed that Georgiana had delayed her journey, but when Mrs. Fitzwilliam did not respond to the letter sent to Georgiana at Alpin, Lady Nora insisted that I travel to Pemberley to deliver the news in person."

Elizabeth's composure faltered. "The Countess sent word to Alpin Hall regarding this false report? When? When was the message posted?"

"Nearly a fortnight ago. I could not leave Father until I was certain of his survival." Rowland tapped the letter's edge against his open palm. "Is it possible for Edward and the letter to arrive in close proximity to each other?"

"I do not see how that could occur." Elizabeth reached for the bell cord. "I had a letter prepared to send to Georgiana with the morning post to inform her of Edward's delay. Let me retrieve it and instead send it with a Pemberley groom. I shall reassure Mrs. Fitzwilliam of the error of the report."

The viscount reached for his gloves. "I despise leaving you to resolve this quagmire on your own. Yet, I feel an urgency to return to William's Wood."

"Of course." Elizabeth followed him toward the door. "You must inform the Earl and the Countess of this change of events."

"May I take this letter with me as proof? My father will want to read it for himself."

"Absolutely." The butler appeared in the doorway. "Mr. Nathan, the Viscount requires a fresh horse, and I shall require a rider to take a message to Mrs. Fitzwilliam."

"Immediately, Mrs. Darcy."

Lindale turned to embrace her. "Thank you, Elizabeth. I came to Pemberley with a heavy heart. You have dramatically lightened my return journey."

"Give your parents my regard," she said as he loosened his grip. "And when next you come to Pemberley, I shall expect your adulation for Mr. Darcy's son—today I shall excuse you for more pressing matters," she said lightly as she laced her arm through his and escorted the viscount to the main door.

"It is a duty I happily accept." He bowed over Elizabeth's hand before taking his leave.

Returning to the house, she searched through the outgoing post. Retrieving her earlier letter from the tray, she hurriedly added a postscript. "Word of Edward's death shall drive Georgiana mad until she knows the truth," she said as she wrote the correction to reassure Darcy's sister. "It is a shame that Mr. Darcy knows nothing of this quandary. He could satisfy Georgiana's mind with more certainty than any words I might offer on paper."

* * *

"Lizzy, I have been searching for you," her father said as he entered the nursery. On the floor, at her feet, Ruth Joseph entertained William with a colorfully painted wooden block.

"Yes, Papa?" Elizabeth hummed a lullaby as she rocked Bennet to sleep. She barely glanced up at her father. "Does something besides my son require my attention?"

Mr. Bennet touched the sleeping child's curled fingers. "Nothing needs your attention more than my namesake." He bent to kiss the top of Elizabeth's head. "It is nothing of import. This letter was mixed in among those Mr. Nathan brought me this morning. It is addressed to Mr. Darcy." He placed the letter in her outstretched hand.

"At least, you managed to forward it to the proper recipient in a timely manner," she teased. Her father held a reputation for procrastination. Yet, that supposition was in error. For though Mr. Bennet was dilatory in undertaking business, he was quick in its execution.

He smiled at his daughter's playful taunt. "It was a great effort, but I persevered for Mr. Darcy's sake. Your husband refuses to ignore his responsibilities."

"Sometimes to the deficit of his own well-being," Elizabeth said good-naturedly. "But Fitzwilliam's dogmatic nature is not among his faults."

Her father chuckled lightly. "Some day, Lizzy, I wish to hear you recite those qualities that you believe to be among Mr. Darcy's foibles. Preferably in the man's presence."

"Do you wish to have Bennet and me taking up residence on Longbourn's entrance step?"

He seated himself beside her. "I would never complain if you should once again wish to live under my roof."

"Thank you, Papa," she said softly. Feeling a bit embarrassed by her father's sentimentality, Elizabeth turned the letter over to inspect the direction. "This is from the housekeeper at the Fitzwilliam estate." No longer reluctant to read Mr. Darcy's mail, Elizabeth handed the sleeping child to Mrs. Prulock and then broke the letter's seal. Rapidly, she read the words that would change everything. Elizabeth paled and her hands visibly trembled.

"Elizabeth?" her father pulled her to her feet and encased her in his protective embrace. "Lizzy, what brings you anguish?" Mr. Bennet removed the letter from her grip and handed her off to Mary Joseph's ministrations. Stepping to the window to take advantage of the light, he, too, read the missive. "This makes little sense," he insisted.

Elizabeth took a deep breath to steady her composure. "The housekeeper claims that Georgiana is...is missing...and presumed dead."

"Yes, I have gleaned that fact." He remained by the window to reread for clarification. "It says that Mrs. Fitzwilliam went riding on the moors and did not return."

"How many times did they search for Mr. Darcy's sister?" Mrs. Joseph inquired.

Mr. Bennet returned to the letter. "It says they sent out searchers for two days straight, but were unable to turn up any clues."

Elizabeth stiffened her shoulders. "I must go to Scotland. Mr. Darcy is to call at the estate. When he is told of his sister's disappearance, or worse yet, of her death, Fitzwilliam shall require my presence."

"What of Bennet?" Ruth Joseph asked quietly.

Elizabeth froze in midstride. "Bennet must come with me. I cannot tolerate a long separation; plus, having his son near will bring Mr. Darcy comfort if this information plays true."

"Ruth and I shall accompany you," Mary declared. "Mr. Joseph will see to Mr. Darcy's emotional needs, but someone must see to yours."

Elizabeth reached for the bell cord. "We shall stay at the Bingleys' estate tonight and be on the road north in the morning."

"Jane and Mr. Bingley have departed for Carlisle," Mr. Bennet reminded her.

"Just the same," Elizabeth insisted. "Mr. Bingley's staff shall have unexpected guests." She reached for the door handle. "Excuse me, I must see to the packing. Mrs. Prulock, I expect you to travel with us. I shall send Hannah to help you pack."

"Certainly, Mrs. Darcy."

* * *

Georgiana surveyed the room carefully. Although the light remained dim, she could decipher the furniture's sparse outlines. She had erred greatly by wandering so far from Alpin Hall. She had thought she knew the way to the ancient ruins, but somehow she had made a wrong turn, and no matter what she had done, she could not recover her bearings.

Then she had heard something behind her, and the Jacks' warnings of highwaymen and mystical beings had played with the little composure she had had remaining, and so she had bolted like a frightened hare. Without considering the consequences, she had raced frantically across the marshy bogs and through ragtag woods. Over rocky terrain. Whatever it was had pursued her for what felt like hours. Yet, she had continued running, with the panic filling her lungs. Then Bracken had reared up. Frightened as well. Sensing her fear. Pawing the air with his sharp hoofs. She had found herself slipping from the saddle with nothing to hold her but her leather gloves against the saddle horn. Slipping. Sliding.

Even then, the sounds of dread pounded in her head. Even as she slammed into the hardened earth. Even when the air rushed from her chest with a great whoosh. With an effort, she had struggled to her feet. Bracken had galloped away, leaving her alone in a vast wilderness. All alone. Just she and the child she had planned to share with her husband. Frightened beyond reason, Georgiana had run. Ran until the pain stitched her side. Ran through bramble that scratched her arms and face. Then it had happened. Her foot had sunk into a rabbit's hole, and she had fallen face first onto the rough outcropping. That was the last thing she remembered until she had awakened in this small room.

I cannot simply lie here, she chastised herself. *I have been here for too long as it is.* Slowly and painfully, she uncurled from the fetal position she had assumed to keep herself warm while she recovered. Pushing herself to a seated position, she straightened her gown over the swell of her abdomen. Tentatively, her fingers splayed across the wrinkled material. "Oh, Edward. Ask God to send me a sign that they are wrong," she whispered to the darkness. "To give me hope." She swallowed the fear that had returned. "I must find a way to Alpin Hall." She touched the ringlets that had escaped from her long braid. Although it hung down her back, surprisingly, the bonnet remained tied about her neck. Untying it, she sat a bit straighter. Mustering her courage, she said, "I require a bit of Elizabeth's tenacity and some of Fitzwilliam's intelligence if I am to survive this catastrophe of my own making." She sucked in a deep steadying breath. *I must survive this madness*, she chastised herself. "I refuse to believe that Edward did not overcome the worst of Napoleon's forces. If he can persevere, then surely his wife can manage to extricate herself from this entanglement." Yet, even as she said the words aloud, a tinge of self-doubt lingered.

Carefully, she lowered her skirts, and using her arms to push herself upward from the small bed, she straightened her knees to shift her weight to a standing position; yet, her best efforts would prove fruitless. An excruciating pain shot through her right leg, and she collapsed upon the hard floor.

* * *

She scrambled to sit on the cot's edge when she heard the key turn in the lock. Shoving the loose strands of hair behind her ear, she searched the disappearing darkness to find two figures by the open door.

"Ah, ye be up," the woman's familiar softness brought the girl a sense of comfort, but the imposing figure lurking in the woman's shadow caused the hairs on the back of her neck to stand on end. "We be movin' ye soon."

"Caution," came a whispered voice from deep within her. With tension creeping up her spine, she could not withdraw her gaze from the man. Memories of the one who had caught her in the woods had plagued her nightmares, and the sounds of what she assumed were others with a similar fate had filled her waking hours. The screams of pain were long and agonizing. Her only escape from the horror had been to slip into a fretful sleep.

Ravenously, she watched the woman place the food on the usual stool, but she made no move to satisfy her hunger. "Are ye not 'ungry?" the woman asked quietly. Unable to remove her eyes from the broad-shouldered hulk filling the door, she shook off the offer. The girl could tell his figure to be squat, but strong and forceful.

Finally, the woman noted her distress, and although the lady remained in partial shadow, the girl saw the frown deepen. "Donnae be afeared of Aulay. He wudnae hurt the smallest of God's creatures. I be tellin' 'im that ye be a smart one. Aulay and I be thinkin' ye might like 'is company. Ye kin play cards or read or just talk together."

"In the dark?" she asked hopefully, but she refused to uncurl from her defensive position.

"Nay, Child. Aulay's brother 'as given permission to move ye later today. Be gettin' you some more clothes—clean water—ye be likin' a bath, wud ye nae?"

She cautiously unfolded her legs, but did not stand. The tingling had begun again. For what she estimated to be the past two days, her legs had felt numb from lack of use. "A bath would be an exquisite pleasure. Please thank your master for the privilege." She continued to eye the man as he stepped into the light's circle. He possessed the same intensity as the one who had taken her prisoner, but his face was softer, with fewer lines and lighter eyes. Younger. Likewise, the dark curl falling over the man's forehead made him appear less formidable.

"I'll leave the door open. Aulay and I be returnin' for ye in an 'our or two." The woman handed the man the wooden plate from yesterday's meal and the used chamber pot. "Ye be eatin'. Ye need yer strength, gel."

"And the light?" she said tentatively. She had hated to plead for any concession from her captors, but keeping the light was more important than the food.

The woman clucked her tongue in disapproval, but the girl did not care. She needed the light to survive. "The light'll remain, gel." She pointedly set the candle on the small table. "We'll be returnin' soon." Then she shooed the man from the room before sweeping out the door. Good to her word, the woman left the door ajar. Cold air rushed into the room. Along with it came the rancid smell of rotting flesh.

The girl straightened before lowering her feet to the stone floor. Wrapping the blanket about her shoulders for warmth, she ignored the pungent odor. All she considered was her need to survive. She would eat the bread and cheese. She would eat for the child growing in her womb. With difficulty, she pressed her weight into her feet and straightened her knees to stand. *Easy*, she warned herself as she shuffled forward. Fiery pinpoints of pain shot through her muscles, and her right leg buckled. She reached for the bed, but the manacle held her in place, and she crashed to the floor. Twisting her torso to protect her child, her head smacked against the dampened stones; for a moment, the light increased, and then everything went dark.

* * *

"Mam!" Aulay burst into her sitting room. "Mam!"

His mother was on her feet immediately. "What be it, boy? What be the fault?"

"The gel, Mam," he choked out the words. "I's go to git her just as you says, but she be on the floor." He paled as he pawed her arm.

She took him by the shoulders. "What mean ye on the floor?"

"Lyin', Mam. Beside her bed," he said with urgency.

"Be she breathin'?" his mother demanded.

Aulay shivered. "Not knowin'. I not be touchin' her."

The woman turned on her heels. "Come along," she ordered as she rushed from her room in the solar. She hurried past arched openings to the chapel and down the narrow muraled stairs leading from the upmost rooms of the former castle to the rooms below the cellar, those which were part of the original monastery. Aulay tripped along behind her. Her youngest son had never moved with the grace that his older brothers possessed, but he had the kindest heart of her four children. Her husband had ignored the boy— leaving her to see to Aulay's upbringing. "The boy be too soft," he would accuse. "And not ret in the heed." Then Coll MacBethan would blame her, saying, "If'n ye not be a bastard's daughter, then yer chillen wudnae be ill born." But she had shown him. Coll had used his fist on her one time too many.

Dolina MacBethan rushed into the girl's room. "Bring the candle closer," she told Aulay as he knelt beside her. She bent her head to hear the girl's heartbeat. "She be breathin'. Go git Blane. We need to move her."

"Yes, Mam." Aulay clumsily staggered from the room.

Dolina lifted the girl's head into her lap. Fishing the key from her pocket, she removed the manacle from about the girl's wrist. "Wot be ye doin'?" she whispered as she brushed the hair from the girl's face. "I'll nurse you and the child ye be kering. Then ye kin marry me Aulay. He not be the smart one, but he'll treat ye well."

* * *

Edward bedded down for the night in a second-class inn. He would have preferred to ride farther, but the rain had come down in sheets of wet blindness. He could not continue on. The thunder had reminded him of the crash of the cannons. The sixteenth and seventeenth of June echoed in his memory, leaving an indelible mark. "Not as torrential as Waterloo's prelude," he grumbled as he stared out the room's small window. Edward could see it clearly in his mind's eye. The storm of monumental proportions had taken its toll on both armies. "Thank God the rain delayed Napoleon's approach and gave the Prussians time to reach Wellington's lines. If not, I doubt the Duke would have known success."

He forced himself to return to the bed. "When the storm breaks, I will be on the road again," he declared as he sought a comfortable position on the lumpy mattress. Concentrating on conjuring Georgiana's face, he attempted to drive away the horrors of those days on the battlefield: The roar of the guns. Rain beating off his shoulders. Thunder. Misfired muskets exploding in the soldiers' faces. Flashes of lightning. The harsh smell of blood. The roar of the cannonballs. The shrill cries of fallen horses. Deadly silence. Over the years, he had seen too many men die. Fate's fickle hand had chosen who was lost, and he was sore to understand the why and the wherefore. For a few moments, the utter chaos of the day dominated his memory, but then the exquisite beauty of his wife's countenance took over his breathing; and its shallowness came from a deep desire to know her again, rather than from the bone-melting fear of battle. "I am coming for you, Georgie," he whispered to the darkness. "Wait for me, my love. I swear that when you are once more in my arms that I will never allow anything or anyone to come between us again."

* * *

He had remained in Carlisle only long enough to pack a change of clothing before continuing north along the London Road. He knew himself to be several hours ahead of Darcy and the clergyman, who would reportedly accompany his old enemy to Scotland. As he crossed into Gretna Green, George Wickham thought of the irony of finally entering the infamous Scottish village. Mrs. Wickham had repeatedly begged him to take her to Gretna Green when they had made that ill-fated flight from Brighton. Little did the lady know that it was a pressing need to escape his creditors rather than Lydia Bennet's charms, which had induced his speedy withdrawal.

Thoughts of those troubled hours plagued him still. One evening, having imbibed in too much drink, he had unburdened himself to his only intimate acquaintance, Lieutenant Jules Norwood. "I acknowledge that her situation and her character ought to have been respected by me. I do not mean to justify myself, but at the same time I cannot leave you to suppose that I have nothing to urge——

that because she was a guest of the Forsters she was irreproachable, and because I was a libertine, *she* must be a saint. If the violence of her passions, the weakness of her understanding—I do not mean, however, to defend myself. Her affection for me deserved better treatment; and I often, with great reproach, recall the tenderness, which, for a very short time, had the power of creating any return. I wish—I heartily wish it had never been."

Of course, Norwood had pressed him for details of said regrets, but even in his most inebriated state, Wickham had not elaborated on the twisted panic that had plagued him daily. When he thought of his lifelong relationship with the Darcy family, he hated the pointy little spears of jealousy that impeded his ability to breathe. The prospect of rejection had reigned supreme, and he had done everything within his power not to be found wanting. Yet, wanting he was. His critics would address him with rather an injudicious particularity. In a situation such as his, he had done everything to be done to prevent a rupture. His actions were couched only to one end. He had recently conceded, "My business was to declare myself a scoundrel; and whether I did it with a bow or a bluster was of little importance. I am ruined forever in Society's opinion. I am shut out forever from their companionship; they already think me an unprincipled fellow; my actions will only make them think me a blackguard one."

He snarled in contempt as he dismounted before a small inn. "I made a terrible error in judgment when I allowed Mrs. Wickham to convince me that Darcy would once again accept my presence at Pemberley," he grudgingly told himself. "Darcy could never understand my world: that limbo between the working class and being a titled gentleman. Never belonging to either," he grumbled as he handed off the reins to a waiting hostler. "But he will learn the depth of my resolve. Darcy will pay dearly for this latest slight. No one offers George Wickham a disoblige and walks away unscathed."

Chapter 8

AS HE TRAVELED NORTH, Darcy could not shake the feeling that he should turn around and race home—that Elizabeth needed him—that Pemberley needed him. As he followed Matthew Joseph through yet another village, he closed his eyes and pictured his wife's countenance. He could easily imagine Elizabeth's eyes—those fine eyes, sparkling and beckoning, a bit of mischief playing across her lips. His heart had engaged long before his mind accepted her reality.

Now, as he shared his afternoon meal in a small clearing northwest of Lochmaben with the clergyman, his desire remained with a sprightly figure in Derbyshire. "I had thought all Galloway cattle to be black," Joseph noted as he unwrapped the large napkin holding the hard cheese they would share. They had observed more than one of the animals grazing on the open ranges as they crossed the Scottish Uplands.

"Nay," Darcy said. He distractedly watched the road they had traveled. "I have seen them with coats of red, brown, and dun. They are nothing like the Aberdeens." He accepted the knife Joseph handed him and began to slice the cheese and bread that would compose their meal.

They ate in silence for several minutes before Joseph observed, "This journey appeared prudent at the time, but I admit to feeling deprived of seeing young William throughout the day. We could be away from our families for weeks." He paused and offered a silent prayer over the food before he took his first bite. "Will my son even recognize me upon my return?"

"Yours is a thought that has crossed my mind during these travels. I have made it my practice to never spend more than eight and forty hours from Pemberley. That is why Mrs. Darcy accompanied me to Newcastle when we first met." Mr. Joseph nodded his empathy. "We have been away longer than that already and have yet to achieve our destination. My only consolation is that my actions will benefit my son's future." It was Darcy's turn to pause in reflection.

A profound silence filled the moment. "It is a decision designed for a man. Women are too practical to search for the golden apple."

Darcy leaned back against a large rock formation and tried not to look smug. "Mrs. Darcy would declare herself content with what we possess and would refuse to leave Bennet behind."

"This plays to accepted stereotypes. Men remain the hunters and women the nurturers," Joseph declared.

He watched as Joseph's mouth twisted bitterly. Companionship had never been easy between them; they were very much of the same nature. Darcy and Matthew Joseph had butted heads in the beginning. It was only through their wives that they had come to respect each other. With a deep sigh of resignation, Darcy stood. "I suppose we should continue. I will bring the horses around if you will see to the remnants of our meal." Catching Palos's reins, he led the gelding to where Mr. Joseph's mount munched on a tuft of grass. "Easy, boy," he said softly as he stroked the animal's hind-quarter. He had sent a string of horses north when he had made the decision to investigate Parnell's business proposal, but the horse Joseph rode was a relatively new one from his stables. In fact, Darcy had never ridden the large-shouldered roan. "Come along, boy," he coaxed. Running his gloved hand along the horse's neck, he reached for the reins. "Time to continue our journey."

Turning the animal in a tight circle, Darcy brought it along-side Palos. "Not much farther." Holding the horse's head still while

Joseph tied the sack to his saddle, Darcy stroked the roan's nose and fed it a small apple he had saved for Palos. "Good horse," he said softly as the animal crunched away at its treat.

Finished with his task, Joseph said, "Let us be about it."

Darcy swung up easily into the saddle. Not as accustomed to traveling by horseback, Joseph moved stiffly to set his foot. Darcy turned his head to the waiting road, and then he saw him: a lone gunman set for the shot. In that moment, everything moved in slow motion. Darcy's heart lurched with dread. In the blink of an eye, he had recognized the man, but before he could react, the sound of exploding gunpowder filled the air.

* * *

Her head throbbed with a sharp pain behind her left ear, but with gritted teeth, she managed to open her eyes. The room felt familiar, but she could not recall when or where she had seen it. The stone walls and meager furniture said it was not a place in which one would wish to dwell, but, somehow, she realized that was exactly what she had done. Yet, she could recall no details of her most recent stay in this unwelcoming place.

Slowly, her wakening awareness spoke of a hard, rough surface, likely the floor. Even without a point of reference, she knew, instinctively, that she did not belong in these surroundings. She had never experienced such conditions previously.

"She stirs," a nervous female voice said from somewhere above her. Yet, despite the comfort of being cradled in another's arms, she knew not the woman's purpose or identity. The realization of that fact sent a shiver down her spine.

* * *

"I have you. " A familiar feeling of safety filled her, and she awoke to find herself lying on the hard cot. She could not recall how she had regained the safety of the crude bed, but she assumed it had something to do with the person with whom she shared the small area. Opening her eyes wider, Georgiana could see the dust flakes as they danced in the shaft of light streaming through a filtered opening. The space appeared more organized than when she had first sought her safety within its walls.

A shadowy figure moved about the room, and she gave her head a shake to bring the person into focus, but try as she might, the edges of the figure's outline remained blurred. Forcing liquid to her dry mouth, she murmured. "Please. Please tell me...to whom...I owe my gratitude." Although the lines stayed in shadow, the familiar figure came nearer, and Georgiana breathed a sigh of relief.

"You know me," the voice said. "I have watched over you for years."

With difficulty, Georgiana turned onto her side. "How did you find me?"

Even without actually seeing the woman's expression change, Georgiana felt the figure smile warmly. The gesture told her that she would survive. "Finding you was never the issue. The question is how to return you to your brother's arms. That may be more problematic."

"But now that you are here..." Georgiana ventured.

The woman corrected, "I have protected you from death's claw, but you are still not completely safe. We must wait for Fitzwilliam and Edward to come for you. Until then, we shall do as best we can with what we have."

"Edward?" Although afraid of the answer, Georgiana breathed the question.

"Is safe," the woman whispered close to her ear. "Rest now. Your husband and your brother shall arrive soon."

* * *

For a brief second, Darcy's brain told him that his vision had betrayed him. It could not be George Wickham aiming one of the military's best personal weapons at him, but he rejected that erroneous assumption immediately. It was Wickham, and Darcy was the target. He spun his horse to charge the man, knowing he must stop his old foe. As he had always done, he would intercept his former rival's machinations. He would protect others from Wickham's deceit, but then from the corner of his eye he saw Matthew Joseph's body lurch first backward from the bullet's impact, and then forward, slumping over the roan's neck. Frightened by the noise and suddenly loose reins, the horse sprang forward and galloped away.

With a curse of alarm, Darcy abandoned his attack; turning Palos, he gave chase. The roan raced helter-skelter over the rocky terrain, bucking and twisting, trying to dislodge his rider. "Hold on, Joseph," he shouted as he urged his gelding closer. Luckily, the skittish horse turned back the way he had come and galloped toward Darcy. As the horse swung past him, Darcy reached out and caught the flailing reins with his left hand, while simultaneously pulling tightly on the bits of both animals. His arms and shoulders revolted from the action, but he gritted his teeth and held on. He now fully understood the concept of being drawn and quartered. Thankfully, Palos ceased his battle with Darcy's right shoulder and turned enough on his own to permit Darcy to tighten his grip on the roan. "Ho!" Darcy grunted as the animal stopped fighting him and came to a halt.

With a shake of his aching arms, he reached for Joseph's reeling body. "Easy, Joseph," he coaxed as he slid from his horse and braced the clergyman's body to the ground. Resting the man against the slight rise of the rolling terrain, Darcy began to search Joseph's body for his injuries. Ripping the handkerchief from his friend's pocket, he said, "Looks as if it is only the shoulder." He pressed the cloth to the wound. "I will escort you to the village. Just stay with me." Blood quickly covered Darcy's fingers. Racing to the roan's saddle, he unrolled the napkins, which had held the remains of the meal they had recently shared. Using the heavy linen as a bandage, he placed it over the wound.

"We need assistance," he grunted as he edged Joseph to his feet. Using his gelding for support, he lifted Joseph's limp body into the saddle. With one hand steadying Joseph, Darcy swung up behind the man he had learned to call "friend."

Allowing Joseph to lie limply in his arms, Darcy turned Palos toward the road where Wickham had staged his ambush. Needless to say, the scoundrel had escaped.

With his head on Darcy's shoulder, Joseph stiffened and caught at the gelding's mane. "Tell Mary I love her," he rasped. "Her and William. Promise me."

Darcy used one hand to press harder against the wound and the other to control the horse's reins. "You will tell them yourself, Joseph. My Elizabeth would demand nothing less, and I am not of the habit of disappointing my wife."

* * *

"How much farther, Mrs. Darcy?" Ruth Joseph asked as she shifted in the coach's seat.

"Mr. Simpson reports that we should be in Gretna Green within the hour. We shall spend the night. I would like to share some time outdoors with Bennet. I miss walking about with my son in my arms."

"From Gretna, where to next?" Mary asked as she searched the landscape.

"Tomorrow, we shall turn toward Dumfries and then onto Thornhill. The next day we shall arrive at Kirkconnel." Elizabeth, too, stared at the changing scenery. "The land seems so hard," she said as she thought of her home. "I once considered Derby and the Peak District quite savage, especially as compared to Hertfordshire. Yet, it was not wild, but wonderfully majestic and as old as time. Now, I look at this rugged terrain and wonder about those who live here in the Scottish Uplands." Elizabeth sighed deeply. "Will these people have nurtured Mr. Darcy's sister? Is she safe among those who eke out a living in this rocky soil? Will such people treat kindly a girl who until not two years prior shrank from her own shadow?"

* * *

"There, there." The woman took her hand. "Ye be safe. We let nothin' happen to you."

The girl opened her eyes wider. The room was cleaner and larger than she had expected. "Where am I?" She attempted to sit up, but the woman pressed her back.

"Might be best not to move too quickly," she said.

The girl sank into the soft cushions. "I am thankful for your consideration, but I would prefer to know the name of my rescuers and of my current direction."

The woman took her hand. The warmth felt good against her chilled fingers. Yet, a warning rang in her subconscious. She could not pinpoint the exact moment that betrayal manifested itself upon the woman's countenance, but it had made a brief appearance. Her breathing shallowed in response. "We be the MacBethan family, and you be at our home in Ayr. Me oldest son is the current laird. Of course, ye know me youngest Aulay." She gestured to a young man in his twenties waiting patiently by the door. "One of arn men found ye and brung ye to arn home. Do ye remember any of wot I tell?"

Her mouth twisted into a frown. "I recall a different room, and I remember your presenting me with a fresh gown."

"And that be all ye remember?" The woman asked curiously. "Nothin' of yer home? Yer family befoe ye came to Normanna Hall?"

The lines of the girl's forehead met. A figure stroking her hair softly fluttered at the edges of her memory. And another of water sucking the air from her lungs. Tentatively, she said, "Only what I have previously said." She would not speak more of the comfort the figure had given her until she knew what she faced in this house.

The woman shot a quick glance at her son. Soothing the hair from her face, she told the girl, "The room must 'ave been the sickroom. Ye be lost on the moor for some time and be in despair. We not be knowin' if'n ye wud live. The family be thankin' the gods for yer recovery."

She stared at the woman who tenderly stroked her arm; nothing of what this woman said rang true; yet, she could not dispute the obvious. She had suffered, and she was a stranger at Normanna Hall. "May I know your name?"

"Dolina MacBethan. Me late husband, may he rest in peace, and now me son be Wotherspoon."

"Dost thou raise sheep?" The girl inquisitively asked before she could resist the urge to know more of her surroundings.

The woman pointedly dropped her hand. "The family surname comes from those who tend the sheep. It be an honest trade. Although our fortunes are now tied to Galloway cattle. The land be not so fit for farmin'."

The girl shoved herself to her elbows. "I meant no offense." The woman's tone reminded her that she would need to guard her impulsive tongue.

As she watched, her hostess purposely smiled. Yet, the gesture did not appear genuine. "Of course, ye not be offering an offense. Ye be part of the family. Or very near to being so."

Suspicion returned, but the girl schooled her tone. "I am a part of the MacBethan family? When did that happy event occur?"

"It not be official." The woman straightened her shoulders. "Ye have accepted Aulay's plight, and we planned a joinin' in a week or so. As soon as ye be regainin' yer strength."

"I am to marry Aulay?" she said incredulously. "How can that be? Until a few hours ago, I held no memory of your son. He is a stranger to me."

Dolina turned quickly toward the door; she shooed her son from the room. "I be givin' ye time to remember yer promise to this family, Lady Esme, and yer lack of gratitude for our takin' ye to our bosom."

"Lady Esme?" The girl called after her. "Is that my name?"

The woman turned to level a steady gaze on her. "Of course, it be yer name. Ye be Lady Esme Lockhart, and ye be Aulay's betrothed."

* * *

"Mam?" Aulay whispered in concern once they were well removed from the closed doorway. "Wot have ye done? She not be Lady Esme Lockhart." He gestured toward the room where they detained the girl. "She no more be Lady Esme than I be Domhnall."

Dolina shushed his protest. "Didnae ye hear the gel? She cannae remember her own name. We kin create the perfect mate fer ye. Do ye not comprehend? I knows ye be slow, but it must be as plain as the lines on me face. She cannae rescind her agreement without jist cause. It not be the 'onorable thing to do. Besides, when the gel recalls the bairn she carries, then she'll be glad to 'ave a man who'll accept another's child."

"But we be tellin' her the truth?" he insisted. "We tell the gel of 'er real family?"

His mother rolled her eyes in exasperation. "Certainly, we'll tell the gel of 'er roots. But for now, she be Lady Esme."

* * *

Unsure of his destination, he had raced from the scene. He had taken what he had thought to be a clear shot, but the clergyman had swung into his sights just as he had squeezed the trigger. When Darcy had charged his position, Wickham had gloried in the possibilities. For years, he and Darcy had fenced their way through life, each besting the other to infinitesimal degrees. Although he had not anticipated a close-quarters confrontation with the man he had despised for his entire life, he had welcomed the opportunity to bury his fist in Darcy's perfect countenance.

"Despite the officious prognostications, we were evenly matched as youths," he told himself. "But he would rue the day he paid for my commission. While the great Fitzwilliam Darcy leads the easy life of a country gentleman, I train for war. While Darcy dines on the best of Pemberley's fare, I make do with the less-than-stellar efforts of Mrs. Wickham. I would hold the advantage in such a battle."

Realizing that Darcy had not given chase, Wickham pulled up on his horse's reins. Looking behind him once more for security, he drew in a deep breath. "It is not likely that Darcy did not recognize me," he reasoned. "And as the man has never felt the wine of common decency towards me, he will not rest until he sees me on the gallows." He dismounted and walked his horse to permit the heavily lathered animal to cool. "I may be required to appreciate Mrs. Wickham's presence, after all. In such a case, Mrs. Darcy would likely intercede with her husband in behalf of her sister. I will keep Lydia in mind if I have no other options. "

He led the horse to a secluded copse where he found a place to rest his saddle-beaten body. "Where should I go from here?" he wondered aloud. "I *should* return to my duty post, but sitting and waiting for Darcy's accusations is not in my nature." He watched the road from his hiding place. "What will Darcy do next, and how much time do I likely have before he comes searching for me?"

Wickham carefully considered both questions. Quickly, he deduced that Darcy must first tend to the clergyman. "If I killed the man..." Wickham shivered from the possibility. He really had not wanted to kill Darcy, and especially not an innocent. All he had wanted was to inflict pain on Darcy—to make his old foe suffer—to wound the man's perfection.

"If I killed Darcy's traveling companion," he forced himself to think only of the immediate crisis, "Darcy will have to arrange for the man's funeral and the return of the clergyman's remains. That will delay Pemberley's master from leading a search. It gives me time to escape." With a deep breath, he settled his nerves. "Even if the man is simply wounded, Darcy will feel obligated to tend to his friend's recovery." It hurt Wickham to think of Darcy having developed a friendship with the young minister. He had once claimed that position in Darcy's life, but his own jealousies and the foolhardiness of his father's shortcomings had doomed Wickham from the start. "I could have a week or so to make my retreat," he reasoned.

He found the flask he had stored in his inside pocket and took a restoring draught of the liquid. "I require funds," he said as he wiped his mouth on the back of his glove. "More than I could get from a penny card game. But whence?" Wickham returned his gaze to the empty road. "Darcy," he grumbled. "You remain the bane of my existence." Silently, he sipped on the warm liquid as he contemplated his options. "If you are the crux of my problems, you should also be my redemption," he told the silence. Striding toward the waiting horse, he made an impetuous decision. "Alpin Hall and the lovely Mrs. Fitzwilliam await. The lady is expecting a husband, and I am willing to serve in the Major General's stead. Plus, there is plenty of silver and riches to support my urgency for funds. Even if Georgiana drives me from the property, I can make my presence felt in the night's secrecy. I can be in and out of the estate before Darcy turns north." Hurtling into the horse's saddle, Wickham turned the animal toward the northern shires. "Let us see what Darcy's family has to offer a weary traveler."

* * *

"I need a surgeon," Darcy shouted as he rode into the inn yard. Matthew Joseph slumped heavily against his aching arms, but Darcy had refused to relinquish the man's care to a country simpleton. He had purposely ridden toward Dumfries because the Scottish town was large enough to host several competent physicians.

"What be the trouble?" A gruff-voiced hostler demanded.

Darcy eased Joseph's body forward. "We were attacked by a highwayman," he growled. Several others rushed forward to catch the horse and to lift Joseph's limp form from Darcy's grasp. "I require a room, and send someone for a surgeon. My traveling companion has been shot."

Motioning for a stable hand to fetch medical care and for the men to carry Joseph inside, the same hostler said, "Who might ye be?"

"A man with a full purse," Darcy snapped. "Now, get out of my way." He shoved the man from his path and followed the men carrying the silent Matthew Joseph into the inn.

* * *

Not certain whether her experience had been a dream or reality, Georgiana eyed the woman whose features remained undefined. Should she trust the woman or not? Unfortunately, despite her qualms, she had accepted her need for the lady's assistance. "My leg," she moaned through dry lips.

"Has received the best medical treatment this cottage can provide," the lady answered. "You shall not be comfortable, but you shall survive the inconvenience."

Georgiana forced a deep breath into her lungs. She smelled clean mountain air and smoke-hampered fireplaces. "Shall I not starve to death before someone finds me?"

"Would I permit you to die?" the woman said saucily. "Have I not always seen to your safety?"

Georgiana shook her head to clear her thinking. "Have you always been my guardian angel?"

"Some would say so," the figure said enigmatically. "Yours and your brother's. Yet, I have not always possessed angelic qualities. I hold the reputation of being quite devilish in my stubbornness and my need for adventure."

Georgiana struggled to bring the woman into focus. No matter how far she turned her head, the lady rested at her vision's edge. "Did you mention food?" she forced the words from her memory.

The figure came closer; yet, she remained misted in Georgiana's vision lines. "There is a water bucket on the hearth with a cup sitting beside it, and there are some dried apples, prepared meats, and a few hard biscuits in the cold room."

"Not my usual fare," Georgiana murmured, "but I would appreciate anything you might bring me." Despite her hunger, sleep pulled heavily at her eyelids.

The woman chuckled lightly. It was a soft rumbling noise that spoke of home and a blazing fireplace and the scent of lavender filling the room. "As much as I would wish to deliver the most luscious meal to your lips, I fear I could not offer you a disservice by cheating you of the pleasure of designing your own rescue."

Georgiana's eyes sprung open. "But I cannot," she protested.

"Georgiana, I have told you repeatedly that you are a magnificent creature. I have whispered those words in your ear. You must have heard them. You wanted your independence when you married Edward. You wanted your own home. To be your own woman. An independent lady would not expect me to act as her servant. She would fight for her own continued existence. What say you, Georgiana? What price shall you pay to know your freedom?"

* * *

He had sent a rider to both Matlock and Pemberley. Although he had left specific orders for Lieutenant Conrad to correct the military's mistake, Edward had not trusted those in command to act judiciously. "Too easy for my request to be placed at the bottom of the stack. Too many crowing over military victories to see to the mundane details of a man's life." He had considered riding to Pemberley just to assuage his need to see to Georgiana's safety within its walls. Yet, his heart knew what his mind thought impossible. She was in Scotland, and some nagging lurch in his chest told him that she was in trouble. "Georgie, Darling," he whispered to the night skies. "Hold on. Whatever it is, stay with me. I cannot imagine my future without you."

* * *

"Lady Esme," Aulay MacBethan said as he bowed. "May I join you?"

She certainly did not wish to share her private time with the young man, but in the woman's absence, she had decided that she required more information regarding her surroundings. "What better way than to ask those involved?" her heart had told her mind. In her dreams, someone, likely the woman called Dolina, had dressed her injuries and had brought her a simple fare. The girl was not certain which part of her dreams were real and which were part of her imagination. She was relatively certain that the woman had fed her hard bread with butter, but the specifics of her recovery remained a blurred memory. It was odd that she could recall some events in minute details and others suffered from her recent injury. Or perhaps, it was from her confinement. One thing was an absolute: Aulay MacBethan was *not* her betrothed. His clumsy, haphazard appearance would never have attracted her. She preferred her men taller and fairer of complexion. MacBethan still possessed those boyish features of a man who had not yet reached his majority. "That would be acceptable as long as the door remains open." She made herself smile at him.

"I thought we might play cards or chess," he offered as he took a step closer.

"Chess," she said softly and motioned to the room's small table.

He turned and said something to the waiting servant before returning his attention to her. "I be grieved that ye be hurt, m'lady." Aulay reached out a steadying hand, and the girl reluctantly accepted it. Her vision spun as she shook her head to clear it, and her ankle remained tender.

"Perhaps, you might assist me in recovering my memory." Although her insides screamed for her retreat, the girl maintained a pleasant tone.

Aulay appeared as nervous as she. He shifted his weight several times. "That wudnae do. Mam be not likin' my rattlin' on."

"Surely, if we are to marry," she said evenly, "you are permitted to share such intimacies. I would hope that you wish me well, Sir."

Aulay frowned dramatically. "I be prayin' fer yer recovery, Lady Esme."

"Could you, at least, tell me why I was found by your men? Was I lost? Please allay my fears: certainly I had not run away?"

"Agin, Lady Esme, me Mam knows these events better than I." He nervously knocked over the chess pieces the servant placed on the table.

The girl's mouth tightened in exasperation, but she controlled the flash of anger. "There must be something of which we are permitted to speak." She nonchalantly moved her pawn. "Might you tell me of your family? Do you have only the one brother? After all, as your intended, I should know the family that welcomes me as one of their own."

Caught in concentrating on the chessboard, Aulay's defenses visibly relaxed. "I be the youngest of four. Only Mam, Domhnall, and I live at Normanna. Mam's brother lives nearby. He be the village butcher. Lilias, me sister, lives in Knovdart. She'll be a mother soon. Islav 'as taken over Mam's family keep near Crieff."

"Your eldest brother has not taken a wife?" Although she wanted to press for Aulay's cooperation, The girl purposely kept her tone conversational.

"Domhnall's wife passed," he mumbled. Reflexively, the girl's heart lurched with from an unknown grief. *Too much death and not enough life,* she thought.

As he manipulated the chess pieces, Aulay appeared totally engrossed in the game. She casually, but deliberately made several miscalculations in her moves. Pretending to consider herself foolish, the girl said with a light chuckle, "I am a miserable partner."

"I be willin' to show ye some of the strategy," Aulay said without looking up from the board.

She swallowed her first words. Instead, she listened to her inner voice, the one which said that she knew the game as well as any man, and the one which also warned her not to display her strengths to these people. The MacBethans expected her to be humble and weak, and that was what she would be. "That would be most pleasant. It would also give us time to learn more of one another."

Aulay nodded absentmindedly. As she watched him, her mind searched for the reason she had come to this sinister place. Lady Wotherspoon had said that she had been previously housed in a sickroom, but the girl could not shake the feeling that the woman had offered her a prevarication. Why would someone sick be shackled to the wall? Why would someone who suffered be kept in complete darkness? *This whole situation does not make sense, and until it does, stay alert*, she warned herself.

* * *

"It will be several days before we know for certain," the surgeon informed Darcy. "The bullet came out clean, and although your friend lost much blood, he is young and strong. As long as infection does not occur, the gentleman should make a full recovery." The surgeon packed away his instruments.

Darcy had appreciated finding an English surgeon at his disposal. "How do we prevent infection?"

"Keep the wound clean. I will leave you several poultices for the laceration, as well as some laudanum for Mr. Joseph's comfort." He picked up his bag. "I shall examine your friend's wound again tomorrow."

"Should I contact Mr. Joseph's wife and sister?" Darcy dreaded informing Mary Joseph of her husband's injury. It was his fault—his and the infernal feud he had maintained with George Wickham. Fault. The word lay heavy in his mind. His fault that an innocent man had come close to losing his life. Could still lose his life.

The surgeon gestured to Joseph, resting under laudanum's influence. "From what you have said it would take Mrs. Joseph two days or more to reach Dumfries, and that does not take into account your sending word to the lady. Would it speed the gentleman's recovery to know his wife was close at hand or would he decide that his wound had challenged her sensibilities? I doubt that Mr. Joseph would want to place his wife in such distress, but if you think it prudent, then we can make that decision after Mr. Joseph has survived four and twenty hours. Those are usually the most perilous with gunshot wounds."

"Then I will wait. There is no reason to worry the lady if Mr. Joseph is on his way to recovery." Yet, Darcy thought of Elizabeth and how having her near to him would ease his troubled soul. Surely, Matthew Joseph felt the same about Mary.

Chapter 9

"I HAD THOUGHT GEORGE WOULD be anticipating my return," Lydia said incredulously. "Could my husband remain out of sorts with me?"

Mrs. Bennet glanced about the shabbily furnished room. It troubled her to witness how far below her other daughters that her favorite child had sunk. Even the small cottage on the Longbourn land, which Mary and Mr. Grange had let, was far superior to the conditions in which Lydia existed. Mrs. Bennet hated to consider how Mary possessed much better sense than did Lydia. "Perhaps Lieutenant Wickham is at his duty post," Mrs. Bennet offered weakly.

Lydia's eyes looked hopeful. "That must be it. Lieutenant Wickham was to be excused from his duties until Monday next, but it is so like my husband to see a need and respond."

"Then we shall see Lieutenant Wickham at supper." Mrs. Bennet made another quick survey of the room's disarray. Things were far worse than she had assumed. Even Mr. Bennet's warnings had not prepared her for the sad state of Lydia's affairs. "Why do we not surprise the lieutenant by putting things aright? A man prefers a well-ordered home."

"I am a miserable housekeeper," Lydia half-whined.

Mrs. Bennet tutted her disapproval. "I did not raise my girls as domestics, but that does not mean that any of them lacks the skills to maintain a proper house. As these are but let rooms, our task shall be a small chore. I shall assist you." She began to gather the clothes strewn upon the furniture. "I suspect Lieutenant Wickham's temper shall be less volatile if he witnesses your efforts to change your circumstances."

"Do you believe it so?" Lydia scanned the room's poor state.

Mrs. Bennet doubted anything would soften Lieutenant Wickham's nature. After all, Mr. Bennet had finally told her the truth of the man's ways, but she would not speak her thoughts aloud. That horrid scene in the curate's cottage had brought her husband's previous warnings squarely to her shoulders. She had once gloried in Lydia's connection to Lieutenant Wickham. Oh, how she rued her former words—those spoken in triumph after news had arrived from her brother Gardiner, announcing Lydia's upcoming marriage to the lieutenant.

"My dear, dear Lydia!" she had cried. "This is delightful indeed! She will be married! I shall see her again! She will be married at sixteen! My good, kind brother! I knew how it would be. I knew he would manage everything. How I long to see her! And to see dear Wickham too! I will put on my things in a moment. My dear, dear Lydia! How merry we shall be together when we meet!

"I will go to Meryton," she had continued in all her ignorance of the situation's truth, "as soon as I am dressed and tell the good, good news to my sister Philips. And, as I come back, I can call on Lady Lucas and Mrs. Long."

And where had all that mirth-filled hope led? To second-class lodgings in Cumbria. Her darling daughter needed instruction on how to survive a loveless marriage, and she could provide such knowledge first hand. Although the man had hurt her in ways she would never confide to another soul, at least Mr. Bennet had never raised his hand to her. Instead, her husband's superiority and sharp tongue often rang with her worthlessness. She had accepted his censure because she had failed him by not producing an heir for Longbourn. Every day, her inadequacy hung heavy about her shoulders. Shoring up her resolve to assist Lydia to a better place, she said, "Let us begin with rearranging the rooms. Remember that a man's heart is easily tamed by the fine design of a female hand."

* * *

"At least, the private room offers adequate accommodations," Elizabeth remarked as she surveyed the open area. "Perhaps, we might place a blanket upon the floor so Bennet and William can stretch their small legs. Children need to move to grow." She handed Bennet to Mrs. Prulock. "I had hoped to reach Thornhill, but Mr. Simpson says the team requires a bit more rest. The terrain is hard on them."

"So we shall arrive at Alpin Hall in the evening instead of the afternoon," Mary remarked as she gestured the serving maid to the table. "A longer night's rest shall do us all well."

Elizabeth heaved a sigh. How could she explain that she must reach Alpin Hall and correct the military's announcement of Edward's death? How might one express the urgency of her assuming the lead in Georgiana's recovery? She had thought to seek Darcy at the Bingleys' summerhouse, but it would likely be several more days before her sister Jane arrived in Newton Stewart. Darcy's and Mr. Joseph's early departures had thrown everything out of order. Elizabeth reasoned that if she could reach Alpin Hall first, she could stymie the rumors that would plague her husband. *There is that blessing*, she thought.

Resigned to a long evening of worrying about her family, Elizabeth seated herself before the serving dishes. "We shall make the best of our time together." However, an anxious knock at the door drew her attention. She motioned Mrs. Prulock to remain seated, and she crossed to the portal. "I shall see to it," she said over her shoulder. "Please. Enjoy the meal while it is hot." Opening the door but a crack, she was surprised to see her trusted coachman. "Is there more trouble, Mr. Simpson?" she asked tentatively. She wanted no further delays.

"Excuse me, Mistress," he whispered hoarsely. "Might I be speaking with you privately?"

Elizabeth nodded and slipped from the room. Closing the door behind her, she asked, "What is it? Difficulty with the team?"

"No, Ma'am." He ran his hat's rim through his nervous fingers. "The horses be seen to properly."

"Then what may I do for you?" she said with more gruffness that she intended.

The man swallowed hard. "It is the Master, Ma'am," he began.

Every nerve in her body came alive. "What of Mr. Darcy?"

"His horse, Mistress. Palos and the roan Garm are housed in the stables."

Elizabeth attempted to calm the man's agitation. "Mr. Darcy sent horses ahead for his trip. He prefers not to let a horse unless necessary."

"No, Ma'am. You misunderstand. The hostlers report a man of Mr. Darcy's description rode in early yesterday afternoon with an injured saddle mate. They were attacked by a highwayman."

Elizabeth swayed as the news swept over her. Mr. Simpson's strong grip on her elbow was a blessing. "Mr. Darcy?" she rasped. "Is my husband still here?"

"Yes, Ma'am. I be asking before I come to fetch you. The Master has the two rooms at the top of the stairs."

Elizabeth caught at his arm. "What do the stable hands say of the injured man?" she asked softly as she stepped away from the door.

Mr. Simpson's expression changed immediately. "They say the man had lost much blood. Mr. Darcy refused to allow the surgeon to bleed him. The Master say Mr. Joseph had suffered enough."

Elizabeth clutched at her chest. "I must discover the truth before I speak to Mrs. Joseph of the incident. Thank you, Mr. Simpson, for your kindness."

"Yes, Ma'am. Tell the Master that Jasper and I await his instructions."

* * *

Georgiana awoke to the late evening shadows filling the small cottage. Her leg throbbed, but the pain was more bearable than earlier. Lifting her skirt, she found a makeshift cast. *How?* she wondered. Then she remembered the woman who had assisted her in those first few crazy hours when she had thought she would die on this wobbly cot. The woman had felt familiar, but she could not place a name or a face. That idea made sense in only the most bizarre terms: the woman possessed no face; yet, she could tell when the lady smiled or frowned or looked upon her with worried eyes, but Georgiana could not actually describe the woman. Had her companion assisted her with her injury? "Has received the best medical treatment this cottage can provide," the voice had said when Georgiana had complained of her injury.

Pushing herself to a seated position, she surveyed the room. Someone had slammed one of the two chairs against the hearth. Wood splinters covered the bricks where the furniture had met the stones. The chair legs, she thought. That explained the brace she wore. Having been tied on with strips from her petticoat and the ribbons from her bonnet, the chair's spindles encased her leg on each side and the back of her calf. Had she done this or had it been the woman? "Are you here?" she called aloud when the room held no more secrets.

"Of course I am with you." The familiar voice caressed her ear, but Georgiana did not turn her head. She understood that the woman could not be behind her. The bed stood close against the wall. Yet, it did not matter. She had felt the warmth of the words as they caressed her cheek. "You should eat to maintain your strength."

Georgiana did not argue. Instead, she reached for the simple meal before her. As if by magic, a tin plate holding strips of dried mutton and several hard rolls had appeared on a low table. Tearing off a piece of the bread, she popped it into her mouth and chewed slowly. Adding a bite of the tough meat, she waited for her mouth's moisture to soften the food. Immediately, her stomach growled. She laughed. "Not as good as Mrs. Olson's bread pudding," she pronounced.

"I miss Mrs. Olson's bread pudding," the voice said.

Georgiana sighed deeply. "Is there water?"

"Beside the table. You should go easy with it. It may be several more days before they rescue you."

Georgiana glanced toward the window. "Do you suppose that Fitzwilliam and Edward search for me?"

"They are yet to know you are missing from Alpin Hall, but they are racing to your side, nonetheless. Neither will rest until you are safely with them."

"And Elizabeth?" Georgiana smiled easily.

The voice chuckled lightly. "Your brother's wife leads the charge."

Georgiana laughed also. "In my dreams, you are Elizabeth."

"Who says you are in error? Would not your sister move heaven and earth to protect you?"

"I hold no doubt that Elizabeth would be an immovable force."

* * *

Darcy read from Mr. Joseph's Bible. It had been among the man's possessions, and he had borrowed it to pass the time. He had sat beside Joseph's bed all night, tending his friend, a man with whom he, in actuality, had but a fortnight's acquaintance: less than a week before Christmas and a sennight since Joseph had called at Pemberley. Yet, he had felt an affinity with the man from the beginning. He recognized bits of himself in the younger man.

"Then it's as Mrs. Joseph asserts? Yours is a love match?" Joseph had smugly challenged as they had examined December's icy road conditions. A blizzard had stranded them at an out-of-the-way inn, and the Darcys had agreed to share their quarters with the Josephs because Mary Joseph's confinement put her well past the time for traveling.

Darcy had felt the sting of the man's tongue. "I would have assumed, Sir, that you, too, cared deeply for your wife. Was I mistaken?"

"You have not erred. My wife holds my highest regard."

"Yet, you refuse to admit to loving your wife," Darcy had observed.

Joseph had countered, "I do not hear your professions, Sir."

Darcy recalled how, at the time, he had found Joseph's prideful display amusing. "I see how it is. If I am man enough to admit to loving Mrs. Darcy, you could claim your own affection. If that is what it takes, Joseph, I confirm that I am hopelessly in love with my wife. You now have my permission to admit your own weakness."

The man had reddened. "I assure you, Mr. Darcy, that I do not require nor seek your permission for anything."

Darcy's smile widened with the remembrance of those first awkward hours of sharing their inn room with complete strangers. He had admired Joseph's loyalty to his wife and family. That is how he had judged the man as being someone he could trust. "And that's how it should be, Joseph. My affection for my wife, my decisions regarding my estate, my sister's guardianship—are all mine. They are none of your concern unless I choose to share them, as your life belongs to you until you care to speak of it. Do not mimic another man's actions, Joseph. Do what is best for you. That is a lesson I learned from Mrs. Darcy."

Only the crunch of their boots on the frosty lane had broken the comfortable silence that nestled between them. For several minutes, neither of them had spoken. Finally, Joseph had said, "I meant no offense, Mr. Darcy."

"You did not offend, Joseph. I spoke because I observed in you my own tentative nature. We men are not free to express our feelings. Women strike up instant relationships. Look at our wives as proof. It is how Society deems our roles, so we must develop confidence in our choices, and, more importantly, we must guard against accepting outside examples as the norm. The true north is what serves you best—what gives you personal satisfaction in your life." From that moment, he and Joseph had found an acceptance. Darcy had found theirs a gratifying connection. He treasured having another male friend with whom to share his experiences, and he would be sorely grieved to lose the man because of Lieutenant Wickham's attack.

A light tapping drove the remembrance from his mind. Marking his place in the Scriptures, he crossed quietly to the door. Expecting the maid with the meal he had ordered earlier, he was shocked to find his wife on the other side of the portal. "Lizzy," he rasped. A heartbeat later, he had scooped her into his arms. "You are a most blessed sight," he said as he rained kisses across her cheeks and eyes. "But how?" As if fearful that she was some sort of apparition, Darcy pulled her closer.

"I followed you," she said simply. "We should speak privately."

Darcy belatedly realized the inappropriateness of kissing his wife in the open hallway. "Come." After closing Joseph's door so his wife could not see the clergyman in repose, he pulled her into the next room. Inside his own rented quarters, he took Elizabeth into his embrace again. "The Lord has answered my prayers."

"And mine," she said as she kissed him tenderly. When their lips parted, she gave a wavering smile. With a release of the pent-up breath she had held since learning of her husband's presence at the inn, she said, "Speak to me of Mr. Joseph's injury. Mr. Simpson says you were set upon by a highwayman."

"Simpson?" he asked.

Elizabeth's tone spoke of urgency. "I shall explain Mr. Simpson's presence in a bit, but please know that Mrs. Joseph is below, and we cannot keep her husband's condition secret."

Darcy released her and began to pace the small open area. "No highwayman. Lieutenant Wickham." His wife paled, and he assisted her to a chair. "The bullet was meant for me. Because of my association with Lieutenant Wickham, Mr. Joseph could lose his life."

"Oh, Fitzwilliam." When he knelt before her, Elizabeth cupped his hand between her two. "You had no way of anticipating Lieutenant Wickham's duplicity."

"But the lieutenant warned us that he would seek his revenge," he countered.

"Yet, not as this," she insisted. "None of us could predict the man would sink to this level."

Darcy released her to pace again. "Joseph must survive this, or I will never forgive myself. My foolish pride has cost an innocent much."

Elizabeth took his hand and kissed his palm. "Lieutenant Wickham constructs one quagmire after another. You are not responsible for his choices."

Darcy bit back his response. He would know regret forever. "Mrs. Joseph should be told of her husband's condition. You and I can debate who bears the most fault at a later date."

"I shall go." Elizabeth nodded to her husband. "Mary is my friend."

"Hurry your return," Darcy pleaded. "I am in great need of your closeness."

* * *

"O God, your Son accepted our sufferings to teach us the virtue of patience in human illness," Mary led the others in prayer. "Hear the prayers we offer for our loving husband, father, brother, and friend. May all who suffer know that they are joined to Christ, for our Lord suffered for the salvation of the world. Protect Matthew and give him peace during this ordeal. Amen."

Darcy and Elizabeth had remained in the background as a very shaken Mary Joseph had tended to her injured husband. She had immediately forgiven Darcy of any blame in what had happened to Joseph. "I would prefer to think that Matthew saved your life because you are needed elsewhere. Mrs. Darcy shall share her own concerns with you." Then she had caught Mr. Joseph's hand and had kissed it tenderly. Ruth Joseph had placed William on the bed with his father before joining her brother's wife in her vigil.

"Come," Elizabeth had whispered. "It is in God's hands now." She and Darcy slipped from the room. "Mrs. Joseph is correct. We must speak privately."

Holding the door to his room open for her, he said, "I had hoped Mr. Joseph's injury was the worst of it, but the constant scowl gracing your countenance tells me otherwise."

"You know me well enough, Fitzwilliam, to know I would not risk Bennet's life on Scottish roads if I did not think it necessary."

He caught her hand and pressed it to his chest. "Although I prefer to think you could not withstand the despair of having me gone from Pemberley, I suppose you should tell me why you have followed me to Scotland."

Elizabeth relished the steady beat of his most loyal heart, and she dreaded the possibility of hurting him. "Although I fear what I have to share shall give you pain, I must speak honestly." She paused to add her other hand. With a sigh of defeat, Elizabeth described Lord Lindale's visit, the erroneous report sent by the military, the gist of his cousin's letter regarding the major general's tardy return to England, and the Countess's attempt to assuage Georgiana's heartbreak.

During her recitation, she had felt her husband's pulse quicken under her fingertips, but he calmly said, "My aunt acted foolishly, but Edward's return will ease any anguish Georgiana may have suffered. I would not wish my sister even one moment of grief, but this is easily rectified. Yet, it does not explain your journey, Elizabeth. As you so aptly stated earlier, you would not risk Bennet's life on the road simply to bring me belated news. Tell me the rest."

Elizabeth lovingly caressed his jaw. This man was her universe. "I had planned to send a rider to Mrs. Fitzwilliam to correct the Countess's too-early assumption, but then Papa brought me a message, which had been mixed in with the Longbourn correspondence." She reached in her pocket to retrieve the folded-over letter. "You should read it yourself."

Darcy reluctantly accepted the papers and stepped away to light another candle. Then he unfolded the page and read the words that set his hands trembling. "This is impossible," he rasped on a sob.

Elizabeth fought for her own control. "Of course, it is impossible. If Georgiana..." She could not say the words. "We would know," she declared with certainty. "Your heart would know, as well as mine."

Darcy ran his fingers through his hair. "I dreamed of my sister last evening," he said hoarsely. "In a lucid moment, Mr. Joseph spoke of his wife and child. Later, as I sat with him, I dozed off. You and Bennet were paramount, but I also pictured Georgiana wrapped in my mother's arms. Just as she was the first time I laid eyes on her. She was perfection, and my mother doted on her."

"Every child is perfection," Elizabeth murmured and rested her hand on her abdomen in that protective way of mothers. Wrapped in thoughts of his sister, Darcy took no note of her maternal gesture.

"Could my dream have been God's warning that Georgiana rests with my mother?" he asked distractedly.

"Did you not also dream of Bennet and me? The letter was addressed more than a week past. Although we have both expressed our anxiousness over Georgiana's early departure from Pemberley, neither of us has sensed danger surrounding our sister. Even your dream was of happy times. Of a time when Georgiana remained protected by her family. You simply continued to grieve for Georgiana's moving into a new phase of her life. You would keep her a little girl forever." She smiled at him. "You have been the best of brothers."

"We should leave for Alpin Hall immediately," he declared.

Elizabeth walked into his embrace. "Not until morning, my love," she said as her arms encircled his waist. "We must see to Mr. Joseph first." His automatically pulling her closer spoke of his need to protect her from harm, and she gladly accepted the unspoken promise. "We must support Mary and Miss Joseph." Darcy did not object, but Elizabeth realized that he would not be easy with the wait. "One of the blacks has taken on a stone near his frog. He cannot continue. I have instructed Mr. Simpson to locate a suitable replacement. We can leave in the morning."

"You have thought of everything," he murmured as he aimlessly stroked her back. Every nerve in Darcy's body sang of his need for action.

Elizabeth tightened her grip. "It is my province to see to your peace of mind, Mr. Darcy. That was my pursuit's purpose.

Tomorrow we shall continue north, and we shall either welcome Georgiana into our embrace, or we shall oversee her rescue. I refuse to countenance the possibility of another ending to this nightmare."

Darcy kissed the top of her head. "Mrs. Joseph requires your sensible counsel as much as I. While you see to the lady, I will speak to Mr. Simpson. I wish to ascertain his progress."

* * *

The girl suspected that the MacBethans had placed something in both her food and her water to keep her mind less engaged. Although she would not refuse the food, she would do what she could to minimize the effects. When the boy-man the family called Aulay had last visited her, she had asked to share his ale rather than to drink from the cool water she had been provided. Lost to the hotly contested game in which they partook, the man had barely taken notice of her sipping from his tankard.

And it had made a difference. She had had the same troubling dreams as before, but this time she had awakened with remnants of the dream still clinging to her memory, and she would use those memories to orchestrate her own release. *First, I should learn more of this place*, she had told herself. *And the easiest way to do so is to appear to accept the path Lady Wotherspoon has chosen for me.*

* * *

He had stopped twice for directions and to listen for any rumors regarding Alpin Hall and its residents. Therefore, it was with confidence that George Wickham released the brass knocker and waited for someone to admit him. As he waited, Wickham examined the capabilities of that end of the house. The lawn, bounded on each side by a high wall, contained beyond the first planted area a bowling green, and beyond the bowling green a long terrace walk, backed by iron palisades, and commanding a view over them into the tops of the trees of the wilderness immediately adjoining. Finally, after several wavering minutes, the door slid open on silent hinges. "Yes, Sir?" an elderly butler asked.

"I am Mr. Hurlbert, the Fitzwilliams' cousin. The family has sent me to deal with the situation which has recently occurred." He spoke with as much military bravado as he could muster. From those at the nearest inn, Wickham had learned of Mrs. Fitzwilliam's disappearance and how the neighborhood had searched to no avail for Darcy's sister.

"We be expectin' the Major General," the man said suspiciously.

Wickham smiled his most solicitous smile. "Wellington has delayed the Major General's return, and Lord Lindale has a new child. Surely, you have heard as such. Besides, I live in Cumbria, much closer than either Lincolnshire or Derbyshire. Now, will you permit a proper admittance or must I tarry on the steps a bit longer?"

The butler blustered as he swung the door wider. "Of course, Sir. I be Jacks. Me wife and I tend the house when the family not be in residence."

"Just the two of you?" Wickham asked as he surveyed the main foyer. He could sleep in luxury for a couple of days before he would need to seek another place to stay. He had assumed that Darcy would wait until he knew the clergyman's fate before giving chase. Wickham knew enough of his long-time foe's pride to realize that Darcy would not inform the authorities of the attack. Darcy had always hidden their interactions because of the previous Mr. Darcy's fondness for his godson. Fitzwilliam Darcy would attempt the impossible to preserve Pemberley's reputation. No, Darcy would come for him himself. Wickham would eventually have to face Darcy, but he did not fear the local magistrate looking for him.

"The family employs some villagers as day workers." The man took Wickham's hat and gloves. "There be a small staff of grooms to tend the cattle and carriages."

"I see." Wickham took note of the shadowy passages. "For tonight, I could use a good night's rest, and tomorrow, I will speak to all involved with the search for Mrs. Fitzwilliam. Might I impose on Mrs. Jacks for a tray in my room, and possibly someone could see to a bath?"

Jacks nodded his agreement. "I will see to it, Mr. Hurlbert. Allow me to show ye to a room, Sir."

* * *

"Mr. Joseph is awake, Fitzwilliam." Elizabeth said softly in his ear. Darcy had joined Mr. Simpson and Jasper in the common room. He often entertained his employees when he was on the road. He considered it a matter of good taste to honor those who offered an honest day's work.

"Please excuse me." He motioned to the bar mistress to bring his men another round of drinks. Then he followed Elizabeth up the inn's narrow stairs. He caught his wife to him in the darkened hallway. "What should I expect?" he asked tentatively.

"You should expect a family thankful for your friendship. For your honor."

Darcy swallowed his trepidation. It was one thing to encounter an opponent, but it was quite another to seek forgiveness from a man he respected. Trailing his wife, he entered the small room and waited for his cue. Finally, Mrs. Joseph motioned him forward, and Darcy pulled a chair close to the bed. "I am thankful to find you awake," he said as he leaned forward to where Joseph could see him.

With the laudanum's lingering effects, Joseph struggled with coherent thoughts, but his voice sounded strong, a fact of which

Darcy took quick notice. "Finding...Mary and...William and... Ruth...made me think...I had found Heaven."

Darcy glanced at the room's furnishings. Although cleaner than many rooms he had encountered over the years, no one would call this particular inn heavenly. "If this is Heaven, it would explain so many seeking hell," he said wryly.

The corners of Joseph's lips turned upward. "A man...knows contentment...in the simplest acts." He closed his eyes as if seeking strength. "How can I tell you...of my gratitude?"

Darcy replied grimly. "I have brought this devastation to your doorstep. I do not deserve your gratitude. I have earned your disdain."

Joseph's gaze cleared. "You shall never know...my censure. Without you and Mrs. Darcy...I would not have Mary and William."

"But it was I that the shooter sought," Darcy protested. "If not for me, you would know no pain."

"If not for you...I could have lain on a dusty road...and bled to death," Joseph countered. "Yet, if it is forgiveness...you require... you have mine." He paused. "And...as a clergyman, I must remind you...that God asks us to forgive...those who...trespass against us. As Jesus did...on the cross...so must we."

Darcy's mouth thinned. His tension was palpable as he directed his wife. "Elizabeth, I am certain Mrs. Joseph and her sister could use a few minutes to freshen their things and perhaps to have a solid meal. I will sit with Mr. Joseph. Young William is asleep at the moment. If he wakes, I will summon you."

Elizabeth did not release his gaze, but she said, "That is an excellent suggestion. Come along, Mary. You must tend to your own needs if you are to properly care for Mr. Joseph."

"But Matthew might..." she began, but her husband's weak smile stopped the woman.

"Mr. Darcy managed…to see me through the worst…of my pain. He is quite capable." He sucked in a shallow breath. "Please see to Ruth, Sweetheart. Both of you…are too pale, and…that worries me. I would rest more comfortably…if I knew you were well."

Mary leaned across him to straighten the blanket draped over her husband's body. She gently kissed his forehead. "You are very fortunate, Sir, that I respond quickly to a guilty conscience."

"I will keep that…in mind…once I am well," he said softly.

Mary caressed his cheek. "I shall count the moments." Then she stood tall before catching Ruth's hand. "May my sister and I use your room, Mrs. Darcy?"

"This way." Elizabeth gestured toward the door. As she exited, she gave Darcy's shoulder a squeeze of encouragement.

With the ladies' departures, the two men remained in companionable silence for several minutes. "We have an acquaintance… of mere days," Joseph observed, at last. "But I feel an affinity…of a much longer duration."

"As do I," Darcy agreed.

Silence continued between them. Finally, Joseph said, "It would be a sin…if you sought revenge…Mr. Darcy."

"How can I not? An eye for an eye. The man who shot you has repeatedly wronged my family. My most excellent father. My innocent sister. Mrs. Darcy's sister. And now you. The man's accounts have been measured. I have spent a small fortune righting the wrongs that my former acquaintance has wrought on the world."

"I would ask you…for my peace of mind…that you abandon…thoughts of revenge. I would not seek it…for myself."

Darcy reasoned, "You are a man of God."

"I am a man…and as such…my first thought is to retaliate." Pause. "Yet, God teaches me…that I should extend…my mercy… to this man you describe."

Darcy rubbed his forehead absentmindedly. "Lieutenant Wickham sees such mercy as a weakness, one of which he gladly takes advantage. I have repeatedly extended compassion, but have been rewarded with new perfidy time and time again."

"Peter once asked Jesus...how many times a person...should forgive those who sin...against him." He paused. "Peter suggested... seven times...but the Lord responded, 'I say...not unto thee...until seven times; but ...until seventy times seven,'" Joseph declared.

Darcy's expression showed his incredulity. "That would mean I should forgive Lieutenant Wickham four hundred and ninety times. It is not likely any man could tolerate so many offenses and each time turn his cheek to the violation of trust."

"That is why...God is the superior creature...but we can strive...to copy his excellence."

Darcy weighed the man's words. "I wish I had your mettle, Joseph, but when I consider the number of degradations..." His thoughts remained in turmoil.

"To not forgive...will cause you more pain...than your enemy will endure...at your hand."

Chapter 10

ESME EXAMINED HER LEG CAREFULLY. When she had awakened from her latest dream, her leg had throbbed with a most unusual pain. It did not tingle as one might suppose when he had slept at an awkward angle. Instead, the pains shot through her upper thigh and into the cavity holding her most private place. If the discomfort had begun in her abdomen and had moved down her leg, she might have thought that the pain signaled trouble with the child she carried. But the pain was most decidedly in her leg; yet, when she searched for the cause, nothing appeared amiss. Not even a bruise stained her skin. *Odd*, she thought as she lowered her skirt and ran her fingers over the wrinkles. She shook off the feeling of dread. "I wonder if I can appeal to Lady Wotherspoon for another gown," she said aloud. "This one has become quite unpresentable."

No more were the words spoken than a soft knock heralded Aulay MacBethan's return. "Mam has given her permission for yer tour of the rooms," he announced.

Still uncertain what plagued her leg, the girl grimaced as she stood to greet him. "I should enjoy that very much."

"Are ye in pain, Lady Esme?" he asked in concern.

The girl shook her head in denial. "I was just thinking how poorly I am dressed. I shall not make a very good impression. Do not misunderstand," she rushed to add, fearing he might relay the wrong attitude to his mother. "I am grateful for the gift of the gown, but I admit to missing my own clothes."

As if uncertain how he should respond, Aulay offered his arm. "I be speaking to Mam. She'll know what to do. For now, we'll see the rooms."

Besides his penchant for games, especially chess, Esme had learned of Aulay's single-mindedness. When given a task, the man Lady Wotherspoon claimed "Esme" had chosen for her husband was singular in his approach. He would attend only to that task until its completion.

Aulay placed her on his arm, and the girl had the distinct feeling that this was not a natural gesture. "I have been practicing," he confessed as they exited the room. She nodded her approval, but her real attention remained on the burly-looking man standing quietly by the portal. When she had previously attempted to exit her quarters on her own, it was this man who had prevented her exploration. She was thankful that today he only glared his disapproval, rather than physically placing himself in her path.

"I wondered about my guard." Although pure inquisitiveness filled her mind, the girl managed to keep her tone nonchalant. The MacBethans may have proclaimed her a guest, but "Esme" knew otherwise. She was most undoubtedly a prisoner. What she could not quite comprehend was why they now treated her with such deference. And were there others hidden away in the house?

"Mam thought it best," Aulay dutifully explained. "Rankin be givin' ye his protection."

The girl teasingly said, "Am I in great danger in this house?"

Aulay looked about as if expecting an appropriate response to drop from the sky upon his head. "The…the house…the house is very large," he stammered.

"Of course," she added quickly to allay his obvious discomposure. "One would not wish to wander aimlessly without a destination."

Aulay smiled in relief. "We live principally in the Laird's Tower, which contains our private chambers and the great hall," he explained in that soft roll of the tongue characteristic of those of Scottish descent. In the past, she had apparently practiced the exclusive speech pattern of British society. The girl wondered how she had come to dwell with these people. "The hall be accessible from the courtyard below or by these stairs."

"Then I am housed in the family quarters?"

"You are," he said simply.

The girl observed her surroundings as they strolled leisurely through the halls. A pale sandstone rubble made up the outer walls. Each doorway arched, and the sign of a patron saint held its marking in stone. Unconsciously, she glanced backward to her door. *Saint Raymond*, she said to herself. *Because I am a prisoner here?* Her mind shouted. "Why Saint Raymond?" she asked her escort.

"The patron saint of ladies enceinte," Aulay said with a blush. "Mam says it be only right as how ye be bringing life to the castle. Domhnall's wife passed shortly after givin' Normanna an heir. Me brother still grieves for Maighread and their lost son. Mam says even if it not be mine ye carry, the child will be a MacBethan. And knowing ye not be barren be a pleasure to the household. Mam says we need to rebuild the MacBethan clan."

She marveled at the number of times the man at her side began a sentence with "Mam says." "Mam says we should marry soon for the child's sake." "Mam says I should see ye to dinner." "Mam says we kin have the house to the north once we marry." It seemed Dolina MacBethan had planned her intended daughter-in-law's future.

"Would you mind if we return to my room?" she said softly. "I am suddenly quite exhausted." She fingered the locket about her neck and wondered if the man in the rendering framed inside would miss her and try to rescue her before it was too late.

"Of course, m'lady," he said as he redirected her steps. "Ye shouldnae overextend yerself."

"Might we try again later?" Despite her suddenly desperate desire to return to the safety of her chamber, the girl quickly realized she could not delay her escape. Otherwise, she would find herself married to this childlike man beside her. Something told her "Mam" would tolerate nothing less.

* * *

"How long has Mrs. Fitzwilliam been missing?" Wickham asked the servants he had gathered in the smallest drawing room. He enjoyed the feeling of power this brief interlude provided him.

"It be a bit over a week," the housekeeper told him. "We spent multiple hours searching before we called off the hunt. The moor be unrepentant when it comes to givin' up its own."

Wickham examined each hired servant. This could have been his life if he not moved so quickly to try to make first Georgiana Darcy and then Miss King his wife. With the latter, he would not have experienced such luxury as what he had found at Alpin Hall, but he could have had a country manor house and several in waiting. "Even if you consider a detail unimportant, I expect to hear of it. My cousin's disappearance has greatly distressed the family." The servants before him dutifully nodded their obedience. "Then I will require a horse. I will survey the area myself."

"Yes, Mr. Hurlbert," the head groomsman responded for the small group.

"I find it hard to believe my cousin could have lost her way. Mrs. Fitzwilliam is an excellent horsewoman."

The groomsman added, "It do appear peculiar. Even the lady's horse be missing. A slip of a girl be one thing, but Bracken would have returned to the stable if'n he be alive."

"Where could an animal of several hundred pounds hide?" Wickham mused.

"That be an accurate assessment," the groom continued. "But it not be the first time a fine animal or a visitor to this area went missing."

* * *

"Have you seen to Mr. Joseph's care?" Elizabeth asked as she and Darcy undressed for the evening.

"I have secured the local surgeon's continued services, and the man assures me he will contract with others to oversee Mr. Joseph's recovery." He shed his tight-fitting jacket. "I paid for the rooms for the next fortnight. Although I expect a week may be the extent of Mr. Joseph's recuperative period, I wished to make certain that he has time to fully recover his strength. Miss Joseph and Mary may use this room when we depart tomorrow."

Before the simple dressing mirror, Elizabeth brushed her auburn waves. "I thought the Josephs might join the Bingleys at Drouot House. Matthew Joseph needs Jane's mothering and my sister's good sense. So does Mary. This experience has taken its toll on my friend's easy nature."

"I am certain Mrs. Bingley's kind disposition will restore Mrs. Joseph's biting wit and spontaneity. Any woman who can enjoy reading *The Heroine* while preparing to deliver her child is quite resilient."

Elizabeth smiled with a delighted twist of her mouth. "By the way, did you finish *The Heroine?*"

Darcy winked at her. "Would I deny myself the pleasure of knowing the ending?"

"Absolutely impossible," she said with assurance. "You are a Renaissance male, one accepting of the female perspective," she taunted lovingly.

Darcy bowed elegantly. "I am either a popinjay or the most progressive man of your acquaintance." His shadowed smile relayed his intentions.

"I choose 'progressive.'" She walked into his embrace. "You would look quite hideous in a yellow waistcoat and pea-green breeches."

He kissed the column of her neck. "On the point of Mr. Brummell's fashion sense, we agree," he said on a rasp before returning to an assault on her defenses.

"Fitz...Fitzwilliam," she said hoarsely. "Are you trying to seduce me?" Her body tensed as his lips trailed fire along her jaw line.

Darcy chuckled as he kissed her ear lobe. "If you must ask, my love, I am failing miserably."

Elizabeth slid her hands under his shirt and massaged the muscles of his back. She rested her cheek against his chest. "There is no place I would rather be than in your arms."

* * *

Wickham bent over the opening in the rock face where he had placed the few items he had managed to pilfer from the estate. Before he pretended to search for Georgiana Fitzwilliam, he had chosen several pieces of silver and a small crystal ornament to stow away as collateral. He would return later and add more to his cache. Wickham realized his time at Alpin Hall would be limited. He had taken only a few items with this first pass through the house. Before he made off freely with the Alpin riches, he would determine the staff's routines.

He covered the opening with brush and used a branch from a hedge to erase his few tracks. Looking about to memorize his bearings in the rugged country, Wickham remounted. "Back to the estate for my afternoon meal. Then a return to this place for a second deposit. By tomorrow afternoon, I should be on the road.

Darcy or the Major General will arrive any day now. If either finds me here, I will face the gallows or transportation."

* * *

Georgiana's eyes slid across the meager furnishings. For a few moments, she could not recall where she was. What was real and what was part of her imagination had blended into a refracted frame through which she viewed her world. What could she actually claim to know? "The room," she whispered. "This room is real."

"Is it?" The familiar female voice said from somewhere behind and above her.

Georgiana did not move——simply concentrated on the wooden table and chair some six feet from her. Yet, try as she might, she could not bring the furnishings into a clear focus. "It must be real," she argued. "Or else...I am dead, and this is one of...Dante's levels of Purgatory."

The voice chortled. "You are most assuredly not dead."

"But shall I die?" Despite her best efforts, tears formed in her eyes' corners.

"I cannot say. It is not part of my domain to change God's plan for you. Yet, I believe a person has the ability to direct his course. What path shall you choose, Georgiana? Earlier, you demonstrated great strength of resolve, but now you regress."

She protested, "I am quite exhausted."

The voice countered, "As weary as Atlas with the world's weight on his shoulders? Or is your lassitude more of Prometheus' nature——a constant pain?"

"Neither describes my state of affairs." Georgiana sighed deeply. "I simply require some rest. This is so daunting."

The voice warned, "I expect you to not surrender to your disillusionment. Your circumstances have an egress. You must believe."

Georgiana's voice trailed off as she closed her eyes once more. "I believe."

"Then sleep, my child," the voice soothed. "I shall watch over you."

* * *

"Esme" forced herself to recall her latest dream. In it, she had pleaded with someone whom she could not identify to permit her a bit more rest. "You must believe," she had heard the person say, but she did not know to what she must adhere. Her only conscious thoughts involved escaping from the MacBethans' hold on her. With a shake of her head to drive away the last of her dream's vestiges, the girl rose and made her way to the door. As she expected, a guard blocked her exit. *If I were truly a guest*, she told herself, *I would have free rein of the house.*

"I would like to continue my tour of the house and grounds. Please send for Mr. Aulay," she directed.

"Yes, Ma'am." The man bowed, but he did not move until she pointedly stepped backwards into the room. A heartbeat later, she heard the key turn in the lock. "Definitely a prisoner," she murmured.

Making herself complete the mundane tasks of repinning her hair and smoothing her gown's wrinkles, she prepared what she would say to Aulay MacBethan. She needed him to share more on this excursion than he had on their last venture. However, those plans flew out the window when the door opened to reveal a man she instinctively knew to be Lord Wotherspoon.

His obeisance offered her respect. "My Lady, I fear Aulay is unavailable. He and our mother are visiting with the vicar's new wife. I am Domhnall MacBethan, Lord Wotherspoon. May I be of service?"

She made herself swallow. Domhnall MacBethan was everything Aulay was not. Unruly dark hair, worn long and tied in a queue. Stern features. Green eyes, like those of a cat. A sensual mouth.

Broad shoulders. He filled the door with his presence. "I...I would not wish...wish to take you away from your duties," she stammered.

He stepped inside the room. "I would be honored to serve as your guide."

"But..." she began. Yet, she accepted his outstretched hand. When the man tucked hers in beside him, she gasped from his closeness. "If you insist." Without another word, he led her from the room.

"What did you see earlier?" He ventured to touch her arm, guiding her around the displays of ancestral armor.

She glanced up at him. "Not much, I fear. My stamina is not what it should be."

"Then you will have the grand tour," he said softly, almost intimately. As they strolled through the passageways, her escort explained some of the house's history. "James III deeded the land to this branch of MacBethan family in the late 1400s, but the family has fallen on hard times. There be few of us remaining. My mother insists we each marry and have many bairns."

He led her up a narrow spiraling staircase. "There be three storeys and a garret. The grand hall consumes most of the second storey. Although we have recently seen to its repair, the original dais remains." He pointed to the low raised platform. "As in most former Scottish keeps, to reach the upper floors and the solar, a person must cross the hall to the opposite corner to ascend a second set of stairs. Such construction deters a man's enemies."

She listened carefully to what he said of the house's design, but also she relished the man's rolling accent. Unlike his brother's uncultured speech, Domhnall MacBethan spoke as a gentleman. "Might I say, Lord Wotherspoon, that I note a bit of an English influence in your speech?"

"I attended Eton and Oxford before making my way in English Society. With my father's passing, I was summoned home," he explained.

"I find the mixture truly inviting," she confessed.

"That be very kind of you, my Lady." As they strolled leisurely through the passages, he noted several of the differences between the original house and the current manor.

Her's mind raced with the knowledge he imparted. She made a mental note of the iron grilles still displayed on many of the windows and the number of niches possibly leading to secret passageways. However, her wariness had left her unprepared for the elaborately decorated chapel he showed her next. A consecrated cross hung over each arched opening, which led to the central altar. "This is magnificent," she murmured.

"This chapel was fitted up as you see it in James the Second's time. Before that period, as I understand, the pews were only wainscot; and there is some reason to think that the linings and cushions of the pulpit and family seat were only purple cloth; but this is not quite certain. It is a handsome chapel, and was formerly in constant use both morning and evening. Prayers were always read in it by the domestic chaplain, within the memory of many; but my grandfather left it off."

"It is a pity," she cried, "that the custom should have been discontinued. It served a valuable part in former times. There is something in a chapel and chaplain so much in character with a great house, with one's ideas of what such a household should be! A whole family assembling regularly for the purpose of prayer is fine!"

"Very fine indeed," said Lord Wotherspoon, laughing. "It must do the heads of the family a great deal of good to force all the poor housemaids and footmen to leave business and pleasure, and say their prayers here twice a day, while they are inventing excuses themselves for staying away."

She declared, "*That* is hardly my idea of a family assembling. If the master and mistress do *not* attend themselves, there must be more harm than good in the custom."

Wotherspoon endeavored to show himself the lord of the manor when he responded, "At any rate, it is safer to leave people to their own devices on such subjects. Everybody likes to go his own way— to choose his own time and manner of devotion. The obligation of attendance, the formality, the restraint, the length of time—altogether it is a formidable thing, and what nobody likes; and if the good people who used to kneel and gape in this gallery could have foreseen that the time would ever come when men and women might lie another ten minutes in bed, when they woke with a headache, without danger of reprobation, because chapel was missed, they would have jumped with joy and envy. Cannot you imagine with what unwilling feelings the former belles of the house of Mac-Bethan did many a time repair to this chapel? The young and pretty virginal ladies—starched up into seeming piety, but with heads full of something very different—especially if the poor chaplain were not worth looking at—and, in those days, I fancy parsons were very inferior even to what they are now."

Having permitted his anger toward the chaos surrounding him to invade his words, Domhnall needed a little recollection before he could say, "Sometimes I think my mother could reside here," he said nonchalantly.

"Then Lady Wotherspoon is very religious?" she asked. The idea set in sharp contrast to what she suspected of the woman.

Wotherspoon's frown lines met. "My mother practices her beliefs, but I would not necessarily call her religious."

She blushed. "I did not mean to pry. I am having some difficulty in remembering the details of my relationship with your brother. It is as if I am learning everything for the first time."

"Who says you have a history with Aulay?" he asked with a bit of irritation.

She reacted immediately. "Are you saying that my acquaintance with your brother is a new one?" Indignation flared in her chest. She did not necessarily want to be engaged to Aulay, but if she had no prior understanding, when had it been decided that she should conjoin with him? And who had made that decision? Did she have family in the area? Had they turned their backs on her? Simply left her under the MacBethans' care? She thought of the child. If she carried another man's issue, she must be an independent woman. That only made sense. Did she possess a widow's pension? If she had accepted Aulay's plight, was it out of desperation? She had hoped this tour would answer some of her questions. Instead, the number of unknowns had increased.

"I be saying, Lady Esme, that few marriages are based on love. You require a husband for your protection and a father for your child. My mother has long wished to see Aulay with a woman who possesses a kind heart." He turned his back on her, symbolically closing the conversation.

As he directed her steps toward her chamber, the girl's mind raced with the new knowledge: as she had earlier suspected, the person who had been her savior, Lady Wotherspoon, was a force with whom she would have to deal. The MacBethan family matriarch ruled her house with a granite fist.

* * *

Domhnall had not anticipated his reaction to the woman his mother had chosen for his youngest brother. His years in England had taught him to appreciate Lady Esme's classic beauty. Even through her current disheveled appearance, she was ethereally elegant. Her golden tresses called to have someone run his fingers through them, and her creamy white neck and shoulders begged to be caressed. The lady was not tall, especially when compared to his stature; in fact, her head did not quite reach his shoulder. Yet, she stood tall, with an air of authority that both amused and intrigued him. *The lady deserves better than a life with a feebleminded man*, he told himself. Unfortunate as it was, his youngest brother had never achieved the maturity expected of a man of two and twenty.

Aulay's birth had been a difficult one for their mother, and the family had, at first, rejoiced with the boy's survival. However, that joy was tempered by Aulay's inability to make his own choices. In many ways, his brother was brilliant—smarter than the lot of them. In games of strategy and of topics with a scientific slant, Aulay was very clever, but when it came to the simplest social interactions, his brother struggled. Only with their mother's assistance could Aulay make the most basic of social conversation.

At first, he had laughed at the hours of practice from which Aulay had suffered at their mother's direction, but now Domhnall envied that time if it brought the lovely Lady Esme into closer contact. He should not be having such thoughts. After all, his beloved Maighread and his child were but eight months in the grave, but, like it or not, he had reacted in a very male manner to their guest.

* * *

The girl was very aware of the man whose muscle flexed under her fingertips. This walk through the house was quite different from the earlier one with Aulay. Instead of being exhausted by the experience, she was completely exhilarated. This was an attractive, yet dangerous, man by her side. She possessed no doubt that he could dispose of another with his bare hands. If she was to survive this situation, she would need to make Lord Wotherspoon her ally.

"You have been kind to show me what is to be my new home," she said softly.

"Then you will accept my brother's proposal?" He brought their stroll to a casual pause in the grand hall's middle.

Bewilderment graced her face. "It was my understanding that I had previously agreed to Aulay's plight."

He said seriously, "A woman can change her mind. Until the vows are spoken, you are not bound to Aulay or to any man. As we are both aware, only death can end the marriage bonds."

She looked at him sharply. "Although I am certain of my husband's demise, I admit with my recent injury that I am experiencing difficulties in recalling our marriage's details."

"Perhaps the locket you clutch holds a clue," he suggested.

"It contains a picture of my husband, but no other identification," she confided.

"Then perhaps it be best if you postpone your nuptials until all uncertainties are resolved."

She said candidly, "I do not expect that Lady Wotherspoon would appreciate the delay."

He looked off as if seeing something she did not. "I will tend to my mother's dudgeon if it occurs." Turning his gaze on her, he said confidently, "I will protect you, Lady Esme. Even from my mother. I am still the laird of this keep."

Before she could respond, a servant rushed forward. "Me Laird. I be sent to find ye. Murdoh needs ye, Sir. Trouble below."

Domhnall caught her hand and brought it to his lips. "I must leave you. Ronald will return you to your room. Take care, Lady Esme." He turned immediately and strode away.

She watched his retreating form. Tension bunched his shoulders, but he still moved with catlike sleekness. A lion in control of his territory.

"Lady Esme," the servant said from behind her. "If'n ye would follow me."

She nodded her understanding, but her gaze remained on the man with whom she had spent the last hour. A sense of loss prevailed.

"Lady Esme," Ronald said more urgently.

She reluctantly followed the servant. "What type of trouble?" she said from curiosity.

Ronald stopped suddenly. "Ma'am?"

"Below," she insisted. "What type of trouble persists below?"

The servant shrugged. "One of the prisoners, Ma'am. He attacked Murdoh."

Chapter 11

WICKHAM SETTLED IN THE LUXURY of the four-poster bed. He had visited his hiding place three times during the day. From the manor house, he had removed pieces of silver, some jewelry, and several interesting-looking ornaments that he thought might bring him ready cash. When he departed Alpin Hall, he would travel to Edinburgh where a man might sell such items without question.

As he had ridden across the estate, he had pleasantly remembered his younger days when he had explored Pemberley and Derbyshire with his father. "Possibly, I can find a similar position to my father's on a Scottish estate or in Normandy," he had told himself. "It is not probable that Darcy will rest before seeing me punished." Even with Lydia's connections to Mrs. Darcy, Wickham held only minimal hope of Darcy's forgiveness. His foolish temper would require him to leave England behind and seek a new life elsewhere. "It is not as if I have never lived by my wits," he said to his room's darkness. Those years of dissipation, after he had departed Cambridge in disgrace, quickly flooded his mind. A deep sigh of anticipation lifted his chest. "It would be good to start over. A pecuniary advantage," he reasoned aloud. "Even with the disgrace, Lydia's family will welcome her return. I will not have to concern myself with my wife's future. As if I ever did," he sarcastically chastised himself. In the past, he had allowed himself great latitude on such points.

Thoughts of his childlike wife brought both pleasant memories and sour ones. Her loyalty and her adventurous spirit he had previously determined were to Mrs. Wickham's credit. She also possessed a sweet temperament, and she readily made friends among his colleagues. His wife could exert all her powers of pleasing without suspicion. Yet, Lydia's having been forced upon him had forever doomed the success of their relationship. He resented how Darcy had bested him.

He had convinced her to accompany him to London. Her mother had provided Lydia with a bit of spending money, and he had needed the stake to escape his creditors. And Lydia was a ready participant. Of course, she had not known what it was he had sought from her. He had gloried in the girl's attentions, but she had not been the one he wanted. If Lydia's sister had had a proper dowry, he might have taken on Elizabeth Bennet. Maybe even have chosen to settle down, but his pursuit of Miss King's settlement had cooled Miss Elizabeth's interest. He had thought to engage her attentions again when the lady had returned from her visit with Charlotte Collins, but Miss Elizabeth had returned home from Kent with a new respect for Darcy. In fact, her opinion of Darcy had altered dramatically. Wickham could readily recall the conversation in which he recognized that he had squandered any chance of regaining the lady's regard.

On the very last day of the regiment's remaining in Meryton, he had dined with others of the officers at Longbourn, and so little was Miss Elizabeth disposed to part from him in good humor that, on his making some inquiry as to the manner in which her time had passed at Hunsford, she had mentioned the former Colonel Fitzwilliam and Mr. Darcy as having spent three weeks at Rosings, and had asked him if he were acquainted with the colonel.

Displeased by her tone, Wickham had masked his surprise and alarm. With a moment's recollection and a returning smile of solicitude, he had falsely assured Miss Elizabeth of the then colonel's very gentlemanlike qualities and had forced himself to inquire of the lady's opinion of Darcy's cousin, a man Wickham had always despised.

With an air of indifference, but with true curiosity, he had asked, "How long did you say the colonel was at Rosings?"

"Nearly three weeks."

Having sensed her possible defection, he asked cautiously. "And you saw him frequently?"

"Yes, almost every day."

Her wry smile should have warned him of her intent, but he had overestimated his ability to bring about the lady's renewed regard. Hoping to regain Miss Elizabeth's goodwill, he had added his usual spill about Darcy's disposition. "His manners are very different from his cousin's."

"Yes, very different. But I think Mr. Darcy improves upon acquaintance."

Her sentiment had shocked him. "Indeed!" But he had checked himself before adding in a gayer tone, "Is it in address that he improves? Has he deigned to add aught of civility to his ordinary style? For dare I not hope," he had continued, while adopting the conspiratorial tone that had proved acceptable to the lady on previous occasions, "that Darcy is improved in essentials."

Elizabeth Bennet's next words had announced her withdrawal from Wickham's favor. "Oh, no! In essentials, I believe, Mr. Darcy is very much what he ever was."

Scarcely knowing whether to rejoice over her words or to distrust their meaning, he had listened with an apprehensive and anxious attention while Miss Elizabeth had added, "When I said Mr. Darcy improved on acquaintance, I did not mean that either his mind or his manners were in a state of improvement; but that from knowing him better, his disposition was better understood."

And now the lady is Mrs. Darcy, he thought angrily, and the silence absorbed his contempt. Darcy had won Miss Elizabeth's hand and her heart, and he had settled for the lesser sister and a substantial monetary payment. Of course, if he had known of Darcy's affection for Elizabeth Bennet, he would have held out for more money. "No further regrets," he reproved. "We move forward from this time."

He had spotted several antique pieces that he would take with him when he rode out tomorrow, but he had no plans to return to Alpin Hall afterwards. A horse with the best pedigree and a small satchel of expensive items would be his ticket. "No more service to country and King," he declared as he punched the pillow to make it more pliable. "Once I have a stake, I will make a new future away from the Darcys and their continual disdain. They will one day say that they knew me when..."

* * *

Edward Fitzwilliam bedded down in an orchard. Some of the aristocracy would find his choice of accommodations abhorrent. He was an earl's son, after all. The "spare" for his brother Rowland. Yet, Edward had always preferred the outdoors and space to a crowded ballroom. It was the reason he had chosen the army over the navy when selecting his military calling. That and the fact that rough oceans made him seasick. "I would have made a deplorable captain in that respect," he mumbled to his horse as he tied the stallion loosely to one of the bushes.

"Another day—maybe a day and a half," he told the animal as he wiped down its coat. "Then you can rest, my friend, and I can bury myself in the sweet scent of jasmine. I have a beautiful wife, you know. A woman to quell the emptiness." He patted the stallion's neck.

He unwrapped the bedding and stretched out under the stars. "At least, there is no rain. No mud. No knee-deep in blood," he continued to talk to himself. "No dreams of the horror that was Waterloo. Only Georgie's beautiful countenance and her sweet body. Heaven on Earth." A smile spread across his face. "A lifetime of proving myself worthy of Georgiana's love," He sighed deeply. "A sentence I will gladly serve."

* * *

"Prisoners." The word beat a staccato in her mind as she reentered the simple chamber with its obvious guard just outside the door. She had considered the idea that she was the MacBethans' prisoner, but somehow she had not previously mustered the panic that now filled her chest. "Prisoner," she mouthed the word. The MacBethans continued to lock her in this small space. "It is obviously not a guest room." She had observed several elaborate bedchambers during her house tour. With its plain furnishings, the room she occupied did not delineate her as an honored member of the household. What would happen if she refused to become Aulay's bride? Would the MacBethans return her to where the others were being held? And where was that exactly? Lord Wotherspoon had rushed toward the lower staircase when he had left her in Ronald's care. "What happens to the other prisoners?" she wondered aloud. "Are they tortured? Killed? Why are they here? What offense have they committed? And if I was one of them, what offense did I practice on the MacBethans to give them dominion over me?"

And there had to be more than one prisoner. The servant had specifically said, "One of the *prisoners*." Her thoughts flooded the room. Could she escape? Could she assist the others? She needed to know exactly where she was being held. She could observe part of the estate's entrance from the room's small window. A better view of the grounds became paramount. If she escaped the MacBethans, could she find someone who would come to her aid? Usually, estates were several miles apart. Could she find a Good Samaritan before Lady Wotherspoon found her? The girl held no doubt that the woman would hunt her down as if chasing a fox in the woods.

"I need more information," she told herself as she paced the small open space. "What can I remember from my so-called sickroom stay?" she mused. The bandage on her wrist was an obvious reminder. Carefully, she unwrapped the cloth to examine the raw scrapes along the pale skin. "What could have caused these lacerations?" She gently touched the deepest cut, which had scabbed over. "I must remember why I felt gratitude for the kindness Lady Wotherspoon has shown me." She rewrapped her wrist so no one would know that she had considered her injuries to result from anything but a simple fall.

"This shan't be easy," she cautioned her rapidly beating pulse. "Lord Wotherspoon reminded me that I must settle my past before I accept the future his mother has designed for me. Yet, I must do so carefully without offending the woman. Domhnall MacBethan has sworn to protect me, but can I trust anyone in this house?"

* * *

"I have sent a message to Drouot House," Elizabeth explained. "I expect Mrs. Bingley to issue an invitation for your family to join them as soon as she receives my letter. As Mr. Joseph and Mr. Darcy were to use Drouot as their base for their business dealings, the Bingleys shall be expecting your husband."

Mary Joseph protested, "Yet, not as a man recovering from a gunshot wound."

"Trust me, Mrs. Joseph," Darcy countered, "Mrs. Bingley would be offended if you did not take shelter at Drouot House. My wife's sister has the kindest of hearts."

"That means that Mrs. Bingley thought highly of Mr. Darcy long before I did," Elizabeth teased. "Yet, my husband speaks the truth. The Bingleys are two of the most obliging adults on this earth. My father has always contended that Jane and Mr. Bingley would do very well together because their tempers are by no means unlike. Mr. Bennet claimed that the Bingleys were each so complying that nothing would ever be resolved upon between them, and that they were so easy that every servant would cheat them and so generous that they would always exceed their income."

Darcy chuckled. "I would call Mr. Bennet's a fair evaluation."

Mary's lips twitched. "Mr. Joseph and I shall quash the urge to make the Bingleys our mark."

"If you are tempted," Darcy returned the smile, "keep in mind that Mrs. Darcy and I will follow you to Newton Stewart, and my wife and I are less inclined to be generous."

"Did you hear that, Matthew?" Mary teased.

The clergyman sat propped against a stack of pillows. Someone had shaved him, and although he still appeared pale, a bit of color had returned to his cheeks. "I would say we have been duly warned, Wife. And we are very familiar with the Darcys of Pemberley's less than charitable natures," he said jokingly. All four knew that if it had not been for the Darcys' generosity, the Josephs' son would have been born in a lowly stable and would have likely died. The couple owed them much more than could ever be repaid. Joseph extended his hand to Darcy. "Be safe, Sir. You and Mrs. Darcy are very important to the Joseph family. You will remain in our daily prayers."

"Thank you." Darcy nodded his understanding. He stood and reached for his hat and gloves. "Mrs. Darcy, we should be on the road."

"Of course." Elizabeth hugged Mary one last time. "Promise me you shall accept the Bingleys' hospitality."

Mary returned the embrace. "I promise."

* * *

Darcy handed her into the carriage. He had taken Bennet from Mrs. Prulock and had deposited his son in his wife's arms. Then he had assisted the wet nurse to a place beside Elizabeth. Traditionally, the nurse and Bennet would have followed in his small coach, but they would make do with the one carriage. He would welcome the nurse's presence if it meant having Bennet in close proximity. His son had brought him a peace that he could not explain to anyone who had never walked the floor with a colicky baby in order to allow his mate a few extra hours of sleep. He and Elizabeth had created this beautiful bundle of arms and legs and joy through their love. He placed his hat and gloves on the seat beside him. "I will hold Bennet," he said softly.

Elizabeth smiled brightly. "You will notice, Mrs. Prulock," she said in that familiar teasing tone he so adored. The one which had disappeared from his wife's personality after her previous miscarriages. It was as if Bennet's birth had given him back the woman Darcy loved with every fiber of his being. "That Mr. Darcy relishes holding *his* son when Bennet sleeps. Yet, let the boy kick up a fuss, and the child is instantly *my* son, not *our* son."

"Wait until the young master be cutting his teeth. He be keeping the household awake with his temper," Mrs. Prulock predicted.

With his fingertips, Darcy traced his child's jaw line. "Even a case of the Darcy stubbornness will not deter my joy at looking at this angelic countenance."

"At least Mr. Darcy did not blame said stubbornness on my side of the family," Elizabeth countered as the carriage lurched into motion.

Darcy did not remove his eyes from his son's face, but he said, "I have learned, Mrs. Darcy, to accept that all Bennet's failings lie at *my* feet while *our* son's more magnanimous qualities are a direct result of *your* influence."

Elizabeth suppressed her grin. "You were difficult to bring to the bit," she teased. "But I am quite content with the end result." They sat in silence for several minutes while each contemplated his own tumultuous part in their coming together as man and wife. Finally, she asked, "How long before we reach Alpin Hall?"

"Seven to eight hours depending on the roads," he said softly.

"I am most anxious to settle what has transpired with Mrs. Fitzwilliam," Elizabeth said.

He nodded as he sat back into the soft squabs. "As am I. I have missed Georgiana."

* * *

"Shall you sleep the day away?" the voice asked in concern.

She turned over to look at the room's ceiling and once more to count the knots in the wood. "Two and twenty," she said to test her voice.

"Yes, two and twenty," the voice spoke with a bit of irritation. "What else shall you do today?"

She said defensively, "What else would you have me do?"

The voice "tutted" her disapproval. "Find a way out of this dilemma. You are a brave, intelligent woman."

"I would beg to differ. If I were brave and intelligent, I would not have succumbed to my doubts, and I would not be at another's beck and call."

* * *

"Shall ye sleep the day away?" Lady Wotherspoon said close to the girl's ear. A splitting headache had driven her to her bed several hours prior. She had searched her memory for details of her life before coming to Normanna Hall, as well as what had happened to her since arriving at the estate. The process had left her exhausted and suffering with a megrim.

The girl shoved herself to a seated position. "Forgive me, Lady Wotherspoon. I thought it best to channel my energies to recovering fully. If I am to accept Aulay, then I must be at my best."

"Of course, ye shall accept Aulay," the woman declared as she began to brush Esme's hair to remove the tangles.

"Esme" frowned deeply. "I have thought much of what is best. I recall..." she paused. "I recall few details of my life prior to my time in this room." She sat quietly for several minutes before saying, "Before I could accept Aulay, I would need to learn more of my child's father." Her fingers splayed protectively across her abdomen.

Her request had, evidently, surprised Lady Wotherspoon. The woman's eyes flared with incredulity, but she quickly masked her true response. "A woman should have pleasant memories to share with the bairn." She braided Esme's hair. "I think it best if ye remember on yer own, but if'n ye kinnae I kin tell ye more of yer life."

"You know of my lost memories?" Esme returned the woman's earlier surprise.

"I's know some of it. Enough to know yer husband be gone. Ye do not wish the child to be barn without a lovin' father. Aulay would be a good companion."

"If I cannot remember on my own, you will tell me what you know?" The girl insisted.

"I shall share it all."

* * *

Lady Wotherspoon rushed through Normanna's intricate passageways until she reached the Grand Hall. Finding Munro, her husband's nephew, drinking with several of the other cousins and distant relatives, with a tilt of her head, she motioned him to follow her into the chapel. Although he was of the MacBethan clan, the man had proved resourceful when she had sent him on previous tasks.

"What be it?" he grumbled when he sat behind her on one of the few pews within the circular room.

"Ye shud not be afeared of God's hand," she said coldly.

He warned, "Tell me what ye need, Aunt, and leave off worryin' fer me soul."

Dolina glanced around to assure their privacy. "I require information on the girl Blane found in the moor. Who might she be? Ride out and check the inns. See if'n anyone be lookin' fer her."

"Why? What hive ye in mind for the lass?"

"Jist do as I say," she instructed. "What I've planned be none of yer doings."

* * *

"Mr. Hurlbert," Mr. Jacks cornered Wickham in the morning room. "I be pleased that I find ye before ye ride out, Sir."

Wickham stiffened. He had loaded a flour sack with several pieces of silver and other valuables and had earlier stashed the items in an arbor in the lower gardens. Immediately, he wondered if someone had discovered his hiding place. As he turned slowly to face the Fitzwilliam caretaker, Wickham consciously placed a smile on his face and began to construct an excuse for the find. "How may I serve you, Mr. Jacks?" he said congenially.

"I have news, Sir," Jacks said hopefully. "A rider has brought word of Mrs. Fitzwilliam's horse."

"Really?" Wickham's curiosity piqued. "Where has the animal been spotted?"

"In Ayr, Sir. In the next shire. A trader says he observed a horse with Bracken's markings on the Normanna estate."

"Where exactly is this estate? On the coast or inland?" Wickham could not control the spark of interest he experienced.

Jacks mopped his forehead with his handkerchief. "On the moor. It be dangerous. I kin't imagine Mrs. Fitzwilliam being so far from the manor house, but we shud see if it be true. We kin send our men."

Wickham quickly sized up the situation. "It may be best if I call at Normanna first. Perhaps my cousin is injured, and the Normanna household has offered her sanctuary. Or perhaps they simply found the horse on the moor and possess no knowledge of its owner. We would not wish to offend a neighbor."

"Yes, Sir. Shud I see to a mount?"

"I will ride out after I break my fast." After dismissing the man, Wickham sat heavily. *I wonder*, he said to himself. *If I could find Georgiana, then Darcy would be honor-bound to forgive me. Mayhap, even reward me. If Mrs. Fitzwilliam is still alive, I could be a hero. Darcy would no longer turn me away from Pemberley. And, if I cannot find the lady, I can always continue on to Edinburgh as planned. It is worth a few hours of actual searching for the long-term familial benefits.*

Finishing off his meal, Wickham strode toward the house's rear. He would take the mount the groom had provided him and then circle the orchard to reach the lower gardens and his hidden treasure. *With that, I will journey into the next shire and see what secrets it holds.*

* * *

"Where dost thou ride?" Domhnall had cornered his cousin on the path leading to the stables.

"Aunt Dolina has an errand for me," Munro said nonchalantly.

Domhnall realized that Munro remained uncertain as to whether Domhnall could handle the family matriarch. His cousin was in for a big surprise. He demanded, "What type of errand?"

Munro smiled purposely, "Nothin' important. Just requires me to speak to her brother on her behalf. They must have had another spat."

Domhnall stepped menacingly closer. "Somehow I do not believe you." He paused. "I would hate to think that you had taken my mother's side against me," he hissed.

Munro retreated a step, bringing him against the stone retaining wall. "Me loyalty lies with the laird of Normanna," he said tentatively.

"Prove it." He paused. "Tell me in truth what game Lady Wotherspoon plays," he insisted.

Munro ran his finger under his tight neck cloth. "Me aunt desires news of the girl Blane brings in. Her name. Something of the woman's family. Aunt Dolina wants the girl for yer brother."

Domhnall's frown lines met. He had other ideas for the woman. Certainly not as a token wife for his puppet of a brother. "Ye'll discover what Lady Wotherspoon wants to know, but you'll report to me first upon yer return. Is that understood?"

"Certainly, Cousin. I wud never step 'tween you and Aunt Dolina." Munro swallowed hard.

"That would be a wise choice on your part."

* * *

Darcy's carriage made its way across the graveled circle before Alpin Hall. The white stone of the façade had given the manor house its name, but red sandstone rubble from the local quarry had been used for the main construction. A draped putto decorated an arched outer door. "Interesting," Elizabeth said wryly.

"Not my style," he grumbled as the coach slowed, and Jasper scrambled to set the steps. Darcy was down first, and he turned to steady Elizabeth's step; yet, his eyes kept glancing at the still-unopened entrance door. "Where is she?" he whispered close to Elizabeth's ear. "Jasper, see to Bennet and Mrs. Prulock," he ordered.

"Yes, Sir."

Finally, the door opened, and the hunch-shouldered figure of Mr. Jacks appeared on the doorstep. "Good day, Sir," the man said with a stiff bow. "Welcome to Alpin Hall. How may we serve ye, Sir?" he said properly.

Darcy braced Elizabeth's footing on the crumbling entrance steps. Although the lawn appeared well groomed, the house was in need of some repairs. He would speak to the earl upon their return to Derbyshire. He wondered if Matlock had hired an inefficient steward. "Mr. Jacks," Darcy recognized the man on closer inspection. "I did not realize you remained with the property."

"I beg yer pardon, Sir. Do I know ye?" He squinted into the afternoon sun.

"Fitzwilliam Darcy. I have not seen you since I was twelve." Darcy looked over the man's shoulder in hopes of finding his sister. "I am Mrs. Fitzwilliam's brother."

To his chagrin, there was no sign of Georgiana, only a small, elderly housekeeper who appeared beside the man. "Himself," she said affectionately. "It be Mr. Darcy." She clutched at Jacks' arm. "My! Ye have turned into a fine gentleman," she gushed.

"Mrs. Jacks?" The Darcys stepped into the front foyer. "I apologize for our unanticipated arrival. This is my wife, Mrs. Darcy, my son, Bennet, and his nurse, Mrs. Prulock."

"A wee bairn," the woman said with glee. "Oh, bless be the days. Please come in." She directed her husband to take their wraps.

"Mrs. Fitzwilliam had a miniature of you on her nightstand. I wud recognize ye anywhere."

As he assisted Elizabeth with her cloak, Darcy explained, "One summer, shortly before Georgiana's birth, Matlock sent Rowland, Edward, and me to Alpin to remove us from underfoot. Rowland's tutor served as our chaperone, but it was Mr. Jacks who kept us in line. Not an easy task with three rambunctious youths free of parental oversight."

Elizabeth nodded her understanding, but her attention remained on the empty staircase. Finally, Darcy could not put off the inevitable any longer. He asked, "Mrs. Jacks, is my sister at Alpin Hall?"

All activity ceased. No one moved. Not a sound could be heard in the house. Not even a tick of the nearby grandfather clock. The woman bowed her head in reverence. "We be tenderin' our regrets," she said softly.

Darcy felt Elizabeth's hand slip into his grasp. She said, "Then it was you who sent the missive to Pemberley?"

"Aye, Ma'am."

She knew he had no words for the complete anguish that filled his heart, so his incomparable wife assumed control. "Mr. Darcy and I would speak to you of the letter's specifics. Might we step into the drawing room?" She glanced about the foyer. "Is there someone to see Mrs. Prulock and our child to the nursery?"

Darcy heard the activity around him, but he could not respond. His mind raced toward the unthinkable possibility that he had lost his sister forever. He could barely breathe as the dread crept up his spine.

"We keep a small day staff, Ma'am," Mr. Jacks explained to Elizabeth. "I'll see to yer accommodations. Mrs. Jacks kin answer yer questions. I'll tell Mrs. Jordan of yer arrival and ask her to bring ye refreshments."

"This way, Mrs. Darcy." The housekeeper gestured to a nearby room.

Darcy automatically placed Elizabeth on his arm. She was his strength, the reason he still existed at this moment. Without her, he could not face the news of Georgiana's possible demise. He marveled at how well his wife handled the highs and lows of their relationship. When he floundered, Elizabeth covered his foibles, and when she stumbled, he stepped forward to assume the lead. His marrying her had been great fortune, almost as if Fate had place Elizabeth Bennet in his path for that purpose. "Thank you," he whispered.

"You avoided the obvious, Mr. Darcy," she said softly.

Darcy swallowed hard. "I did. Yet, my gratitude exists for more than just this moment." He seated Elizabeth comfortably in a wing chair and then stood stiffly to face the unavoidable. "Mrs. Darcy has shared your letter. What we require is an explanation of what led to your writing it."

Mrs. Jacks slumped heavily in her chair. "I shan't explain how pleased we be to have Mrs. Fitzwilliam among us and how the house anticipated the return of Master Edward. Besides being a beloved member of the Fitzwilliam family, the Major General be a grand war hero. And his wife being yer sister, Mr. Darcy, only made Mrs. Fitzwilliam more welcomed.

"Your sister be so elegant, very much like yer mother Lady Anne, she is. And Mrs. Fitzwilliam possesses the kindest of hearts," Mrs. Jacks said fondly. "However, yer sister, Sir, be highly disappointed with her husband's delay, and then she be receiving the letter from the Countess. If I had known, Mr. Darcy, what the letter say, I be not givin' it to yer sister. I wud have sent for you or the Viscount."

"The Viscountess has delivered the Matlock heir," Darcy explained. He was surprised that no one had apprised the Jackses of Lady Lindale's healthy delivery. The news affected their futures also. Again, he wondered about the efficiency of the Alpin steward.

"We be unaware until Mrs. Fitzwilliam told us. It be happy news among the staff," Mrs. Jacks explained politely.

"Would you explain exactly what happened the day Mrs. Fitzwilliam read the Countess's letter?" Elizabeth redirected the conversation.

"Mrs. Fitzwilliam had just returned from her morning ride. Expecting news of the Major General, your sister broke the seal and quickly began to read, but then she turned pale, and Weir, he steadied her. I thought Mrs. Fitzwilliam might collapse. But instead she ran. Ran from the room. From the house. From where the groom be returnin' her horse to the stable. She be taking Bracken's reins from the groom's hands. When I picks up the letter and sees its contents, I allowed her to leave. I thought it best, at the time, to permit yer sister to grieve in her own way. I wish now that I had had the sense to send Weir after her.

"When the lady didnae return, we mustered up several searches. We looked for eight and forty hours straight, Mr. Darcy. Day and night. Unfortunately, it be a wild land, and the moors keep their secrets. It be not unusual for a stranger to find himself lost in one of the bogs."

Elizabeth shuddered, but Darcy's resolve hardened. "Despite it being more than a sennight since, I plan to resume the search. I must assure myself that there is not some error, and that Georgiana has not found sanctuary elsewhere."

Mrs. Jacks looked hopeful. "Mr. Jacks has arranged for riders to come to Alpin Hall at dawn. Me husband anticipated Mr. Hurlbert needin' assistance with the MacBethans. They be an ornery bunch, at least, according to Weir, whose cousin married one of the clan."

"Mrs. Jacks, I am afraid I do not understand," Elizabeth said. "Who are the MacBethans, and what do they have to do with Mrs. Fitzwilliam's disappearance?"

"Oh, Mrs. Darcy, I apologize. Ye kin not know. We received word earlier today that Bracken be spotted in the MacBethans' stables. The horse never returned after yer sister went missing. Mr. Hurlbert thought it likely that he could find out if the MacBethans know anything of Mrs. Fitzwilliam's whereabouts."

"Who is Mr. Hurlbert?" Darcy demanded. "The estate's steward?"

"No, Sir. Mr. Hurlbert," she said the name slowly as if Darcy had gone daft. "The Matlock cousin sent by the Earl to coordinate the search. He be here for two days, Sir."

Darcy said incredulously, "I assure you, Mrs. Jacks, there are no Hurlberts listed upon the Matlock family tree."

Chapter 12

AULAY HAD RETURNED to her chamber, but she barely took notice. He played both sides of the chess board, totally engrossed in his strategy and ignoring her completely. She suspected it was a common occurrence with the man. She had no desire to speak to her supposed betrothed, but she made herself ask, "When we marry, must we remain at Normanna? I mean, should we not have a place of our own? Away from your mother and Lord Wotherspoon? Something not close to the manor house?"

Aulay frowned emphatically. "I kinnae imagine my mother wud be pleased. I've never lived any place without Mam."

"A house cannot have two mistresses," she said defiantly.

"If we stay on Normanna's land, Mam remains the mistress of the great house while we cud play games and do what we wish. I enjoy games."

She shook her head with regret. "Aulay, I am to have a child soon. Any games I play shall be with the baby I carry."

"Mam says I kin teach the child to play chess," he protested.

She touched his hand tenderly. It was not his fault that he did not understand. "Not right away," she cautioned. "It would be six or seven years, at least, before the child could grasp even the game's basics."

Aulay's mouth twisted in disgust. "That long? I thought..."

A knock at the door brought a close to what he would have said next. Without an invitation, the door opened to display Domhnall MacBethan. He filled the frame with his broad shoulders; and despite her best efforts to control her reaction, she felt her chest constrict.

"I beg your pardon, Aulay," the man directed his words to his brother. "If you have no objections, I would show Lady Esme the courtyard."

With his brother's entrance, Aulay had taken a step backward. "If'n...if'n Lady Esme wants...wishes to see...to see the gardens," he stammered.

"Aulay, neither Lady Esme nor I have time for you to construct an answer of which ye think our mother would approve. This be my estate. I know it better than you, and I will show the gardens to the lady." He extended his hand. "Will ye join me, m'lady?"

She glanced quickly to Aulay. He stood with his eyes averted. If the man could not even muster an objection against his own brother, how would he protect her from the world? And was that not a husband's duty? To protect his wife? She had a sudden feeling of loss. Of an emptiness that she could not explain. Lord Wotherspoon noted it immediately. "Are you unwell, m'lady?" he said softly. "We kin walk in the gardens at a later time if you feel poorly."

She needed to see more of this house than the passages the Mac-Bethans had shared. If she were to escape, she must possess intimate knowledge of what lay beyond the house's walls. She turned to Aulay. "I shall see you at dinner, Sir." With that, she placed her fingers in the elder MacBethan's hand. Surprisingly, when he folded his hand around hers, she felt safe.

As he closed the room door behind him, Wotherspoon said close to her ear. "I thought you would prefer my company to my younger brother's for dinner."

She slid her hand into the crook of his elbow. "Is that a command, my Lord?"

"It is a dream, m'Lady."

REGINA JEFFERS

"Your dreams are more pleasant than mine, Lord Wother-spoon. Mine are peppered with nightmares of my previous life. I am uncertain what is real and what is a dream."

He spoke without looking at her. "I would venture that my mother has offered to refresh your memory."

She glanced up in surprise. "She did."

A long silence followed as he directed her steps through a finely draped door to the outside. Stepping into the hazy summer sun, she closed her eyes and tilted her head back to accept its warmth. She inhaled deeply. "A bit of moisture on the air," she said automatically.

He chuckled lightly. "The English are known for their talk of the weather." An awkward pause followed before he said, "In Scotland, there always be moisture on the air. We are inland, but the coast be not so very far." He directed her to an arbor bench. "Oftentimes, I think of riding for the coast and taking the first ship I encounter to anywhere but here."

"Do you not love your home, Sir?"

Domhnall reached for a cultivated eyebright. With its yellow-petaled flower base opening to six rose-colored buds—flowers with a flower—it held renewal's promise. With a small knife, he cut the stem at an angle and handed it to her.

"It is lovely," she said as she inhaled the bloom's fragrance.

"You are lovely," he said softly and then looked off to the distance. "On the moors, the heather blossoms. Purple and pink. I love it, but I despise it. Does that make me a madman? It is the most beautiful land on earth, but this land is a dangerous mistress. Hard and unforgiving. A man must fight to survive."

She followed his gaze, and although the fields were not visible, she saw what he did. "Your responsibilities must be enormous."

He turned slowly to her. "A man makes decisions for the good of his people, but those choices can eat away at his conscience—his soul—until nothing remains. Excrement." Domhnall caressed her cheek. "Then a brief flash of sunshine flickers, and his foolish heart takes flight."

Esme sucked in a quick breath. What would she do if she were placed between Wotherspoon and his mother? Could she survive such a struggle of wills? And did this man speak the truth of his heart or was she a game piece in some bizarre chess match, one to be claimed by the most ruthless player? "I do not know how to proceed, m'Lord. Your mother has saved me for your younger brother."

"My brother, Lady Esme, cannot be taught to appreciate a woman. To Aulay, you are a diversion from his games of strategy, a respite that my mother has convinced him that he would enjoy. Yet, Aulay tires of everything but his chessboard. You deserve a man who would see you as someone he could worship." He brought her hand to his lips. "Did your husband appreciate you, m'Lady?"

Although she could not understand why she spoke so openly to this man, she confessed, "I have no memories of my husband. How shall I tell this child of his father?" Her fingers traced a small circle upon her lap. "Any details I am provided shall be slanted to Aulay's benefit. Unless my memory returns, shall I ever know the absolute truth?"

Domhnall placed her on his arm again. They stood, and he led her toward the ungroomed area beyond the gardens. "The truth may be unpleasant. Are you strong enough, Lady Esme, to learn both your secrets and mine?"

* * *

"Lieutenant Wickham," Elizabeth whispered into the room's deadly silence. "Is it possible?"

"I will kill him," Darcy growled. "He has taken my sister's disappearance and made it into one of his schemes to thwart this family."

"Mrs. Jacks," Elizabeth said firmly. "How long was this 'Mr. Hurlbert' in residence at Alpin Hall?"

"Less than two days, Mistress." The woman's hands visibly shook. "The gentleman seemed so familiar with the family. Knew of Lord Lindale's happiness. Of how both you and the Major General were as boys." She swayed in place. "I be horrified, Mr. Darcy. How cud I've permitted a stranger to defile the Fitzwilliam family? I be turning in me resignation immediately, Ma'am." Tears streamed down the woman's face.

Elizabeth caught the housekeeper's hand and assisted Mrs. Jacks to a seat. "That shall not be necessary, Mrs. Jacks. But we do require your assistance." She shot a glance to her husband. Although she did not think herself in error, she said, "Fitzwilliam, we may be mistaken." She had never witnessed Darcy so angry. "Might you describe Mr. Hurlbert for us, Ma'am?"

Mrs. Jacks dabbed at her eyes. With a quivering lower lip, she said, "The man has a wonderful play of feature. He possessed a most gentlemanlike appearance. Mr. Hurlbert had a certain air. He wanted nothing to make him completely charming." The lady swallowed hard. "His appearance was greatly in his favor; he had all the best part of beauty—a fine countenance, a good figure, and very pleasing address." Elizabeth's heart stilled. She had described Mr. Wickham in similar words when he had first come to Hertfordshire.

Her eyes continued to meet her husband's steady gaze. "Lieutenant Wickham," he said the words with pure disgust.

Elizabeth nodded her agreement. "Mrs. Jacks, you will assemble the staff. Mr. Darcy shall need to speak with each individual who interacted with this fictitious Mr. Hurlbert."

"Yes, Ma'am."

"I shall examine Mr. Hurlbert's chambers, and I want you to inventory everything, especially the silver and other portable goods."

"Does ye think the gentleman stole from the estate?" The housekeeper appeared faint again.

Darcy grumbled impatiently. "I will warrant it. I doubt Mr. Hurlbert will make another appearance at Alpin Hall."

* * *

Wickham had ridden as far as Cumnock before he stopped for a bit of drink. On his first day in Kirkcudbrightshire, he had spent a diverting afternoon in the Cumnock inn's common room playing cards. On that particular day, he had won more hands than he had lost, and with a fresh stake, he could not quite pass the opportunity by. *Perhaps there is news of the lovely Mrs. Fitzwilliam*, he smirked to himself. *I still am uncertain whether it would be best to spend my time searching for the Major General's wife or making my way east to Edinburgh and then to ports in Northumberland.* He glanced up at the two-storey inn. "First things first," he said as he entered the darkened room.

* * *

"And what is this area?" Esme asked as they reached a barren strip of land between the manor and the open moors.

"A fire border," he said, while steadying her step on a low stone wall. "The heather is this area's life blood. The deer. The grouse. The cattle. Man. We all depend on it, but the heather extends no mercy. She has conquered the once-mighty forest. If a person looks closely, he might find patches of bluebells and wood anemones from when the trees outnumbered all the animals combined. But, now, only the heather remains."

Esme looked out over the open land. If they were on a proper English country estate, the land before her would be well-manicured lawn. She had no idea how she knew such a fact, but she knew it nonetheless. He remained by her side, but not as if he wanted to keep her in check. Instead, Lord Wotherspoon appeared to require her closeness. She said softly, "I ask again, do you despise it so?"

"I loathe how it holds me as its prisoner," he said grudgingly, and Esme wondered whether he meant man's constant battle with the land or whether his ties to the estate had made him a different sort of prisoner.

"We are all prisoners in some form," she observed. "I am a prisoner to my lack of memory." She would have liked to point out that he and his family had posted a guard outside her door, but she planned to remain silent until she had determined how best to proceed.

"What if I told you my mother has sent a man—our cousin—to learn more of your life prior to your coming to Normanna Hall?" He stared out over the land.

She fought for control. What would Lady Wotherspoon do with the information, and how would she know the truth when she heard it? "Is my name Lady Esme?" she asked tentatively. Her head began to pound, and a voice warned her to beware what this man offered.

Domhnall remained steadfastly silent for several minutes. "I doubt it. *Esme* is the name my mother had chosen for Aulay, if he had been a female child. It means 'esteemed' or 'loved.' I am certain it would have been easier on my mother if her last issue had been an *Esme* rather than an *Aulay*. As she ages, Lady Wotherspoon must see her beloved son into another woman's care."

"Would not Lady Wotherspoon experience the same regret for a female child with Aulay's particular eccentricities?" She walked a bold line with these questions, but she needed all the information she could muster.

"A female child could be placed in the care of the Sisters. Trained as a nun. Taught to care for her nieces and nephews. A dozen different scenarios. Aulay is a gentle soul. Too gentle for a man in this rough, hard country. He requires a wife of very superior character to any thing deserved by his own. An excellent woman. Sensible and amiable. One who would never require indulgence after the vows were spoken. A woman to humor and soften and conceal his failings. A woman who could promote his real respectability. It is my mother's wish," he said flatly.

She winced. Lady Wotherspoon had "chosen" her for such a life. "What is your wish, my Lord?"

"To find a woman who would share my desires and my adventures."

It was of what every woman dreamed. Wotherspoon looked upon her with a hopeful heart. Life with Normanna's lord would not be easy, but if she were truly alone in this world, it would be better than an alliance with his younger brother. Gingerly, she lifted her hand to his cheek. "Do you consider me such a woman, my Lord?"

With a devilish smile, he said, "So much so that I have instructed my cousin that he will know my wrath if he does not bring any news he may discover of your prior life to my attention first. I would give you your past in order to claim your future." A shiver of fear ran up her spine. What would the MacBethan cousin discover of her former life? And what of her past would have brought her to these lonely moors?

* * *

Wickham did not care for the man sitting across from him. Despite the fellow's congenial pose, he suspected the man lacked scruples. Likely lower than his own. Until this journey to Scotland, he had never done more than to cheat at cards, to walk out on a few debts, or to tell a pretty woman what she wanted to hear.

But the man with whom he shared a card table was of a different nature. The stranger turned a palm-sized glass disc in his free hand. Red-orange streaks of color met in a yellow cat's eye in the center.

The prop spoke of the hunter who had a desire for the unusual. The one known as *Munro* to the locales would be in the thick of whatever was thrown at him. In it for good or evil.

Wickham knew his own limits. His skills rested in the area of manipulation, but this stranger possessed untold skills. Like a chameleon, the man assumed the color of his surroundings. His black gaze fell on Wickham, and George shifted uncomfortably. "What be yer business in Cumnock?"

He tensed and waited for the group's attention to lessen before he forced himself to nonchalantly say, "I have been sent by my family to address an issue at Alpin Hall."

"There be truble?" Munro asked suspiciously.

"No trouble. Some concerns for my cousin." The fact that this man insisted on questioning him came as a warning. Men of Munro's disposition did not make simple conversation. In fact, his presence would normally be statement enough. Despite despising every moment of his service in the British army, Wickham was still a soldier, and he had developed specific skills to recognize an enemy. He had endured hours of training to fight a foe he had never met. His instincts now said that the man called "Munro" could be involved in Georgiana's disappearance. As he carefully observed the man through slitted eyes, he added, "My cousin has lost her way on the moor."

Munro rearranged his cards, but Wickham became aware of an unusual stillness about the man—a stillness that spoke of death. "What be the gel's looks? Mayhap we be seeing her." The other men at the table chimed in their agreements.

Wickham took no heed of the others. Only this dangerous stranger mattered. He thought to tell Munro a lie, but then he reconsidered. It would be best to observe carefully the man's reaction. "Mrs. Fitzwilliam is of a little less than twenty years of age. In truth, it has been several years since I last beheld her, but I suspect my cousin has altered little. She should be to my shoulder in height, very lithe, with golden blonde hair, and eyes of blue."

One of the other men asked, "Ye say the lady be a missus. Where be her husband?"

Wickham constructed his tale as he shuffled the cards. "In all reality, the Major General likely lies on a bloody battlefield in Belgium."

"So no one searches for the lady?" Munro rearranged his hand.

"Only me and a few the Earl's staff."

The men nodded their understanding. "Too busy to search for their own," the man on his right grumbled.

Realizing he needed a bit more legitimacy, Wickham added a significant fact he had discovered over a similar game in Pemberley's stables. "With the Major General's long-overdue arrival, I imagine the Earl is seeing to his heirs. If the spare is gone, the eldest son's newborn has taken on more significance than usual. The family's bloodline is reduced to the Viscount and his son."

"Ye be not part of the inheritance?" Munro asked.

Wickham's frown crumbled, and he laughed robustly. "Not unless I could arrange to kill off the four poppycocks ahead of me in succession."

"Fer the right price," Munro said menacingly.

Wickham said haughtily. "If I had the right price, I would not be in a public inn in Ayrshire."

"No, I donnae suppose ye wud."

* * *

With a few discreetly placed inquiries, Wickham determined that the menacing Munro was part of the MacBethan family, which oversaw Normanna Hall. *The same estate at which the trader reported seeing Mrs. Fitzwilliam's horse*, Wickham said to himself as he enjoyed a brief respite from the card game with an evening meal. He watched as Munro MacBethan claimed another pot. *I imagine the gentleman is a poor loser, as well.*

Wickham scowled as he considered his options. If he were to tarry in Ayr, he must first determine if Georgiana Fitzwilliam had taken refuge at Normanna Hall, and if she had, had the lady done so of her own free will? He continued to wonder about the sensibility of pursuing his former friend's sister. *But it could shift the power to my grasp,* he observed silently. *Honor would require Darcy to act against his natural arrogance. At a minimum, Darcy would have to permit me my freedom. There is also the possibility of a reward. Darcy's pride would require it.*

* * *

They had circled the manor house and crossed the lower gardens and the pastureland. "We should return to the house." Domhnall noted the increasing shadows.

The girl sighed deeply. "Thank you, my Lord. The exercise and the fresh air have bolstered my spirits."

"As they have mine," he said intimately.

She had fidgeted when he leveled his gaze upon her, but his tone created a calm. "You might think me brazen, but I must know: why have you spoken to me so personally? What do you expect of me?"

Domhnall curled his fingers hard around her wrist. "I have no way of explaining it. I cannot allow my mother to manipulate another to her own ends." Realizing his grasp bruised her pale skin, he released his hold and then gently kissed the inside of her wrists.

Her breath caught. "What would you do with me?"

"I would bind you, m'Lady, to me forever."

She gave herself a small shake to clear her thinking. This situation had become more bizarre than ever. She had no clear memory of her family or her former life. She was relatively certain that Lady

Wotherspoon had taken her as a captive with the purpose of placing her in Aulay's way. She knew absolutely that the MacBethans currently held her prisoner. Now, the eldest, Lord Wotherspoon, offered her a position as his wife. At least, she thought he meant to marry her. Perhaps Domhnall MacBethan meant to make her his mistress. "Without the truth of my past, I have no future."

* * *

After questioning each of the Alpin staff who had come in contact with their recent guest, Darcy held no doubt that their intruder was none other than George Wickham. "How much did the man pilfer?" Darcy asked flatly.

Elizabeth watched him with those sometimes hazel, sometimes forest green eyes that seemed always to speak to his soul. "Mrs. Jacks has not completed her accounting, but she reports several pieces of silver and two sets of candlesticks of note."

"Likely very much more," Darcy grumbled as he strode to the window. "I have considered how we must proceed."

"It is late in the day," Elizabeth noted.

Darcy's anger rose to a red haze, and he struggled not to alarm her. "I have sent the head groomsman to the village. I want additional men scouring every inch of the estate and the surrounding area with the first streaks of light. Until I find my sister, no rock is to remain unturned."

Elizabeth observed cautiously, "There is an abundance of rocks to search."

Darcy wished to rail at her about the injustice of it all. How could a benevolent God have permitted anything foul to happen to Georgiana? "What if my sister suffered alone?" he asked in pure frustration. "What if Georgiana died on the moor and her remains are even now being abused by some wild animal?"

Elizabeth rushed to his side. "Fitzwilliam, you must stop this madness. Georgiana is not dead. I refuse to accept our sister's passing. She may not be well, but Georgiana has not left us. Your sister is a part of you. Do you truly feel her loss?"

Darcy reached for her hand. "I feel the white, serious heat of my anger. The severe ache chipping away at my heart. I try to fight the images conjured up by my own ineffectiveness. Yet, I cannot permit my mind to consider Georgiana's absence from my life." He sank heavily onto the window seat.

Elizabeth knelt before him and caressed his chin. "Oh, my love. Do not despair so. We are in Scotland, and we shall not rest until we find our sister. Georgiana is much stronger than you give her credit for being. She is likely injured, but we can rectify that quickly enough. She may even be in a place where she cannot send us word of her survival, but my heart tells me that Georgiana has not met our Maker."

Darcy turned his cheek into her palm and accepted her tenderness. He said valiantly, "I will place my hopes in your most capable hands, Mrs. Darcy." He kissed her inner wrist.

Elizabeth pulled over a footstool upon which to sit. "Then let us plan the search. Besides sending the groomsman to recruit others, what should we do?"

"I plan to call at the MacBethan estate tomorrow. It is the only clue we possess. Did Georgiana's horse wander in? Is she recovering at this family's expense? If my sister is not at the MacBethan estate, and the family has no knowledge of her existence, then I want to ascertain where the horse was found."

Keeping her voice even, Elizabeth asked, "And what of Lieutenant Wickham? Do you think him likely to use what he knows of Georgiana's disappearance to feather his bed?"

Darcy's jaw tightened as if a sharp pain frayed his nerves. "Absolutely. If he can benefit from the effort, Lieutenant Wickham would

defy the Prince Regent. Lieutenant Wickham has no way of knowing whether I have brought the law after him after his attack and
Mr. Joseph's injury. The man is many things, but unintelligent is
not among them. He must realize that I will not rest until justice
is served. That I will not turn my head and offer the other cheek.
The man has repeatedly slapped away my proffered hand. Lieutenant Wickham's continued perfidy has tarnished my revered father's
memory. My promise to my father no longer holds my allegiance."
He sighed deeply. "You must realize, Elizabeth, that I can no longer
protect your sister. The man set out to kill me."

"Of course not," she said automatically. Darcy knew her loyalty
had deep roots, but he gratefully accepted her decision to choose
her life with him over her need to protect her sister. "You have been
most generous to the Wickhams. No one may say otherwise."

* * *

When Munro MacBethan called it an early night, Wickham waited
long enough for the man to resaddle his mount before making his
own excuses. He had ordered his horse held in readiness. Watching
Munro ride away into the darkening shadows, Wickham mounted
and turned his horse in a tight circle before giving pursuit. "Let us
see which way our pigeon flies," he said to the stallion as he allowed
it to break into a canter.

* * *

The girl sat to Domhnall MacBethan's right. The man's mother had
excused herself from the table when she realized what her eldest
son had planned. Lady Wotherspoon had taken Aulay with her, leaving her alone with Domhnall on the raised dais in the Grand Hall.
Nearly two dozen family members and respected individuals on the
Normanna staff sat at the tables below them. It was a scene from the
fourteenth century, with the laird of the manor setting to his meal

with his men. "This is very reminiscent of an early Scottish keep," she said softly to the man who bent his head to hear her over the boisterous voices.

Domhnall laughed easily. "It be appropriate, my Lady. Normanna is built over the ruins of a medieval monastery and my family's ancestral home." He leaned closer to speak more intimately. "Of course, if this were a traditional lowland keep, my men would cheer if I chose to kiss you before them."

She blushed thoroughly. "Please, my Lord. Our friendship is too new for such intimacy."

"A man knows his heart," he declared.

She counted to ten before responding. Part of her enjoyed this man's company and attentions. He had refined manners, but with a touch of wildness. Caution warned that this man was as danger-ous as his mother, and that she was the piece of meat over which two wildcats fought. "We shall continue our acquaintance after your cousin returns to report his findings."

"As you wish, m'Lady."

She turned to the meal. It featured several courses. As she picked at the fish, she wondered if the household ate thus every evening. For the past few days, she had eaten hard bread and cheese and had been thankful for the offering. Now, she dined on fish and beef and fine sauces. If she were truly a guest, would she not have been afforded such food previously? Ignoring her urge to break into a run to escape the panic building in her chest, she made herself ask, "How extensive are the ruins?"

"Many of the monastery's silent passages remain," he said as he motioned a server to remove their plates. "Quite dank and dark. The narrow passages lead to an escape into an underground karst. There are not many such structures in this part of Scotland—too far inland. There be a cave and several streams that vanish into the rock face. I would offer to show it to you, but it is dangerous and very narrow in places."

Wotherspoon had not noticed the perturbation spreading through her body. As soon as her host mentioned the hidden passages, she remembered her horror at being dragged into a small cell. At having fought her jailer's attempts to touch her. At begging the man not to leave her fastened to the wall. At praying for the darkness to go away.

She saw it all. As plainly as if she still remained within those walls. The heavily grated doors. No windows. A pair of long corridors. Black shadows draping every corner. And the screams! Men pleaded for their lives. "Prisoners," Ronald had said. She had been among them, but she had been spared. *Why?* she wondered. Then the worst of the memories intruded. Blood drained under the doors of the other cells. Doors behind which no one cried for mercy. The acrid smell. Blood had stained her boots. Unconsciously, she glanced at her dress slippers. *These are not my shoes*, she recalled belatedly.

"Lady Esme?" Wotherspoon whispered in concern. "You be very pale."

She swallowed hard, forcing air into her lungs. "I…I am well, my Lord," she stammered. Trying to conjure up a legitimate excuse for her sudden anxiety, she glanced around quickly. Her eyes fell on the approaching servant. "I…I have eaten so little of late that the food is almost too rich."

Lord Wotherspoon caught her hand and gave it a squeeze. "Although your figure is quite pleasing, m'Lady, I would not have you too thin. You must consider the bairn. Please say that you will permit me to see to your care."

She made herself maintain his gaze. "Your tender concern is most appreciated, my Lord. You are felicitous in your attentions."

Chapter 13

HE HAD FOLLOWED THE MACBETHAN cousin long enough to be certain that the man planned to investigate Georgiana's disappearance. "Probably wants to warrant what I shared," Wickham told the horse as he watched Munro cross the open area leading to the undeveloped parts of the Matlock estate. "While MacBethan verifies my honesty, I will verify his." Wickham turned his horse away from Alpin's lands. "Let us determine if the lovely Georgiana is a 'guest' at Normanna Hall." As he rode away, Wickham calculated what he might earn as a reward for recovering Darcy's missing sister.

* * *

She dreamed of her favorite foods and of dining at a fine table set with polished silver and sparkling crystal. The man beside her spoke in intimate tones, and Georgiana anticipated the pleasure of knowing him better. Yet, part of her feared his regard.

"I would bind you to me forever," he whispered in her ear, and Georgiana felt herself blush thoroughly. It was Edward's familiar accent—a mix of aristocratic exactness and merchant-class authority, but something was amiss. A Scottish brogue caressed many of his words, and her mind revolted against the incongruity. "I would wish you beside me. My future intertwined with yours."

"Without the truth of my past, I have no future," she said softly.

His breath caressed her cheek. "I am part of your past. The truth will never hurt us. A man knows his heart."

* * *

"What is it?" Darcy had staggered through the unlit room to answer the persistent tapping at the exterior door. Although the Alpin staff had prepared adjoining rooms, he had been sore to leave Elizabeth's side, especially after all that had transpired. Watching her breathe the breath of a restless sleep, he had lain beside his wife for hours, but even as she thrashed and murmured through her fretful dreams, he had taken comfort from her closeness. What turn would this journey have taken had she not trailed after him? How his heart had lurched with joy at the sight of Elizabeth at the Dumfries inn! How Fate had delivered her to the safety of his arms just when he had needed her the most! Had placed Elizabeth in his path just as the Fickle Lady had done in Hertfordshire. He was nothing without Elizabeth.

Irritated, he yanked the door open to see a disheveled Mr. Jacks on the other side. "What is it?" he repeated harshly.

"A rider, Mr. Darcy," the man said through a sleepy drawl. "Be here in a moment."

"Maybe our Mr. Hurlbert returns," Darcy observed cautiously. "Go admit the rider. I will be down immediately."

Jacks bowed. "Yes, Sir."

As he turned into the room, Elizabeth appeared beside him. "Lieutenant Wickham?" she asked hesitantly.

"Very likely." He caressed her arm before moving to relight the candle he had blown out not thirty minutes prior. "I want to confront him if it is he."

Fully awake, Elizabeth followed in his footsteps. "That makes little sense. Why would Lieutenant Wickham return? Surely, he realizes it is only a matter of time before someone becomes aware of his thievery."

"How am I to understand the man? Lieutenant Wickham lacks a sense of proper decorum. He will likely try to convince me that

I owe him my continued allegiance." Darcy pulled a shirt over his head. "You are to remain here," he said as he slid his breeches over his hips. "One can never predict Lieutenant Wickham's behavior. Especially in desperate circumstances."

"You shall not fight with him?" Elizabeth pleaded. "Lieutenant Wickham's volatility has led him to make poor choices. He has attacked you once, Fitzwilliam," she warned.

Darcy looked up suddenly. "More than once," he confessed.

"Lieutenant Wickham's actions are insuperable," Elizabeth declared. "But please be careful. Neither Bennet nor I can survive without you."

"Nor I you." He kissed her forehead and left the room. He had hoped that he had hidden from her view the small pistol he normally carried in his inside jacket pocket when he traveled.

* * *

He was so exhausted, Edward nearly fell from the saddle, but he managed to hand off the reins to an equally sleepy-eyed groom. "Give him some feed and wipe him down. You can brush him in the morning. He needs some rest." Edward patted the animal's neck. "Thank you, old friend. You have served me well."

Edward watched the groom lead Porteus away before resignedly accepting his next task: explaining to his wife that the army had erred in reporting his death. He had considered spending the night at an inn and riding in fresh tomorrow morning, but the thought of spending another night without Georgiana in his arms had driven him to reach the estate this night. "Oh, my sweet Georgie," he murmured as he mounted the steps.

He released the knocker and waited impatiently for someone to answer. Surprisingly, the door opened almost immediately, and a familiar face stared back into his.

225

* * *

Elizabeth had noted how Darcy had palmed the small pistol he had fished from his jacket pocket when he thought her mind more fretfully engaged. "Well, Mr. Darcy, I am not so easily fooled." She reached for her most practical day dress—one she could lace herself.

Pulling the last of the laces together, she draped a shawl over her shoulders to cover any sagging of the material. Stepping into her dress slippers, she followed her husband to the main stairs. Creeping slowly down the steps to where she could spy on the encounter between Darcy and Mr. Wickham, Elizabeth's eyes fell on a most welcome face.

* * *

Remaining in the shadows, Darcy had paused at the bottom of the steps. He did not want Lieutenant Wickham to bolt before the Alpin staff could corner the man in the open foyer. When the knocker sounded, he nodded solemnly for Mr. Jacks to respond, and then he aimed the gun in the door's direction. From the semi-darkness, an eyebrow rose in surprise as he looked upon a familiar face.

* * *

The door had swung wide, and Edward had breathed relief's sigh. He was home. Not his actual home. Not Matley Manor. Not Yadkin Hall. Yet, home, nevertheless. Wherever Georgiana resided was his home. The girl whose skinned knees he had once bandaged now held his heart in her delicate hand. He had returned to England from the American war to find a woman where a child had once stood. He still could not understand how it had happened.

He had stepped into Pemberley's foyer that December evening, very much as he had done a hundred times prior where he had expected to find his cousin and Mrs. Darcy and his ward. Instead, a blizzard, which had blanketed the northern shires, had waylaid Darcy and Elizabeth at an out-of-the-way inn, and the young girl he had expected to find had transformed into the most beautiful woman he had ever seen. And from the moment that Georgiana had propelled herself into his welcoming arms, everything had changed. He could not resist Georgiana's allure. One look. One soft pout of her lips, and Edward had lost the battle.

They had married in March before he had shipped out to join Wellington's forces. In fact, out of the seven months since that eventful night in December when he had discovered the love of his life, they had spent less than four days together as man and wife. Edward was looking forward to making up for lost time.

"Mr. Jacks," he said as he stepped into the dimly lit hallway. "Do you remember me, Sir?" Then Edward's eyes fell on the gun pointed at his chest. An eyebrow rose in surprise. "I know you never totally accepted my marrying your sister, Darcy, but your objections are a bit late." He casually handed his hat, gloves, and crop to Jacks. Then he looked over the caretaker's shoulder at Georgiana's inscrutable brother. "Well, Darcy?"

Before his cousin could respond, someone shoved Darcy out of the way and launched herself into Edward's waiting embrace. "Thank God, you have returned to us!"

* * *

Elizabeth had silently crept closer so she would be able to hear everything her husband said to Lieutenant Wickham, but the voice she heard did not belong to her sister's husband, at least, not the husband of her natural sister, but her sister in marriage would know happiness again.

"I know you never totally accepted my marrying your sister, Darcy, but your objections are a bit late," the voice said. And then Elizabeth was on the move. In a panic, she realized Darcy pointed a gun at his cousin and best friend, and something bad could happen. Therefore, Elizabeth put herself between the two men. She rushed past her husband, shoving Darcy to the side and springing into the Major General's open arms. "Thank God, you have returned to us!"

"Now, that is more in the nature of the welcome I had expected." Edward lifted Elizabeth from the floor and swung her joyously about in a circle. "Embracing a lovely woman." The Major General laughed aloud and placed a wet kiss on Elizabeth's equally happy mouth.

Darcy cleared his throat with intent. "That lovely woman belongs to me, Cousin." He had not lowered the pistol.

Elizabeth laughed breathlessly as Edward settled her to the ground. She slid her arms around Edward's waist, but she spoke over her shoulder to her husband. "Mr. Darcy speaks in the Parliamentary sense of possession rather than of my willingly giving the man my heart."

Edward smiled down at her. "Absolutely, Mrs. Darcy. Even a relic such as my cousin knows better than to exercise his territorial rights with a man who has just returned from history's worst battle."

Darcy slid the gun into his waistband. "I assure you, Cousin, that I would not hesitate to confront any man who dares to place an inappropriate hold on Mrs. Darcy."

Elizabeth gave Edward's cheek a gentle pat. "I adore it when men posture like lions in the wild. It makes a woman feel very desirable. Much more flattering than words of poetry or jewelry."

The Major General winked at Darcy. "You have a most insensible mate. Yet, I would imagine you the most fortunate of men."

Darcy reached for her and brought Elizabeth into his own loose embrace. "'Fortunate' does not come close to describing my marital bliss."

Elizabeth maintained a hold on Edward's hand. "Come," she said. "You must be exhausted. Mr. Jacks, might you secure refreshments for the Major General?"

"Yes, Ma'am." The servant disappeared into a side hallway.

Edward's gaze slid to the staircase. "Is my wife such a sound sleeper?" Elizabeth felt him tug on her hand to free his, but she tightened her hold.

"Come," she said again. "We will explain all. You should know that Georgiana is not at Alpin. My sister needs your expertise to bring her home."

* * *

Edward's heart clinched in protest. Surely Mrs. Darcy made a poor jest. Georgiana was to wait for him. Her last letter had told him such. It was the reason he had raced to Kirkconnel from Kent. The reason he had slept but a few hours each night. So he might reach her more quickly. "Georgiana," he groaned. "It cannot be."

Darcy had reached for Edward's arm in a sign of support. "Mrs. Darcy is correct. This will take some time to explain. Come along. As we have always done, we will solve this together. I am heartened by your presence, Edward."

He allowed Elizabeth to lead him to a room of which he was completely unaware, but he did not resist. His mind remained on the truth of what Elizabeth had said: Georgiana was not at Alpin Hall.

When he had first experienced Elizabeth's happiness at his return, Edward had rejoiced in her very feminine response. He had survived an extraordinary battle—a battle where thousands had fallen—a battle of blood and rain and mud and the screams of the dying. He had survived Waterloo because his demise would have killed his mother and father. Because he wanted to see his nephew grow into a man. Because he needed to be available for his godson Bennet. Because without him, Roman Southland would have lain on a rain-soaked battlefield and bled to death. Because Anne's hopes and dreams deserved fruition; and mostly, he had survived for her— for Georgiana. Because only in her arms had he found peace, and a balm for the loneliness that had plagued him through more than a decade of war.

If exhaustion had not rattled his thinking, he would have known that Darcy had no reason to be at Alpin Hall, and his cousin's presence should have set Edward on alert. But it had seemed so natural to find Darcy wherever Georgiana was that Edward had not considered how the "welcome home" portrait in his mind hung askew. Edward shook his head to clear his thinking: Darcy had held a gun on him. Edward stopped suddenly. "Why did you greet me with a loaded gun, Darcy?" He spoke in hushed tones although it was not necessary. "Surely, you did not expect trouble. Did you expect an intruder to knock on the front door?"

Darcy's lips set in a grim line. "Actually, Cousin, I had thought the sound of the door signaled Lieutenant Wickham's return."

* * *

"Are you certain the girl is not free to come and go as she pleases?" At a secondary inn close to Normanna Hall, Wickham had stumbled across a man related to several of the MacBethan servants. In finding the man, his luck had held. Of late, the cards had treated him well, and he had a few extra coins to buy this Scotsman's allegiance.

"Like I says before, me cousin told me so himself. Blane carried the gel from the cells and puts her in one of the smaller rooms. He say the laird's mother had saved the gel for the yanger boy, but

Aulay, he not be ret in the head. Now, the laird has set his eye on the gel. Domhnall's wife, she died deliverin' his bairn. The babe didnae survive either. The new gel be with child or so the missus tells Blane. Lady Wotherspoon be thinkin' to wed the gel to Aulay and then collect the dowry. Domhnall has different plans, tho. At least, that be what Blane be sayin'."

"Did your cousin describe this woman?" Wickham asked cautiously.

"Dinnae say much exceptin' that she be very fair. Light hair and very small in frame. He dinnae say more of her looks, but she must be pretty because Blane be tongue-tied around pretty gels."

* * *

Feeling dreadful presentiments, Edward demanded, "What the hell would Wickham be doing at Alpin Hall?"

Darcy nodded toward the drawing room. "What else? Pretending to be something he is not."

Elizabeth softly added, "And, of course, pilfering the silver."

Edward shot a knowing glance at Darcy. The glance said that he understood how much Darcy must truly love Elizabeth to have aligned himself with a scoundrel such as George Wickham. Indirectly, he, too, was part of Wickham's extended family. However, ice would blanket Hell's fires before he would allow the man anywhere near Georgiana.

He had counseled Georgiana to face the worst of her fears after Darcy had aborted his sister's attempt to elope with Wickham. Edward had hated what a person's sudden demise did to the man's family, and even though he had spent what felt like a lifetime as a warrior, he had never killed a man in cold blood. Yet, he had considered killing George Wickham because the man had preyed on Georgiana's naïveté. Had disregarded it as if Georgie's girlhood innocence was not the most precious gift a man could ever receive from a woman. Had robbed Georgiana of her schoolgirl dreams of romance. To satisfy his need to revenge himself on Darcy, Wickham had manipulated, undoubtedly by design, Georgiana's first experience with love—souring her relationships until she had committed herself to their marriage.

"I would hear it all," he grumbled. Edward's heart experienced the creeping doom that the shadows held. Georgiana had disappeared, and the loneliness loomed like an apparition.

They quickly settled in the chairs, and Elizabeth lit several braces of candles while Darcy explained Georgiana's departure from Pemberley, their denying the Wickhams a presence at Kitty's party, Darcy's journey with Matthew Joseph, Mr. Wickham's attack along the road, Darcy's frantic ride to Dumfries to save the man's life, Elizabeth's meeting with Edward's brother Rowland, the news of the Countess's letter to Georgiana and of Mrs. Jacks' note chronicling Georgiana's disappearance, and of Elizabeth trailing Darcy to Scotland. During this time, Elizabeth had handed Edward a hastily prepared plate, which he had devoured without thinking.

"How long has Georgiana been missing?" Edward asked as he returned the plate to Elizabeth's waiting hands.

"A sennight." Darcy swallowed hard, and Edward noticed his cousin struggling for composure. "We have a lead. It is believed that Georgiana's horse has been located at an estate in the next shire. On the moors."

Edward understood his cousin's unspoken warning. When they had spent youthful summers at Alpin, their chaperones had warned them repeatedly to exercise caution around the moors, with their bogs and juniper scrubs and fields of heather. The moors were beautiful, but dangerous. "Then you and I will call at this estate tomorrow morning."

"Mr. Jacks and I have recruited extra staff. I want a more thorough search of the area. Georgiana cannot be very far away. She could be injured, or my sister may not recall from whence she came. Possibly, the horse threw her." Darcy refilled Edward's glass of brandy.

Edward thought of how expertly Georgiana sat a horse. The likelihood of her being thrown was slim, but it was possible in such rough terrain. "We will find her, Darcy. My wife is lithe and elegant, but she is also tenacious and intelligent. If anyone can survive for such a period, it is Georgiana."

"I have assured my husband," Elizabeth said softly into the silence between the men, "that Fate would not be so cruel as to bring you and Georgiana together and then separate you forever."

Edward's gaze fell on the woman. "I do not feel Georgiana's loss," he murmured. "That is why I was so certain she would be at Alpin when I reached it."

"Neither do I," she confirmed. Silence rose again. Finally, Elizabeth stood and picked up a brace of candles. "I shall confirm your room's readiness. You and Mr. Darcy finish your plans, and then I expect both of you to seek your beds. I realize it will be difficult to sleep, but you must make the effort. Georgiana requires a brother and a husband who are fully rested to save her."

Edward caressed her hand. "My wife is blessed to have you as her sister."

Elizabeth bent to kiss his forehead. "And I was blessed the day Mr. Darcy brought you into my life."

* * *

She waited until all in the household had taken to their chambers before she eased her weight from the small simple bed she had occupied for the past few nights. Death's images, those which had emerged during her earlier conversation with Lord Wotherspoon, had lingered, and now she felt compelled to know the truth. Her palpable fear held her in suspension. Her foot halfway to the floor. *Could she do this? Could she find her way to the cells? Could she learn the truth?*

Swallowing her incapacitating fear, she slid her feet into the half boots before making her way to the door. When Normanna's lord had escorted her to her room, he had lingered long enough for her to ease the room key from the peg beside the door. She had hidden it under a book he had brought her from the estate's library.

Now, she retrieved it and silently slid the key into its hole and turned it to the right…slowly…waiting for the soft click…breathing at last. Her damp palms reached for the knob. Her heart seemed to cease beating as she drew the door inward—just a crack. A wall sconce offered a flicker of light along the passageway, and in the weak shadows she could observe Rankin, the ever-present guard, sleeping on a pallet along the wall. The urge to quickly reclose the door and return to the relative safety of her bed nearly stayed her movement, but she forced herself to open the door wider. She kept her eyes focused on the sleeping figure. A slight gurgle deep in his throat indicated the man slept soundly. With a deep breath to steady her nerves, she slid through the narrow opening and set the door ajar. She sidestepped her way along the wall, keeping her gaze locked on her jailer until she could see him no longer, and then she raised her skirt and raced in the direction she had seen Lord Wotherspoon go when summoned by the servant Ronald only yesterday.

Not a sound came from inside the great hall as she slid into its emptiness. For a brief moment, she wondered what it would be to act as the mistress of this estate. If she pursued what Lord Wotherspoon offered, would he place his mother elsewhere? A household could not divide its allegiance between two mistresses. As dark and mysterious as Domhnall MacBethan appeared, she much preferred him to his younger brother. At least, the estate's master had a future and had had instruction as a gentleman. With Aulay, she would be a mother twice over.

Bracing her courage by forcibly relaxing her hunched shoulders, she crossed the open area to the stairs leading to the lower levels. She would have liked to take a candle, but she would not risk anyone's notice. Her normally soft tread echoed loudly in her ears, but no one else stirred. She had waited for the clock to chime one before executing her escape.

Following the narrow spiraling stairway, she held tightly to the wall's stones to steady her step. At the northwest corner, the stairs took a deeper slant into what most likely was the cellar. Again, she spent a moment to bolster her composure before plunging further into the darkness. The air had cooled dramatically. Lord Wotherspoon's description of the monastery's ruins had reminded her that she descended into the earth, as if she stepped into a grave.

A shiver ran down her spine as the stairs opened to a narrow, uneven passage. She wished once again for a candle, but she could not chance it. Allowing her fingertips to slide along the damp walls, she edged forward. Praying not to encounter a rat or other creature of the night, she stepped carefully into the darkened passageway. *Slowly,* she silently cautioned herself. The space opened further with a cross passage, and for the span of several heartbeats, she panicked. The wall she had been following suddenly disappeared, and she fought the feeling that she was falling into a pit. Into the nether regions. Into the ash-filled memories. Panic ricocheted through her like a bolt of lighting. Stifling her own scream, she reached for the wall and was thankful to find the bricked corner. Clawing at it for safety, she embraced it with both arms. "Thank God," she murmured.

Righting her position, she fought to discern anything in the complete blackness. She could not tell whether to continue straight ahead or whether she should follow one of the cross halls. Would she walk into another wall if she continued along this route? Concentrating on the openness, a pinpoint of light gave her hope. She turned to the right and walked toward the flicker of truth awaiting her. With each of her tentative steps the light grew more pronounced, and her heart pounded harder.

For a brief second, she wondered whether she truly wanted to know what the light held, but she continued her slow progress toward the unknown. Finally, she reached a locked door. With her fingers, she traced the hinges, the handle, the door's width. Nothing moved as she went on tiptoes to peer through the grated opening. The light remained far removed, and the shadows held their secrets in a tight grasp. She had failed to discover the truth. She would have liked to see what the door held behind it, but she felt the pressing need to return to her room. She had tarried long enough.

Reluctantly, she turned toward the blackness behind her. Lifting her hand to trail along the wall again, she had taken no more than a half dozen steps before a blood-draining scream filled the depths of the ruins. Frozen in place, she debated whether to run or to return to the door. Finally, her curiosity won out: she had to plumb the door's mystery.

Moving quickly, she stumbled toward the grated closure. She leaned once more against the wooden door and stared through the small opening. At first, she knew disappointment, but then two figures stepped into the circle of light.

"That be a difficult one," the first figure said.

"I expect no more trouble." The voice was one she knew well: that of the house's mistress. "I want him prepared by mornin'."

She heard the finality in Dolina MacBethan's tone. She needed to escape before someone found her. Turning to the wall again, she traced the bricks. Lifting her skirt, she moved quickly away from the opening until she reached the corner. Her hand grasped the wall's edge and she stumbled, but she had no time to worry about the sudden pain in her weak ankle. A scraping sound announced the door's opening. In a panic, she raced to the stairs and climbed to the main level. She fought to keep her balance on the narrow, damp stairway.

The footsteps quickened behind her as she reached the grand hall. She glanced about to assess the open area before breaking into a run. Like many of the traditional Scottish keeps, Normanna Hall required anyone wishing to reach the private quarters and the battlements to cross the hall to the second staircase. Previous lairds had designed their houses with security in mind, but at the moment, all she wanted was the secrecy of the upper passage.

"Lady Esme!" Dolina's voice rang out in the empty hall.

Caught, she skidded to a stop, but she did not turn to face the woman. Fear crept up her spine. They would return her to the cells below ground, and she would meet the same fate as the person she had heard screaming only moments earlier. Lady Wotherspoon's purposeful approach held her in its grip.

"What be ye doin' here?" Dolina hissed close to her ear.

Terror ran rampant through her chest. Her throat would not permit a response. She simply shook her head in denial. Of what? She could not think: denying her presence seemed paramount. Yet, she could not.

"I ast ye a question, gel," Dolina said threateningly.

A familiarly calm voice took both women's breaths. "I asked Lady Esme to meet me here." Domhnall MacBethan stepped from the shadows and placed his arms about her. Instinctively, she slumped against him. "I would show the lady the battlements. The stars are brilliant when the world is silenced by sleep." His hand brought her head to rest against his chest.

Dolina protested, "Lady Esme's room..."

"Will remained unlocked," Domhnall announced. "Lady Esme has earned my trust. Is that understood, Mother?" The girl felt him stiffen with the recognition of his mother's presence. His tone spoke of disappointment, of hatred, and of revulsion, but the girl had never felt safer in her life. Tentatively, her arms encircled Domhnall's waist. Evidently, she had made her choice in the Mac-Bethans' battle of wills.

Chapter 14

HE SAID NOT ONE WORD as they climbed the steep stairs leading to the battlements. Domhnall had rarely felt such strong feelings: such anger that she had placed herself in danger and such thankfulness that he had reached her in time. Unable to sleep, he had wandered through the deserted passageways of his ancestral home. He had done so on a regular basis ever since he had returned to Normanna and had discovered the evil his mother had welcomed to the manor's every corner. Of late, he had spent his time grieving for Maighread and their son. His grief was too much to bear in the daylight. He had failed Maighread. He had failed his ancestors. He had failed his descendants, because he had not acted quickly enough to put an end to this madness.

Tonight he had spent several hours divining ways to extricate the family name from his mother's immorality. He had allowed the woman free rein, and she had betrayed him and all the MacBethans. Had not his father warned Domhnall on more than one occasion of Lady Wotherspoon's deviousness? His mother had never been the type to coddle her children—except for Aulay. He and his other brother and sister had raised themselves and each other. It was the reason he had tarried in England after his years of schooling. He had never wanted to return to the coldness that permeated Normanna's walls. Even when he had returned to visit his family—and those incidents had grown further and further apart over the years—everything had appeared normal. Little had he known of the struggle between his parents—how much his father had despised the woman he had married, how Coll MacBethan had turned to others with ulterior motives rather than true benevolence, and how his mother's despair had taken a twisted slant. At first, he had been grateful for the unexpected income. It had settled many of the debts from Normanna's former lords. Now, only abhorrence remained; yet, even his father could not have imagined how his mother had set the family roots on a rocky base before grinding them into the dirt with the heel of her boot.

The woman beside him stumbled, and he automatically caught her to him. "Thank you, my Lord," she whispered hoarsely.

He realized belatedly that he had been walking too quickly for her. Startled by the loss of his flawlessly varnished control, Domhnall glanced down at her flushed face. He studied her shad- owed profile. "I apologize," he said contritely. "I allowed my anger to set a punishing pace. I have neglected the fact that for a woman the steps are difficult to negotiate. They are steep and uneven in spots." Her liquid blue eyes held him.

"The steps were steep, but I did not object to the ascent," she said with a frown.

She was like no woman of his acquaintance, and Domhnall was sore to explain his attraction to her. To touch her would be over- whelming pleasure. Every time he looked at her, he approached a fever point. He tightened his grip on her hand. "Then let us finish our climb."

Domhnall had brought her here because to him this was the most romantic place in the keep. Standing on top of the battlements, he could imagine reaching up and catching a shooting star as it flashed overhead. "This is magnificent," she said softly as they stepped into the open. Her head tilted backward to absorb the view.

Unable to control his desire for her, Domhnall encircled the girl with his arms. Her head rested on his shoulder, and her back plastered his chest with her warmth. "You make it magnificent," he whispered in her ear. A long silence ensued. Finally, he felt the sobs shaking her shoulder. "Tell me," he said as he brushed the hair from her face.

She turned her head into his palm and brushed her lips across his hand. Her tenderness rocked his composure. He had to protect her at all costs, even if it meant choosing her over his flesh and blood. "I saw…saw the cells…heard the screams. I…I remember," she sniffed. "The cold…the smell of blood…the prayers…" Her voice broke on a sob. Domhnall turned her in his arms and pulled her closer. His hand stroked her back, and he whispered endearments. "How can…how can a man…a man of your tenderness… keep prisoners in his home?" She clutched his shirt as if holding on to her only lifeline.

"I never knew," he rasped. "You must understand. I never knew. I should have. It was my responsibility. As Normanna's lord, I should have known." He cupped her face in his large palms. "My wife. My child. They were taken from me. And then my Da passed. I was thrust into a life I was not ready to live. She be my mother. I trusted her. I thought she had found a solution to my father's growing debts. I never questioned her methods." He searched her eyes for understanding. For empathy. A moment of breathless anxiety followed.

"What do we do?" she whispered. Strain showed in her eyes.

The lady's use of the word "we" had delighted Domhnall. It meant that she would not run from him. "I have taken steps to deal with the chaos, but, Esme, I cannot see her in prison. Despite everything she has done, she is still my mother. I will send her away, where she can never hurt another."

With a tightening of her shoulders, she sought to rationalize his motives. "I wish I could say something that would relieve your anguish, my Lord, but I fear that I cannot reconcile myself with your tolerance of what Lady Wotherspoon has done, even in the name of love."

Domhnall shivered as apprehension ran up his spine. He had spoken to no one else of the horrors he had discovered under his roof. He wanted Esme to understand how he had made great strides to correct the wrongs. "We will speak of this in detail tomorrow. It is late, and we cannot reason without proper rest."

She shrugged from his grasp. "As you wish, my Lord."

Domhnall brought the back of her hand to his lips. "I told my mother that your door was to remain unlocked, but promise me you will lock it from the inside, and you will keep the key with you."

"I promise."

* * *

With the break of dawn, Darcy and Edward prepared to ride out; Elizabeth had insisted that both men have a proper breakfast, and to ensure their doing as she asked, she had filled their plates and had sat beside them to encourage their appetites.

"You did not say what has happened to Mrs. Wickham," Edward remarked as he consumed the ham Elizabeth had placed on his plate. Although both he and Darcy had argued against the necessity of the meal, they each ate heartily.

"My mother has escorted Lydia to Carlisle. Of course, we all assumed Lieutenant Wickham had returned to their let rooms. As we erred in that assumption, I am certain Mama and Lydia are at their wits' end." Elizabeth placed preserves on her toast. She had begun to think with assurance that her pregnancy was real. Of late, the smell of certain foods affected her hunger or lack thereof.

"Perhaps you should send Mrs. Wickham news of her husband's true nature," Darcy observed with bitterness.

Elizabeth scowled. "Neither Lydia not Mrs. Bennet deserve our censure. Let us please direct our disdain to my sister's husband. I certainly cannot send word of the man's attack or of his thievery without bringing on a case of the vapors. What would you have me say, Fitzwilliam? Instead, I think it best that I send word to Papa. He should travel to Carlisle and speak to Mama and Lydia personally. Someone must take control of the hysterics that are likely to follow. We would not want news of the man's perfidy to become common knowledge."

Darcy said flatly, "For my satisfaction, I would not mind seeing Lieutenant Wickham receive his due."

Elizabeth set her teacup down with emphasis. "Fitzwilliam, despite your contempt for Lieutenant Wickham and despite Lydia's naïveté, it would not serve either the Darcys or the Bennets to have the situation become a court issue. You have fought for over a decade to protect the Darcy name from Lieutenant Wickham's schemes and prevarications. You may have washed your hands of the man, but the Darcy family has not. Bennet's name and the names of any future children with which we may be blessed shall not be associated with that of a convicted criminal. I shall not have it. You must set your mind to a solution."

Darcy's lips turned up in amusement. "As you wish, Mrs. Darcy."

Elizabeth sighed impatiently. "I despise how easily you read me, Mr. Darcy."

Darcy placed his napkin on the table, stood, and then leaned down to kiss the top of his wife's head. "Not easily enough, my dear, but I am very aware of your familial loyalty and am blessed by it."

Elizabeth smiled brightly. "Be off with you." She stood as the Major General finished his meal. "Ride safely, Fitzwilliam. Please bring Georgiana home to those who love her."

Darcy caught her hand and tugged Elizabeth along behind him. "Kiss Bennet for me."

"And me, as well," Edward added as he accepted his hat and gloves from Mr. Jacks.

"Send word if you are delayed," Elizabeth ordered.

Darcy kissed her fingertips. "You will know what we discover."

* * *

The early morning light had invaded the space, and although she had fought for sleep, the day brought her a flicker of hope. Would this be the day? The day someone would find her? The day someone would rescue her, and she could return to her family's bosom?

During the night, she had dreamed of a dark evil chasing her through the blackness. Georgiana had never felt such fear, but then Edward had stepped from the shadows and had taken her into the safety of his embrace. The alarm had not disappeared, but with her husband's acceptance, she had known love.

"It is time to escape from the confines of these walls," she chastised herself. "Edward would expect it, Fitzwilliam would require it, and Elizabeth would challenge me to follow through. Yet, where do I begin?"

* * *

Wickham had found a secluded setting where he could observe the comings and goings of those residing at Normanna Hall. He had observed a young man, likely the one known as Aulay, depart with an elderly lady in a farmer's wagon covered with a heavy canvas. From the descriptions Kerr had provided him, Wickham recognized the woman as the MacBethan mother. Strangely, rather than the young man, the woman picked up the reins. "Namby pamby," Wickham grumbled. "What man permits a woman to handle a ride? Maybe if he is wooing her, but never otherwise. And why does the lady of the house drive a farmer's wagon—one meant to carry supplies?" The lack of reasonable answers to his many questions draped heavily about his shoulders.

After the wagon's departure, for the next hour he simply watched the staff going about its business, but finally a man and woman appeared on the upper ramparts. Wickham sat back against the rock cropping so the pair could not observe his presence. He would like to know of what they spoke, but he could not safely move in closer to listen. Instead, he drew from his pocket a small spyglass he had taken from the blue bedroom at Alpin Hall. At the time, he had removed the glass on a whim, but now he was pleased with his choice in doing so. Bringing the glass to his eye, he focused his attention on the woman.

He could not decipher many details regarding the woman's appearance, but he could see her face. He recognized the golden blonde hair and striking facial features of Kerr's earlier description. "Well, well," he said to himself as the man bent his head to kiss the woman's lips. "Not what I had expected, but perhaps there is a way to profit from this information." Closing the glass, he eased backward to hide more completely from view. "Who might be interested in a man stealing a woman away from her family? And who might be interested in recovering their loved one? I suspect I know the answer to both of those questions."

* * *

"Thank you for agreeing to walk with me," Domhnall said as they reached the lowest level of the house's parapet. He had thought to revisit the upper floors where last evening she had accepted his comfort after the confrontation with his mother.

"It is my pleasure, my Lord." She had yet to look at him, and Domhnall feared he had lost her.

He held her hand fast to his arm. "We should speak honestly of what happened last evening."

Surprisingly, she raised her chin in a regal manner and stilled him with her gaze. "I spent most of the night trying to understand how you could permit men to be held as prisoners in your home. I thought I had taken a measure of your merit, but I erred completely."

Domhnall's heart slammed into his chest wall. "I am not the ogre you describe," he protested. "Again, you must believe that I was unaware of my mother's actions. When I discovered her deviousness, I put an end to her designs."

"I do believe you did not participate willingly in what is happening here, but you have done nothing to release those imprisoned below," she declared.

Domhnall caught her hand and brought it to rest above his heart. "I wish you to hear that my heart speaks the truth. I have not released those kept below because to do so would be to see my mother brought before the courts. She has committed a great crime, but I love her. She is my family. Yet, I have ordered extra food and blankets to increase the others' comfort until I can determine how best to proceed."

Her countenance darkened. "It was you," she rasped. "You brought me the extra warmth."

Domhnall nodded. "And was mesmerized by your exquisite beauty."

She blushed, but she did not look away. "Would you tell me how I came to be at Normanna?"

"I assume in the common way. My mother gathers those who travel alone. Some have lost their way and have sought shelter behind these doors. I was not in residence when you came here, but I understand that one of those loyal to my mother found you alone on the moor. It is supposed that your horse had thrown you. The animal is housed in the Normanna stables if you care to see it. Perhaps it will jar your reminiscence."

The girl appeared to be searching for the memory he had provided her. "Why does Lady Wotherspoon take them? Not everyone who is lost has someone who could pay a ransom for his return. What of those who have no families?"

Domhnall could not speak of the horrors he had discovered below stairs. Instead, he said, "It is complicated, but for now know that I will not condone what has happened previously as the normal for my household. I will make things right. I have pledged myself to see it so. Please say that you will permit me to demonstrate my sincerity."

She touched his cheek in a tender caress. "I shall allow you time to recover your honor."

"Would you also allow me the favor of a kiss?"

She grew quiet, and Domhnall knew her mind searched for a memory upon which to hang her hopes. Finally, she rose on tiptoes in acceptance, and he lowered his head to touch his lips to hers. Pure joy, the first he had known since the day he had learned of Maighread's being enceinte, rushed through his veins. Esme would accept him. Even with her doubts, Lady Esme would stand beside him. Just the idea of her brought contentment. Her lips held her doubt, but they also held gentleness. Warmth surrounded her, and Domhnall felt her innocence in his bones. His groin reacted to her closeness. He warned himself to go slowly. Instinctively, the girl pulled back, and Domhnall's gaze sought hers. Passion flickered but did not flare. He would have to wait to know the depth of the lady's desires, but he thought it possible that they could find happiness together.

"Thank you, my dear." He motioned her toward the stairs. "I will return you to your room. We will dine together, but I suspect that you could use some rest after last evening. Meanwhile, I will proceed with my plans to unravel what this house hides."

* * *

The girl allowed Domhnall MacBethan to escort her to her chambers. With his withdrawal, she locked the door, as he had suggested the previous evening, and then she collapsed into the nearest chair. "Oh, my," she gasped. Overcome with emotions, she dropped her head into her hands. "What am I to believe?" she moaned. "Who am I to trust?"

She had not asked Lord Wotherspoon why the man cried out last evening. What had Dolina MacBethan done to the prisoner to bring on that agonizing scream? And what had the woman meant by "I expect no more trouble; I want him prepared by mornin'"?

"Prepared how?" she whispered to the empty room. "And for what purpose?" She knew of only one way to prepare a person: prepare a body for burial. Had Lady Wotherspoon permitted her henchman to kill one of the prisoners? Or worse yet, had she done the deed herself? "I would not place such an action outside the woman's realm," the girl declared.

Silence surrounded her. Instinctively, she looked about the room for some sort of weapon with which she might protect herself if Lady Wotherspoon came for her. "It is time to escape the confines of these walls," she declared as she stood reluctantly and walked toward the bed. For reasons she did not fully comprehend, she remained bone tired—barely able to move. "Is it the realization of what I must face within these walls? Or is it the weariness of not knowing my future? Or recognizing my past?" She glanced as the unkempt bed. "A few hours sleep while I design a way to leave this madness behind." She stretched out on her back and stared at the ceiling. "Lord Wotherspoon already trusts me. I can build on that. Perhaps I can convince him to take me away from here."

* * *

"Where is my mother?" Wotherspoon demanded as he entered the final passageway leading to the cells. His heart thundered in his ears. All the anger and misery of his childhood had exploded before his eyes. Over the years, he had schooled his emotions never to show the feelings of loneliness. Of his mother's scowling indifference.

The man known as Blane scrambled to his feet. "Me cousin and Aulay take out the wagon, m'Lord," the man said in that mocking attitude that Domhnall had come to hate.

Without thinking, he spun the man about and placed a dagger to his throat. "Permit me to make myself clearer to your side of the family. Perhaps my mother's father raised simpletons," he growled in the man's ear, "but the MacBethans do not sire half men." Domhnall tightened his hold. "I am the master of this house. Whether you like it or not, you remain at Normanna only with my good graces. It would not be wise to cross me." The man clawed at Domhnall's hold, but Domhnall never gave the slightest notice. "I want to know what happened last evening. I want to know why my mother has taken out the supply wagon this morning? Nod if you understand what information I seek."

Blane's face had turned first red from anger, then pale from fright, and finally an ashen color as Domhnall increased his pressure on the man's throat. With the slightest of nods, Blane surrendered to Domhnall's wishes. Hating to release his maternal cousin, Domhnall gave Blane one more tight squeeze before physically shoving the man from him. "Now tell me what you know." He brandished the dagger at the man for whom he had never cared.

Blane rubbed at his neck, and with some satisfaction, Domhnall noticed a trickle of blood from where his dagger had left a cut. "A man..." Blane began hoarsely. "A man...passed during the night. Dolina...takes the body...where no one...sees it."

"Did the man pass of natural causes or did my mother aid his leaving this world?" Each time Domhnall thought the situation could not become more troublesome, it did.

"The man...be sick," Blane offered lamely.

Domhnall groaned. "I see." His mother had lied to him. Even though he had vehemently warned her against continuing her evil ways, she had defied him again. "This will be the last one. Make no bones about it. The last one!" His voice echoed from the stone walls. "I mean to have this house cleansed of blood!" He stormed away. When his mother returned, he would deal with her. Perhaps, he might even place her in the prison she had made.

*　*　*

"Damn," Munro growled when he observed the wagon making its way toward him. He had purposely circled the series of lochs and had approached from the east. He had stopped only twice after he left the card game in Cumnock: once to question several of the temporary workers at Alpin Hall and then again in the late morning hours in Ruthwell. Some of his clansmen thought him foolish to leave his meager savings at the Ruthwell Savings Bank, but Munro had tolerated their taunts because he had his eye on a small piece of land near where Islav MacBethan had settled. He desired to be far from his aunt and the power struggle between her and his cousin. Domhnall had seen the evil too late to fully take control of Aunt Dolina's schemes. Once Munro had saved enough to purchase the land he had previously scouted on his journey to Crieff, he would leave this craziness to his aunt. She might fight her own societal wars without his assistance.

As he approached the Awful Hand, he had thought himself safe, but Aunt Dolina and Aulay had made their way along the Hand's Merrick appendage, and in the moor's open terrain, a person could easily pick out his movements.

The Awful Hand, a series of north-south mountain ranges, had earned its unusual name because from Waterhead, the mountains formed a gnarled hand: Minnoch, Tarfessock, Kirriereoch, and Merrick made up the fingers and Benyellary the thumb. Kirriereoch and Merrick were some of the highest peaks in the Southern Uplands, but Munro realized Dolina was not out for a pleasure ride. His aunt had business on the moor.

"Ho!" she called as she brought the horses to a halt. "Ye be back early," she noted suspiciously. "Ye found wot I ast?"

Munro knew better than to look away—to show any weakness. His Aunt Dolina observed him carefully for any signs of betrayal. He also knew she would have no qualms in killing him where he sat in the saddle. He had promised Domhnall to report his findings to his cousin before sharing them with Dolina, but neither he nor Domhnall had anticipated this scenario. "I did." He brought his horse closer to where she sat upon the wooden bench.

"And?" she asked emphatically.

He could likely find a position on another estate, or he could borrow money from Lilias Birrel's husband. Domhnall's only sister had married well, becoming Lady Carmichael, the lady's husband heir to a viscounty. Lord Carmichael had always welcomed Munro to his home. The decision was made: he could no longer tolerate what went on under Dolina's reign at Normanna. He wanted away from the madness. Never one to walk away from a fight, he, at first, thought it admirable that his aunt had discovered a way to make the estate profitable, but then he had discovered what Dolina did to innocent victims; now, he just wanted distance between him and Coll MacBethan's widow. He would leave for Knovdart tomorrow. He would no longer be a pawn in Dolina's games. He circled the horse in place so he might have a moment to school his countenance before facing her again. Should he tell her the truth? *Tell them both the truth*, he chastised himself. *Allow mother and son to fight it out while you escape north.*

He cleared his throat before saying, "I met a man in Cumnock."

"Playin' cards?" Dolina interrupted.

"We each cherish our own games, Aunt," he said testily. "Do ye want to hear wot I discovered or not?"

She grudgingly said, "Go on."

Munro smiled smugly. "This man speaks of a cousin he seeks from over near Kirkconnel. The girl, she leaves the estate and does not return at dark. They search for two days, but no one has seen her."

"Be the gel Lady Esme?"

Munro shrugged. "If she be so, the gel's name be not Lady Esme. She be Mrs. Fitzwilliam, and her husband be a great war hero."

"The gel say her husband be dead," Dolina protested.

Munro thought to prevaricate, but he reminded himself of the pledge he had just made to leave the others to deal with the turmoil of their ultimate confrontations. "The estate be closed, but the gel bring in workers because she expect her husband's return. Unfortunately, she received word from his mother, an English countess, that Major General Fitzwilliam was among those lost at Waterloo."

"A countess?" Dolina said greedily. "I knew Lady Esme be from quality."

Munro ground his teeth in frustration. He knew what Dolina had planned for Lady Esme before Domhnall had stepped in and put a stop to his mother's schemes. "She not be Lady Esme. The gel's name be Georgiana Fitzwilliam. Her brother reportedly owns the biggest estate in Derbyshire. When she learned of her husband's fate, she rode away, and no one be seeing her since that day."

"Must be when Blane finds her and brings her in," Dolina mused. Her jaw tightened, and the darkness returned to her eyes. "I shan't be fightin' Domhnall if he chooses the gel."

"But ye be promisin' Lady Esme for me," Aulay protested.

Dolina's frown lines met. "Mrs. Fitzwilliam be related to an earl. She has a powerful brother. The gel be needin' a powerful husband. A man with his own title and land. They be payin' to keep her reputation sound. Domhnall has demonstrated his regard for the gel."

"She be English," Munro observed. "Once she remembers her past, Mrs. Fitzwilliam may not wish to remain in Scotland."

Aulay turned pointedly away. "Domhnall always be takin' the best of everything."

"We shan't speak of this again," Dolina ordered. "Your brother be needin' a wife and an heir, and Mrs. Fitzwilliam kin provide an influx of economy to stabilize the estate. Domhnall must press the gel to marry him immediately. We be requirin' the deed done before her family be discoverin' her presence at Normanna."

Munro backed the horse up a few steps. "Ye should hurry along. Yer delivery's beginning to smell."

"Me brother Oliver knows wot to do with the deliveries I bring him," she said as she rearranged the reins between her fingers. "Ye shud return home. Tell no one of our meetin'," she instructed. "I be speakin' to Domhnall upon my return."

"As ye wish," Munro said contritely. Yet, he would speak to his cousin. Then he would pack his meager belongings. Tomorrow, he would leave Normanna Hall forever.

•

* * *

"How should we play this?" Edward asked as they dismounted before the manor house.

Darcy glanced toward the red sandstone monstrosity. "We ask about the horse. No one has admitted knowledge of a female taking refuge within. Let us see if the lord of the manor volunteers information on Georgiana's presence."

Edward adjusted his horse's straps. "I do not like it. Something about this place feels wrong."

Darcy removed his gloves as a groom rushed forward to claim their reins. "I agree," he said softly. "We should listen to what is not said by our host. Our instincts are rarely wrong."

Handing off the horses to the groom, they climbed the few steps leading to the main door. "This place makes one appreciate Pemberley's clean lines," Edward said under his breath. "It feels as if each generation added on to the main house without regard to the previous generation's vision."

Darcy released the knocker. "A person could literally become lost in the house's many wings and passages."

"That is what frightens me the most. Is Georgiana lost within?"

Chapter 15

AFTER SEEING ALL THERE WAS to see at Normanna, Wickham had reached for the saddle's stirrup with his booted foot. He had mounted the waiting horse and had ridden away from the Scottish property. "What should I do with what I have discovered today?" he had repeated aloud several times. How best to twist the situation at Normanna for his own good nagged at him. Looking off in the distance, he scanned the horizon. "A storm is brewing." He shaded his eyes from the dust stirred up ahead of a line of dark clouds. "I require shelter." Leaving his thoughts of profit and revenge behind, he turned his mount toward the south.

* * *

Rain pelted the windows, but she had more problems than the sudden downpour. She needed to discover a means of escape. She had remained in this room too long. It had offered her a brief sense of security, but now the walls had closed in and had robbed her of her very breath. Yet, the hope of freedom flickered within her chest, and she had resolved to alter what had held her immobile for so long. "There must be a way out." She stared out the small window at the darkening clouds. "As soon as the storm clears, I must make a move to extricate myself from this place. If I remain much longer, I shall surely die behind these walls."

* * *

"Yes, Sir." A proper servant swung the door wide just as the heavens had opened again. Darcy and Edward stepped through the opening into the house's main foyer. The droplets splattered against the dust-covered steps, leaving penny-sized marks in their wake.

Darcy removed his hat and presented his card. "Mr. Darcy to speak to your master," he recited the words automatically. They were ingrained on his tongue. Such formality was so familiar that he often wondered if he repeated the phrase in his sleep.

Edward placed his card beside Darcy's on the tray. "Major General Fitzwilliam," he said evenly.

The manservant accepted their hats and gloves. "If you gentlemen will follow me, I will inform Laird Wotherspoon of yer arrival."

"Thank you." Darcy glanced about the hall as he and Edward followed the servant to a small alcove. It was not the traditional English sitting room. Rather it was a recessed area off a large open room that could serve as a ballroom or a large stateroom. When the servant disappeared into the house's bowels, Darcy let out the breath he had held.

"What do you think?" Edward asked under his breath.

Darcy frowned. "I have never encountered such an unusual house. Parts of it take on the architecture of a medieval church."

Edward's eyes searched for any sign of his wife. "True." The Major General's voice took on threatening tones. "Heaven help us if Georgiana is being held within. How will we ever find her?"

"I hope it will not come to that," Darcy assured. He nodded toward the walls. "Did you notice the faded paper where once hung several portraits?"

Edward spoke through clenched teeth. "I noticed." He pointed to a nearby setting with a nod of his chin. "I would say the furniture has seen much wear."

"Perhaps Lord Wotherspoon is in need of financial assistance," Darcy observed. "Perhaps there are certain advantages which His Lordship is now obliged to forego through the urgency of his debts."

The sound of approaching footsteps cut short their analysis. They rose to their feet as a man in his early thirties strode toward them. The gentleman was dressed with an English influence rather than in the typical Scottish garb that Darcy had expected.

"Mr. Darcy." The man came to a halt and offered a bow. "Major General." He showed Edward similar respect. "You gentlemen have surprised me. I had not known we had English visitors in the neighborhood." He gestured toward the chairs they had recently abandoned. "I am Domhnall MacBethan, Lord Wotherspoon." He sat across from Darcy.

Darcy's curiosity won out. He had instantly sized up the man before him. His late father had preached the importance of first impressions. Of course, Darcy had learned his lesson regarding the misconstruction often associated with assessing someone on first look when he had met Elizabeth Bennet, but he still placed a value on such imprints. "You have studied in England, Lord Wotherspoon?"

"I have, Mr. Darcy. Since I was a small boy. I have only recently returned to my ancestral land." Wotherspoon leaned back into the chair's cushions and relaxed. "It is a pleasure to speak to someone from Derbyshire. Might I offer you gentlemen a drink? Some refreshments? I fear my mother, who serves as my hostess, is away from my home today. She will be sorry to have missed you." When Darcy and Edward declined, Wotherspoon smiled widely and said, "How might I serve you?"

Darcy kept control of the conversation. Although he, too, wanted to grab Wotherspoon by the man's expensive jacket and demand to know immediately if Georgiana was in this house, he recognized his cousin's increasing fury. "My cousin and I have only recently arrived in Scotland, but it was brought to our attention that one of my uncle's thoroughbreds is missing. Unfortunately, that same report says that the horse has been spotted among your stock."

* * *

The moment that his servant had presented the two embossed cards, Domhnall had expected the worst. The visitors would see his mother and the rest of the household to the gallows unless he could divert their questioning. He had watched their expressions as he attempted an amiable presence, but Domhnall realized that it was only a matter of time before the whole world knew of the evil his mother practiced behind these doors.

Now, these Englishmen sought information on the horse Lady Esme had ridden the night she was taken prisoner by Blane and placed in the cells by his mother. A part of him wanted this madness to end, but another part still clung to the hope that his ethereal prisoner would choose to stay with him. He had convinced himself that only Lady Esme could bring him happiness. Shifting his weight to appear concerned over the gentleman's request, Domhnall said, "I assure you, Mr. Darcy, that no one at Normanna would purposely keep a horse that did not belong to the property." He was thankful that his cousin had ridden out on the horse in question when his mother had sent Munro to search out Lady Esme's true identity.

* * *

Darcy watched carefully as the Scot shifted nervously. Wotherspoon sat ramrod straight. "I assure you, Mr. Darcy, that no one at Normanna would purposely keep a horse that did not belong to the property."

Darcy intentionally kept his tone even. "No one is accusing you, Lord Wotherspoon, of devious transactions. We simply assumed that someone found the horse and did not know to whom it truly belonged. It is not our mission to place blame—only to retrieve the animal if it is at Normanna Hall."

"Of course you have my permission to inspect the animals in my stable. I have nothing to hide. Allow me to send for my head groomsman to expedite the search."

"That is most kind of you, Wotherspoon," Edward said with strained politeness.

Wotherspoon's sullen wariness showed. "Might I ask of the horse's rider? If the animal is of pure lines, surely he did not escape his tethers."

Darcy's slight flick of his wrist kept his cousin silent. "A groom was exercising the animal. Something spooked the horse, and he threw his rider."

"Really?" Wotherspoon said with a look of skepticism. "It seems unusual for a man schooled to train horses to lose his seat."

"Yet, it does happen," Darcy said brusquely.

"True." Wotherspoon stood. "Permit me to escort you personally to the stables."

Darcy and Edward rose also. "That is most gracious of you." Disappointment rode Darcy's shoulders as they followed the man through the halls toward the main entrance. They would have no opportunity to search for Georgiana under Normanna's roof. "I have taken the liberty of bringing several grooms from the estate with us to better identify the animal."

Wotherspoon nodded his understanding. "That would prove most advantageous on your part, Sir." They stepped out into the open. "Ah, the storm has passed." The Scot gestured toward the clearing skies. "Very typical for the uplands. Fierce rain followed by a complete stillness."

"It is a rough terrain," Edward observed. Darcy heard his cousin's restraint sharpen. Edward likely imagined Georgiana lost in such territory.

"Difficult to eke out a living," Wotherspoon shared.

Darcy, too, stared at the rocky landscape. "Farming must be near to impossible."

Wotherspoon nodded toward the expanse. "We have converted to sheep and Galloways. The land provides little of our staples."

"Then you deal with the butcher rather than the miller?" Darcy motioned to the Alpin men to follow Edward.

"It is a difficult life," Wotherspoon noted. "When I returned to assume my duties, the herds had been depleted from lack of proper care and from a localized drought. We welcome these sudden downpours to refresh the land. Without them, we might lose everything."

Darcy slowed his step as they approached the stables. "But you have found a means to continue?"

Wotherspoon paused as if he chose his words carefully. "My mother did the best she could following my father's passing, and we are thankful for her frugality. She saw the estate through the worst of it."

Edward and the groom reappeared. "We could find nothing of Bracken among Lord Wotherspoon's stock," Edward said begrudgingly.

Darcy frowned. "Forgive us, my Lord. It appears we have been misinformed. I pray we have offered no offense."

"Naturally, not, Mr. Darcy. You did the honorable thing by speaking to me before seeking the local magistrate. I hold no animosity."

Edward addressed Darcy. "We should return to Alpin. It is a long ride. If the weather does not hold, we should seek an inn."

Darcy paused to see if Wotherspoon would offer lodging. When the man remained silent, Darcy nodded his agreement, and they remounted. "We bid you adieu, Lord Wotherspoon," he said as he reached down to shake the Scot's hand. "May we meet again under more pleasant circumstances."

Wotherspoon said reluctantly, "I would greatly prefer such a scenario."

* * *

He had escaped the questioning from the two Englishmen, but Domhnall understood that they would soon return, and Mr. Darcy and the major general would bring the law's weight with them. He would have Munro take the horse out on the moor and release it. It was the only thing that tied Lady Esme to this house. Domhnall would be hard-pushed to release her to Mr. Darcy. Instead, he would use his best means of persuasion to take the girl away from Normanna. "She belongs to me," he whispered to the wilderness. "I will fight to keep her with me."

* * *

With interest, she had watched the rain from the privacy of the small room the MacBethans had assigned her. "There must be a way out of this place," she had declared. Only moments before, she had observed the riders as they had entered the circular drive. She could not see the men well enough to know who the visitors might be, but the fact that outsiders had come to the hall had given her renewed hope. Immediately, she had raced to her room's door and turned the key, but Rankin scowled at her.

"Ye be goin' nowhere," he growled.

She slammed to a halt. "Lord Wotherspoon has permitted my freedom," she argued.

"It be 'is Lairdship's orders," the man said with confidence.

"But…" She began before a modicum of sanity settled her reeling emotions, and she retreated into the room's relative safety. Closing the door with emphasis, she returned to the window to stare out at the rain. "So, Domhnall speaks of freedom in one ear, but offers imprisonment in his orders." Below her, strangers—

possibly her salvation—kept company with Lord Wotherspoon. Would anyone know she was here? In a limbo halfway between being an honored guest and a captive? Did anyone care about her recovery? "As soon as the strangers depart, I must discover the best way to proceed." Deceit bubbled from every crack in Normanna's walls. Her every instinct said that this place spelled death for all who remained under its roof. "I cannot trust Lord Wotherspoon any more than I can his mother."

* * *

They did not pause until they were well out of sight of the main house. "What did you think of Wotherspoon?" Darcy asked as they took shelter in a small copse.

"I am not much of a gambler, but I would wager that the man hides something."

"Yet, we found nothing unusual," Darcy countered.

Edward's mouth set in a thin line. "You found nothing of suspect, Darcy?"

"On the contrary. The man offers us a series of untruths, but does Wotherspoon hide the theft of another's horse or something more devious?"

"Did you feel Georgiana's presence?" Edward asked as he turned his head to look the way they had come.

Darcy shook his head in the negative. "I felt His Lordship's unease, but I cannot say that I detected my sister's essence at Normanna Hall." He noted his cousin's knitted brow. "We will find rooms close by and ask a few questions."

"I want my wife safely in my arms," Edward growled.

Darcy muttered a silent oath before saying. "Between us, we will not rest until Georgiana is home among her family. You have my word."

"Mr. Darcy," one of the Alpin men said with urgency.

"Yes?" Darcy reluctantly looked to the man.

The groom pointed to an approaching rider. "Bracken, Sir."

"Are you certain?" He rose higher in the saddle for a better look. The rider had not seen them.

"The white foreleg, Sir. I be certain," the groom said with determination.

Edward said quietly behind him, "Let us greet this unknown rider and see what he can tell us of how the horse that Wotherspoon swore no knowledge of came to be at Normanna Hall."

* * *

For the past half hour, he had openly cursed his decision to travel to Scotland. "To this God-forsaken landscape!" he shouted into the storm. Not a stitch of his clothing remained dry as he crossed yet another swollen burn. The rock surface channeled the water through cracks and crevices, creating ponds where dry land had stood not an hour earlier.

He had taken a different route—one less traveled—toward Kirkconnel. Before the rain arrived, he had convinced himself to return to the Fitzwilliam estate and determine whether he might cheat Darcy's bid for the information Wickham had garnered in Ayr. Now, he thought to abandon his quickly concocted plan for simply heading for the coast. With Napoleon's fall, the European populace would welcome an English soldier. "Maybe Italy," he grumbled as he pulled his coat tighter across his chest. "Always wanted to see Rome."

Water streamed off his hat and poured onto his thighs and down the horse's shoulders. "Not a blessed shelter anywhere!" Wickham said incredulously. Then he spotted it: a dilapidated-looking hut huddled on a rocky ledge. Its rear backed into a recessed area of the rise. Automatically, Wickham turned the horse in the direction of the whitewashed building. "Any port in a storm," he announced as he kicked the animal's flanks.

However, the shelter remained deceptively out of reach. He wove his way through yet another overflowing berm before he entered the narrow valley below the rocky ledge. A marshy moor flanked by thick heather awaited him, and Wickham urged his horse cautiously forward. "Easy," he said calmly, although he felt anything but calm. He wanted to be free of the constant downpour. He wanted dry clothes. He wanted to escape Scotland, his past, and Darcy's revenge.

The horse stepped gingerly. A sucking noise following each release of its hoofs. "Not much farther," he said as he stroked the animal's mane, while encouraging it forward with his knees. "There is bound to be a lean-to."

One step. Then two. Step by step closer to a few minutes of dry shelter and the opportunity to weigh his options. Where to go next? What to do about Lydia? How to avoid Darcy's retribution? All his choices remained out of his reach—nearly as elusive as the cottage's shelter. With regret, he had watched Darcy and the clergyman from a distance. Briefly, he had envied the camaraderie between his former friend and the man with whom Darcy had shared a mid-afternoon meal. It had reminded Wickham of the hastily made sandwiches he and Darcy would pilfer from the Pemberley kitchen before they would head off to the nearest stream or lake to fish or to sail the cork-bottomed miniature boats Wickham's father had carved for them. The allure had drawn him closer, but Darcy's and the clergyman's conversation had proven that he had lost that opportunity for normalcy. For a devoted wife and children and an honest income.

He could have turned away at that point. Could have ridden toward the Scottish coast or back to Carlisle and Lydia. Could have started over and made a new future. Yet, something in the way Darcy had moved had brought back the memory of his once-upon-a-time friend's dismissals: first at Cambridge, then with Georgiana, again with his buyout of the Kymptom living, and later with Darcy's insistence that Wickham marry Lydia Bennet. It was nothing more than the characteristic lift of Darcy's chin. A look of disdain toward the waiting road. As if the man had expected the dusty Scottish roadway to bend to his wishes. Something in Wickham snapped, and he had found himself reaching for the gun he had strapped to his saddle. Sighting his target along the line of his shoulder, he fired.

It had been one of his most ill-conceived moments. A disaster in the making, but he could not alter the course he had chosen.

Deep in thought, he had not seen the snake until the last second— unfortunately, several seconds after the Fitzwilliam-owned stallion did. The horse reared up on its hind legs...iron shoes clawed the air in fright, and Wickham felt himself sliding backwards over the strapped-on supplies. He tightened his grip, but again he was several heartbeats too slow in his reaction time. In the next instant, Wickham's backside slammed into the marshy bog. The wetland had been surprisingly hard, knocking the breath from his lungs.

With a "whoosh" of air and a "quish" of water, he found himself lying spread eagle. The rain pelted his face and clothing on the front, while the standing water of the bog seeped into his coat and breeches. A curse passed through his lips as the stallion skittered away. Rolling to his side, he groaned, "Christ!" as the pain shot through his chest.

* * *

Munro replayed in his head the encounter with Dolina. "What be her design?" he asked himself as he leisurely rode along Normanna's pike road. "Dolina not be deliverin' no hindquarters and flanks to the butcher. McCullough's be the other direction." Reasoning it out, Munro turned his head to glance back the way he had come. Then the answer hit him. "Damnation!" he cursed. "She cannae be doin' what I think she does!"

* * *

With the slightest hand gesture, Edward motioned the Alpin men into position, and when the Scotsman turned his head to look behind him, he and Darcy led his recently recruited "warriors" forward. They burst from their wooded cover and surrounded their prey. Edward leveled his gun on the man. "We do not mean you harm, but we require information, and you will provide it if you know what is best."

The Scotsman paled, but he did not appear surprised by their presence on the Normanna land. He automatically raised his hands in surrender. Edward eyed him cautiously. "Take the man's reins, Darcy," he said without lowering his gun. "Weir, you three follow us," he instructed the Alpin men. "Keep your weapons on him." To his new prisoner, he said, "We will take the gentleman to the nearest inn. We will eat and drink and speak honestly. Is that understood?"

"Aye, Sir. I be requirin' a spot of ale." Their captive lowered his hands slowly and repositioned his grip on the saddle horn and the horse's mane.

"Move out," Edward ordered.

* * *

Munro, had, at first, thought to fight when the men had charged at him, but in the next instant, he had welcomed their approach. If he left with the strangers, he would not have to face Dolina's close scrutiny upon her return. The realization of the evil his aunt had practiced clung heavily upon his heart. He had lost his desire to be anywhere near Dolina MacBethan.

His captors, at least, the military man and the one called "Darcy," were English. Likely, they had traveled from Galloway. If his memory served him well, the three who followed behind wore the colors of the Alpin livery. The Englishmen had come for Lady Esme. Munro held no doubt of that fact, and with that knowledge, he saw an opportunity to bargain for his freedom.

If he engaged the Englishmen with honesty, he could probably earn a reward—maybe one large enough for the Crieff property. He sat easily in the saddle. Although the military man brandished a gun, Munro experienced less fear than he had earlier with Dolina. Coll MacBethan's widow's pure contempt for all that was holy made her a dangerous opponent. Despite the Scotsman's natural dislike for anything English, Munro would gladly take his chances with his southern foes.

* * *

"I will see to the rooms," Darcy said as he dismounted. His cousin remained in the saddle; Edward masked the gun he carried in his coat's fold.

"You sit upon a horse reportedly stolen from my family's estate," Edward had hoarsely whispered to the man. "I may be English, but I am an earl's son. My word will go far even in a Scottish court. You do understand the implications?"

"Aye, Sir." The man had glanced anxiously toward Darcy. He had nodded his encouragement while keeping his countenance stern. In all honesty, something about Edward's intensity bothered Darcy. His cousin was normally the sensible one. When Darcy had wanted to tar Wickham for his perfidy against Georgiana, it had been

267

Edward who had stopped Darcy from doing the man bodily harm. When Darcy had lost all form of reason after Elizabeth Bennet had refused his honest proposal, Edward had counseled Darcy through weeks of desperation and despair.

Now, his cousin possessed a singular thought: recover Georgiana. Of course, he, too, wanted to secure his sister's safety. Yet, Edward's time on the battlefield had hardened the major general. His cousin required time to leave the horrors behind. Instead, Edward had remained in the midst of the carnage while seeing to his aide's healing. "In order to protect our dear Anne and to prove myself worthy of Captain Southland's devotion," Edward had stated his reasons for remaining so long on the Continent. And now, his cousin fought the nightmare of Georgiana's disappearance. Darcy worried for the man's mental state.

Within a few minutes, he returned with room keys. "Everything is settled," he said softly. He motioned a waiting hostler to take the major general's and the Scotsman's horses.

"You lead the way, Darcy," Edward said ominously. "I have Weir and Jasper standing by in the common room in case we need them."

Darcy responded with a mere tilt of his head. They had learned long ago to converse without words. As they entered the darkened room, Darcy paused briefly for his eyes to adjust to the smoky lighting, and then he turned toward the narrow staircase.

"Munro!" One of those lounging in the open room called, and their captive stumbled to a halt. "Come share a pint and some cards."

The Scotsman flushed with color, but Darcy was certain that no one enjoying the comfort of the open room would notice. They waited in shadows. The man known now to them as "Munro" turned easily to his friend. "Got me some business with these gentlemen," he said evenly. "I be down a bit later to take yer money, Cairn."

The man lifted his mug in a polite salute. "Ye be tryin'."

Munro nodded agreeably and followed Darcy toward the waiting room.

"Nicely done," Darcy heard Edward whisper as they ascended the stairs.

"I may be a Scotsman," Munro declared in hushed tones, "but that donnae make me an ignorant bumbler. I know the danger of wot we do."

Darcy opened the door and motioned Munro through. Edward followed closely on the Scotsman's heels. "I have ordered a meal sent up and refreshments for the Alpin men. I thought this might take some time."

Edward's mien appeared bleak. "If I have my way, there will be no delay in our guest's telling us what we require."

* * *

Edward placed his sword on the small table where he might easily reach it. He had gestured the man they had taken prisoner to a straight-backed chair and had assumed the one directly before him. From the moment the groom had recognized the Alpin horse, Edward could think of nothing but the fact that this man knew something of Georgiana's disappearance. His wife was close. He knew it in his heart, but he could not pinpoint how the MacBethans had involved themselves in Georgiana's survival.

"Tell us your full name," he said coldly. The Scot leaned back casually in his seat. Although the man had given up quite easily when they had surrounded him, Edward did not fool himself into thinking this man had not a mean streak of his own. He had learned to recognize cunning and bravery. This Scotsman possessed both.

"Munro. Munro MacBethan," the man said evenly.

"Do you reside at Normanna Hall?" Darcy asked as he moved a chair from the corner to join his cousin in the questioning.

The man did not appear nervous, which bothered Edward extensively. Would this Scot purposely lead them astray?

"Aye, Sir."

"And how are you related to Domhnall MacBethan?" Darcy continued.

Surprisingly, the man seemed to speak without craftiness. "Domhnall be me cousin. Me father, Ashe, and Domhnall's father, Coll, be half brothers. I come to live among the MacBethans when Islav, the second brother, needed to return to his property in Crieff. Islav ast me to assist Lady Wotherspoon's overseein' the estate. Domhnall jist returned a few weeks ago following 'is father's passin'. His mother, Dolina, be runnin' the estate fer nearly a year as Coll lay ill for many months."

Edward relaxed his hand on the gun he still held on the man. Possibly, they would not need to use force on their captive. He had witnessed enough brutal examinations to last a lifetime. "How did you come by the horse you rode today?"

"Blane brings him in maybe a sennight prior. I required a sturdy animal for me travels," the man admitted.

Edward asked warily, "And your travels took you to..."

"Tuv over yer way, Major General." The Scot smiled smugly.

Darcy leaned forward to emphasize his point. "Did you have a particular destination in Galloway?"

"Me Aunt Dolina tasked me with an errand on her behalf."

"Did you succeed in completing your charge?" Edward's hackles stood at attention.

The Scot casually stretched his arms behind him to release his shoulder tension. "Other than the miles, it not be a difficult task. Play me some cards. Drink me share. Listen to wot others 'ave to say."

Darcy cleared his throat. "So you found the stallion in your cousin's stables. Lord Wotherspoon claimed no knowledge of Bracken. Why would His Lordship offer a prevarication?"

"I doubt Domhnall knew of the horse's presence. It not be likely that me cousin saddles 'is own mount. And if'n 'e thought the animal 'ad at one time been at Normanna, Wotherspoon wud believe the animal no longer there."

Edward leveled a deadly stare on the man. "Explain," he demanded.

"Me uncle leave Domhnall many debts. Before my cousin returned, Aunt Dolina discovered ways to keep the tax man from the door."

Cocking his head, Darcy gazed hard upon their prisoner. "I do not understand."

The Scot offered up an innocent smile, as if he shared an obvious secret that neither Edward nor Darcy comprehended. The expression sent a shiver of dread down Edward's spine. Only on the eve of a battle had he felt such trepidation. He knew the Scot's revelation would change everything. "Normanna depends on the success of its herds. Last year, we experienced first months with no rain and then months with more rain than we cud 'andle. The herd suffered greatly, but Aunt Dolina found a means to supplement the estate's bounty. A few nags. A neighbor's lost sheep or Galloway."

"Are you telling me," Darcy clarified, "that your aunt passed off the meat of stolen animals, including horses, as the estate's Galloway cattle?"

"Easy enough to do when Dolina's brother McCullough be the village butcher," the Scot declared.

A knock at the door indicated their meals had arrived. Darcy rose to answer the summons. A girl entered with a heavily laden tray. Darcy indicated a nearby table. "We will serve ourselves," he said.

"Yes, Sir." She curtsied. Twice, in fact. Once with his dismissal and a second time after he handed her a coin for her trouble.

With the door's closing, Edward remarked, "Are these the extent of your cousin's sins?"

The captive craned his neck toward where Darcy dished out bowls of stew. "Ye should know the inn do not buy from Oliver McCullough."

It took a second for both Darcy and Edward to comprehend the Scot's reference. "Quite humorous, Mr. MacBethan," Darcy said with a frown.

"I jist thought ye should know before ye took yer first bite. Mr. Shadlow care not for McCullough's ways. They's had quite a row 'bout three years prior." He took the bowl Darcy handed him. "Thank ye kindly. I've not et since I left Ruthwell."

"Do you know anything of Bracken's rider?" Edward ignored the food Darcy placed before him. He needed to stay sharp, and hunger had always kept him on alert. It was how he had survived so many battles. He refused to eat or sleep before an attack. Others thought him foolish, but he believed the self-imposed fast made him "hungry" to survive.

The Scot shoveled another spoonful of stew into his mouth before he answered. Wiping his mouth with the back of his sleeve, he said, "Ye be askin' abut the gel. About yer Mrs. Fitzwilliam."

Chapter 16

DOLINA STRODE INTO DOMHNALL'S study without knocking. He refused to look up or to acknowledge her lack of respect for his position as the lord of the manor. It remained a truth that he had been slow to claim his title after his father's passing. He had hated to relinquish the life he had carefully crafted in London's Society. Even the birth of his child had not brought him home. Maighread had written. Had begged him not to desert her and their child. But he always assumed that his mother had coerced his wife into demanding his return to his ancestral home. Therefore, he had purposely stayed away. Had ignored his family obligations. Had refused the shackles placed on him by an estate and a title he had never wanted and had always assumed that he could not manage. Not surprisingly, his prediction had proved itself correct.

He had not wanted to abandon Maighread to the Scottish Uplands, but she had refused to follow him to England. He had offered to find a small manor house in the English countryside. He had no desire to live solely in London, but Maighread had reasoned that her thick accent and lack of genteel education would produce disdain from their English neighbors and, therefore, him. Her adamant refusal had left him no option, for he could not live in a house dominated by his mother, and he could not banish the woman he had once admired from the land she cherished.

However, if he had held any inkling of his mother's pure evil, he would have confronted her in order to protect Maighread and his child. He had not loved his wife, but Domhnall had respected

273

the woman who bore his name. He had held a deep affection for Maighread. Sometimes, he wondered if he had not been so weak, if Maighread would have survived. He had spent the last eight months trying to forgive his foolish lack of foresight.

Now, Dolina had turned her sights on Lady Esme, and this time he would not fail. He would protect the woman against his mother's manipulations. "What might it be, Mother?" he asked with more contempt than he intended.

She seated herself without his permission. "I understand ye had visitors," Dolina said coyly.

Domhnall made a vow to dismiss all of the servants and rehire new ones once he had freed Normanna from his mother's grip. He would not have those in his employ who had remained loyal to Lady Wotherspoon upon his return. Once he had driven his mother from his home, he would wipe the slate clean of her influence.

"Two gentlemen sought a missing horse. Someone had reported the animal as having been seen at Normanna. Unfortunately for them, the report was in error." He had purposely continued his correspondence. Without even raising his head in an acknowledgement of her presence, Domhnall sanded the page and blew on the foolscap to dry the ink faster. He had positioned the paper so that she would have to peer over a stack of books to read what he had written. He realized his mother would not openly appear curious about his communication. Yet, he held no doubt that she would return to the study late in the night to search his desk. Of course, by that time, it would be too late. As soon as he finished with her, he planned to send the message to the inn for the next mail coach.

"That be the extent of it?" she grudgingly asked at last. "No inquiry about the gel?"

"Only of the horse." He sat back in his chair. "Do you know anything of the animal, Mother?" he asked pointedly. He had made it his business to discover every fact he could of Lady Esme's sudden appearance in the estate's cells. From the first moment Domhnall had laid eyes on the girl's sleeping form, he had wanted her; therefore, he became quite aggressive in discovering what had truly brought the girl to his care.

His mother's mouth twisted into a mocking smile. "Why would I know of the English pig's horse?" she protested. "Ye 'ave asked me to think deeply on my previous means to support this family, and I 'ave done everything ye required. Likely, those who spoke out agin me in the past 'ave repeated their allegations to these so-called gentlemen."

"How can it be a coincidence that Lady Esme arrives on our doorstep on foot, and then a short time later these men come calling and asking about a horse with pure blood lines?" He would not tell his mother that he had uncovered her twisted truths regarding Lady Esme's arrival at Normanna.

Lady Wotherspoon's countenance held a strange expression that Domhnall wished he could identify. "If there be a connection between Lady Esme and the missing 'orse, would not the Englishmen ask of the lady's presence?" she asserted.

Domhnall rested his forearms on the desk. "You should know that I intend to ask Lady Esme if she has any knowledge of Major General Fitzwilliam or of Mr. Darcy. If the lady proves part of the mystery, I will return her to her family."

"And if she be not of the Englishman's line?"

"I plan to cut my younger brother from your plans. I will make the lady my wife and replace you as this house's mistress. I want your legacy erased from Normanna's history."

"Beware, my son. Erasing my name removes your heritage, as well. We share the same blood," she warned.

"Your blood runs in streams along stone floors. I will wash it from every brick in this house, and if that means my claim to the title disappears with the cleansing waters, then so be it. I want none of the wealth you brought to Normanna. I refuse to permit your habitual disdain for the MacBethan name to sabotage my life. We will find another way."

Dolina stood suddenly. "I caution you, Domhnall. Sometimes our most fervent prayers are answered by the Devil."

* * *

Wickham rolled to his side just as the horse skittered away; yet, that was not his most pressing concern. He brought his knees up so he lay like a babe cradled in his crib. He could barely breathe. "Christ!" he groaned as he quickly assessed the situation. No horse. Pouring rain. Substantial pain.

Forcing himself to his hands and knees, Wickham raised his head to survey the area. He had to reach the small cottage. He could not remain on the soggy bog. He had no choice but to fight his way to the only shelter available.

With water streaming down his cheeks and seeping into his neck cloth, Wickham took a deep breath that he hoped would bring him new resolve, but instead it blurred his vision further as a sharp pain shot through his chest. He forced himself to a standing position by walking his hands up his thighs. He remained hunched over, but he was able to take a tentative step forward. He moaned audibly as his boots sunk into the marshy soil, but he kept the cottage in view. It would be his salvation. He would not fail to reach it.

Painfully, he struggled, but would not accept defeat. Instead, he chastised himself with reminders of how much Darcy would enjoy seeing him in such a predicament. How much pleasure his old friend would take in knowing not only of the pain Wickham suffered, but also of the desperation that had crept into his heart. He used Darcy's imagined scorn to shore up his determination. A way to prove that he could overcome anything God placed in his path. "Anything but a stupid snake," he growled. "Since the time of Adam and Eve, snakes have spelled disaster for mankind."

"Gruph!" he exhaled as he stumbled on the rough paving stone leading to the cottage's entrance. The cottage certainly did not look like much. He just prayed that it would be a dry place where he could reevaluate what to do next. He took another lurching step forward and braced himself by catching the door's framing. "Not yet, Darcy," he whispered as he tilted his head backward to bring his eyes to the heavens. "You have not bested me, after all, my friend," he swore. Then he reached for the door.

* * *

"Ye be askin' about the gel. About yer Mrs. Fitzwilliam."

Every nerve ending came alive as Darcy set his own bowl of stew on the small table with a loud thwack. Out of his eye's corner, he had seen his cousin stiffen. "What do you know of Mrs. Fitzwilliam?" he demanded.

The change in his tone must have warned the Scot that the man trod on dangerous ground. Their captive swallowed deeply. "I 'ave been 'onest with you. Even spoke ag'inst me own family."

Darcy threatened with his tone. "Your point being what, MacBethan?"

The Scot shot a glance at Edward's menacing scowl. "I want out. Want me own place, but I's need a stake to start ag'in."

"If what you say proves true," Darcy said before Edward could respond, "then you will be fairly rewarded. However, if you lead us a merry chase, I will permit my cousin to take out his frustrations on you." Darcy leaned closer to the man—his face mere inches from the Scot's. "I assure you, MacBethan, the Major General has learned his lessons well on both the battlefields of the American front, where the Indians scalp their captives, and on the Continent, where the guillotine takes a different cut. Mrs. Fitzwilliam is his wife. He would not take kindly to your playing games with us."

Once more, MacBethan's Adam's apple worked hard to swallow his fear. "I understand, Sir," he said on a rasp. "I'll tell ye the truth." It was the first time that the Scot had lost some of his swagger, and Darcy judged the man to be speaking honestly.

"How do you know of Mrs. Fitzwilliam?" Edward's voice held the cold restraint Darcy had expected.

MacBethan eyed them both with caution. "I's met a man recently over a card table in Cumnock. He be English, and he tells a tale of a missin' cousin."

Darcy shot a glance at Edward. "Could you describe the man?"

"We be callin' him handsome. Like a woman only with a touch of manliness. His appearance be greatly in 'is favor; he 'ad all the best part of beauty—fine countenance, a good figure..." His voice trailed off as if he recognized their interest.

Darcy nodded to his cousin, who understood completely that the Scot spoke of Wickham. "Go on," Darcy encouraged. "This man spoke of Mrs. Fitzwilliam?"

"Aye, Sir. But I be suspicious when I leaves the card table. I's ride to Kirkconnel to learn more of the lady. I be on me return when ye stop me on Normanna's lands."

Darcy demanded, "Did you hope to profit from Mrs. Fitzwilliams's disappearance?" Even though MacBethan answered honestly, he despised how the man told only bits of the truth. Why could the Scot not tell the whole story without their questioning him so thoroughly? What was the man hiding?

"Not until I's sees me aunt earlier in the day. I be thinkin' when I come across Aunt Dolina out on the moor that I need to escape Normanna. If'n I kin find a way, I be foolish not to take advantage of me opportunities."

Edward purposely fingered his sword's blade to make a point. "Your tale makes little sense. You meet an Englishman and then ride out of your way to learn of a woman whom you have never met."

MacBethan's eyes followed Edward's gesture. "I be leavin' out why the Englishman's speech brings me to seek out Mrs. Fitzwilliam." He turned his head to speak directly to Darcy. "Aunt Dolina had set me a task."

Darcy fought the urge to roll his eyes in exasperation. Would the man never complete his tale? "And that would be?"

MacBethan continued cautiously, "To discover Lady Esme's true identity."

"Lady Esme?" Edward's scrutiny increased.

The Scot winced. "The gel Dolina 'as chosen fer her youngest son Aulay, although word 'as it that Domhnall 'as taken a liking to the gel."

"Then Lord Wotherspoon purposely hid the woman's presence from us?" Darcy accused.

"I doubt me cousin saw it as such," MacBethan said. "Domhnall jist be discoverin' of late the extent of his mother's maneuverings. Did ye ask Wotherspoon about Mrs. Fitzwilliam?"

"No," Darcy said softly. Did all Scotsmen despise the English so much that they would purposely lie rather than to help his fellow man? "We thought it best only to ask of the horse."

"As Domhnall likely knew nothing of the 'orse, me cousin most naturally dinnae judge the connection. And even if he did consider on it, he likely be cautious in disclosing the lady's presence to complete strangers."

Edward refused to deem what Lord Wotherspoon did or did not know. Darcy's cousin simply wanted straight answers. He demanded, "What task did Lady Wotherspoon set?"

The Scot's confidence faded when he looked upon the major general's banked anger. "Dolina be savin' the gel for Aulay. Lady Esme 'olds no memory of her life before comin' to Normanna. Dolina sent me to discover wot I cud of the gel's history. Me aunt means to marry off the woman as soon as possible."

"If this woman is Mrs. Fitzwilliam, she already has a husband," Edward hissed.

"Then Dolina asks fer a reward to keep quiet. Besides the gel claims her husband be dead. She 'as no father fer her child."

"A child?" Edward's voice exploded in the small room. He was on his feet immediately. "Georgiana is with child?" He turned pleadingly to Darcy.

"Not to my knowledge," Darcy said quietly. "But my sister has been away from Pemberley for nearly six weeks. Perhaps she wished to tell you before telling the rest of the family. But allow me to caution you, Cousin. We do not know for certain that Lady Esme is our family."

Edward paced the open area. He ignored Darcy's suggestion of prudence. "We must recover Georgiana, Darcy."

Darcy stood before his cousin. "We will, but we require more information before we can go using a battering ram on Normanna's door."

Edward nodded curtly. Then he pulled his chair to where Mac-Bethan would see only him. "You will tell us everything you know of this Lady Esme and where she is being held inside Normanna Hall."

* * *

Domhnall knocked sharply on Lady Esme's door. He had set himself the task of ridding his home of his mother's influence and that exorcism would begin with Lady Esme Lockhart. When the door opened to reveal the woman who had quickly captured his heart, Domhnall breathed more easily. "Would you walk with me, my Lady?"

A quick nod signaled her agreement. She closed the door behind her and accepted his proffered arm. Domhnall turned their steps toward the garden's entrance. He waited until they were well away from the house before he spoke. "Normanna had visitors today."

She kept her eyes diverted from his gaze, which worried him more than Domhnall would have cared to admit. "I observed the gentlemen from my window."

"Did you recognize them, my Lady?" he asked with more calmness than his racing heart would betray.

Her eyes sharpened. "Should I have?"

"The gentlemen inquired of a missing horse, but I wondered if they knew of your presence at my home," he confessed. "If they be your family, my Lady, I will return you safely to their bosom."

"And if I am not part of the gentlemen's families?" she asked tentatively.

He brought her fingertips to his lips. "I have developed an affection for you, Esme. Without destroying everything for which my ancestors stood, it is my wish to clear Normanna of all vestiges of my mother's reign. I would claim you as my own and pledge to spend my days as your husband and protector. I would raise your child as my own and offer him or her a fine settlement upon his coming of age."

"Tell me of the gentlemen, Lord Wotherspoon," she said simply.

Domhnall seated her on a wooden bench, but he did not relinquish her hand. "They were a Mr. Fitzwilliam Darcy and Major General Edward Fitzwilliam, whose family owns a property in Galloway." Domhnall reached into his pocket to retrieve two calling cards and handed them to her. He watched closely as Esme examined the cards carefully before she returned them to his open palm. "Do you recognize either name?" he asked anxiously.

She shook her head in the negative, and Domhnall expelled the breath he did not know he held. "I do not believe the gentlemen are my kinfolk," she said with some disappointment.

Domhnall squeezed her hand. "In many ways I am sorry for it, my Lady; yet, my heart speaks a different language. I wish nothing more than to bestow my name upon you."

"Yet, I maintain the need to know of my past, my Lord. Before I can make a commitment, I must know the truth of how I came to Normanna."

* * *

"Could you describe the woman known as Lady Esme?" Darcy asked with more calm than he felt. He had to keep Edward focused while attaining as much information as he could from Munro MacBethan.

"Ye will see me paid fer me information?" the Scot asked tentatively.

Darcy's gaze narrowed. "If what you say proves true, then you will earn my gratitude, but if you waste our time with some perverted scheme, you will find Scotland too small to escape my wrath."

The Scot nodded his understanding. "I only see the gel twice. Once when she be in the cells and once when she walked about with Wotherspoon." Neither Darcy nor his cousin responded, so MacBethan continued his tale. "The lass be fair of hair and lithe of figure."

"How tall?" Edward asked.

"Mayhap to me shoulder," MacBethan responded.

Darcy said softly. "Taller than Georgiana." He meant it as a caution to his cousin not to place all his hopes on MacBethan's story, but Edward was singular in his thoughts. Darcy understood the major general's urgency; he felt it also. Every day that Georgiana went unfound decreased their chances of locating his sister alive, but something about MacBethan's tale spoke of sclerous devices operating at Normanna.

"What else can you tell us of the woman?" Edward sounded remarkably calm for a man whose face held such sorrow.

"The gel be English in 'er speech and 'er manners," MacBethan declared. "That be probably the reason Domhnall 'as taken a liking to Lady Esme. He spent most of 'is life in England. Me cousin could never convince 'is first wife Maighread to reside in England, while Domhnall could not tolerate livin' in 'is homeland."

Darcy took up a position by the window. He attempted nonchalance. He would ask questions not of Georgiana's disappearance but of Wotherspoon's obvious nefarious actions. "You spoke previously of this woman, Lady Esme, being held in a cell. What type of cell?"

"There be cells from the monastery's ruins. Even religious men have enemies." A shiver shook MacBethan's shoulders. "It not be a place for good men, Mr. Darcy."

"And what happens to those held in the cells?" Darcy asked cautiously. He thought he knew the answer, but he would have MacBethan spell out the truth.

The Scot paled. "I be there only once. It was I who found Lady Esme below and told Domhnall about the lass. I be curious, but..." His head dropped as if in sorrow. "A man should not see such evils and not go blind."

MacBethan's words caused Darcy's shoulders to stiffen. His heart lurched in his chest. "Explain, Mr. MacBethan."

"The men held there...they be allowed to die."

All the air in the room fled as his dread mounted. "Were those who found themselves placed in Normanna's lower levels...did they find themselves in the same situation as the appropriated animals of which we spoke earlier?" Darcy's voice betrayed his emotions.

"Aye, Sir." The Scot sobbed.

Edward was on his feet in an angry explosion. He caught Mac-Bethan up by his lapels. With his face inches from their captive's, Darcy's cousin snarled, "Men were held as a source of food? You expect us to believe such preposterous lies?" He gave MacBethan a good shake.

Darcy pried his cousin's hands from the Scot's body. "We need to hear MacBethan's story, Edward," he said as he placed himself between their only source of information and the Major General.

Edward glared at him, but he accepted Darcy's warning. With a curt nod, he strode away. Darcy turned to MacBethan and patted the man's shoulder. "Your tale is not an easy one to swallow for several reasons. The Major General worries for his wife." He would offer no other excuse for his cousin's actions. The man they had taken prisoner had an active knowledge of the atrocities perpetrated by the MacBethan household on innocent travelers, but he had done nothing to bring a halt to those reprehensible activities. How could he trust such a person to speak the whole truth? Yet, he possessed no other leads to the mystery of his sister's disappearance. He gestured to MacBethan to return to his seat, and he took the one Edward had abandoned. "How long have the cells been in use?"

"Donnae know fer certain. I dinnae come to stay at Normanna until Domhnall's father Coll passed, and even then I be traveling back and forth between Normanna and Islav's place in Crieff. Coll be ill a long time, and Aunt Dolina ran the keep. I dinnae learn of wot happened below until after Domhnall's return."

"Does Lord Wotherspoon know of this travesty?" Darcy initially thought the man a tormented soul, but now he considered Normanna's lord as evil as the others.

"Domhnall and Dolina have had a battle of wills of late. As with the animals, I assume me cousin negligent by ignorance, not by intent. Wot man wud consider his mother capable of such evil? He seemed surprised when I told him of the girl's presence. He swore he wud get to the bottom of what went on under his roof. I wud guess that Domhnall has possessed only limited knowledge until recently."

"And what has Lord Wotherspoon done to correct the wrongs?" Edward demanded coldly.

MacBethan shook his head in disgust. "Not enough to please the likes of you." He swallowed hard. "Domhnall tried to avoid the scandal."

Edward ran his fingers through his hair. "Why not allow the local authorities to deal with Lady Wotherspoon's madness?"

"Me aunt holds great sway in the neighborhood. Normanna be the largest house, and she be its mistress the last quarter century. Plus, her brother be respected in the village. She 'as a smatterin' of cousins in the area. I suspect Domhnall knows not whom he can trust. Many of me cousin's servants express their loyalty to Aunt Dolina."

Something still did not feel right. "Besides the shame of his mother's treachery, what else does Lord Wotherspoon have to hide?" he demanded. "What scandal haunts Normanna's master?"

"Me family not be always MacBethans. Some five hundred years prior, we be Beans and MacBeans. Our roots be in East Lothian, near Edinburgh."

Edward tersely demanded, "What does this have to do with these alleged heinous crimes?"

The Scot appeared irritated that the major general did not make the connections. He countered, "We became Bethans because the name means 'life,' and after our most famous ancestors' antics it seemed only appropriate."

Darcy asked cautiously, "And those ancestors would be?"

MacBethan returned Darcy's steady gaze. "Have ye not heard of Sawney Bean, Mr. Darcy?"

Darcy pressed his lips together. His forehead crinkled in a puckered brow. "Unfortunately, Mr. MacBethan, I have. Are you saying your aunt mimicked the celebrated escapades of a fourteenth century legend?"

"Not exactly," the Scot said evenly. "But the saga of Coll's predecessors gave me aunt her motivation. Rather than dine on her captives' pickled flesh herself, she mixed the pickings with that of the other animals and Normanna's Galloway cattle. It doubled the profits."

"I thought Bean's legend to be the creation of last century's broadsheets and chapbooks. We often played at mysterious caves and bloody executions as young boys when we stayed at Alpin."

"There be more truth to it than the family cares to admit, Mr. Darcy," MacBethan assured. "Ayrshire wud never forgive the MacBethans for revisiting such scandalous misdeeds. Domhnall tries to save the family name."

"By doing nothing?" Edward accused. "By holding an innocent woman in a medieval cell. As if she...as if none of the Normanna prisoners had a right to a life of his own."

Darcy directed his words toward his cousin. "We must access Normanna Hall, and I doubt Wotherspoon will invite us through the front door a second time."

Edward's expression remained unfathomable. "Our newest friend," he nodded toward MacBethan, "will assist us with a means in."

"Just a minute," MacBethan protested. "I agreed to tell ye wot ye required. Dolina will 'ave me killed if'n she discovered wot I did."

"Then tell us how to reach the cells without being seen." Darcy insisted.

MacBethan ignored Edward's glare. "There be a karst," he said at last. "Some parts be too narrow to stand straight, but the passage will bring ye into the monastery's ruins."

Darcy spoke to his cousin. "I shall leave it to you to make the arrangements for what we require. Perhaps, Weir should ride over to the next village for a few extra men."

Edward picked up his sword. "I will see to it." He put the gun in a holster under his jacket. "I assume you have a weapon, Darcy." He did not wait for a response before he strode to the door. Without turning around he said, "If anyone has laid a finger on Georgiana, he will know my fury." The sound of the door slamming throughout the small inn brought the world to a stand still.

Chapter 17

"YOU HAVE A MESSAGE from Mr. Darcy, Ma'am." Mr. Jacks presented Elizabeth a note on a silver salver.

She watched as her son rolled from his stomach to his back. Bennet had learned the skill perhaps a week prior. Unfortunately, Darcy had been absent when their son had reached this milestone, and she had yet to share it with her husband. It would grieve him not to have seen Bennet's accomplishment. "At least, you have not mastered a complete rollover." She chuckled as she placed Bennet on his stomach once more. The child seemed never to tire of this half rotation. "I hope your father will discover on his own how strong you are becoming, my son." She patted Bennet's small bottom while he pulled up his knees as leverage to roll to his back once more.

Elizabeth loved the way Bennet babbled, congratulating himself on his new skill. Her son amused himself with a variety of new sounds. She placed a rattle close by to see if he would reach for the colorful gourd filled with dried beans. He cooed and waved his arms about in excitement. She bent to kiss his forehead, and Bennet stilled to accept her sign of affection. "Just like your father," she said softly. Rising from the floor, she sat in the wing chair she had abandoned earlier. Reaching for the note Darcy had seen fit to send her regarding his investigation, Elizabeth knew before she read her dear husband's words that he had not located Georgiana. She had known somehow that Darcy and Edward's quest would be more difficult than either man anticipated.

She read his summary of his meeting with Lord Wotherspoon and the recovery of the horse Georgiana had ridden that fateful

REGINA JEFFERS

day that her sister had gone missing. "They should all have listened to their hearts," she murmured. "One cannot love the way I love Darcy and not know of his loved one being in danger." Elizabeth closed her eyes and easily brought the image of her husband's countenance to mind. "Always frowning," she chuckled, but did not open her eyes. "Probably why I find the man's smile so addictive. He uses it so rarely."

She opened her eyes to watch Bennet wave around the colorful scarf that her son had taken a liking to. In fact, the boy would not sleep unless he held the end of the scarf in his tiny fist. "Too fastidious," Darcy had grumbled when he had seen his son's choice, but Elizabeth had noted her husband's fighting an amused grin.

"Oh, my boy," she said softly. "You can do no wrong in your father's eyes." Her praise brought several loud squeals and a hard shake of the blood-red cloth. Elizabeth chuckled at his antics. "Shall you be willing to share your favorite things with a younger brother or sister? Somehow, I doubt it shall be necessary. Mr. Darcy shall likely buy each of you your own suite full of toys." She allowed her fingers to stroke the place where a new baby grew within her womb. She had missed her second menses, and a familiar tenderness had returned to her breasts. "When this madness is complete, I shall share the good news with your father."

Mrs. Prulock appeared at the door. "Shall I take the young master to the nursery, Ma'am?"

Elizabeth sighed deeply. "It is probably best. I did not sleep well last evening. I may revisit my bed for a few hours." She bent to lift Bennet from the floor. "I love you, Little One," she said as she kissed the hand holding tightly to the silk scarf. She handed the boy to his nurse. "Mr. Darcy and his cousin still seek Mrs. Fitzwilliam. So we shall dine together. Would you mind bringing Bennet to me a bit later?"

"Yes, Ma'am, and I shall ask Cook to set us a table in yer rooms. No sense in keeping a full dining room for just us two. Never mind the fact," the woman said with confidence, "that you need to conserve yer energies for the new baby."

Elizabeth's head snapped around in surprise. "What makes you believe I am with child?"

Mrs. Prulock chuckled lightly. "The fact that ye did not deny me words speaks the truth of what I say. Besides, I be tending babes for years. I know when a woman's body houses a wee one." She cradled Bennet close to her. "Mr. Darcy will be beside himself with joy when he discovers yer secret."

Elizabeth smiled in earnest. "The man was built to be a father many times over."

* * *

Lydia stood looking out the window of her let rooms onto the busy street below. "I do not think Mr. Wickham is ever coming home," she said dejectedly. "I have completed all this work for nothing." She gestured to the sparkling clean rooms.

Mrs. Bennet, head bowed over a pair of the lieutenant's socks, said calmly, "Lieutenant Wickham is not required to report for duty until Monday next. We should not expect the man before that time. Permit your husband time to howl at the moon. Lieutenant Wickham will not risk being labeled a traitor by deserting his post."

"Where might he be?" Lydia's attention returned to the street. She brushed away her tears and sniffed loudly for the dramatic effect that Lydia preferred in her interactions.

Mrs. Bennet swallowed her true thoughts of the man her youngest daughter had married. This trip had been a real lesson in what happens to one who does not think before acting. "Mr. Bennet writes that a man resembling Lieutenant Wickham played cards with many of the temporary servers employed by Mr. Darcy for Kitty's engagement party. Your husband reportedly won the pay owed two of the men."

"Then you think that George is trying to earn enough for his fare to Carlisle?" Lydia said hopefully. She attempted to convince herself of her mother's version of the truth.

Mrs. Bennet no longer held such delusions regarding Lieutenant Wickham's good intentions. She knew the man for what he was—a scoundrel, a gambler, a womanizer, and a blackguard. Lydia. Poor, poor Lydia. Her daughter's impetuous choice would be Lydia's life sentence. Nothing would change the fact that her darling child would live a life of misery. Over the past few days, Marjory had instructed her daughter in ways to keep a cleaner house, to stretch her husband's pay to keep them from debt, and to find her own worth in something besides Lieutenant Wickham's praise. If only the lessons would stick, then Lydia might survive her joining to the infamous Lieutenant Wickham. She had never before wished someone to his grave—not even Mr. Collins, who would jerk her beloved Longbourn from under her feet when Mr. Bennet passed. Yet, she wished Lieutenant Wickham to perdition. Anything to free Lydia from her husband's hold on the girl. "I imagine Lieutenant Wickham knows his duty and is doing what is necessary to return to his home."

* * *

He did not know how long he had lain slumped against the door's frame, but the evening shadows approached, and the rain had stopped. Wickham moved gingerly, but still the pain radiated through his chest. "Damn," he growled through clenched teeth. "Now what?" He allowed his weight to rest against the sandstone walls of the cottage. "I need rest. Things will seem different in the morning," he said with a less-than-optimistic snarl.

Wickham forced himself to his knees. Using the door's frame to support his weight, for the second time this day, he reached for the door's handle. However, unexpectedly, the portal gave way, and he found himself pitching forward to smack the floor of hardened earth and paving stones with his chest and face. "Arrgh!"

* * *

Barking orders with each step, Dolina rushed through Normanna Hall. "I want to leave in the mornin'," she told the maid who trailed in her wake. The girl, out of breath from the whirlwind activity surrounding her mistress, did not answer. She simply made a small notation on a scrap of paper she had taken from Lady Wotherspoon's room. Years of dealing with the Lady of the Manor had taught the young maid that if all her mistress's orders were not executed as she instructed, there would be hell to pay. No one crossed Dolina MacBethan without meeting the lady's wrath.

"Yes, Ma'am," she mumbled when she realized her mistress's stare had settled on her.

"Remind the staff that I'll not be toleratin' anyone aidin' Lord Wotherspoon. Do ye hear me, gel?" she demanded.

The maid swallowed hard. "Yes, Ma'am." However, the girl would not pass those orders on to the rest of Normanna's workers. Like the majority of those who held employment at the estate, the girl needed the new lord's goodwill. Few positions paid as well as this one. When Lady Wotherspoon took her leave of the house, the girl would give her loyalty to Dolina MacBethan's replacement.

* * *

Elizabeth awoke with a start. Her dream's shadow remained as she bolted upright. "Oh, my," she gasped as she tossed the coverlet aside. "What could this mean?" Over the years, she had learned to listen to her dreams and premonitions. Only once had they failed her. Her initial reaction to Darcy's too-quick evaluation of Elizabeth's family connections had clouded her interactions with the man. Of course, if she had admitted the truth she would have realized that flutter she had felt in the pit of her stomach every time they had met was not disgust, but genuine regard. Instead, she had convinced herself that she felt disdain rather than affection for Fitzwilliam Darcy.

"It was my defense," she had told Jane a few days prior to the weddings that would so please their mother. Jane had inquired how Elizabeth now justified her change of heart regarding Mr. Darcy. "I thought to protect myself from the hurt Mr. Darcy's biting remarks had inflicted upon me. I had never felt more confused and uncertain. There were simply too many contradictions between the man Mr. Bingley admired and the one whom Lieutenant Wickham defamed. I began to comprehend that Mr. Darcy was exactly the man who, in disposition and talents, would most suit me."

Shoving thoughts of those tumultuous days with Darcy aside, Elizabeth concentrated on what she could recall of her most recent dream. She swung her legs over the bed's edge and slid her feet into her waiting slippers. Like Darcy, she thought better on her feet. Without considering the state of her clothing, she began to pace.

Images of Darcy's sister easily rose to her mind's eye. Georgiana was in a sparsely furnished room, and her sister appeared a bit worse for wear. Yet, the girl was alive. Elizabeth could see a few scratches and bruises upon Georgiana's arms and face, but it was her awkward movements that worried Elizabeth. With Georgiana in the dream was another presence, one Elizabeth did not recognize, but one she sensed meant no harm to Darcy's sister. Instead, she realized the other person held a great affection for Georgiana. "Who is she?" she whispered as she came to a sudden halt.

Wrapping her arms about her waist, Elizabeth closed her eyes to relive the moment, but nothing more came to her memory—

just the same scene replaying over and over: the woman hovering over Georgiana's shoulder. "I wonder if I describe what I have dreamed to Mr. Jacks if either he or the others might know of such a place in the area. It was too real not to be true."

Hurrying to the mirror to right her clothes and to repin her hair, Elizabeth could not help but feel optimistic. She did not worry over whether the Alpin staff would think her eccentric to believe in dreams. "It shall be well worth the raised eyebrows if we can reclaim Georgiana," she announced to her reflection. "What care I for their censure if Darcy's sister is safe within the Major General's arms."

* * *

"Ye shud not be here," Dolina hissed as she rushed into the room. Her brother's presence was not something of which she wished Domhnall to become aware. Having socked away a solid fortune of her own, she held plans for another beginning, and Dolina would not rile her eldest son any further than she had previously.

Oliver McCullough caught her arm and roughly pulled her into his body. "I want tuv know wot transpires at Normanna. Ye be keepin' secrets, Dolina."

She attempted to ease herself from his grasp, but Oliver's fingers tightened about her arms. "No secrets," she asserted. "Domhnall be thinkin' of makin' the gel Blane brung in his wife."

"But she 'as knowledge of what ye did here," McCullough growled.

"Wot *we* did at Normanna," she corrected.

McCullough's smile widened. "Ye always be the sharp one," he said easily. "And we always be together. Even after Lars McCullough planted ye in Coll MacBethan's bed."

"The old bastard thought Coll too drunk to know what he be doin'; but Coll fooled us all. He took me so fast that I's barely had time to remove me gown," she stated matter-of-factly. She slid her arms about McCullough's waist and rested her head on his chest. Those years of the streets—living hand to mouth—still haunted her. Dolina recalled how the hunger had gnawed at her insides and how the cold never seemed to leave her. It was why she had demanded large fires in all of Normanna's hearths. McCullough's plan seemed plausible at the time, but it had gone nothing like they had assumed. Coll MacBethan had been gentle, but persuasive, and despite promising Oliver that she would not succumb to the man, she had secretly wanted to escape to a world she would likely never know. So, she had lain with a man who thought of her as nothing more than a whore. It was only afterwards that she had learned to despise Coll MacBethan. When he reminded her of her low connections. When he threw his many trysts into her face. Only then did she return to the one person who had always loved her.

"Lars had no way of knowin' ye had known a man before Coll, and yer husband could not recall that he was not yer first." He stroked Dolina's back.

She snuggled into his chest. "Lars be lockin' me away until I be missin' me menses and then he dragged me off to Coll's doorstep. At least, me husband be honorable."

"That be the only honorable thing 'bout the man," McCullough grumbled. "He be takin' ye from me."

"But not fer long," she countered. "No one be keepin' us apart. Not ever."

"No, me, gel. Not ever," he said softly. "MacBethan could order me from his house, but not from yer life." He kissed her forehead. "Wot do we do now?"

Dolina raised her chin so she might observe the steadiness in his countenance. Her eyes locked with his. "We leave together."

* * *

Weir had proven invaluable in locating additional hands in the next village. He had a cousin named Linden living in the area; including the two of them, there were now six willing men to follow Edward's instructions. Darcy had left Bryn, the oldest of the three Alpin footmen they had brought with them, to guard Munro Mac-Bethan. They would not release the man until they had recovered Georgiana. "We do not know exactly what we will find within the Normanna cellars," he warned. "If half of what we suspect proves true, you will experience life's worst horrors on the other end of this cave." The men nodded their understanding; yet, neither he nor Edward had described what they expected. It was too heinous to put into words, and secretly, Darcy had prayed to be wrong regarding what Lord Wotherspoon had permitted to be practiced in his household.

Edward handed out small lanterns he had procured for their descent into the karst. "I would prefer that no one lose his life in this endeavor," he said ominously. "But do not allow that fact to keep you from discovering Normanna's secrets."

Darcy did not like the anger his cousin had brought with him when he had returned from the war. Edward had always been the reasonable one, but something played heavy on his conscience. All Darcy could hope was their finding Georgiana would act as a balm for his cousin's troubled soul.

"The Major General will lead the way," he said as the men lined up behind him. "Stay close and be aware of the hand signals of the person ahead of you. Especially as we approach the actual house."

As karsts went, Darcy did not think this one much more than a well-developed cave system. He had been in much more elaborate rock formations in the Dark Peaks of Derbyshire. Nor was it anything like the limestone karsts his father had shared with him near Loch Slapin. He had been nine when his father had allowed Darcy to accompany the elder Darcy on a journey into Scotland's interior. All the karsts of which he knew were on raised shorelines; yet, an underground lake could cut into rolling hills in much the same manner. The day's earlier downpour showed in the water trails that vanished underground. The men lit their lanterns as they started forward into the opening's depths. "It narrows up ahead. Be careful."

Darcy followed his cousin through the twists and turns, but he also kept a careful eye on the additional six men they had hired as part of their force. Edward had drafted a plan of sorts. They knew how difficult it would be to reach the chambers where the girl they suspected to be Georgiana was kept. They would first fight their way through the cellars and then across the upper halls to the private quarters. Darcy wondered if ten armed men would be enough. The element of surprise would aid them, at least initially, but he doubted they would get through this night without someone being injured or killed. He thought of Elizabeth and Bennet. When his party had departed Alpin less than four and twenty hours prior, he had hopes of quickly locating Georgiana and returning to his family's comfort. Now, he questioned whether they would find Georgiana and whether he might survive the upcoming battle. Not a battle in the strictest sense of the word—not a battle as Edward had experienced—but a battle nonetheless.

He lowered himself to wedge his way through the small opening. Edward waited impatiently on the other side. With both their lanterns swinging from one hand, his cousin stared distractedly into the darkness, as if seeing something not there. Finally, through the tight opening, Darcy rose to stand beside the man he admired and trusted above all others. "If she is here, we will find Georgiana," he said softly behind his cousin.

"And if she is not?" Edward asked hoarsely.

"Then we will search elsewhere," Darcy assured. They stood in silence for several minutes until each of the men they had hired had likewise come through the opening. "We are prepared. Lead on, Cousin."

* * *

"Yes, a room with one high window on the side and a smaller one on the front," Elizabeth explained.

Mr. Jacks concentrated on her every word. Elizabeth had found plain paper and charcoal in Georgiana's belongings and had sketched the room of which she had dreamed. "It resembles a reivers' hut," he said as he scratched the day's growth of gray stubble adorning his chin.

"This far inland?" Elizabeth asked. "I thought those were only found along the border."

"Some clans set up a line of safe places in case they be chased by the English. Mayhap, it be one of them," Jacks reasoned.

Elizabeth turned the sketch where Jacks might see it better. "I need to know where the closest of these huts is located," she insisted.

"Let me show this in the stables and see if any of the boys recognize it. It be many years since I be farther than the village."

"Thank you, Mr. Jacks. This is important." As she watched him make his way toward the servants' exit, Elizabeth said a prayer that he would return with news of her hunch proving correct. "At least, Mr. Jacks did not consider me deranged," she said with a chuckle. "Hold on, Georgiana. We are getting closer."

* * *

"Wot be that odor?" one of the hired men whispered. After thirty minutes and more than one missed turn, they now peered through a grated opening into the Normanna chambers.

"Rotting flesh," Edward said harshly. Anger flared deep in his gut.

Darcy looked over Edward's shoulder at the darkened passageway, which was lined with iron doors. "I had hoped MacBethan had exaggerated," he said with a resigned sigh. "How should we handle this?"

Edward did not turn his head. His eyes remained fixed on what lay ahead. "I will go through first. Reconnaissance. Depending on what I discover, I will either motion you to follow or send you back the way you came." They had left three lanterns burning on the other side of a large boulder. Trying to return in complete darkness would be foolish.

"Be careful," Darcy cautioned. Using their handkerchiefs to muffle the scraping sounds to a minimum, they eased the grate from the crumbling stones. "I will give you no more than ten minutes, Cousin. Then I follow you into this pit."

Edward nodded before sliding through the opening feet first to land standing in a circle of muted light from a high wall sconce. Without looking back at Darcy, he pulled his gun from his holster and moved away into the blackness.

Edward felt his chest constrict as he moved along the passageway. As he checked each of the locked doors, memories of those pits in which he had found his fellow countrymen flooded his mind. Despite the difference in circumstance, panic filled him. He had tried to save those he had discovered in a makeshift prison outside of Belgium. It had been a fine house, such as this one, in which he had discovered some fifty Englishmen locked in five rooms in the house's cellars. The men lived in filth and surrounded by death. It was some two weeks after Waterloo, and he had led a ragtag unit of men to round up the last of the French who hid in the area. He had received word one day as he kept vigil beside Southland's bed in a makeshift hospital of a house and a community that had hidden the French during their retreat.

Needing to find redemption for surviving the terror known as Waterloo, Edward had made a command decision. He had gathered men he could trust and set out to know the truth of this alleged betrayal. Signs of the French were everywhere in the house and in the neighborhood, and Edward's long-held temper snapped. He ordered the building burned to the ground after allowing his men to take what they wanted from the house's treasures.

It was not his crowning moment as a leader, and his superiors had not been pleased, but he had not regretted the decision because his impetuous action had saved the lives of some thirty good men and had given honor to the remains of another twenty. "Thank God," he murmured as he tried yet another lock. This time the door gave way, and Edward noiselessly pulled it from its frame and entered the cavity. The smell of urine and feces choked the breath from his throat, while complete blackness blocked his vision.

To his left, a groan and a creak of furniture said he was not alone, but he could see none of what the room held. "Be someone there?" A raspy voice came from the direction of the previous groan. "Be it time for more food?" The sound of chains straining against the walls spoke of imprisonment.

"Not quite," Edward whispered through gritted teeth.

A long silence followed. "Ye be English," the voice accused. "I always thought God be a Scotsman."

Edward could not help but smile. "Not God," he said softly, "but you will have to tolerate being saved by an Englishman. Will you mind terribly?"

He heard the man shift again. "I be changin' me allegiance and callin' meself English if that be so," the hoarse voice whispered.

Edward made no effort to see the prisoner. It was enough to know the man was alive. "That shan't be necessary. For now, rest easy. This may take a few minutes, but you have the word of the son of an English earl that this is the last hour you will spend in this cell. I will return for you."

The prisoner rattled his chain in a grim reminder. "I be goin' nowhere for now, m'Lord."

"Soon," Edward whispered and retreated to the passage. He eased the door closed behind him before slowly letting out the breath he held. His conversation with the prisoner reminded him that there was more at stake than simply finding Georgiana. Others needed him as much as his wife.

* * *

Claiming a megrim, the girl had avoided having dinner with Lord Wotherspoon. Her emotions had played havoc with her all afternoon, and she was no closer to knowing what to do than she had been the first day she had awakened in this house. One moment she had thought to trust Lord Wotherspoon and the next she reminded herself that it was he who had ordered her to remain behind when the strangers had arrived at Normanna.

Wotherspoon had rattled her senses. He had shown her a great kindness and true tenderness; yet, the man concealed his mother's keeping prisoners in the cellar. And for what purpose? Why would someone kidnap peddlers and villagers and tradesmen? What good would they be to the estate? How could commoners bring about Normanna's solvency? And Wotherspoon had said his mother had saved the title with her schemes; yet, he had countered with the idea that Lady Wotherspoon had committed the ultimate sin. What did His Lordship mean by "save the title"? What sin, exactly? In her mind, the ultimate sin was murder, but surely Lord Wotherspoon could not lay such accusations at his mother's feet. Despite her misgivings regarding the woman, the girl knew full well that it was Lady Wotherspoon who had nursed her back to health. And where did she fit into this situation? How would Lady Wotherspoon react to His Lordship's plans to replace her? None of it made any sense.

"Could Lord Wotherspoon's affections be honest?" she wondered aloud. "Or is it all part of a devious plan to baffle me?"

The girl loosened the tumbler holding the door closed and edged it open no more than an inch. She had quickly learned Rankin's habits and knew when he retreated below stairs for a quick meal. Seeing his mat empty, she opened the gap wider and stuck her head out into the hallway to search for Rankin's replacement. With no one about, she slid into the open passageway and silently closed the door behind her. She had taken several pillows and covered them with a blanket to give the impression that she slept; but with a closer inspection, anyone would notice that the three small cushions could not possibly be an actual human form under the coverlet.

Turning to her left, she clung to the wall as she moved stealthily through the shadowy passages. She knew only one way from the house—through the gardens. On foot and with the approaching nightfall, she had not calculated her chances of success as very high, but she had to try. The only way she could ever think clearly was to put distance between herself and this house—between herself and Lord Wotherspoon. Her feelings for the man were tangled in the mystery of this house, and until that was solved she would not know her true regard.

Hiding in an empty room, she anxiously waited until two maids hurried past before she continued toward her single goal of reaching the gardens and the lands she had viewed beyond. She realized that she held no understanding of what lay beyond the groomed lawns nor which way led to safety, but she reasoned that she could never feel secure while under the Wotherspoon's roof. "Please, God," she prayed silently. She had just turned toward the stairs leading to the side entrance when an uproar below warned her that her situation had suddenly become dire. *Run*, she thought. *Run for your life*.

* * *

Edward had no more than closed the door to the prisoner's cell when a burly-looking attendant stumbled into view. The man carried a tray with several food plates, but when he spotted Edward, he tossed the tray against the stone wall and immediately sent up a call for assistance. The man brandished a cudgel he had left resting against the stone walls.

"Damn!" Edward growled. From behind him, he could hear Darcy and the others scrambling through the small opening while racing feet rushed to the Scot's defense. "Just you and me," he said ominously. Motioning the man to face him, Edward stepped into the light.

He could have fired his pistol and effortlessly ended the confrontation, but Edward had had enough of killing. Instead, he relaxed and waited for his opponent to charge. No more than two heartbeats passed before his wait ended. Raising his weapon, his adversary lumbered forward. A shout filled the space as Edward easily sidestepped the man's lunge. He landed a straight punch to the man's solar plexus and a back fist to the fellow's nose as he avoided the Scot's best efforts. His foe had had no formal boxing training. Instead, he stumbled his way through the steps and offered only poorly placed punches.

A second pass left the Scot on his back and his cousin at his side. "My friend there sounded an alarm. We need to hurry."

"The cells?" Darcy asked as the others stacked up behind them.

"The people inside are going nowhere. We need to secure the house first." Edward moved toward the sound of their next physical encounter. Immediately, Darcy fell in beside him. Edward thanked his lucky stars that his cousin would allow him to work through this madness without censure. "Be careful," he warned Darcy as a metal-edged door opened to reveal a dozen and a half angry men eager to defend Normanna.

Edward hit the first man with an uppercut to the point of the fellow's chin and sent his adversary tumbling backward, taking down several of the others with him.

Darcy stepped around Edward to take on the next intruder with a quick jab to the man's ribs and a counterpunch to his jaw.

Edward approved of his cousin's efforts. Standing back to back, they took on all comers. If he could have had Darcy with him during his many battles over the last decade, perhaps he would not so desperately need Georgiana in his life. Maybe, the despondency could have been held at bay. He shoved one of their attackers toward Linden and then turned toward the open passageway. "Come, Darcy," he yelled over his shoulder.

* * *

An overly anxious Aulay drew Dolina's attention from her daydream. Seeking refuge in the small chapel's pews, she had been contemplating how she might maneuver Domhnall into giving her the small property near the Achmore plateau before Aulay's urgent entreaty called her away. "Mam! Mam! Please!" Flushed with agitation, her son stood beside her.

"What be it, boy?" she demanded resentfully.

"Men," Aulay gasped for breath as he leaned heavily against the wooden bench. "Men in the cells, and they be not ours!"

Chapter 18

DARCY HAD NEVER SO MUCH admired his cousin as when he trailed Edward through the twists and turns of the monastery's ruins. His cousin's sense of direction and his ability to defuse each situation they encountered left Darcy in awe. Edward moved just ahead of him, but he had placed himself in the position of protector, assuring that Darcy remained safe. He had heard tales of his cousin's exploits on the battlefield, of Edward's heroism in protecting his men. Now Darcy fully recognized the man of which these advocates spoke. This man was not only his cousin; he was *his brother's keeper*. Darcy admitted to never taking well to Georgiana's marriage, but at that moment, he came to accept the brilliance of his sister's decision.

From the beginning, Darcy had suspected that Georgiana had chosen Edward because she felt *comfortable* with the man. Darcy's sister had never taken well to Society's demands, but with Edward's name and his honored position, Georgiana would win over half the *beau monde* without raising a finger. Add to that inducement Edward's tenacious nature and his cousin's need to safeguard complete strangers, and it became quite evident that Georgiana had made the perfect match for a woman with his sister's sensibilities.

"This way!" Edward encouraged as they emerged into Normanna's cellars. Again, a few loyal servants brandished makeshift weapons, but Edward left each sprawled upon the hardened earthen floors. As they reached the kitchen's entrance, his cousin came to a halt as he peered into the now-empty room. Fires burned in the hearth. Bowls rested upon the roughly hewn table. But not a person moved within the space.

Darcy leaned over Edward's shoulder as his cousin knelt for a better view. A nagging unease returned like a powerful blow to his gut. "I count two dozen so far," he said softly. Darcy heard Weir and Linden moving closer. As Edward waylaid each of their attackers, the Alpin men had finished them off. "How many more?" Darcy whispered into his cousin's ear.

"Even with the grooms, it cannot be more than another dozen," Edward said cautiously as he positioned himself to explode into the room.

"We have been fortunate," Darcy reminded him.

Edward did not remove his gaze from the room. "Pray our luck holds. I do not imagine that Lord Wotherspoon will be so accommodating."

Darcy expelled a deep steadying breath. "Let us finish this."

The words had barely left Darcy's mouth when Edward charged into the warm kitchen. This time his cousin allowed his gun to lead the way, so Darcy mimicked the seasoned warrior and did likewise. With the wooden floor from the above storey serving as the kitchen's ceiling, the space seemed cramped, especially to two men several inches taller than six feet.

"Nothing," Darcy noted as they turned in circles to survey the area. The Alpin men checked the storage areas for those possibly hiding inside.

"Then we continue our climb," Edward said flatly as he turned resolutely toward the steep, narrow stairs.

Surprisingly, they met no one, and the lack of confrontation set Darcy's nerves on alert. They passed through an open area, evidently, part of the foyer where the butler had greeted them earlier in the day. No sound came from the main entrance, and Darcy wondered for a second if they had made a wrong turn, but then a half dozen poorly armed footmen stepped from the shadows. With a shout, the Normanna men charged into the melee.

* * *

Elizabeth nearly jumped in excitement when Mr. Jacks returned with the news that one of the workers had recognized the building in her sketch. "Oh, Mr. Jacks," she said in a gush. "Please send the gentleman to see me, and ask the stable to hitch up a gig or a phaeton."

"You do not plan to be goin' out, Mrs. Darcy? Himself will not like it if ye be having trouble like his sister," Jacks warned.

Elizabeth granted, "I do not plan to make Mrs. Fitzwilliam's mistake. Yet, I must investigate. If Mr. Darcy's sister is at the cottage, we must find her."

"But Mr. Darcy takes our strongest men with him," Jacks protested.

Elizabeth frowned deeply. "I do not need one of Alpin's best men, I simply require a vehicle, someone who is competent to escort me, and a confirmation of the cottage's location," she said in her best Mistress of Pemberley voice.

Her tone must have served well because Mr. Jacks bowed. "Yes, Ma'am. I'll see to it immediately."

"I want my sister found this day," she announced for good measure, but as she watched Jacks make his way to the stable, Elizabeth wondered if her instincts were accurate. The Major General and Darcy believed Georgiana was at Normanna Hall. Was she setting out on a wild goose chase? *I must see this through. If there is the slightest chance that Georgiana is not at Normanna, I must know the right of it.*

* * *

Domhnall rushed through the halls circling Normanna's turret. Earlier, he had climbed the spiral staircase to the parapet's watch post. Even when he hated his life under Coll MacBethan, he had always loved to peer out over the land's wildness, and for the first time in many years, he had known the comfort in doing so. He had met his demons and had dealt with them. He had decided to send each of the seven prisoners housed below to a different part of Scotland and to start anew. He would present each man with a bag of gold and demand that he not return to Ayrshire. He could think of no other solution. He would not have another lose his life because of Dolina MacBethan, but he could not bring himself to place his mother in the local magistrate's hands. After the prisoners were freed and the estate set aright, he and Lady Esme would take an extended holiday in Europe while awaiting any repercussions.

The thought of Lady Esme brought a smile to Domhnall's countenance. He had found a woman who might return his affections. He had long hungered for a soft touch—to know the feel of someone else's care. "God only knows that my mother offered no such tenderness to any but Aulay," he had murmured. He would assist Lady Esme in raising her child, and they would have children of their own. For the past few nights, he had dreamed of making love to the woman. He imagined her hair spread across his pillow and her lissom form pressed to his. Just the thought of it brought a tightening of his groin and a quickness to his breathing. He would delay his urge to know the woman, but he prayed that her resistance would not be of a long duration. "At least, in Scotland, one must not wait for the calling of the banns," he told himself.

Deep in the images of the lady's sweetness, at first, Domhnall had not heard his valet's racing panic. "My Laird," the man gasped for breath. "There be a skirmish below. Yer mother holds Lady Esme prisoner, and intruders have entered the cellars."

Domhnall swayed and silently swore. For a moment, he considered pitching himself over the cap house to the ground below. To end it all before his dream could crumble. But that would brand him as a coward. Also, he held no doubt that his mother would want no witnesses to her crimes. She would kill Lady Esme. Only he could save the woman.

With a deep sigh of resignation, he turned toward the stairs. Over his shoulder, he shouted at the man following him, "Where is Lady Wotherspoon?"

Stumbling after his master, the elderly dresser rasped, "In the main hall."

With his heart pounding in his ears, Domhnall left the man behind as he raced toward impending doom. Finally, he burst into the open hall. Skidding to a stop on the raised dais, he coldly uttered, "Let her go, Mother." He leveled his pistol at the woman who had given birth to him.

* * *

When she had exited her room, the girl had anticipated encountering someone who would force her to return to her quarters or even to the cells below, but she could not have predicted being held at knifepoint by Lady Wotherspoon. Crossing the Lord's Hall by clinging tightly to the masonry and timber walls, she had watched the portal, which led to the family's private quarters, but the attack had come from the direction of the small chapel.

The turmoil below had signaled trouble, and she had broken into a run, but she had taken no more than a dozen steps before slamming hard into Aulay's shoulders. The man had, literally, stepped into her path, and the girl had stumbled backwards from the impact. Before she could recover, Lady Wotherspoon had caught her from behind.

With a strong forearm across the girl's throat, Lady Wotherspoon placed a knife to the soft spot at the base of her neck before the woman hissed, "Plan on goin' somewhere special, m'Lady?"

The girl would have denied the woman's words, but even capturing a breath had proved impossible. Instead, she concentrated on Lady Wotherspoon's ominous tone and the strength of the woman's hold.

Aulay stood nearby, mouth agape. He fell away from the horror. "Mam?" he protested weakly, then turned on his heels and ran from the scene.

Biting her lip to quell the desperate sob that strangled her, the girl's eyes followed his retreat. She had foolishly hoped that Aulay might sway his mother from Lady Wotherspoon's intended punishment, but the boy-man's nature remained too weak to oppose his strong-willed mother.

"Did ye think the boy wud be yer savior?" Lady Wotherspoon whispered menacingly into the girl's ear. "Silly gel. Aulay only does my biddin'."

The girl's fingers clawed at the arm cutting off her breath. She felt herself swooning from the effort. In moments, she would die, and no one would be the wiser. But, a familiar voice brought an end to her struggle.

"Let her go, Mother." Lord Wotherspoon's voice boomed through the open hall. The girl felt the woman stiffen, and Lady Wotherspoon's grip minutely relaxed. With the change, the girl sucked in a quick breath, and her vision cleared.

"Don't ye see, boy? The gel be sneakin' off. Lady Esme chose another. Yer not who she be wantin'."

The girl wanted to defend herself, but a further opening of the pinpoint cut on her neck left her speechless. All she could do was to speak to Lord Wotherspoon of her regret with her eyes.

Domhnall took another step closer. For a long, painful moment, his gaze lingered on her. The man had asked her to be his life's partner. "That is between Lady Esme and me," he said threateningly. "I repeat. Release Lady Esme and walk away." The girl slid her fingertips under Lady Wotherspoon's grasp. She had a chance if she could break the woman's hold on her.

"I think not. The gel be me warrant. The intruders come for her," Lady Wotherspoon reasoned.

Yet, before Domhnall could respond, two men burst through the door: the same two English gentlemen the girl had spied from her window earlier in the day. They truly had come for her, and her hopes soared. Yet, her troubles had not come to an end. Using her as a shield, Dolina MacBethan pulled her closer. The intruders slid to a halt. The one in the uniform trained his pistol on Lady Wotherspoon, while the gentleman in the waistcoat took aim at the woman's son.

* * *

Edward had hoped to find his wife under Lord Wotherspoon's roof, but the scene enfolding before him shattered those dreams. He had fought his way through three levels to find a girl who resembled Georgiana, but was most assuredly a stranger.

"Mr. Darcy. Major General," Lord Wotherspoon said coldly, but his eyes remained on the two women. "I suppose the trouble below is of your making," he accused.

Darcy took a half step to the side. Edward realized his cousin would kill Lord Wotherspoon rather than allow Normanna's master to harm the girl. She might not be Georgiana, but the woman was, obviously, in trouble. Neither he nor Darcy would turn away. The girl ceased her struggling and waited for the next moment. "As you did not see fit to make us your guests for the evening, my Lord, we invited ourselves," Darcy said tersely.

Wotherspoon flashed Darcy an indignant expression. "As you have made yourself at home without a care for my approval, you will excuse me if I am less than welcoming at the moment."

Edward recognized his cousin's anger before Darcy masked it. "Perhaps, if you had not tolerated evil under your watch, we would not have had to take matters into our own hands."

Something flared in Lord Wotherspoon, but he squared his shoulders and continued to take an account of the older of the two women. "You have no idea, Mr. Darcy, what your neighbor conceals behind his doors nor how he plans to reconcile the horrors he encounters," the man said sadly.

Edward caught the expression of bewilderment in the girl's eyes. The elderly woman did not relinquish her hold on the younger female. "We know more than you may suspect, Wotherspoon: how you returned to claim your title to find your estate in financial straits and how your own family members explored heinous methods to correct those shortcomings." He noted the increasing desperation of the family member in question. "I assume this would be your mother, Lady Wotherspoon, and the young lady who has piqued your interest, Lady Esme."

Wotherspoon growled, "It is as you have noted."

Edward continued, "What we do not know is what you plan to do to resolve this madness."

"What choices do I have?" Wotherspoon sneered.

"Ye kin kill them all," Lady Wotherspoon growled her anger. "Then we start anew. Surely ye donnae mean to turn on the woman who brought ye into this world."

Wotherspoon snorted his disgust. "And what a world you have carved for our family! We had the opportunity to leave Bean's legacy behind, and, instead, you have resurrected it. You bring infamy to our doorstep!" He took an agitated step toward his mother.

"Tell me, Madam, what actually occurred with Maighread and my child."

Rich in Scottish pride, Lady Wotherspoon responded. She said with careful formality, "I suspect somethin' my wud-be successor ate dinnae agree with Maighread."

Indifferent to his surroundings, Wotherspoon accused, "You poisoned my wife? My child? Your own grandchild?"

"Maighread shud 'ave followed ye as you asked. Instead, she sought yer own brother's arms fer her cumfert. I love Islav, but it not be right. Maighread be yer wife, not Islav's. The bairn be a MacBethan, but we know not whether the babe be the rightful heir. I protected yer line, my son."

His voice lowered to an intimidating rumble. "You protected your position as the mistress of this estate," he snapped. "You care not for my feelings or my regard."

Edward had eased closer to Lady Wotherspoon during this exchange, but he still did not have a clear shot. He would not risk hurting the girl who had been caught in the middle of this madness. Her eyes never strayed from Wotherspoon's countenance, and Edward recognized the familiarity that passed between the couple. The girl had engaged Wotherspoon's heart.

With the barest of nods, Edward directed Darcy's attention to the Scot, and his cousin responded with a raised eyebrow. It had been a boyhood gesture, but Edward believed Darcy understood. When they had challenged each other to be the first to jump into the deepest part of the lake or to explore the darkest recesses of a cave or to sneak into the earl's study for another piece of a brandy-soaked sugary treat, they would count down to one before they moved. Where their friends might recite, "We go on three," he and Darcy had developed a silent count. The "challenger" would hold his hand loosely at his side. First, he would extend three fingers and then curl each digit back into his fist. When the hand closed, they would charge into whatever adventure awaited them. It gave neither of them an advantage, and he and his cousin often remarked how they had preferred it to other childhood teases.

Now, as Wotherspoon faced off with his mother, Edward pointedly dropped his hand to alert Darcy of his intentions.

"How kin ye think so ill of me?" Lady Wotherspoon pleaded.

Wotherspoon glared at his mother. "Besides the chaos you created below, you hold a knife on the woman I would have replace you as this estate's mistress."

His words brought an expected reaction from Lady Wotherspoon's captive. As if His Lordship's words had inspired the woman, she began to squirm and kick at her assailant.

Edward seized the opportunity. *Three—Two—One—Go*, his fingers announced. As he launched himself at the two women, his cousin executed a sliding takedown of Wotherspoon. The Scot's gun flew from his hand and crashed with a loud explosion against the polished hardwood floors as Darcy spun to straddle the man.

Meanwhile, Edward made a similar move. He did not go for the hand holding the knife precariously close to the younger woman's jugular. It was too dangerous. Instead, he dove for Lady Wotherspoon's legs. Wrapping his arms about both women's knees, he sent them tumbling sideways. He allowed the girl to roll away from him as he wrestled an infuriated Lady Wotherspoon to the floor. The woman clawed at his face, but Edward managed to avoid the worst of her efforts. Irritated at having to subdue a violent female, he pressed his weight harder. "I have never struck a woman," he growled, "but it does not mean that I am above doing so."

"Yer a pig!" The woman snarled as she spit into his face.

Edward responded accordingly. A right cross caught the woman's chin. Her head snapped to her right, and the lady fell silent. He struggled to bring his breathing under control. He pulled his handkerchief from an inside pocket and wiped the offending saliva from his cheek.

A quick glance assured him that Darcy was assisting a bloody-nosed Wotherspoon to his feet. "Darcy?" Edward asked as he stumbled to right himself.

His cousin smiled in amusement. "Easier than yours," Darcy said as he spied the still-unconscious woman on the floor.

Edward gestured to where the woman laid crumpled in a heap. "Next time you take the female."

Weir emerged from the lower level. "Mr. Darcy?" he asked as he surveyed the scene.

"Everything secure below stairs?"

"Aye, Sir. Found a young laird hidin' in the cold pantry. They all be bound."

Edward suggested, "Find another length of rope for the lady. Secure her hands and feet and place someone to guard Lady Wotherspoon."

"Aye, Sir."

Darcy directed his remarks to Wotherspoon. "I will demand your honor as a gentleman, Sir."

His Lordship agreed with a nod, but he watched the younger woman push to a seated position. "See to Lady Esme's safety, and I will agree to anything," he said flatly.

Edward automatically extended his hand to assist the woman to her feet. "I pray you have not suffered unfairly, my Lady," he said in apology.

Although her voice remained raspy, the woman said, "I am...I am well, Sir. How may I...speak my full gratitude?" She struggled to her feet as she straightened her gown. Pushing her hair into place, she stammered, "I owe...I owe you my life."

Edward braced her weight with his forearm and shoulder. "If you are well..." he began, but his words hung in the room like an icy rain. Watching her adjust her clothing and hair, her movements had led him to discover something he hoped never to see anywhere but about his wife's neck. In the room's utter silence, Edward reached for the chain entangled in the girl's hair. "How did you receive my wife's locket? And what do you know of Georgiana Fitzwilliam?"

* * *

Georgiana had heard the disturbance outside the cottage. With a great effort, she had pushed herself to a seated position. Instinctively, her fingers smoothed the wrinkles of her dress before she realized how foolish that was. If someone had truly come to her rescue, he would understand her disheveled appearance. Escaping this dilemma was more important than regrets over a heavily soiled gown.

Excited by the possibility of finally knowing her freedom, Georgiana struggled to stand. She could not support her weight fully on her right leg so she wobbled to balance on her left. Using the single chair as support, she stood tall as the door swung wide and a figure pitched forward, slamming against the floor. Shocked, Georgiana screamed.

* * *

One moment, he had supported his weight with his shoulder and forearm against the doorframe, and the next, George Wickham reached for a door that was no longer there. He slammed face first into the cottage's harden dirt floor. With a whoosh of air, his breath escaped into the small room before a sharp pain shot through his chest. He heard himself groan "Aarrggh," but another voice drowned out his pain, that of a female in distress. With a gargantuan effort, Wickham rolled to his back to look up into the anxious face of Georgiana Fitzwilliam.

"Cease!" he growled as her screams continued, and, miraculously, she went instantly silent. "It is I, Georgiana...George Wickham," he said with distaste. With a deep grunt, he rose to his elbows.

"Mr....Mr. Wickham." Her lips moved, but the sound remained weak. He could read her countenance easily: Staring blindly at him, Georgiana Fitzwilliam's worst nightmare had come to life. The acknowledgment of that fact would play to his advantage.

Wickham tightened his lips as he shifted his weight to come to his knees. Instinctively, he clutched at his chest. The pain announced that his ribs needed binding. "I am certain," he said through clenched teeth, "that I am...the last person...you expected...to find in a cottage...in Scotland; yet...I am here."

"The prayer the Devil answers," she said softly.

Despite the pain that ricocheted through his body, an ironic chuckle escaped his lips. "Still repeating...that old adage...are we? It was...a favorite of your father's." Bracing his ribs with his forearm, he stumbled to stand straighter. "You will excuse me...if I... offer no bow of respect. I seem to have...accumulated both a soaking...and a injury to my ribs."

Georgiana ignored his excuse for his bad manners. The idea of it bothered Wickham more than he would care to admit. It was if she expected him to act without decorum. "You do not appear surprised to find me here?" she said cautiously.

With a painful effort, Wickham managed a smile. Georgiana was no longer the weak, impressionable girl he had once known. He wondered if his betrayal had anything to do with her current strength. "In truth, my dear...the prospect...of finding you in this," he gestured with his free hand to the room in which they faced off, "shepherd's cottage...was not part...of my mental landscape...while I fought the elements...to reach this *pleasant* dwelling." His smile widened in a conspiratorial smirk. "Yet, if it appeases your curiosity...I will admit to cursing your brother...with each step I took."

Georgiana stiffened. Her grip tightened on the chair, and Wickham noted how her chin rose with that damnable air of superiority that he despised in all the aristocracy. He often wondered if those of elite bloodlines were born with the propensity to look down their aristocratic noses at others. He had often practiced the gesture in the mirror, but it did not come naturally to him. "What has my brother to do with your misfortunes this time, Lieutenant Wickham?" she demanded. "Surely, you cannot lay blame for the weather at Fitzwilliam's feet. My brother's influence does not extend to natural phenomena."

"Perhaps not," Wickham said ruefully. "Yet, much of my misfortune...can be traced to my former friend." He took an awkward step forward. "Our elopement..." he began, but Georgiana finished his thoughts.

"Was a mistake," she asserted. "A foolish whim of a too-shy schoolgirl who thought our familiarity would bring her happiness."

"And you have no regrets...for your brother's interruption...of our plans?" Wickham said coldly.

Georgiana shook off his words. "How could I? If we had known success, then I would never have experienced the joy of knowing my husband's regard."

"And how is the Major General?" he said gravely.

Instantly, Georgiana paled. Grief and regret shafted her. She swayed and sat back heavily on the cot. "My husband...reports say that Edward was lost at Waterloo." Tears formed in her eyes, and she turned her head to hide her grief.

Her obvious anguish touched Wickham. Would anyone regret his passing? Would Lydia truly mourn for him or would Mrs. Wickham flaunt her newfound freedom? He said with a touch of empathy, "And do you...believe these reports?"

"I should not have considered the possibility," Georgiana chastised herself with a shake of her head. "Now I question my emotional response. If Edward were lost to me forever, my heart would know. My heart speaks a different language."

Wickham straightened stiffly. "Then you imagine yourself in love with the Major General?" he said through tight lips.

Georgiana sat perfectly still. With her face lifted in defiance, she declared. "There is no imagining involved, Lieutenant Wickham. The Major General knows my deepest affections."

With a contemptuous snort, he said, "Personally, I never cared for the man."

"I am certain that my husband's natural intuition told him how base your motives could be. Edward would see through your cleverness." Her eyes spit fire.

"Does not your brother possess this same natural intuition? It would appear to me that Darcy considers himself a good judge of character," he disputed. Wickham found he actually enjoyed this brief encounter. When he had pursued an alliance with Georgiana Darcy, he had done so for very selfish reasons. He had desperately desired her thirty-thousand-pound dowry. He could have finally owned a bit of the luxury he had always coveted; and, of course, having Darcy forced to acknowledge him as family would have been an added inducement. Yet, despite her beauty, he had never thought the shy, retiring Georgiana could have long held his interest. Now he thought otherwise. He found the woman's loyalty and her innate intelligence very engaging. "Darcy once considered me one of his closest acquaintances."

As if suddenly aware of their surroundings and the shocking intimacy of their conversation, the lady's lips quirked. "Both Fitzwilliam and I have our father's trusting heart. Yet, we each learned a valuable lesson at your hands, Lieutenant Wickham. A lesson in those who present Janus's face."

Wickham's gaze shifted from her countenance to the hearth. He said ironically, "We could debate my finer qualities all evening, but for the moment, I require a warm fire, or I will catch my death. Do you mind helping with the wood? I know it is not normally within a lady's realm, but I find my ribs are unforgiving." He walked stiff-legged toward the ingle.

From behind him, Georgiana stirred. He had made his knees bend so he might reach the opening, but her words curtailed his efforts. "I cannot assist you, Lieutenant Wickham. My leg will not bear my weight. If it could, I would have walked out of here days ago."

Wickham turned his head with renewed confidence. "I see," he said impertinently. Standing again, he smiled deceitfully. "I will attend the fire." He worked his way about the room tossing flimsy furniture and the broken chair into the fireplace. He felt Georgiana's eyes on him. Intently, she followed his every move. The knowledge that she could not escape this deserted cottage without his assistance pleased him. Darcy would pay well for his sister's return.

With difficulty, he managed to kindle a small blaze. "That should serve us well for the moment," he said softly.

"Now what?" Georgiana crossed her arms over her chest as if to protect herself from him. .

The movement spurred him on. Wickham wanted her off balance—wanted the lady a bit afraid of him. He began to unbutton his waistcoat. Then he wiggled out of his jacket and removed the vest. He draped the clothing over the remaining furniture.

"What are you about, Sir?" Her voice rose in apprehension.

Wickham smiled deviously. "I am removing these wet items before they bring on the ague." He flipped his shirt from his body and over his head. "And you are welcome, Mrs. Fitzwilliam, to look your fill."

Chapter 19

EDWARD GROWLED, "I REPEAT, Madam. How did my wife's locket come into your possession?" Despite the heated exchange, Edward shivered. He felt completely alone. Would he never find Georgiana? Was his wife lost to him forever?

The girl's energy surged from her. She swayed as he held her by the shoulders. Her eyes seemed to double in size. "I…I cannot explain," she stammered.

Edward shook her soundly. "That is not good enough. My wife is missing, and you wear the locket I presented to her as a wedding gift. I want to know how you came by it."

"I wish I could say." Tears pooled in the corners of her eyes.

Behind them, Lord Wotherspoon said pleadingly, "Permit me to explain. The lady has suffered a head injury. She has struggled to recall her coming to Normanna and something of her past."

Edward did not release the woman, but he loosened his grip. "What do you remember?" His gaze demanded that she continue to meet it.

"I see that it is your image in the sketch. All along I thought it was my husband's countenance staring back at me. I understand now why the image never brought me the comfort I sought. I am sorry, Sir. I truly possess no recollection of Mrs. Fitzwilliam." The tears began to flow freely.

Edward dejectedly released her. "Where do I look next?" he murmured to no one in particular.

The girl loosened the latch and placed the locket in his palm. She closed his fingers about it. "When you find Mrs. Fitzwilliam, please present this to her as a symbol of your continuing regard."

Darcy guided Wotherspoon to a nearby chair, so Edward directed "Lady Esme" to sit beside the man. Deep in his own thoughts, he abdicated the necessary interview to his cousin while he watched over Lady Wotherspoon until Weir's return.

* * *

Darcy eyed his cousin cautiously. He could never recall Edward being so distraught. If they did not find Georgiana soon, he thought, his cousin's normally even temperament would explode, and Heaven help the person on the receiving end of Edward's wrath.

While keeping the hunched posture of the major general in view, Darcy addressed his questions to Wotherspoon and the woman. "Would you explain to me why you tolerated such degradation under your watch, Sir?"

The earl looked off as if imagining the scene they had discovered. "It was derelict of me to not attend to all the details of my succession, but I so despised my return to this house that I did not perform my duties as I should have. It was easier to permit others to carry on as they had in my absence." His countenance grew studiously grim. "It may appear insignificant to one whose family name contains no stains, but I had no desire to inherit the MacBethan legacy."

Darcy diplomatically acknowledged, "We are aware of the legend associated with the Bean family."

"It is no legend, Mr. Darcy," Wotherspoon averted his gaze from Darcy's measuring one. "In England, few made the connection of the name MacBethan to Sawney's descendants, but in Scotland, one must face it every day. Can anyone blame me for wanting to leave the association behind?" The man did not wait for a response before he continued, "To make no further excuses, I ignored my responsibilities until I stumbled upon the evil lurking in the branches of this family's tree."

"And what did you do when you discovered what was happening below?"

Wotherspoon buried his face in his hands. "Obviously, not enough. Another man died yesterday." Only the girl's whimper could be heard in the room's silence.

"Explain your actions," Darcy said evenly.

Wotherspoon raised his head slowly. The images would haunt the man forever. Darcy held no doubt of the fact. "I came across the hell on Earth my mother has created one night when I had gone looking for a bottle of wine in the lowest cellars." He turned to the woman who sat beside him. Despite the tension between them, the lady took Wotherspoon's hand in both of hers. The Scot intertwined their fingers. "I thought my cousin Munro daft when he insisted that I be the one to retrieve the wine. Little did I know at the time what I would discover under my very nose. It was the first time I ever laid eyes upon you, Lady Esme. Your lovely countenance stung my soul, my Lady."

The macabre image of the horrors below brought a grimace to Darcy's lips. "You were a prisoner?" he directed his question to the woman.

Before the lady could respond, Wotherspoon said, "Lady Esme was unfortunate in the respect that she was found on the moor by one of my mother's henchmen. I lied to you earlier when I said I knew nothing of the horse you sought. Lady Esme rode the animal when Blane captured her. I possess no knowledge of the horse's whereabouts at this time."

Darcy noticed his cousin's stature shift. Edward listened carefully to their exchange. "We are in possession of the horse and its rider," he disclosed.

The girl said, "I vaguely recall riding a horse across the moor, but little else of how I came to be there."

Edward stalked toward them. "But that means if you rode Georgiana's mount that you must have met Mrs. Fitzwilliam. Can you recall anything of her?" He opened his pocket watch to display a likeness of his wife. "Did my wife seek your assistance? Could you have been on an errand of mercy?"

The woman examined the rendering closely. "Mrs. Fitzwilliam is quite lovely, but I fear I am of little use to you, Sir. It is not a countenance that I hold in my memory."

In frustration, Edward snapped the watch closed. "Finish it, Darcy. I want to be on the road soon."

Darcy nodded his understanding. "We can surmise your shock when you finally discovered the scale of your mother's perfidy. Explain what you did when the situation became apparent."

"I demanded that Lady Wotherspoon cease her operations. The prisoners were to be fed small portions at regular intervals. With the first one I tried to nurse to health, we fed him large portions, thinking that be what the man required after having been nearly starved to death under my mother's orders. Yet, believe it or not, he ate so much that it killed him. From then on, I have gradually increased their portions."

"You claim charity, but there are still men housed below in the darkness. They are chained to the walls!" Edward's voice boomed throughout the room. He slammed his fist against a small table, sending its contents crashing to the floor.

Wotherspoon looked away in regret. "I did not know what else to do. You must believe me, Mr. Darcy. I have made moves to alter what has happened with my mother's orders, but I could not change everything at once. Please understand. Those men have been taught to expect the worst. I am trying to wean them from their dependence on Lady Wotherspoon's whims. I have already moved two of the victims to other parts of Scotland. I have bestowed a settlement on each to better his life."

"You paid them not to testify against Lady Wotherspoon," Edward accused. A cloud crossed his countenance.

Wotherspoon looked to where his mother lay bound and gagged. "She is still family," he said flatly. "I meant to see her sent away." He shook his head in disgust. "It was all I could think to do. In hindsight, it was not enough."

Lady Esme pointedly released his hand. "Was that why you proposed marriage? So I would not testify against your family?" She stood suddenly as if to leave, but Edward's hand on her shoulder forced the woman to resume her seat beside Wotherspoon.

The earl caught her hand to his cheek. "Look at me, Esme," he insisted. "My feelings are sincere, but I thought to clear my family name before I permitted you to become involved." He kissed her palm. "You must believe me. I swear in the name of Saint Margaret. Just as the Queen Consort ferried pilgrims from Dunfermline Abbey, I would see all my mother's victims safe."

The lady's eyes grew wide and her skin paled as she once more shot to her feet. "Margaret," she gasped. "Lady Margaret Sarah Caldwell." She swayed as her hands unconsciously lifted to massage her temples.

"I beg your pardon," Edward said softly as he encouraged the girl to sit once more.

She turned to Darcy. "Lady Margaret Sarah Caldwell." She paused to gather her thoughts. "Second daughter of Viscount Penworth. Surely you have heard of her. Of me."

"Good God!" Darcy exclaimed. "Do you claim to be Lady Margaret? Everyone assumes her to be dead. Lady Margaret disappeared at least two months ago."

The lady's hands trembled, and tears pooled in her eyes. "On June 3...the day...Mr. Vincent and I raced toward the border." A sob swallowed her words, and Wotherspoon slid his arm about the woman's shoulders.

Darcy finished the tale. "When the younger of the Earl of Hamby's heirs drove his carriage off the road and into a rain-swollen stream—robbing Lord Hamby of his spare and the older of Hamby's sons of his intended. The incident was in every scandal sheet, as well as in the more legitimate papers."

With tears streaming down her cheeks, Lady Margaret took up the story. "My father and Lord Hamby had come to an agreement when the future earl and I were but children; I was three and Stephen Vincent nine, but I had not yet met Samuel Vincent. Men deride women's belief in love at first sight, but at my sixteenth birthday celebration, I saw Samuel Vincent across a crowded ballroom, and my heart became engaged. For over two years, we denied the attraction. Initially, it was easy because we were rarely in each other's company, but Lord Hamby had insisted on my Presentation, and so my family made the trek to London.

"Stephen resented having to play attendant upon his future bride, so he had passed my companionship to his brother. Things progressed quickly." Her cheeks flushed with color; it would not be politic to admit the nature of her relationship with Mr. Vincent. And although she never said the words, the three gentlemen understood that she and Samuel Vincent had anticipated their love. "We saw no other way from the engagement," she said softly.

Darcy asked, "What happened on the road?"

Her gaze dropped to her intertwined fingers. "We thought ourselves so clever. We realized my father and the Earl would give pursuit, and that they would assume we would journey to Gretna Green. Samuel said we should travel further into Scotland. We would marry before our families could deny us."

Darcy asked incredulously, "Did Hamby truly send a professional tracker after his own son?"

"Samuel had shamed his brother, and the Earl would have none of it. Thinking ourselves safe, we traveled more leisurely once we crossed into Scotland. At the end, Samuel raced toward the nearest village, but Lord Hamby's men had given chase. Samuel saved me when the carriage tumbled after us on the slope. He took the brunt of the coach's weight. It pinned him under the water. I tried to free him, but I could not budge the carriage, and seeking their release, the horses dangerously pawed at the coach. Samuel touched my lips with his fingertips and then shoved me clear of the animals. My dreams destroyed, I permitted the current to carry me downstream. Finally, I caught a limb and pulled myself to freedom." Her gaze returned to Darcy's face. "I knew my parents would force me to marry Stephen if I returned, and I could not spend my life with the brother of the man I loved. I ran. For days. For weeks, I roamed the moor. Taking shelter where I could."

"Is that how you found my sister's horse?" Darcy asked the question to which his cousin wanted to have an answer.

The lady shook her head in the negative. "I still do not hold a memory of how I came to be riding the horse in question, but I shall put my energies to giving you something useful."

Darcy sighed deeply. "Then perhaps we should decide how best to handle the chaos below."

* * *

Elizabeth stared intently at the cottage nestled in the side of the hill. It sat on a plateau, and the craggy slopes held the small building tightly in their grip.

"Be this the one ye dreamed?" Mr. Jacks asked as he pulled up on the gig's reins. When Elizabeth had insisted on searching for this place, Mr. Jacks had agreed to drive her rather than permit Himself's wife to become lost like her sister. He was more familiar with the area than some of the younger Alpin workers were, and he had insisted that he could competently handle the carriage he had chosen for the journey. It had taken them over an hour to reach this deserted area of the moor.

"I believe it is," Elizabeth said distractedly. She stared at the small window on the front of the cottage. "I wish I could see the left side to observe whether there is a window there as well."

Jacks pointed to the rising smoke. "Someone be taking shelter within. Maybe we should be thinking twice before we venture forward," he cautioned. "There be a rough sort roaming the moors, Ma'am."

Elizabeth did not want to turn back. She had vividly dreamed of Georgiana in such a shelter, and she would not leave until she had proved herself wrong. "I mean to know whether Mrs. Fitzwilliam is within," she said as she clamored from the carriage before Jacks could scramble to assist her. She dug in her reticule and pulled out a small pearl-handled pistol, which Darcy had given her on her last birthday. "Bring your musket, Mr. Jacks." Elizabeth began to climb at a steady pace.

The incline was steeper than it appeared. Halfway up, the Scot caught up to her as she stopped to catch her breath. Being enceinte made it more difficult to maintain her momentum. "I see no movement from inside," Jacks observed. "Whoever be within do not know we be coming."

Elizabeth glanced about as she inhaled several deep, steadying breaths. "A person has a good view of the whole valley from here," she said softly.

"Better to keep enemies in check." Jacks supported her step. "Allow me to go first, Mrs. Darcy," he said as he raised his musket higher.

Elizabeth stepped to the side to permit him easier access on the narrow path. Then her eyes caught the slightest of movements near a cluster of scraggily looking trees. "Mr. Jacks, what is that over in the bushes?" Her arm directed the man's sight to the spot.

"Don't know," the man said gruffly, "but we best be finding out. Don't want no surprises." He led the way off the path and down the hill to the shrubbery. As they closed in on the place, he said sharply, "Well, I be." He lowered his gun.

"What is it?" Elizabeth could not see around the man. She stepped further to the right for a better view. "A horse?"

Jacks shot a glance at the cottage. "Not just any horse, Mrs. Darcy, but the one Mr. Hurlbert, or whatever be the scoundrel's name, rode out on right before you and Himself arrived at Alpin."

Elizabeth, too, allowed her eyes to drift to the cottage. "The prayer the Devil answers," she mimicked her husband's favorite saying. She had no doubt that she had found Darcy's sister, but this was an unexpected development. "Lieutenant Wickham is likely inside," she said aloud to confirm her suspicions. She thought of Georgiana and of the number of years Darcy's sister had suffered from the insecurities following her experience with George Wickham. She and Darcy had carefully guarded Georgiana's encounters so there would be no opportunity for Darcy's sister to "accidentally" encounter the man who had once shattered the girl's illusions about romance. Now, Lieutenant Wickham likely had Georgiana cornered and at his mercy. Anger coursed through Elizabeth. "Mr.

Jacks," she ordered, "I want you to take the gig and find Mr. Darcy at the Ayrshire inn from which his last message came. Tell him that I have discovered Lieutenant Wickham's whereabouts, and that the gentleman likely has Mrs. Fitzwilliam with him."

"What be you planning, Ma'am?" Jacks asked suspiciously.

Elizabeth lifted her skirt and began to climb once more. "To keep my husband's worst enemy away from his sister."

Jacks caught up to her. "Himself won't like this, Ma'am. I cannot allow ye to do this alone."

Elizabeth turned on the man. "Mr. Jacks, you are wasting precious time and daylight. I mean to see to Mr. Darcy's sister, and I insist you follow my orders. Lieutenant Wickham is my sister's husband and my former suitor. He is a thief and a womanizer, but he is not a murderer." Elizabeth shoved from her mind the nagging reminder of the man's attack on Darcy just two days prior. "He will not harm me. Obviously, Lieutenant Wickham either is too injured to ride or he has no knowledge of the horse's presence. The animal is not tethered where Lieutenant Wickham might make a quick escape. I shall have the element of surprise and this." She palmed the gun. "But I shall need Mr. Darcy's timely assistance. Now, shall I have the Earl sack you and Mrs. Jacks without a pension or will you do as I ask?"

The man shifted his gaze to the gig. "It likely be two or three hours before yer husband be arriving. Will you be well until then?"

"I have no doubt the time will fly by," Elizabeth said ironically. Again, she began her climb. "Please hurry, Mr. Jacks. Mrs. Fitzwilliam is likely in distress."

"Then I will take the horse and leave you the gig," he said urgently from behind her.

Elizabeth placed her hands on her hips—a defiant stance she had learned from her mother. "Do you imagine that even with our combined strength that you and I could carry either or both of the cottage's occupants down this incline without injuring them or ourselves? I need Mr. Darcy's assistance, and I need it now. Do you understand?"

"What if Mrs. Fitzwilliam not be within?" Jacks protested.

Elizabeth stubbornness laced her tone. "Mr. Darcy's sister is inside that cabin." She gestured to the small, cozy-looking structure. "I know it here. In my heart." Elizabeth touched her bosom. "I know it is true. I shall host no doubts, and neither should you."

Jacks held her gaze for a brief moment before nodding his agreement.

"Then go," she shooed him on his way. "And tether Lieutenant Wickham's horse to that tree. I want to know where it is if I require it."

* * *

"What are you about, Sir?" Her voice rose in apprehension.

Wickham smiled deviously. "I am removing these wet items before they bring on the ague." He flipped the shirt from his body and over his head. "And you are welcome, Mrs. Fitzwilliam, to look your fill."

"How dare you!" Georgiana accused. "You will act as a gentleman or you will leave this moment."

Wickham sat gingerly upon a small stool and removed his boots. "It may not have occurred to you, Mrs. Fitzwilliam, but I no longer take orders from the Darcys." The first boot hit the floor with a loud "thwack." "If my actions offend you, then I suggest that you should be the one to leave."

"You know I cannot do that," Georgiana said petulantly.

Wickham feigned real concern. "How will my leaving dissolve this dilemma? My departure would increase the possibility of my succumbing to a case of the chills. The choice of traipsing about in wet clothing on the damp moors lacks merit," he reasoned. "Yet, if I stay, I will expose you to the seedy side of life." He laughed softly. "I suppose you might cover your eyes for the next eight to twelve hours while my clothes dry."

Georgiana retorted, "Your lack of empathy is noted, Sir."

Wickham snarled, "Why should I care of your weak sensibilities? When have the Darcys ever given a second thought to what happened to your father's godson?"

"Fitzwilliam has repeatedly provided you with a proper living, but like your mother, you have always wanted more than what even a generous spirit would allow." Georgiana recalled her brother once telling Elizabeth, "Old Mr. Wickham's conduct in the discharge of his trust naturally inclined my father to be of service to him, and on George Wickham, who was his godson, his kindness was therefore liberally bestowed." They had not realized that she had taken refuge in the window seat to reread Edward's latest letter. She had not expected Lieutenant Wickham to be the discussion topic between her brother and his wife. They certainly went out of their way to not mention the man before her. "My father supported him at school, and afterward at Cambridge—most important assistance, as his own father, always poor from the extravagance of his wife, would have been unable to give him a gentleman's education." Fitzwilliam and Elizabeth had moved away, but Georgiana had cherished that bit of information because it had not only confirmed how foolishly she had acted in her affairs with Mr. Wickham, but also how fortunate she had been to have a family who loved her enough to forgive her schoolgirl mistakes.

"What do you know of my mother?" Wickham accused. "You were but a child when she passed."

Georgiana wanted to correct his lie. Edward had confided in her—treating Georgiana as an adult in the wake of her failed elopement. It was likely the basis of her growing regard for her cousin. "Mrs. Wickham departed when you were still in the nursery. The lady ran off with a baronet. No one knows what became of her. Old Wickham searched everywhere. There was once a report of her living with an Italian diplomat, but nothing came of it." She recited the gossip, which had surrounded her father's steward, but the look of devastation that flitted across Lieutenant Wickham's face softened her response. "I should not have repeated idle gossip," she said repentantly. "It was incogitant of me to speak out of turn. You are correct, Sir. I have no personal knowledge of your home life before you lost your mother. Nor much of it afterwards."

Wickham stood stiffly, but Georgiana took notice of the defeat in his shoulders. It was a moment she never expected to know. "We have returned to the issue of your feminine frailty." He spoke with renewed contempt. "I am assuming you have looked upon a man's body, and I will not shock you thoroughly." He reached for the buttons along his placket.

Georgiana squeezed her eyes shut. "Lieutenant Wickham!" she gasped.

"What?" he taunted. "There was a time you wished to know me as your husband." He openly chuckled. "I will promise to leave on my small clothes."

"You will leave on more than that, Sir!" Elizabeth's voice filled the cabin with loathing. "Opening that buttonhole shall be the last move you ever make."

Georgiana's eyes shot open. "Elizabeth! She said you would come for me, but I did not believe it possible!"

Wickham eyed the pistol pointing at his chest. "Mrs. Darcy. Kind of you to join us. Welcome, Sister Dearest, to our humble abode."

* * *

One part of her had wanted to sing out in celebration when she had seen Georgiana sitting primly on the small bed, but the window had also revealed a half-naked George Wickham; Elizabeth's instinct to protect those she loved accelerated. Dread filled her as she had edged the cabin's door open far enough to hear Lieutenant Wickham threaten to disrobe before Darcy's sister.

Without considering the best way to handle such a delicate situation, she had charged into the room and had threatened Lieutenant Wickham with the gun she carried. "Georgiana?" Elizabeth said cautiously. At this moment, she thoroughly despised Lieutenant Wickham's devil-may-care attitude. In Meryton, she had known a congenial young man with a pleasing address. Yet, had she really known him? Who was this man who stood bare to the waist before her? Why had he assumed this persona? Could George Wickham truly have a bit of lechery coursing through his veins or was it some sort of show to keep others at arm's length?

"I am well." Georgiana's words refocused Elizabeth's thoughts. "Except that I seem to have a broken ankle."

Despite her need to rush to Georgiana's side, she said, "I assume you will conduct yourself as a gentleman, Lieutenant Wickham," she warned.

"Of course, Sister Dearest, this is all in the family," he said mockingly.

Elizabeth rolled her eyes in exasperation. "If you call me 'Sister Dearest' again or do not cease this absurd mockery, I shall forget that I am a lady and shoot you just to wipe the smile from your lips."

Wickham's eyes widened. "As you say, Mrs. Darcy."

"And cover up," she gestured to his nakedness.

He started to protest, but Georgiana finished Elizabeth's thoughts. "With this." Her sister extended a small blanket to the room's other occupant.

Graciously, Wickham offered a nod of gratitude and took the coverlet from Georgiana's hands. "Much appreciated, Mrs. Fitzwilliam," he mumbled.

Elizabeth motioned him away from Georgiana. "Could you see to the fire, Lieutenant Wickham?" she ordered as she came to stand between the man and Darcy's sister.

"Lieutenant Wickham claims an injury to his ribs," Georgiana said softly from behind her.

Elizabeth eyed her brother in marriage carefully. It would not surprise her if the man feigned an encumbrance to gain Georgiana's sympathies. "Then please have a seat, Lieutenant Wickham. I shall see to Mrs. Fitzwilliam first; that is, unless you are in extreme pain."

"The pain is intense," he said with his usual flippancy, "but never let it be said that I put my needs above a lady's."

"No one could ever think such dastardly thoughts of you," Elizabeth said sarcastically. She handed the gun to Georgiana. "If I were you, Sir, I would attempt a tone that rings truer than the one you have assumed." She crossed to the still-open door. Stepping outside, she returned with three chunks of wood to add to the fire he had already started. As she bent to stir the flames and catch the kindling, she continued, "I am well aware of your attempt on Mr. Darcy's life..."

"Elizabeth!" Georgiana gasped.

She glanced to the girl. "Your brother suffered no harm," she assured Georgiana. Elizabeth stood and dusted off her hands. "But Mr. Joseph nearly lost his life because of Lieutenant Wickham's selfish mantra. I am not likely to forgive the pain he has brought to poor Lydia, to my family, to the Darcys, and now to the Josephs." She leaned down menacingly over the man and whispered close to his ear. "Please give me an excuse to shoot you, Brother Dearest. I have built up an arsenal of resentment where you are concerned." Standing tall once more, she turned her attention to Darcy's sister. "Now, Georgiana, permit me to see to your care." Elizabeth knelt before the girl. "I expect you to avert your eyes, Lieutenant Wickham," she said over her shoulder.

"And if I choose to ignore your request?" The man had lost some of his sauciness. Undoubtedly, he required her assistance, and he would not jeopardize what goodwill she was willing to provide him. Plus, as she was well aware, Lieutenant Wickham was a gambler. He would play the hand dealt him and bluff his way to win the pot.

Without looking at him, Elizabeth said deviously, "When Mr. Darcy presented me the gun Mrs. Fitzwilliam now holds, he obtained a similar one for his sister. I am ashamed to say that my husband's sister exceeds my skills in hitting a target consistently." Elizabeth squeezed Georgiana's calf through the girl's gown as a warning not to give away her deception. In truth, Georgiana feared guns. Her sister's willingness to accept the one Elizabeth had placed in Georgiana's hand was a true testament to the girl's desperation. *I see your bet and raise the ante, Lieutenant Wickham,* Elizabeth thought.

A long pause said that Wickham considered his next move. "You are quite good at this game, Mrs. Darcy," he said with respect.

"I learned my lessons well, Lieutenant Wickham. Now, please show Mrs. Fitzwilliam the respect she deserves."

Chapter 20

ELIZABETH RAISED HER EYES to meet the deep blue of Georgiana's. "I have never been so happy to see anyone." She was on her knees before the girl. Instantly, Georgiana caught her up in a strong embrace.

"I had lost hope," Georgiana whispered.

Elizabeth caressed the girl's cheek. "You should know that neither your brother nor I would rest until we found you."

"Where is Fitzwilliam?" Tears began to trek across Georgiana's cheeks.

"Your brother will arrive shortly," Elizabeth said softly. She glanced to where Lieutenant Wickham obviously eavesdropped on their conversation. "As crazy as it sounds, I had a vision of where I might find you. When I described this place, Mr. Jacks located a groom who recognized my sketch of the cottage's exterior."

Georgiana grinned widely. "I believe it wholeheartedly. I had dreams of someone tending to my needs, and I imagined it was you. Actually, at first, I thought it was my mother."

Elizabeth wiped away the girl's tears. "Who says it was not Lady Anne? I am certain that the former Mrs. Darcy looks down fondly upon her children." She kissed Georgiana's cheek. "Now, allow me to tend your ankle; otherwise, the Major General shall have my head if you suffer further."

Georgiana caught her breath on a sob. "Edward is here?"

"Oh, yes, the man is quite adamant about finding you quickly." Elizabeth teased, "You must do something to calm our cousin's surly nature." She winked at Darcy's sister before lifting Georgiana's skirt to examine the girl's ankle. However, she could not wipe the smile from your words when she noted how Georgiana sat taller and how the girl unconsciously tried to straighten her hair. "I expect both the Major General and Mr. Darcy shall shower you with affection." Elizabeth braced Georgiana's foot on her lap. "This is quite unique. However did you conjure up the idea?" She carefully turned the girl's leg to admire the makeshift splint.

Georgiana giggled nervously. "I really do not remember how this came about. I woke from a dream in which I had tended my leg to find I had broken the chair and tied the rundles to either side of my ankle. Did I do it properly?"

"I would say that it was an exemplary effort." Elizabeth untied a few of the cloth strips that Georgiana had, obviously, torn from her petticoat. She retied them carefully. "As it shall take some time to return you to Alpin Hall, it is probably best to leave your creative medicine in place. It shall assist the bone in healing faster. Do you have other injuries?"

Georgiana shook her head in the negative. "A few bruises which have already turned lighter in their healing and more scrapes than I care to mention. A major dent in my pride."

"I assure you, Mrs. Fitzwilliam, that your brother has enough pride for the two of you," Wickham said sarcastically from behind them.

Elizabeth gently returned Georgiana's foot to the floor. Turning toward where Lieutenant Wickham sat with his back to them, she picked up a torn sheet from the bed and came to stand beside him. Motioning for the man to remove the blanket, she sat about examining a bruised area under his left arm. Enjoying bringing the man a bit of physical pain, she pressed a bit harder than necessary against his injury. Smiling sweetly, she said, "So you believe Mr. Darcy has too much pride?"

Wickham winced as she poked the swollen area below his left nipple. "You once said...the same...of the man," he countered.

Elizabeth used her thumb to massage the multicolored area. "You speak the truth, Lieutenant Wickham. I once thought Mr. Darcy was eaten up with pride. Yet, now my husband's pride does not offend me so much as pride often does, because there is an excuse for it. One cannot wonder that so very fine a young man, with family, fortune, everything in his favor, should think highly of himself. If I may so express it, he has a right to be proud. And despite what you may accuse, Mr. Darcy has never been idle. He has nearly doubled Pemberley's wealth."

"I could easily forgive Mr. Darcy's pride if he had not mortified mine," Wickham said harshly.

"Pride," Georgiana observed from where she remained on the cot, "is a very common failing. By all that I have ever read, I am convinced that it is very common indeed; that human nature is particularly prone to it, and that there are very few of us who do not cherish a feeling of self-complacency on the score of some quality or other, real or imaginary. Vanity and pride are different things, though the words are often used synonymously. A person may be proud without being vain. Pride relates more to our opinions of ourselves; vanity to what we would have others think of us. I would pronounce Fitzwilliam as possessing pride."

Wickham had turned his head to watch her carefully. "I suppose that means that you would pronounce me vain, Mrs. Fitzwilliam," he said scornfully.

Georgiana raised her chin defiantly. "Those are your words, Lieutenant Wickham."

Elizabeth bit back her cheer. Georgiana had suffered so after the girl's botched elopement with the man. Mr. Wickham had recommended himself to Georgiana, whose affectionate heart had retained a strong impression of his kindness to her as a child, so much so that she was persuaded to believe herself in love, and to consent to the elopement. But fifteen and unable to support the idea of grieving and offending a brother whom she looked up to almost as a father, Georgiana had acknowledged the whole of the matter to Darcy. Elizabeth's husband had protected his sister without public exposure of Georgiana's credit and feelings. Yet, even with the girl's shame hidden from everyone but Darcy and Edward Fitzwilliam, it was many years before Georgiana would willingly meet another's eyes. Darcy had required Elizabeth's assistance in handling a romantic-hearted girl straight from the schoolroom. Over the past three years, she and Georgiana had shared every female confidence possible. They were more than sisters in marriage. "Permit me to wrap your ribs, Lieutenant Wickham," Elizabeth said as she distracted him from his fixed glare on Georgiana's countenance. She pressed the heel of her hand against an especially tender spot on his chest. Taking the sheet and tearing it into strips, she began to tightly wrap Wickham's ribcage. "There. That should assist in the healing, but you should seek a surgeon's opinion as soon as possible."

Testing his movements, Wickham stood slowly. "I am eternally grateful for your *tender* care, Mrs. Darcy, but I will take my leave of you lovely ladies." He reached for his still-damp shirt. "You require private time to reunite, and I cannot imagine that Darcy will approve of my accompanying you and Mrs. Fitzwilliam."

Elizabeth straightened and began to clear away the mess. She tossed the pieces of cloth into the fire and casually reached for the water pitcher. "We shall take our loss with a saddened heart," she taunted. Finally, she paused in her tidying. "Might I ask, Lieutenant Wickham, how you planned to escape our company?"

Wickham stirred uncomfortably. He considered carefully before speaking. "Although I respect your and Mrs. Fitzwilliam's newfound proficiency in weaponry, I am well aware that neither of you has the desire to shoot an unarmed man. It is not within your natures." He slipped the shirt over his head and began to stuff the ends of it into his breeches. "Besides, I do not believe you would purposely create widowhood for Mrs. Wickham," he said confidently.

"You are likely correct, Sir," Elizabeth observed. "I doubt if Lydia would relish the idea of wearing black for a year. Although I must admit the idea of enjoying my sister's company on a regular basis does have its merits. I can hardly extend an invitation to Pemberley to the man who tried to kill my husband," she said tartly.

Wickham chuckled ironically. He resumed his seat and worked his feet into the water-saturated boots. "I understand your objection, Mrs. Darcy." He stood again. "I do not suppose there is any chance you rode astride?"

"Astride, Lieutenant Wickham?" Elizabeth said coyly. "Actually, I traveled by gig. I have forsaken equestrian pleasures for the time being." She glanced over her shoulder at Georgiana. "I have not told Fitzwilliam. I wanted to find you first. I am enceinte again. Bennet will have to share his father's attention with a younger sibling."

Georgiana's face lit with delight. "Oh, Lizzy, that is wonderful. We shall raise our children together."

Elizabeth was instantly in Georgiana's arms. "Edward will be beside himself with happiness. The Countess will ask the bishop to celebrate your child's christening."

On the other side of the room, Wickham cleared his throat loudly. "I hate to be the damp sponge in this family reunion, but I require a horse or a carriage."

Elizabeth said with a great deal of enthusiasm, "That may be a problem, Lieutenant Wickham. I sent Mr. Jacks with the gig to find Mr. Darcy. Until my husband and his cousin arrive, we shall have to make the best of our situation. Of course, I suppose you could set off across the moor on foot, but as it shall be dark soon. I would not recommend it."

* * *

Edward's patience with the situation had worn thin. "Could we not settle this madness? My wife remains on the moor, and I mean to find her," he said harshly.

"I have instructed Weir to release each of those held below. He has moved them into the smaller bedchambers and has arranged food and clothing," Darcy said. "Those who fought in Lady Wotherspoon's behalf are locked away in the cells they once protected."

"A taste of the horrors they inflicted on others," Edward said ironically.

Darcy smiled wryly. "A fit ending." He gestured to where Wotherspoon spoke softly to Lady Margaret. "We cannot hide what has happened here. Too many people possess a knowledge of Lady Wotherspoon's evil to mask the events."

Edward said softly. "What do we do with Wotherspoon and the woman? Lady Margaret has, obviously, suffered enough—first with Samuel Vincent's death and then as Normanna's prisoner. She is enceinte. Has no husband. Has been embroiled in one scandal after another. I am not certain the lady can withstand another. Not in her condition."

"Lord Wotherspoon appears to hold Lady Margaret in affection," Darcy observed.

"Are you suggesting that we permit Wotherspoon to escape?" Edward said suspiciously.

Darcy leaned closer to maintain privacy. "Wotherspoon would be termed completely inept in his handling of his mother's lunacy, but he attempted to protect those taken against their wills, as well as salvaging his family's legacy. I cannot fault his heart—just his methods."

Edward said with disgust, "*Inept* is too kind of a word for the gentleman's efforts."

Darcy spoke with sympathy for what his cousin had witnessed during the war. "I disagree. Wotherspoon treated the prisoners with kindness."

"Kindness?" Edward hissed. "I was in one of those cells. Filth. Darkness. Starvation. Chained to the wall!"

Darcy countered, "Under Lady Wotherspoon, it was as you have said, but His Lordship made changes. He permitted the prisoners to reclaim their lives. He did it in small increments to allow those kept below time to resume their dignities. Then he bestowed a settlement on each in order that he might rebuild his life. You know better than I the horrors those held as prisoners suffer. You have seen it first hand. But you have also seen how those men continue to suffer when they return to society. I do not know whether Wotherspoon's method could prove kinder, but the man considered how those who had experienced the worst of Lady Wotherspoon's evil would resume their daily lives. His actions were not malicious."

"If it is as you say," Edward conceded half-heartedly, "then what do you advise?"

"We *suggest* that Wotherspoon and Lady Margaret retreat to the Continent. The man has evidently proposed previously," Darcy reasoned.

"I concede to your insights," Edward said grudgingly. "I will oversee what happens below stairs. You should speak to the couple."

* * *

"How did you manage to reach this cottage?" Elizabeth asked Georgiana. She ignored Lieutenant Wickham's grumblings and mutterings as she tended to Darcy's sister. She had unbraided Georgiana's hair and had combed it with her fingers.

"Everything is a blur. When I ran from the truth of the Countess's letter, I meant to seek the ruins of a medieval castle I knew in the area. I had visited it several times since coming to Kirkconnel. It is a place I knew I could be alone with my thoughts." As she had always done with Georgiana, Elizabeth simply listened. She did not judge or put her own interpretation on the tale. She allowed Georgiana to explore her own feelings. "When Bracken stumbled, I felt I was in a race with a terror I could not see, but one that existed nevertheless. Does that sound odd?"

Georgiana turned her eyes to Elizabeth as if she expected censure, but Elizabeth busied herself with smoothing the tangles from the girl's hair. "The moors hold many dangers. Who is to say what is real and what is not. If you believed someone or something pursued you, then so do I. You have never told me an untruth."

Georgiana's eyes filled with tears. "Thank you, Elizabeth," she murmured. "Even after Bracken galloped away, I ran, but my foot caught in a rabbit hole, and I went down. When I first woke in this cabin, I could not recall how I had come upon it, but over the days since, I have remembered bits and pieces of how it happened. There was a woman. Pretty and fair. She found me on the moor and assisted me to this place."

"The same woman of whom you spoke earlier?" Elizabeth asked.

Georgiana noted that Lieutenant Wickham had abandoned his plan to leave and now listened to her tale. "At first, I believed so, but my rescuer left me to find assistance. She never returned. The woman who saw me through those early days spoke of Fitzwilliam and Edward, and even of you, Lizzy; and she ordered me not to forsake hope. She told me I was resourceful and strong. The lady taught me how to find food and how to protect my ankle."

Elizabeth slid her arms around Georgiana from behind. She nuzzled the girl's cheek. "Your mother," Fitzwilliam's wife whispered into Georgiana's ear. "Your guardian angel."

"What is that you are saying?" Wickham demanded. "What is it you are talking of? What are you telling Mrs. Fitzwilliam? Let me hear what it is."

Elizabeth released her, but the feeling of love remained. Georgiana raised her eyes to the man she once had allowed to define her self-confidence. With Fitzwilliam and Edward and Elizabeth, she had discovered a woman she so much preferred to that foolish girl. Mimicking Elizabeth's earlier tone, she said teasingly, "We speak of angels and of the Devil, Lieutenant Wickham, and whether we would recognize either if he appeared before us."

* * *

Darcy approached Normanna's master and Lady Margaret. "We must speak honestly."

Wotherspoon stiffened. "Of course, Mr. Darcy. It be time to summon the magistrate."

Darcy gestured to a private alcove. They had bound Lady Wotherspoon, but he had noted how the woman had quieted when Lady Margaret told her tale. Darcy would not have the house's mistress know of what he would suggest. "Keep your voices low," he cautioned the couple as they settled where he still could observe what occurred in the main hall. "As you say, Wotherspoon, we must inform the authorities."

The man glanced to where his mother fought against her ropes. "It is to be expected," he said with resignation.

Darcy cleared his throat. "I had another thought."

Wotherspoon's brows met in a deep frown. "I fear I do not understand, Mr. Darcy. Will you or will you not announce Normanna's shame to the world?"

"The crimes perpetrated by Lady Wotherspoon will become the business of the Scottish government, but to my knowledge, the head of the Wotherspoon family would have known nothing of what has transpired under Normanna's roof, as the gentleman in question has taken himself off to the Mediterranean to grieve over his father's passing."

Wotherspoon's countenance held his surprise. "You would permit me to save face?"

"I would," Darcy said flatly. "I am not certain at this point what tale I will give the authorities, nor can I warrant how much of your name I will be able to salvage. Too many people know what has occurred under your mother's reign to maintain your family's honor completely. Yet, I will promise to soften the public's opinion of your involvement in what has occurred." He turned to the woman. "Lady Margaret, if you desire to return to the safety of Viscount Penworth's home, I will have someone to escort you."

"In my condition, I doubt that I would be welcomed," she observed. "I shall find my own way. However, if you could send a discreet note to my mother advising her of my continued health, I would appreciate it. The Viscountess deserves to know her youngest daughter lives."

"As you wish, my Lady, but perhaps I could send her news of a happier nature. A note to explain that her daughter has found a man she esteems and with whom she intends to begin a family."

Wotherspoon caught Lady Margaret's hand. "Mr. Darcy is correct. Marry me, Margaret. We will abandon our shame and build a life elsewhere. I will devote my days to making you happy."

Lady Margaret shot a glance at Darcy, but before giving them their privacy, he warned, "I have instructed my men to wait six hours before they ride for the authorities. Not one second more. Am I understood, Wotherspoon?"

"Absolutely, Mr. Darcy. You will hear no more from me on the matter."

"I wish you happiness, Wotherspoon. Lady Margaret."

* * *

"So, I am the Devil. Is that how it is, Mrs. Fitzwilliam. I bear the label of the ultimate sinner. You think yourself so far above the rest of us," Wickham charged. "You and the Darcys and the Matlocks and the Fitzwilliams; and, you are nothing but a spoiled, insecure girl."

Georgiana felt Elizabeth's hand slip into hers. Her brother's wife gave Georgiana permission to exorcise her own demons. She could return to Lieutenant Wickham all those retorts that she had concocted over the years.

"Your insecurity does you no credit, Georgiana. It fools no one into believing you humble," he persisted. "Your insecurities are pride in disguise."

Georgiana squared her shoulders. "I admit to my insecurities, Lieutenant Wickham. At times, I have acted quite imprudently, but my mistakes were those of young woman finding her way in the world. How will God judge you, Sir? How will our Maker judge a man who requires the world's approval? Who cannot accept his lot and would steal another's identity? Who accounts his failures at another's hands? Who cannot bear his own reflection in the mirror?"

"And whence comes this expertise on the follies of man, Mrs. Fitzwilliam? What makes you an authority on my life?" he asked caustically.

Georgiana squeezed Elizabeth's hand in a moment of solidarity. "I have said previously that your life remains a mystery to me, and I should not judge you. When the Israelites were given into Midian, the Bible says that Gideon cried out to God. 'Oh my Lord, if the Lord be with us, why then is all this befallen us? And where be all his miracles, which our fathers told us of, saying, Did not the Lord bring us up from Egypt? But now the Lord hath forsaken us, and delivered us into the hands of the Midianites.'"

"What is your point, Georgiana?" he demanded.

"As Gideon found, it is easy to blame others for our failures. When I returned to Pemberley after our aborted elopement, I blamed you for my shattered dreams. For my near ruination. Even for your quick desertion of a young girl who had placed her trust in your words of love. Yet, I found an aberration of my own making. To emerge from my arrogance, I had to face the knowledge that God sees our strengths rather than our weaknesses. The weaknesses are our domain. The faults we see in others are often found within our own souls. When I thought you had betrayed my trust, I was slow to admit that I had accepted your attentions because I could not accept my own insensibility. I had sought my identity in someone else's eyes. Humility requires us to not place ourselves above others. There are no exemptions in life—only arrogance. We bring judgment upon ourselves. My advice, such as it is, suggests that instead of ignoring one's critics, it is better to embrace them, for they speak the truth. As the Bible says in Matthew 7, 'Cast out first the beam out of thine eye, and then thou will see clearly to cast out the mote of thy brother's eye.'"

* * *

"Jasper, what are you doing here?" Darcy asked tersely. "I thought you were guarding the gatehouse?"

"This came for you, Sir. A messenger delivered it from the inn. I thought it important. It is from Mr. Jacks."

Darcy nodded his acceptance. "You did well, Jasper." He rarely reprimanded his men, but the current craziness had had him on edge.

"What is it, Darcy?" Edward appeared at his side.

"A message from Jacks," he said as he stepped closer to a wall sconce for light.

"News of Georgiana?" Edward asked. His eyes followed Darcy's every move.

Darcy unfolded the paper and scanned the short note. "Jacks has word of Lieutenant Wickham's whereabouts." He read further. "Damn! Elizabeth has confronted the man." He turned toward the side entrance. "I must leave."

"Take my horse. It stands in wait," Edward called after him. "I will see to the final details and then follow."

"Jacks is at the inn," Darcy called over his shoulder.

"Jasper," Edward instructed Darcy's footman. "Here is what I expect you and Weir to do..."

* * *

He had bidden Wotherspoon and Lady Margaret farewell and had given Weir and Jasper specific orders on when to contact the magistrate and what to tell the man of the Fitzwilliam family's involvement in capturing Lady Wotherspoon and her cohorts. Now, Edward rode with a purpose. He had checked at the inn to find that Darcy had followed Mr. Jacks's gig to an unknown destination. Edward knew he must overtake his cousin. He had read the note shoved into his hand as Darcy raced from Normanna. If Mrs. Darcy truly had located Lieutenant Wickham, Darcy's former friend could lose his life and Darcy himself his freedom. Edward did not think the world would regret the passing of George Wickham. For what the man had intended to do to Georgiana, Edward would gladly dispatch Wickham to hell himself, but he would not have Darcy tried for murder. If Wickham had laid one finger on Mrs. Darcy, it would be difficult to control his cousin's response.

He followed the well-marked road. He and Darcy had always carried several packets of flour in a cloth handkerchief in their saddle rolls. They had learned the trick from an old poacher on Pemberley's grounds. The man had convinced the two excessively curious boys that they could mark their trails and never become lost. Over the years, the cousins had explored several expanses of the Peak District with no qualms regarding the terrain. The flour would mark the way with a powdery arrow.

Yet, it was not Normanna's secrets or Darcy's troubles with Lieutenant Wickham, which continued to plague Edward's mind. Instead, it was the disappointment he had experienced when the unknown woman in Wotherspoon's care had proven to be Lady Margaret rather than Georgiana. The woman's possession of Georgiana's locket and horse said that Lady Margaret had encountered Georgiana, but the lady claimed no memory of the incident. And as much as he hated to admit it, Edward believed her. The shock of all the girl had experienced would be enough to drive the truth from her mind. "Oh, Georgie," he groaned as he pulled up on the reins of Darcy's gelding to check another of his cousin's markings. "Where are you, Sweetheart?"

* * *

Darcy grumbled, "Mr. Jacks, are you certain that this is where you left Mrs. Darcy?"

They knelt at the bottom of a steep hill. "When last I saw yer missus, she be climbing that path." Jacks pointed to a tethered horse. "And that be the animal yer Lieutenant Wickham stole from the Alpin stables."

Darcy examined the area once more for possible intruders. Could Wickham have made "friends" who would offer protection? He doubted Jacks would be of much use if Darcy had to lead an assault on the building. He certainly did not want to walk into a trap. If Wickham was within, he could be lying in wait to kill Darcy.

"Mrs. Darcy dreamed that Mrs. Fitzwilliam be inside," Jacks shared.

"She what?" Darcy's head snapped around to glare at the caretaker.

Jacks backed away from Darcy's anger. "I thought I had explained that. Mrs. Darcy wakes up from a sleep, and she describes this place. One of the grooms knows of it, and yer missus be determined."

Darcy rolled his eyes heavenward. "She always is." With that, he started the climb. "When my cousin arrives, tell him we may have found my sister."

Chapter 21

"AS WE HAVE REACHED AN IMPASSE," Wickham said bitterly, "I will bid you ladies adieu." He picked up his gloves; he had lost his hat when the horse had thrown him. "Thank you, Mrs. Darcy, for your nursing efforts. I fully understand the true benevolence behind them. When you see Mrs. Wickham, please explain the situation to her. I fear my wife will not take well to the idea of my leaving her behind, but I have confidence that you will find a way of convincing Lydia that my actions are for the best."

"You mean to leave my sister a widow's existence, but without the option of seeking another union?" Elizabeth asked incredulously.

Wickham winced when he moved too quickly. "What would you have me do? My hanging from the gallows would, obviously, free Mrs. Wickham to remarry, but, on a personal level, I find that option less than appealing," he said. With an aristocratic nod of his head, he turned to Georgiana. "My current misfortunes prove that your confessing our elopement plans to your brother was very astute. I am certain that realization will give you comfort." To Elizabeth, he said, "I assume you will not hold me prisoner if I decide to walk away from this abode."

"If I thought it would solve your dilemma and, therefore, save my sister from anguish, I would detain you until Mr. Darcy's arrival, but I cannot see how your presence shall bring anything but complications. Go with God, Lieutenant Wickham," Elizabeth said softly.

Georgiana shook her head as if disagreeing with Wickham's decision. "Perhaps this time, you should consider what is best for others and permit yourself to experience giving, instead of receiving."

Wickham gave her a bittersweet smile before he wistfully replied, "Oh, Georgiana, I wish it were that easy. There are too many collapsed bridges, and I have no skills to repair them, but I do appreciate your compassion. The Major General has won the purest of hearts. Perhaps..." he began, but then thought better of it. "I wish you both happy." Elizabeth stood as if to delay his departure so Wickham quickly reached for the door and swung it wide. "Au revoir, Ladies."

* * *

Darcy had run up the steep hillside without concerning himself with the pebbles tumbling down its curved slope. Nor had he given a thought to Lieutenant Wickham's knowledge of his presence. His mind held only one image: George Wickham accosting Elizabeth. He possessed no doubt that Lieutenant Wickham would take advantage of Elizabeth. He had witnessed his former foe manhandling her in Pemberley's drawing room, and reports existed of the man's heavy hand with Elizabeth's sister. And now, his Elizabeth had placed herself in Lieutenant Wickham's way.

Reaching for the gun he had carried earlier in their assault on Normanna Hall, Darcy wondered how his life had come to this moment. Was he not supposed to be at Pemberley? Making love to his wife? Contentedly raising a brood of children? Living the life of a country gentleman? Instead, he fought with Canibales, searched the Scottish countryside for his missing sister, and scaled an incredibly steep upland to fight with his long-time enemy over Darcy's excessively obstinate wife. If it were not so extraordinarily serious, he might have had a good laugh at his own expense. Yet, real life, he had found, played stranger than fiction.

As he reached the plateau upon which the cabin sat nestled into the hillside, he would have preferred a moment to catch his breath before having to meet Lieutenant Wickham, but the cottage's door swung wide, and his forever foe, literally, walked into Darcy's grasp.

Giving the man a shove, Darcy drove Wickham backward until they slammed hard against the cabin's rear wall. Without hesitation, Darcy lifted his fist and smashed it into Wickham's jaw. "I should kill you and free the world of another piece of dung," he growled as he landed a second punch in Wickham's gut.

Even if Mr. Jacks had not told him that Elizabeth had set her mind on investigating this place, Darcy would have known she was in the room. It had been that way from the moment he had entered the assembly hall in Meryton. As he had crossed the crowded room at Bingley's side, he had become aware of her eyes on him. The whole room had silenced upon their entrance, and Darcy had known from experience that every fawning mama and blushing innocent had carefully assessed his and Bingley's separate fortunes. Yet, it had been Elizabeth's gaze that he had engaged. Briefly, they had held one another's eyes before they had both looked away. Later, he had admitted to his cousin that he had fallen in love with the future Mrs. Darcy with that brief glance.

Yet, knowing Elizabeth was in the room and having her, literally, hanging from his upraised fist were two different realities. "No! Do not kill him!" she pleaded.

Wide-eyed and trembling with anger, he hissed, "Give me a reason why I should not dispense with my family's darkest shadow."

She held fast, but she said with tears in her eyes. "Because I shall not see you tried for murder, and because he is my sister's husband."

For an elongated moment, Darcy searched his wife's countenance for some unknown detail that kept from him. A secret. It was there for a brief second before Elizabeth brought it under control, but he had seen it nonetheless. Gently, he lowered his arm to set her feet squarely on the floor. He released Wickham, and the backbiter slid like a rag doll down the wall. Darcy immediately forgot about the rascal. Instead, he caught Elizabeth to him. "Do not ever..." he rasped as he buried his face in his wife's hair. His arms clutched her to him, and he relaxed into the sensation of Elizabeth's body aligned with his.

"Fitzwilliam." A soft melodic voice called to him from across the room. Raising his head, he glanced toward the sound, but his body resisted what his mind had recognized. His maleness wished to remain with Elizabeth, but his brain won out.

"Georgiana." He released Elizabeth slowly as the realization rocked him. To his wife, he said, "You found her," but he was moving toward his sister. "You are the most beautiful sight I have ever witnessed."

He was reaching for his sister when his wife ordered, "Wait!" Darcy stumbled to a halt. "Wait? Whatever for?"

"Georgiana has a broken ankle," Elizabeth smiled through her words. "I imagine a brother who has paced the floors in worry would pull his sister to her feet and swing her around with happiness upon finding her well."

Darcy's lips twitched. "As much as I adore you, Elizabeth Darcy, there are moments that I would love to turn you over my knee for your insolent tongue."

He knelt before his sister. On his knees, he rocked Georgiana in the safety of his loving arms. "I feared the worst," he whispered into her ear as his hands searched his sister's face and arms to assure himself of her presence.

"As did I." Georgiana clung to him. "But the Voice told me to believe."

"Voice?" For an explanation, Darcy glanced over his shoulder to Elizabeth.

"Your sister's guardian angel," she confirmed as she joined them in a group embrace. "In her despair and pain, Georgiana turned to God, and He sent his angel to protect her."

Georgiana touched Darcy's cheek. "I thought it to be Elizabeth, but the Voice said I had to be patient and to wait for Lizzy's arrival."

Elizabeth whispered in Darcy's ear as she turned her face into his shoulder. "Your mother. Lady Anne."

Darcy's eyebrow rose in disbelief, but he kept his comments to himself. "I am thankful for whatever kept you safe." He kissed Georgiana's temple.

She accepted his gesture before her eyes returned to the still-open doorway. "Where is Edward?" she asked with disappointment.

* * *

He had followed Darcy's hastily marked trail and had easily discovered Alpin's overseer tending to two horses and the gig at the bottom of a good-sized incline leading to what appeared in the moonlight to be a reiver's cottage. What he had not expected was to hear Jacks announce that not only had Mrs. Darcy located Lieutenant Wickham's hiding place, but the lady had likely discovered Mrs. Fitzwilliam, as well.

Just the mention of the possibility of Lieutenant Wickham intimidating Georgiana had sent him scurrying up the hill, often clawing at the loose gravel as he reached out to maintain his balance. He had never cared for the way George Wickham had weaseled his way into Old Darcy's life. How the man had tried to insinuate himself into Darcy's place. How Wickham had taken advantage—first at school, but then more venomously with Georgiana. Edward had thought the family might lose her. To her core, Georgiana had felt the shame of her actions. He had spent countless hours counseling and comforting her. Hopefully, not for naught.

Edward, as he had sat in the mud and the blood of Waterloo, had considered the years when Georgiana had been most vulnerable. Had his intimate feelings for her originated when he had held a weeping fifteen-year-old in his embrace? He would acknowledge that only in her presence had he ever experienced the feeling of finally being cleansed of the harsh smell of blood, which constantly plagued him. When he had returned to Derbyshire this past Christmas, a vibrant young woman had met him at Pemberley's door, and he was lost to her perfection. He would not permit Wickham's baseness to destroy all she had become.

As he reached the still-open door, he heard her say, "Where is Edward?"

"Here," he announced as he stepped across the stoop. Out of his eye's corner, he noticed the slumped over form of Lieutenant Wickham stir to life. He also observed how Darcy and Elizabeth retreated from the figure on the cot. There in all her glory sat the woman he loved more than life. He gazed upon the countenance he had feared never to see again, and desire reared its head. "Georgie," he murmured before crossing the room in three long strides.

He dropped to his knees before her. "Thank God," he said on a rasp, his happiness complete in that moment. He pulled her toward him until he heard Elizabeth caution, "Careful." Edward froze. He cupped Georgiana's chin in his large palm. "Are you injured?"

"Badly bruised," she admitted.

"Her ankle." Again, Mrs. Darcy's voice cut through the pure bliss of looking upon his wife's countenance.

Edward raised Georgiana's skirt carefully. "What have we here?" He examined the makeshift dressing carefully. "Is this device of your making, Mrs. Darcy?" he asked over his shoulder.

Elizabeth's pure joy played through her words. "While you and Mr. Darcy were skulking about the countryside, our Georgiana devised her own rescue. All I did was to provide a tightening of the strips about her ankle. Our girl has been quite ingenious."

Edward kissed Georgiana's temple before lowering her skirt. "I always knew my wife possessed more than just a beautiful countenance." He tenderly caressed her chin.

Darcy playfully whispered in Elizabeth's ear, "A gentleman never skulks," before saying, "We are both blessed with remarkable women. Yet, neither should have encountered Lieutenant Wickham on her own," he chastised.

"In my defense," Georgiana said tartly from Edward's side, "I did not chose to greet Lieutenant Wickham under any circumstance, and, especially, not such a dire one."

"And although I perhaps stumbled into a hornet's nest, at least, I brought Delilah with me," his wife countered.

Darcy rose in amusement. "Where is Delilah?"

"Here." Georgiana grinned widely as she uncovered the pistol hidden in her gown's folds.

Edward chortled. "Delilah is a pearl-handled pistol? Where is Sampson?" he asked with an all-knowing smirk.

"In my boot," Darcy confessed. He supported Wickham to the stool Elizabeth shoved his way. "If you move a hair, I will shoot you in both knees," he threatened.

Edward stood. "If you can tolerate it, I would return you to Alpin Hall tonight," he said to Georgiana. "I will not rest easily until you have been seen by a physician."

"I cannot descend the hill," Georgiana said softly.

"You may do so in your husband's arms," Edward assured. "And if I fail, you have a brother who would attempt to walk on water to save you."

"You will not fail," Georgiana assured. "You have never failed me."

* * *

Darcy strategized, "We will place the women in the gig with Mr. Jacks. Elizabeth, you will assure that Georgiana's ankle sustains no further injury. We are perhaps an hour from Alpin, but at night, it will take longer."

Wickham stirred. "And what of me? Can I hope that you will turn your head and permit me to find my own way?" he said with his last stand of defiance.

"It is not likely that you will ever be free of me," Darcy snapped. "As I am to never know the pleasure of our relationship's end." He took the pistol from Georgiana's grasp and returned it to his wife. "Keep it close," he ordered. "As for you, Sir," he directed his comments to Wickham, "you will return with us to Alpin until I decide your fate."

"Do you expect me to walk behind the gig?" Wickham sarcastically asked. "It is not likely that the carriage will hold four passengers, and I cannot imagine that either you or the Major General will wish to share your seat with me."

Edward snarled, "I would not share a cup of tea with the likes of you."

Elizabeth asked softly, "With your injury, are you capable of riding a horse, Lieutenant?"

"What injury?" Darcy asked suspiciously.

Elizabeth slid her hand into her husband's. "I wrapped Lieutenant Wickham's ribs. He was thrown from his horse."

Darcy's brow knitted. "*You* treated the lieutenant's injury?"

Elizabeth moved closer. "I could hardly permit Georgiana to do so." She allowed the importance of what she said to soften Darcy's irritation. He nodded his understanding. They would speak more of this in private.

"Pardon me for interrupting these tender exchanges, but the issue of whether I can ride remains on the table," he said with renewed contempt. "*If* I possessed a horse, I could stay ahorse," he declared.

Elizabeth doused the fire with the bucket of water. "We should send supplies to restock this but and ben," she told Darcy. "If our sister had not found bread and fresh water, she would not have survived this ordeal, and the place requires new linen and furnishings. A future traveler will sing our praises."

"I will see to it." His wife clearly had a secret she kept from them all. Her tone was a familiar one. It spoke of some mischief she would practice, and he suspected that Lieutenant Wickham was about to receive a lesson in the magnificence of Elizabeth Darcy.

Wrapping Georgiana in the cottage's thin blankets, Edward carefully lifted her into his arms. "Madam Wife." He teasingly nuzzled her cheek. "You are as light as a feather."

Georgiana snaked her arms about her husband's neck. "Let us see if you say the same thing when we reach the gig."

"I assure you that I will feel nothing but elation."

Elizabeth cleared her throat. "If everyone is prepared, then let us see to Georgiana's safety."

"There is still the matter of a horse for me." Wickham grudgingly rose to his feet when Darcy prodded him with the toe of his boot.

Elizabeth smiled deviously. "Then I suspect the horse upon which you arrived will have to do."

Wickham blustered, "Do you mean there has been a horse at my disposal all along, and you said nothing? "

"Did I not mention the possibility of a horse earlier? I suppose I should have made a point of it when you declared that you wished to depart before Mr. Darcy's arrival." With that, she led the way from the room.

Wickham stumbled after her. "How dare you?" he stormed. "You planned for your husband to have his revenge on me!"

Elizabeth spoke over her shoulder as she began her descent. "Actually, I wished for Georgiana to face her nightmares. My sister proved herself self-sufficient by first withstanding these terrible conditions and then by confronting a man who treated her poorly. Now, there will be no second-guessing on her part. The fact that my husband will earn a similar opportunity is an added benefit."

"Deceitful," Wickham grumbled as he watched her move gingerly on the loose footing.

"Exquisite," Darcy corrected from behind him. "I could have told you from the beginning that you were not equal to the lady. I am just thankful that Mrs. Darcy overlooks the fact that neither am I." Darcy gestured to where Elizabeth ran the last few feet to the bottom of the hill. "You are next, Cousin. Take your time. I will close up the cottage when you are at the bottom."

Edward started forward. "We will be waiting at the gig, Darcy."

Wickham asked with a wintry smile, "What will be my sentence, Darcy? What will be the end to this madness?"

"Personally, I would prefer to be rid of you forever; and with what you did to Mr. Joseph, I am inclined to turn you over to the local magistrate," Darcy said ruefully.

Accusingly, Wickham said, "You will demand your pound of flesh?"

Darcy motioned Wickham toward the hill. "Perhaps." He watched the man sidestep his way to the waiting horses. What had Elizabeth meant by Georgiana finally knowing freedom from Lieutenant Wickham's hold? And how would he ever achieve such independence? As much as he wanted to never lay eyes on George Wickham again, Darcy knew he would ultimately protect Elizabeth's sister from shame. He would devise another solution besides turning the man over to the authorities. Sighing with resignation, he doused the lantern and closed the cottage's door. As he followed the others, he did not want to consider the concessions he would make; he preferred to imagine Lieutenant Wickham on the receiving end of several forms of torture about which he had once read in a book on medieval warfare.

* * *

"There we are, Mrs. Fitzwilliam." Edward lifted Georgiana to the gig's seat. Elizabeth and Mr. Jacks watched Wickham's and Darcy's descents. "Still light as a feather." He tucked the blanket in closer around her for warmth. "I will ask Mrs. Jordan to make her most decadent meals to put some healthy weight on my wife's limbs." He kissed the tip of Georgiana's nose. "Thank God, you will lie once more in my embrace."

Georgiana ignored his intimate comment. She knew she should wait until they were alone, but she had kept her secret for too long. Speaking of it would make the child's existence real. "So, you think your wife too slender?" She traced Edward's lips with her fingertips.

He kissed her palm. "You are perfection in my eyes, but you have not had a proper meal for nearly a fortnight."

"Then I shall eat for two," she said enigmatically.

Edward's eyes remained locked on hers. "Now, that you have returned to my arms, I shan't be neglectful of my duties, including enjoying good English fare. I suspect we both could do with a bountiful repast."

Georgiana smiled brightly. "Even once you have sated your appetite, I shall still eat for two."

She watched as her words registered in his consciousness. Her husband's eyes grew in surprise. "Tell me it is true, Georgie. We are to be parents?"

"It is true," she said softly. "I hope the news pleases you."

"Pleases me?" he rasped. He crawled higher on the gig's frame to cover her mouth with his. "My God. You are unequaled. How have I ever lived without you?"

"You have not," she said matter-of-factly. "And neither have I lived without you. Only when we are together is life perfect."

"I love you, Mrs. Fitzwilliam," he whispered as his lips touched hers again.

Georgiana's face lit with happiness. "And I you."

"You will permit me to tell Darcy?" Edward said mischievously. "I will relish your brother's reaction."

"Trust me. I have no desire to speak those words to Fitzwilliam."

When the others approached, Edward edged away from her. "I will tell him when we return to Alpin. Then I will lock us in my chamber until your brother's rancor cools."

Georgiana giggled, "That may take several weeks."

Edward laughed easily. "I am willing to suffer your brother's acrimony if it calls for us to seek shelter together, Georgie."

She protested, "You think Fitzwilliam will truly not approve?"

Edward whispered, "The man will adore his nephew or niece, but he will not be happy with the image of how you became enceinte."

Georgiana blushed, and she fanned her face despite the cool evening. With another giggle, she said, "I suspect your words to hold some truth."

Elizabeth climbed in the carriage beside Georgiana. She squeezed closer to permit Jacks room to drive the gig. "Let us escort you home," she said as she slid her arm about Georgiana's shoulders. "We have been without you too long."

* * *

Edward could not eliminate the silly smile from his face. Georgiana was to give him a child. Someone who would love him and to whom he would devote his life. *When?* he wondered. As he traversed the moonlit road, he calculated the date when he might expect to know the pleasure of saying the words "my family." He and Georgiana had only known each other as husband and wife for less than a week prior to his deportment to the Continent. He counted forward from those days. As he estimated his child's delivery, he realized that his wife must be between four and five months. "If so," he said to himself, "then we should expect our child close to Christmastide." *His family.* The words ricocheted through his body.

A child for Christmas. Sharing the festive days with the birthday of our Lord. Only last Christmas, he had returned to Pemberley, broken-spirited, his desire to go on nearly at an end, but then Georgiana had given him hope. How long had he gone without hope? The question had lingered as he tried to make sense of what was happening between him and the girl whose scrapes and bruises he had once tended. With a secret waltz in a shadowy study and a kiss under the mistletoe, she had become his whole existence.

He looked up to see Alpin's gatehouse coming into view. He glanced to Georgiana, slumped against Elizabeth's shoulder. The day Fitzwilliam Darcy had brought Elizabeth Bennet into their lives, his cousin had given Georgiana a future. His wife had needed a confidante. He had told the earl so when his father had questioned Edward regarding Darcy's choice of a wife. Now, he looked on the woman's quiet strength with new admiration. Using pure female intuition, Elizabeth had found Georgiana when the rest of them had failed miserably, and the lady had rushed to protect his wife from Lieutenant Wickham. If he had not already held Elizabeth Darcy in the highest esteem, he certainly would now.

* * *

"Cannibalism!" Elizabeth gasped. "In Scotland? In the British Empire?" She and Darcy dressed for the evening. Upon their return to the manor house, Edward had ordered a bath for Georgiana and had sent for a surgeon to attend her. Darcy had placed Wickham in the root cellar with a footman standing guard. They would have the surgeon tend the man's injuries once he had seen to Georgiana's. Elizabeth did not inquire as to what her husband would do about his long-time enemy. She trusted Darcy to come to a just decision. "Cannibalism!" she repeated in disbelief.

"Not in the strictest sense of the word—not as Christopher Columbus meant during his explorations around Hispaniola," Darcy assured. "Lady Wotherspoon did not serve her captives to her guests. Yet, she did share the bodies with her brother Oliver Mc-Cullough, who is the local butcher. I am quite certain that people will be speaking of these atrocities for some time." He paused in his explanation to stare into the late evening fire in the hearth. After several minutes of quiet anguish, her husband said matter-of-factly, "Edward has seen too much devastation. My cousin efficiently dispensed with those protecting Lady Wotherspoon's secrets, but the look in his eyes spoke of how the insensibility of the situation affected him. Edward has been at war for too long. I am concerned for Georgiana's sake."

Elizabeth slid her arms about Darcy's waist from behind. "The Major General requires your sister's presence in his life. Without her, Edward would continue to suffer. Only with Georgiana will your cousin manage to leave the desolation behind."

"Do you truly believe so?" He turned in her embrace to wrap his arms about her.

Elizabeth rested her cheek on his chest. The steady beat of her husband's heart spoke of a man of principles. A man who placed his family above duty and wealth. "Implicitly. Edward will thrive because of Georgiana's love."

"As I do under your watch." He kissed the top of Elizabeth's head.

For long telling moments, they clung to one another. Finally, Elizabeth eased from his embrace. "We have responsibilities yet to see to tonight, Mr. Darcy. I wish to visit with our sleeping child and tell him of my love. Afterwards, I desperately wish to spend four and twenty hours wrapped in your arms." She lifted her chin for his kiss.

"Make it eight and forty," Darcy countered. He touched his lips to hers.

The tenderness of the moment tugged at Elizabeth's heart. Not a kiss of overwhelming passion, but one of infinite devotion. "Fitzwilliam," she murmured as his lips lingered above hers.

"Yes, my love," he said with a grin.

"I have something of which we must speak," she began softly. "But...there never seemed to be the right moment."

Darcy frowned. "The right moment for what?"

"For this." Elizabeth kissed each of Darcy's knuckles; then she turned his wrist to place a feathery kiss to his lifeline before she guided his hand down the length of her body to rest on her abdomen. During the exchange, her eyes remained locked on his. She had seen his curiosity when her lips met his clenched hand, had noted the tenderness when her mouth grazed his palm, had gloried in the desire as his fingertips skimmed her body, and had known the instant that the realization of her news registered in her husband's consciousness.

Gently, he touched the place where his child grew within her. "Lizzy?" he whispered.

"It is true." Elizabeth had expected him to lift her into his arms. She had not expected her strong, virile husband to sink to his knees before her. His hands cupped her buttocks, and he pulled her closer. Darcy kissed his wife where the child lay, and despite the folds of her gown, Elizabeth could feel the warmth of his mouth against her skin. Her body reacted as it always did to his touch. He pulled her closer still; yet, this time it was he who rested his cheek against her. Darcy closed his eyes in a silent prayer. Elizabeth stroked his head. "You are happy with the news?"

Still on his knees, Darcy leaned back to look up to her. "Elizabeth Bennet Darcy, you are by far the smartest decision I ever made. You have brought me, Georgiana, and Pemberley, the greatest happiness. I remain on my knees before you in reverence to your goodness."

Elizabeth dropped to her knees also. "I have never desired your reverence, Fitzwilliam. Treat me as you have always done: as a woman you protect, but also as a woman that you have chosen as your partner in life. There is nowhere else on earth I would prefer to be than in your arms."

"You are everything, Elizabeth." Darcy caressed her cheek. "My world."

"A world large enough for me, Bennet, and this little one?" she teased.

Darcy grinned as he assisted her to her feet. "A world large enough for you and all our children." He lifted her chin with his fingertips. "When?"

"Mid-February."

"A new year brings us a new beginning."

Chapter 22

"IN TRUTH, MR. DARCY, I know not how to proceed." They had had but four hours sleep before the magistrate had arrived on Alpin Hall's doorstep. Before retiring the previous evening, they had heard the full of Georgiana's tale, had permitted the surgeon to set her ankle with a proper cast, had tended to Lieutenant Wickham, and had decided among the three of them what version of the truth they would tell the authorities. They would speak of what could not be easily dismissed, given the word of an earl's son and that of a respected English couple as corroboration.

Elizabeth had spoken her reasons for Darcy to demonstrate kindness to Lieutenant Wickham, but she assured him that no matter his choice, she would support his decision. With the utter chaos surrounding them, Darcy had not given the disposition of his foe's future his full attention, but he had agreed to move Wickham to a smaller servant room, one without windows, for the man's recuperative period. He had placed a guard inside the room and another without. Lieutenant Wickham's part in the adventure would not be made known to the authorities until Darcy came to a decision regarding the man's fate.

"That is understandable," Darcy responded. "It is an unusual situation. Perhaps it might be advisable to seek the aid of someone with more experience in criminal cases." He had quickly assessed the magistrate's lack of sophistication. "Besides requiring justice for the victims, you will wish to curb idle curiosity. The circumstances will play out poorly in the newspapers, and the area will suffer."

Mr. LeEvans nodded his agreement. "It be a great shame for the shire. I will send to Edinburgh at once."

Edward cautioned, "Keep the investigation as private as possible. The fewer people who know of it, the better."

Darcy had taken note of how his cousin had permitted the deference that the Alpin staff and the magistrate had given Darcy. He suspected Edward felt uncomfortable in the role of a country gentleman. Give his cousin a group of men to lead, and the Major General excelled. The events of last evening had proven that. Edward had spent a generation away from the responsibilities of being an earl's son, and Darcy realized that if his cousin were to be successful in this new realm, he would need to begin immediately. Georgiana's future happiness depended on it. "As Mrs. Darcy and I will tarry at Alpin only long enough to assure my sister's recovery from her separate ordeal, I suggest you actively involve the Major General in your query. He has an extensive background in questioning enemy prisoners. I am certain his skills could be of use."

Mr. LeEvans looked with admiration upon Edward, and Darcy took great satisfaction in seeing his cousin sit a bit taller. "I be proud to have such a distinguished officer guiding us."

Edward sat forward. "What else did you learn from Normanna's men?"

"Not much from those who followed Lady Wotherspoon, but the woman's youngest son be more cooperative," the magistrate said with satisfaction. "Aulay MacBethan be tellin' us where his mother and uncle be dumpin' the bodies. Not likely we be findin' any remains, but I will examine the spot meself. The bog already has a reputation of sorts. Some say ghosts be seen walking about there. It makes sense if Aulay's tale be true."

"Why would this man tell you anything of his mother's activities?" Edward inquired.

The magistrate explained, "Aulay be a man in stature, but he has a simple mind. When he viewed his mother bein' restrained, he spoke to us of his fear." The magistrate ran his finger under his collar in a nervous gesture. "I beg yer pardon, Gentlemen, but I must ast ye what ye know of Lord Wotherspoon? Yer men say nothin' of Normanna's laird, but some of Lady Wotherspoon's men say Normanna's master knew of what happened below stairs."

"Wotherspoon was an associate during his stay in England," Darcy lied baldly. "We were of a bowing acquaintance, and when he heard that my cousin and I had come to Scotland to search for my sister, Lord Wotherspoon sent word, seeking a meeting." Darcy paused to sip his tea. He knew from business dealings to provide enough details to prove his point, but not so many as to sabotage the truth of what he offered. The pause gave the appearance of being relaxed.

"In her last benevolent act, Lady Wotherspoon had rescued a young woman, and Normanna's master wanted to assure himself that the lady in question was not my cousin's wife. Wotherspoon had developed a *tendre* for the lady, but she had suffered an injury and could not recall her past."

"Was the lady one of Lady Wotherspoon's captives?" The magistrate made notes on a folded piece of paper.

Edward took up the tale they had agreed upon. "Lord Wotherspoon offered nothing of the kind, and the young lady made no reference to the horrors Lady Wotherspoon executed. Luckily, Mr. Darcy recognized the young woman as Lady Margaret Caldwell, the Earl of Penworth's youngest daughter. Surely, you are familiar with the tale of Lady Margaret's assumed demise."

Whether or not Mr. LeEvans knew of the search for the English aristocrat's daughter, he assured them that he was quite familiar with the case. "A tragic event."

"Certainly, we were aggrieved to find that the woman Wother-spoon entertained in his home was not Mrs. Fitzwilliam, but we took pleasure in knowing that Lady Margaret had found a hero in Wotherspoon. With full knowledge of the lady's indiscretions, His Lordship offered Lady Margaret marriage. As they held a growing affection for each other, the lady accepted. Her reputation remains in shreds, and Wotherspoon's marriage had ended in tragedy. If they can find comfort in each other, I applaud their joining."

Edward added, "The couple prepared for a speedy marriage to bury Lady Margaret's ruination with an honorable proposal."

"Wotherspoon's family be knowin' its own infamy," LeEvans shared.

Darcy assured, "No one of whom I am familiar speaks of the legend that follows the MacBethan family name. In England, few make the connection. Perhaps, that is the reason that Wotherspoon remained on English soil for so long."

LeEvans agreed. "Likely true. Now, might you explain why you and the Major General returned to Normanna after yer visit with Wotherspoon and how ye discovered the prisoners?"

"The answer lies in Fate's hands. As we exited Wotherspoon's property, one of Alpin's footmen recognized the horse Munro MacBethan rode. It was the one upon which Mrs. Fitzwilliam had ridden on the day she went missing. Naturally, we detained the man to ascertain how the horse came into his possession."

LeEvans said, "I asked several of the regulars at the inn, and each be sayin' that Munro appeared to go with ye willingly."

Darcy recognized his cousin's irritation when Edward said dryly, "I am appreciative of the fact that we passed muster."

Darcy added, "We questioned MacBethan, but we also provided him with a meal and a place to sleep while we assured ourselves of the truth of the man's tale. As remarkable as it was, veracity rang through it."

"And so ye took it upon yerself to enter Normanna through the caves that Munro described?" LeEvans asked.

Darcy hid his amusement. Perhaps the magistrate possessed a better mind than he had first suspected. He would match wits with the man. "Being Englishmen, we assumed a Scot would not accept such a charge lightly, especially without proof. We searched for the proof that Munro MacBethan guaranteed existed. Besides the Alpin staff, who accompanied us, we recruited several from the area to assist us and add validity to our discovery. The Major General led the men because we did not wish anyone hurt unnecessarily."

"I see." LeEvans put his paper and pencil away. To Edward, he said, "We certainly be pleased yer wife be found, Sir." The magistrate picked up his teacup and finished off the brew. "Ye be fortunate that Mrs. Darcy followed her vision and located her sister."

Darcy said good-naturedly, "I am certain that Mrs. Darcy will remind me of her success when we have a domestic disagreement."

LeEvans stood to take his leave. "They always do. Women plague us with their foolish ideas, and we men be at their mercies."

"I am the exception to your rule, LeEvans; Mrs. Darcy is the one person whose opinion I trust above those of all others," Darcy countered. "I imagine the Major General holds similar sentiments regarding Mrs. Fitzwilliam."

"Absolutely, Darcy." Edward joined them at the door. He shook the magistrate's hand. "You will keep us informed of the developments in the case."

LeEvans nodded and disappeared into Weir's care. As Edward closed the door, he said, "There is something of which we should speak. I wanted to discuss it with you upon our return last evening, but I felt my duty belonged with Georgiana."

"Certainly." Darcy gestured to the chairs they had recently vacated.

When they were settled, Edward spoke with evident happiness. "Georgiana has informed me that we are to expect our first child in December. You are to be an uncle, Darcy."

Darcy's heart lurched. "Will Georgiana's ordeal affect her delivery?" He immediately imagined his sister's difficulty in delivering the child. The horror of it slammed into his soul.

Edward shook his head in the negative. "We cannot know for certain, but the surgeon did not believe it so. She suffered no internal injuries, and other than losing a few pounds, she appears in good health. The physician suggested that she rest for at least a week before she attempts anything too strenuous. Her ankle injury will force Georgiana to take life at a slower pace, and I will welcome the excuse to tend her." Edward shifted his weight nervously. "I had hoped that by now you could offer your sincere congratulations, Cousin."

Darcy smiled to temper his remarks. "I celebrate anything that brings both you and Georgiana happiness."

Edward's irritation showed, "Yet?"

"Yet, I worry for my sister's health. Childbirth is a dangerous exercise under the best of circumstances."

"And?"

"And I possess concerns regarding your transition to civilian life. I have heard tales of Waterloo and its destruction. And from your own lips, I am aware of the devastation you have witnessed first hand during the past eleven years. The future will not be easy for you."

"Do you think I have not previously considered all you say?" Edward asked tersely.

Darcy responded evenly, "On the contrary. You likely had these same thoughts the moment that you decided to ask Georgiana to accept your proposal. However, as her brother and your cousin, I would consider not speaking of my qualms a dereliction of my duties."

Edward stared at a spot somewhere over Darcy's left shoulder, but Darcy refused to turn his head. The grim line of Edward's mouth relaxed. Finally, Edward said, "It will be a trial, but please believe me when I say that only Georgiana can see me through this. During that crazy snowstorm at Pemberley last Christmas, I was presented with the most exquisite creature I had ever seen, and suddenly I felt as if God were saying it was time for me to come home. To leave behind man's greed, and to know the love of a wife and a family. Georgiana will know no pain at my hand. She is my world, Darcy."

"Then I give you my hearty congratulations. It is time that you had a bit of happiness all your own." He leaned forward and extended his hand to his cousin. "A December baby will make Christmastide even more joyful."

Edward smiled easily. "Maybe a daughter as a match with your Bennet," he suggested.

"Or a son for the daughter I will welcome in February," Darcy rejoined.

"Mrs. Darcy also?" Edward's smile widened. "Are we not the most fortunate men in England?"

Darcy stood. "Speaking of the ladies, we should join them in Georgiana's chambers. I am certain their curiosities are steeped with questions regarding LeEvans's visit."

"What will you do about Wickham?" Edward said as they climbed the main stairs.

Darcy's brow knitted. "I cannot permit Lieutenant Wickham to return to Carlisle without some form of punishment. He intended to see me dead. Yet, I will not bring shame to the Bennets. It is a conundrum for which I possess no solution."

"Then we will keep the man under lock and key until you see your way clear to deal with him decisively, but also logically."

* * *

Three days later, the Major General and Elizabeth watched as Darcy pushed Georgiana in a tree swing. "My sister's color has returned to her cheeks," Elizabeth observed.

"Georgiana appears to be recovering well." Edward's smile widened. "My wife is quite resilient. A fact for which I am most grateful. Otherwise, I might have lost her." He paused to watch Darcy send Georgiana higher. "Does she not have the most infectious laugh?" he asked wistfully.

"A laugh none of us have heard often enough of late; but with your return, Georgiana's heart grows lighter." Elizabeth shaded her eyes by pulling her bonnet's brim lower. "You and Mrs. Fitzwilliam will remain at Alpin for a few weeks?"

"I want Georgiana on her way to good health before we return to Derbyshire. My wife has expressed a desire to open Yadkin Hall before winter arrives. She plans to see the child born in our home."

Elizabeth reached for his hand; they interlaced their fingers. The comfortable familiarity they had always shared wrapped them in sunlight. "Permit Georgiana to give you what you most need. It has been too many years since you have had roots. Plant yours where Mr. Darcy's sister may nourish them."

Edward's hand tightened over hers, and Elizabeth could feel her cousin's close scrutiny. "*Home* is a word I have had little practice saying, but one I am anxious to claim as part of my vocabulary." They sat in companionable silence as they watched Darcy spin the rope into a tight knot and then release it to Georgiana's loud shrieks of delight. "They have always been so close," he observed.

"I suppose it was necessary under the circumstances: my husband and his sister have found a special bond. Sometimes I feel quite misplaced at Pemberley," Elizabeth confessed.

Edward chuckled. "I understand. It is almost as if Darcy and Georgiana were twins. People say that twins feel each other's pain. That is the way of them. Darcy knew of Georgiana's impending elopement before she had executed the deed."

"Thank God," Elizabeth murmured.

"Yes. Thank our Lord that Darcy arrived in time to foil Wickham's plans," he said hoarsely. "The thought of Georgiana under Lieutenant Wickham's influence still brings my anger. If Darcy's good sense had not ruled the day, I would likely have disposed of the man and spent my life on the Continent rather than to see her suffer such degradations."

Elizabeth asked tentatively, "Do you have suggestions for dispensing with Lieutenant Wickham?"

"None that does not involve hot tar and feathers," he grumbled. "The man lost any sentiment I might offer when he chose to undress before my wife." A dangerous lethality laced his tone.

"I am surprised that Georgiana told you of how I discovered Lieutenant Wickham in a state of dishabille. I would never have confessed it to Mr. Darcy. I fear my husband might have called the lieutenant out. Mr. Darcy's anger at finding Lieutenant Wickham in the reiver's cottage with Georgiana was frightening enough."

Edward released her hand and refilled Elizabeth's lemonade. "What would you have your husband do with Lieutenant Wickham if you could choose?"

Elizabeth mouth tightened in a serious line. "Actually, Mrs. Fitzwilliam and I have landed on an idea. We believe Mr. Darcy should send Lieutenant Wickham to America—possibly under Mr. Buckley's supervision. Considering the American's manipulation of Caroline Bingley, we suspect that Lieutenant Wickham and Mr. Buckley might do well together. The gentlemen appear to possess like qualities."

Edward leaned closer to assure their privacy. "I find the prospect quite compelling. Have you approached Darcy with the idea?"

"Not yet. Georgiana and I assumed that Mr. Darcy would believe that I sought to protect Lydia; also, I promised Fitzwilliam that I would leave the decision to him. Despite my concern for my youngest sister's situation, it is truly my husband's name that I wish to preserve. I do not want Fitzwilliam involved with Lieutenant Wickham's future any more than is necessary."

"What if the proposition came from me? We must do something soon. Lieutenant Wickham's wounds heal quickly. Darcy cannot keep the man prisoner forever."

Elizabeth sipped her cool drink. "Georgiana suggested that part of the agreement for permitting Lieutenant Wickham to leave England be that the man cannot return for a decade. My sister reasons that if the lieutenant stays away from English shores for an extended period that the man will no longer feel a dependence on the Darcys' goodwill, and he will have no desire to return."

"America would offer continual opportunities for Lieutenant Wickham to exercise his skills. Perhaps he can aid Mr. Buckley's bid for political office," he said ironically. "However, I am a bit disturbed that my wife has once again retreated from the hold Wickham poses over her. It sounds as if Georgiana seeks to send the lieutenant as far from her sight as possible."

Elizabeth shook her head in denial. "You did not witness Georgiana's confrontation with Lieutenant Wickham. My sister has placed that odious episode behind her. Instead, I am persuaded that she fears her brother will do something that will haunt Fitzwilliam forever. To kill a man in cold blood would darken my husband's soul. For her own escape, Georgiana has you to thank for her ability to face her fears. Your love has given Mr. Darcy's sister a strength she did not know she had."

"I would attribute much of my wife's newfound resolve to your tender guidance," Edward said softly.

"I would like to think we each had a hand in guiding Georgiana into womanhood; you, Fitzwilliam, and me." Silence returned as they watched Darcy tease Georgiana's neck with a shaft of wild grass. Finally, Elizabeth spoke her thoughts aloud. "You should trust Mr. Darcy's sister with your confidences."

"I fear I do not understand." His voice remained casual, but Elizabeth noted how Edward's shoulder muscles flexed with caution.

"The war. The years away from your family." Elizabeth touched Edward's arm. "Even in the short time of our acquaintance, you have changed, Edward. The American front affected you more than you care to admit." She paused. "I have heard men speak of the horrors of Waterloo. Even the mightiest of men would know regret. A man cannot see such devastation without it affecting his outlook—his hopes and dreams."

Edward's hands fisted, and his posture slumped. "Look at her. My wife is the most beautiful creature I have ever beheld. And look at me. I am three and thirty, and I am far from handsome. What do I have to give Georgiana besides the protection of my name? I have known nothing but war."

"You might give her your respect." Elizabeth stifled his objection with a flick of her wrist. "Not that type of respect. Men always think we women wish to be protected from all the evils of the world. In reality, we want to be respected for our intelligence, our nurturing natures, and our empathy. Give Georgiana the part of you that you withhold from everyone. Share with your wife what you have kept secret."

"She would hate me," Edward said hoarsely.

"Georgiana could never hate you," Elizabeth said adamantly. "Some of what you relate shall shock my sister. Some shall distress her, but none of it will make Georgiana turn from you. Mr. Darcy's sister desires to be treated as a woman rather than as a schoolgirl. Trust Georgiana with what haunts you. It will heal your soul and give your wife a different role in your life: You will not only be Georgiana's guardian, but also, she will be yours. You will be her partner in a life that you shall forge together."

Edward swallowed hard. His Adam's apple worked intensely to clear his throat. "I will consider it." He paused. "What makes you so intuitive, Mrs. Darcy?"

Elizabeth relaxed. The major general had not taken offense at her intrusion into his private life. Her eyes sparkled with mischief. "There are things I do not know."

Edward's shoulders shook with suppressed laughter. "Such as? It seems my cousin's wife is capable of holding her own with some of the Matlock family's most stubborn males."

She smiled genuinely. "For example, I do not know why the Jackses refer to my husband as 'Himself.'"

Edward chortled. "That is easy to resolve. When Darcy was ten or so, we made a trip to Alpin. During those days of summer pleasure, the Jackses continually remarked on my cousin's being a near-replica of his respected father, to which Darcy vehemently declared that he did not wish to be George Darcy. 'I wish to be myself,' he demanded. From that point forward, Mr. and Mrs. Jacks referred to Darcy as *Himself*. At first, my cousin thought it a disparaging remark, but Rowland convinced Darcy that such a moniker was only given in Scotland from respect."

Elizabeth attempted to hide her amusement when she said, "Of course it is a signal of respect."

"Do not fool yourself, Mrs. Darcy," Edward good-naturedly corrected. "Nowadays, I am certain the Jackses mean it in a respectful manner, but at the time, Mr. Jacks likely felt Darcy's attitude a bit stinging."

Elizabeth fought hard to keep a straight face. "I cannot imagine anyone thinking Mr. Darcy to bear false pride."

"It is difficult to consider that any person, say an intelligent female such as yourself, could be that misguided," he taunted. "Now, if you will excuse me," he set his glass on a nearby table, "it is time I win one of my wife's playful smiles."

Elizabeth watched the major general stride across the lawn. He and Darcy congenially tugged at the ropes supporting Georgiana's swing. For a moment, she recognized the two boys they must have been all those years ago. Saw how far they had come and how much they had remained the same. "They are the best of men," she whispered.

* * *

Darcy relinquished the swing's ropes to his cousin. Despite not having acknowledged it to his wife, he had come to a like mind with Elizabeth regarding Georgiana's marriage. Edward was the perfect choice for his sister. His only concern now lay in his cousin's extensive military background. Could Edward actually abandon the blood and the gore and become a country gentleman? Darcy glanced over his shoulder to where Edward whispered something personal in Georgiana's ear.

"They shall be fine, Fitzwilliam," Elizabeth said softly. "Although his scars run deeper than hers, the Major General knows he must respect Georgiana as his wife. It shall not be uncomplicated, but he will see his way clear to including her in his recovery."

A knot formed in Darcy's stomach. He took the seat his cousin had recently vacated. "I am not certain I want Georgiana exposed to what the Major General has known on the battlefield," he said defensively.

A smile tugged at the corners of Elizabeth's lips. "In case you have not noticed, Mr. Darcy, such decisions are no longer in your realm of care for Georgiana. Your sister is a woman of age. A wife. And very soon a mother."

"That does not mean I will ever abdicate my concerns to another," he said testily.

Elizabeth heaved a sigh of exasperation. "No one, least of all Edward or Georgiana, expects you to simply step aside, Fitzwilliam, but you must permit your sister and your cousin to find their own way. For the Major General to reclaim his life, he must speak of the time since accepting his commission in the King's service. It is very much a part of the man Edward has become. The man your sister loves. Trust them to see their way through this together. I am certain that if Georgiana needs us—needs you—that she shall not hesitate to seek your counsel. You have been her universe for too long for your sister to desert you completely."

Darcy's eyes remained on the playful interactions of the newlyweds. "You believe this is so?" he asked flatly.

Elizabeth sounded firm. "You must permit Georgiana her freedom, Mr. Darcy."

Her eyes flashed in a way that made Darcy feel the comfortable heat of desire. "I will do my best, Mrs. Darcy, but I can promise nothing beyond that."

Mr. Jacks cleared his throat. "Post, Mr. Darcy."

"Thank you, Mr. Jacks." Darcy accepted the folded over pages before examining the direction and seal. It did not bear the familiar scrawl of Charles Bingley as Darcy had expected.

"From whom does it come?" Elizabeth asked curiously.

Darcy's mouth twisted in amusement. "Spare me a moment, my dear, and I will satisfy your inquisitiveness." He reached for a knife from the serving tray to break the wax seal. He did not look at her, but he suggestively said, "By the way, you are deliciously appealing when you squirm in querying interest."

"Mr. Darcy, you are incorrigible," she protested, but she squeezed his arm affectionately.

Darcy winked at her before turning his attention to the letter. "It is from Lord Wotherspoon," he said as he read the first few lines of the letter.

"Did the gentleman and Lady Margaret escape Scotland's shores?" Edward asked as he placed Georgiana gently in one of the empty chaises. "There, my love," he said softly as he caressed her cheek.

Georgiana sighed deeply. "I am unaccustomed to being a lady of leisure," she said shyly.

"Yet, you will follow the physician's orders to please both your husband and your brother," Edward instructed.

Georgiana blushed at having everyone's notice. "I shall permit my husband his way in this matter," she said definitively.

Edward kissed the tip of her nose before he sat beside Darcy. "So tell us. What news of Wotherspoon?"

"MacBethan and Lady Margaret married near East Linton. They managed to secure passage to Crete. Wotherspoon writes that they will continue on to Italy from there."

"I sincerely hope they may find some measure of happiness together. Both Lord Wotherspoon and Lady Margaret have known enough devastation in their lives," Edward observed. Darcy was well aware of this turn in Edward's opinion of the Scottish earl. Only days earlier, his cousin had thought to skewer the man for Wotherspoon's lack of action.

Darcy continued to recapitulate the earl's letter. "Wotherspoon has sent a statement to the local magistrate in which he presented evidence against his mother and several of the lady's henchmen in behalf of his wife. He has made arrangements for Aulay to live with their brother Islav. He dismissed the Normanna staff and closed the estate until his return, which appears to grieve him. For a man who desired none of his title, the Earl speaks eloquently of his responsibility to the neighborhood."

"Perhaps we could secure the services of some of Wotherspoon's staff for Alpin Hall. I am certain my father is unaware of the estate's need for repairs," Edward noted.

Elizabeth added, "It is uncharacteristic of Matlock to neglect a family property, even one at a great distance."

"I had meant to speak to my uncle upon my return to Derbyshire," Darcy explained. "I suspect the steward is either incompetent or cagey."

"What say we offer the position to Weir's cousin Linden? We simply require someone to oversee the annual harvest and the upkeep of the manor house," Edward proposed.

Darcy smiled easily. "As you need the practice, Cousin, I will leave those details in your very capable hands."

Edward stretched his long muscular legs before him. "I suppose if Mrs. Fitzwilliam and I are to open Yadkin Hall for the holidays that I might also examine the Alpin books. That is, of course, if my beautiful wife has no objection to my spending some time daily on righting the obvious wrongs circulating about my father's estate."

"Uncle Matlock would expect as much," Georgiana agreed.

Darcy handed across a folded sheet to Georgiana. "This one is for you."

"For me?" Georgiana looked surprised. "Why would there be a message for me among Lord Wotherspoon's words?"

Elizabeth chortled, "None of us shall know, Dearest, until you read it."

Georgiana tentatively opened the single sheet. She read aloud,

Mrs. Fitzwilliam,

I pray that your family has found you, and you have returned safely to your husband's waiting arms. This note shall serve two purposes: In case the above wish has not been fulfilled, it will explain to your family where I left you: After a horrendous fall, you came upon the reiver's cottage in which I had taken refuge. Surprisingly, your horse had followed your path across the moor. I observed your approach from the cottage's safety. Realizing you offered me no danger, I brought you under my care. I took your horse to find assistance for your injuries, but, unfortunately, Lady Wotherspoon's man intercepted me before I could complete my task.

"It sounds as if the lady's memory has returned," Edward noted. "Thank God Mrs. Darcy found Georgiana when she did. Otherwise, it might have been too late." A noticeable shiver shook the Major General's shoulders.

Georgiana appeared bewildered. "I had thought the woman who initially came to my assistance was part of my imagination." She looked closely at Elizabeth. "Remember, I spoke to you of the one who told me that each of you searched for me? Could it have been Lady Margaret, after all?"

Elizabeth tilted her head thoughtfully. "I would imagine parts of what you recall come from your interaction with Lady Margaret, but some of what you have relayed to me would not be of the lady's understanding."

"What do you suggest, Mrs. Darcy?" Edward's voice sounded a bit strained.

"Only that Georgiana had a special angel looking over her shoulder during this incident," Elizabeth said confidently.

Edward frowned notably. "I do not believe in guardian angels, Mrs. Darcy."

Elizabeth shrugged. "We each must choose our own way to reason what we cannot explain. You shall not approve, Edward; yet, I cannot conceive how a man with your military history could walk through purgatory's jaws again and again without serious injury. I would like to think that it was God's will. That he saved you for Georgiana and for your family."

Darcy interrupted, "What was Lady Margaret's second purpose for writing?"

His sister returned to the note.

Second, I beg your pardon, Mrs. Fitzwilliam, for having failed you miserably. You deserved better than my feeble efforts.

Lady Wotherspoon

"Quite an unusual note," Elizabeth said softly.

Darcy observed, "I imagine Lady Wotherspoon is still struggling with the realization of her past. It must all be quite disconcerting."

"I suppose," Georgiana observed. "Perhaps if we hear from the MacBethans again, I shall write to her directly to discover what is real." She refolded the page and slipped it into her pocket.

As the others spoke of the unusual connection that had developed between Lord Wotherspoon and the former Lady Margaret Caldwell, Georgiana reflected on the coincidences that had brought her to Lady Margaret's notice: Their lives held several parallels. From what her husband had told her, Georgiana knew of the similarities in their physical appearances, but it was equally odd that their paths had crossed at a secluded reiver's cottage in the Scottish Uplands. When Georgiana considered the result of Lady Margaret's desperate race to Scotland's border, a shudder racked her shoulders. Such a fate could have been hers. She could certainly have succumbed to George Wickham's persuasion—she had thought herself in love with the man. Mr. Wickham was rawly handsome, and he amiably twisted her reasoning powers, leaving her a quivering mess of feminine insensibility. Had Lady Margaret encountered equally mesmerizing qualities in Stephen Vincent? And Georgiana held no doubt that if she had carried through with her elopement, both Darcy and Edward would have given chase. The realization that she had narrowly escaped Lady Margaret's shame rode heavily on Georgiana's heart.

Darcy finished MacBethan's news. "Wotherspoon says they will write to Viscount Penworth once they have reached Italy. They will explain to Penworth the truth of how they have come to join their families. He hopes that I will speak to the Viscount personally if Penworth has any question as to how the events unfolded."

"And will you?" Edward inquired. "I mean will you defend Wotherspoon?"

"I previously promised Lady Margaret to speak discreetly to the Viscountess Penworth; therefore, I have no qualms in addressing the honor that Wotherspoon offered Lady Margaret after her dis-astrous elopement, and I will encourage Penworth to downplay MacBethan's connection to the infamous Bean family and instead to speak of Wotherspoon's English education and training, as well as the man's ancestral title, which his daughter's children will inherit."

Georgiana pondered aloud, "The perils of a tragic love tale play hard on the truth."

Chapter 23

ELIZABETH STOOD AND straightened the seams of her gown. "I believe I shall see if my son is awake. It has been several hours since I have known the pleasure of inhaling Bennet's scent."

Darcy chuckled. "And you find this soothing somehow, Mrs. Darcy?"

"It is the scent of Heaven," she said dreamily.

Edward observed, "From what I recall of baby cloths, the odor is far from heavenly."

Elizabeth shaded her eyes with the back of her hand. She inhaled deeply. "Do me the gift of a favor, Major General. Inhale the sweetness of this late summer day. Smell the sunshine and the clouds and the faint hint of heather. Implant the memory solidly in your mind. Then in December, compare it to the lovely fragrance surrounding the babe you hold cradled in your arms. Even with a dirty cloth, I imagine you shall find the baby's scent superior to anything on this Earth. So, it is, therefore, 'heavenly.'"

Darcy followed his wife to his feet. "I believe the lady has outwitted you, Cousin."

Edward smiled easily. "England could have employed Mrs. Darcy in the diplomatic services." He inclined his head. "I bow to the lady's authority."

Darcy snaked his arm about Elizabeth's waist. "Although I consider my wife exceptional, I would not wish to share Elizabeth's attentions with the world. England will have to embrace other reasonable philosophers."

Elizabeth reached for her husband's hand. "Come, Mr. Darcy. For such praise, you deserve a bit of Heaven."

* * *

"I am not helpless," Georgiana protested as Edward carried her toward the bed.

He nuzzled her neck. "On the battlefield, I imagined moments such as these. Do not rob me of my dream."

His wife tightened her hold about his neck. With a deep sigh of contentment, Georgiana rested her cheek against his chest. "I have thought of nothing else for years," she confessed.

Reverently, Edward lowered her to the bed. Earlier, he had removed the pins from her hair. Now, he spread the white-gold locks across the pillow. "You are so exquisitely beautiful," he rasped. "And I am blessed among men."

Georgiana caressed his cheek. "I love you," she whispered.

"And I you." Edward stretched out beside her. "My heart forgot how to beat. When I was away from you, part of me ceased to exist." He leaned across her and kissed Georgiana tenderly. "I came to you a man blind to love, but I lie beside you with the knowledge that together we are a powerful force. One special moment can change a man's destiny."

Georgiana's eyes misted with tears. "All my previous fears make this moment with you more precious. We have our own tale to write." She kissed him with the passion known only to those new to the wedding bed. "Claim me as yours, Edward," she whispered softly as she pulled his head toward her. "We have waited too long to begin our life together."

* * *

"There you are," Edward said as he entered the library.

Darcy placed his newspaper to the side. "I apologize, Cousin. I was unaware that you wished to speak to me. I assumed you would be spending your time becoming reacquainted with my sister."

"I assure you, I have no plans to ignore my husbandly duties."

Darcy's mouth twisted into a tight line. "If you have no objections, I will not dwell on the image of my sister meeting her wifely obligations."

Edward good-naturedly slapped Darcy on the shoulder as he passed. "As you wish, Cousin." He took the seat opposite Darcy. "Have you and Mrs. Darcy considered when you will depart for Newton Stewart?"

"Do you wish to be rid of us?" Darcy teased.

Edward shrugged his shoulders. "I am always pleased to spend my time with both you and Mrs. Darcy, but I would offer a prevarication if I said I did not want private time with Mrs. Fitzwilliam. Yet, that was not my intention when I spoke of your removal to Mr. Bingley's summer retreat. You have business to conduct, and I am certain you wish to assure yourself of Mr. Joseph's continued recovery."

Darcy nodded his agreement. "The Ayrshire magistrate has forwarded word that the former Lady Wotherspoon and her brother are being brought before a public inquest in Edinburgh. The gentleman assuming responsibility for the case, a Mr. Tolliver, has asked that we be present for the proceedings. I had thought to join the Bingleys the following day."

Now, it was Edward's turn to indicate his agreement with a simple tilt of his head. "Then we should come to an accord on how to dispose of Lieutenant Wickham. According to Mrs. Darcy, Wickham's leave ends this upcoming Monday. After that day, the man is in violation of his military orders."

"Then let us keep Lieutenant Wickham away from his duty post long enough that the British army locks him away forever," Darcy grumbled. "As long as I do not have to see him again, I will be satisfied."

Edward expelled a wicked chuckle. "It is a tempting scenario, but there are holes in your logic. First, the lieutenant is likely to implicate our families in his delay to return to his post. We may balk at announcing to the world that Lieutenant Wickham is a distant relation, but I would place a wager that Wickham holds no such qualms. He would risk his own reputation to sully yours." Edward paused to permit Darcy's protest, but when his cousin remained tight-lipped, the major general continued. "In addition, military protocol has gone the way of smuggled brandy. Sometimes procedures are followed, and other times, no sense of order remains. It is likely with the discharge of so many war veterans that those in charge may overlook Wickham's absence."

Darcy's frown lines met. "I suppose you have a point," he said testily.

"My *point* is that we need a creative solution. Our ladies have placed their lovely heads together and have landed on an idea that might prove advantageous. They suggest that we send the Wickhams to America; perhaps even place Lieutenant Wickham under Mr. Buckley's tutelage."

Darcy sat forward in concern. "Why would Mrs. Darcy or my sister not discuss this idea with me? Am I that unreasonable?"

A rumble of laughter escaped Edward's lips. He recognized Darcy's irrationality on the topic of Lieutenant Wickham's contin-ued duplicity. "I suspect our womenfolk thought that Lieutenant Wickham had offered you the final offense. Yet, neither lady wishes to see you consumed by your hatred. Both Mrs. Darcy and Geor-giana recognize how honorably you have acted."

"If I agree to this scheme, how might it serve the Darcys?" Darcy asked grudgingly.

"Besides removing Lieutenant Wickham from our immediate notice, it would seem a ready source of information for Mr. Bingley regarding his sister. I understand that Mr. Bingley has known frustration in seeing to his sister's future, and I imagine that Mrs. Bingley would readily correspond with her youngest sister." Edward allowed the first of his points to take root.

Darcy sank back into the chair's cushions. "I am intrigued," he said softly.

"If Mrs. Bingley is aware of the Wickhams' activities, so shall you be through your joint connections to the Bingleys." Edward noted how Darcy interlaced his fingers across his waistcoat's front. It was a favorite gesture when his cousin was deep in thought. "It is also less expensive to live in America, and not so easy for Mrs. Bingley or Mrs. Darcy to send their pin moneys to salvage the Wickhams' latest upheaval. It would force the Wickhams to live within their means."

Darcy growled, "I doubt that is possible." He shifted his weight forward again. "How do we assure that Lieutenant Wickham takes passage to America?"

"I have been thinking on Mrs. Darcy's suggestion. Why not send someone to escort the Wickhams?"

"Did you have someone in mind?"

"How about Munro MacBethan? The man requires a stake to purchase the land in Crieff. He would not permit Wickham to escape. For the right price, MacBethan is likely to deliver the lieutenant bound in a cargo net."

Darcy observed wryly, "That is a pleasant image."

"I propose we provide MacBethan his purse and give the Wickhams the equivalent of two years' pay. After that, they would receive no financial assistance from either of us. I have promised Georgiana that as part of this agreement Lieutenant Wickham must remain absent from British soil for a decade. If word of his return were to reach our ears before the ten years expire, we would file attempted murder charges against him. He would be a wanted criminal. If you agree with this plan, I will make the necessary arrangements for Lieutenant Wickham's dismissal from his military assignment."

Darcy sat perfectly still. A gamut of emotions crossed his face. "It is a solid plan," he said flatly. "And better than any I have devised. I suppose you should see to Lieutenant Wickham's release. I will contact MacBethan regarding the journey."

"Permit me to *reason* with the lieutenant. Once I have his agreement, I will write his superiors."

Darcy sighed heavily. "I will be pleased to wash my hands of the man. Lieutenant Wickham has haunted my peace of mind for too many years."

* * *

"Elizabeth?" Darcy asked eagerly as he stood mesmerized by his son's antics. "Have you seen what Bennet has accomplished?"

His wife joined him in his sitting room. "What would that be?" Her voice betrayed her amusement.

Darcy turned his head to glare at her. "I suppose Bennet's turning from his knees to his back is not a recent achievement?"

Although she attempted a sympathetic countenance, Elizabeth's smile widened. "If it is of any consequence, your son has only mastered the rotation in the last week."

Darcy threw up his hands in frustration. "That settles it! I refuse to be away from my family ever again. Bennet grows too quickly as it is. Each day brings a new triumph. I will not miss the special moments when my children first experience the joy of exploring their worlds. It is the last time, Elizabeth. Hear me well. If I am to travel from Pemberley for any extended period, so will you and the children. You will learn to adapt to journeying. I will have it no other way. When I depart for Drouot House, you and Bennet will accompany me. We will tarry with the Bingleys until my business is complete."

Elizabeth gently massaged his temple as she said, "Wherever you are, Fitzwilliam, that is the place our children and I shall call home. You are the strength upon which we depend."

With just the touch of her fingers, his frustration dissipated. She had that effect on him. "Then you will stay at Newton Stewart while I see to the railway proposal?"

"Of course, Bennet and I shall remain with you." She caught his hand. "Come. Let us enjoy our son while he is still young enough to require us in his life. Soon enough, he will be off to school and to new adventures."

"Do not remind me," Darcy grumbled. "How will I ever part with him? I still grieve with the knowledge that I have lost Georgiana forever."

Elizabeth slid her arms about his waist. "Oh, my darling." She rested her head upon his chest. "We in this family are blessed by your loyalty. And you must know that even if our sister and, eventually, our children do spread their wings, they shall always fly home to Pemberley. The shades of Pemberley tie each of us to the land and to you."

* * *

"Then you agree to this venture?" Darcy had cornered Munro Mac-Bethan outside the Edinburgh courtroom where the initial hearing would occur for Lady Wotherspoon and several of her former employees.

Munro carefully watched those who entered the governmental hall. Only his hand displayed the agitation he felt. MacBethan repeatedly worked a colorful glass marble through his fingers. "It be best for me to disappear from this part of Scotland for a spell," he remarked. "Islav's welcome in Crieff will disintegrate after I give me testimony today. Even Lord Carmichael, Lilias Birrel's husband, intends no longer to call me friend."

"I grieve that you have lost the goodwill of Lord Wotherspoon's siblings. I am certain His Lordship will welcome you to Normanna upon his return," Darcy observed.

Munro shifted his weight nervously. "It may be many years before me cousin knows Scottish soil."

"That is true," Darcy reasoned. "Then this offer comes at a fortuitous time. When next you arrive on Scotland's shores, you will possess a small fortune to begin anew."

"For that, I be grateful. Perhaps this Mr. Buckley will have a position for a man who be not afeared of hard work."

Darcy thought of Beauford Buckley's deviousness. "Although I have the highest respect for your ability to prove useful to Mr. Buckley, I would prefer to see you increase your fortune with people of your ilk. There is a large Scottish settlement in the mountains north of Charleston. You might find happiness among those who have ties to your homeland."

"I will consider it."

They remained in companionable silence until Edward motioned them to join him. "You will come to Alpin Hall on Saturday. The Major General should have everything in place by then."

"Aye, Mr. Darcy. I be there." He gestured to the open door. "We best we getting' this over."

* * *

"May I approach, Mrs. Darcy?" Elizabeth played with Bennet on the Alpin front lawn. Georgiana had taken to her bed for a restorative sleep, and Elizabeth had decided to enjoy the mild weather with her son.

She debated on accepting Lieutenant Wickham's company. Her doing so would not please Darcy, but she wanted to know if the man would accept the "punishment" that she and Darcy's sister had designed for him. If so, Elizabeth would write her father to prepare Mrs. Bennet and Lydia for the upcoming journey. She disliked the idea of separating her mother from her youngest sister, but Elizabeth could conceive of no other solution. Lieutenant Wickham must be sent away from Darcy's notice, and although sending Lydia away would create chaos in her father's household, it would be far better than having Lydia in a state of perpetual widowhood.

"It is acceptable." She nodded to the Alpin footmen who flanked the lieutenant, and they withdrew to a respectful distance. Under the major general's order the footmen permitted Lieutenant Wickham two daily half hour sessions out of doors. Yesterday, they had walked the lieutenant toward a distant loch, but with Darcy's and the major general's departure for Edinburgh, the Alpin staff had chosen to escort their prisoner toward a nearby orchard.

Elizabeth lifted the boy to her and fell into step with her sister's husband. Instead of the orchard, they turned toward the lower gardens. They walked in silence for several minutes before Elizabeth said, "I should not spare you even one second of my time, Sir. You played at God with my husband's life. I feel nothing but contempt for your presence in my family."

They paused beside a high wall, and Elizabeth shifted the child to her other hip. Surprisingly, Lieutenant Wickham reached for the boy. "Would you permit me to carry young Master Darcy for you?"

Elizabeth stepped back and stared suspiciously at the man. "I think it best that I decline your offer, Lieutenant Wickham. Mr. Darcy is quite particular regarding the interactions of his heir. I doubt he would approve of your association with his son."

Wickham blinked away her insult. In a cool, matter-of-fact voice, he said, "I shan't taint Pemberley's anointed son with my touch, Mrs. Darcy."

Elizabeth could not keep the scorn from her tone. "Nevertheless, I insist that Bennet remain with me."

His eyes narrowed, but Wickham gave her a curt nod. He gestured to a nearby arbor. "In that case, perhaps we should sit."

Elizabeth permitted him to assist her to a seat on a wooden bench. She adjusted her grip on the child and began to rock the boy in the way of mothers. Finally, she said, "Have you considered the Major General's proposal?"

Wickham said bitterly, "Do I possess another choice?"

"Of course, you have always had choices, Lieutenant. When you and Jonathan Lowell caroused your way through the Derbyshire countryside, it was of your own choosing. When you refused the Kymptom living, the choice belonged to you. And when you persuaded my youngest sister to flee Brighton as your companion, it was an act of your design."

"You sound very much like your husband," Wickham accused. "I recall a woman of more discerning tastes."

Elizabeth fought the urge to recoil. "I am ashamed of how easily I once misinterpreted my dear husband's goodness. When Mr. Darcy's actions proved honorable multiple times, I could no longer hide behind a veil of innocence. From the very beginning, I was unwilling to admit the painful truth: the man consumed my every thought." She forced a smile to her lips. "Why do you suppose that

I found him so disagreeable? Mr. Darcy's opinions mattered, and I feared to be found wanting."

Wickham reached out to brush one of Bennet's dark curls from the boy's cheek. "Darcy will never be able to deny this child," he said softly. "The boy is the image of his illustrious father."

"A fact that pleases both of Bennet's parents," Elizabeth said with a note of satisfaction. She shooed a pesky bee from a nearby flower.

Wickham continued to stare at the boy's countenance. "I have often wondered how it would be to have a family of my own." His lips curved into a wistful smile.

"It is not too late," Elizabeth encouraged. "Use this opportunity to start a new life—one for you and Lydia."

He shrugged noncommittally. "Have you ever..." he began and then looked away.

"Say it," Elizabeth demanded. "Whatever rests heavy on your shoulders must be whisked away if you are ever to be free of this continual struggle with Mr. Darcy."

Slowly, he returned his gaze to the resting child. Eventually, he said, "Have you ever considered how it might be if I had not sought my fortune with Miss King?"

Elizabeth chose her words carefully. She would not fuel the jealousies between Lieutenant Wickham and Mr. Darcy. "There was a time I might have welcomed your addresses, but those early points of interest had cooled long before your defection for Miss King's dowry."

"Then you truly held me with no regard?" he asked with a note of irritation in his tone.

Elizabeth's ire rose, as well. "You inquired of my feelings, but you refuse to accept my response. Your denial speaks of a man who will not accept that I could care more for the one person he considers his inferior."

"I consider Darcy my inferior?" he asked incredulously. "Should not that fault lie at your husband's feet?"

Elizabeth motioned one of the waiting footmen forward. "Would you return my son to his nurse?" She handed Bennet into the man's awkward grasp. "Have Mr. Jacks send Weir to replace you in your duties."

"Yes, Ma'am." After she caressed Bennet's dark curls, the man rushed away to do her bidding. Then she turned her full attention on her sister's husband. "Mr. Darcy has a multitude of faults, but a lack of compassion is not one of them." Although a head shorter than Lieutenant Wickham, she now seemed to loom over him. Elizabeth jabbed Wickham's shoulder with her index finger, punctuating each of her points. "The Darcy family welcomed you and provided for your future, but your greed overcame reason. If Mr. Darcy views you as his inferior, it is because you have placed yourself in that position."

"I object..." he said with a smirk, but Elizabeth's hands fisted at her waist.

"Did I indicate that I was finished?" she asked brusquely.

Wickham's frown lines met. "Not of which I am aware, but a woman..."

"Has a mind," she interrupted. "You forget yourself, Lieutenant Wickham. I am Elizabeth Darcy, not my sister Lydia. I am permitted my thoughts. My opinions are respected." She sighed heavily. "I would like to think that you truly held me in affection, but as your apparent partiality subsided, I could see it and write of it without material pain. My heart had been but slightly touched, and my vanity was satisfied with believing that I could have been your only choice had fortune permitted it. I was never much in love; for had I really experienced that pure and elevating passion, I should have detested your name, and wished you all manner of evil. But my feelings were not only cordial toward you, they were even impartial toward Miss King. I continue to think her a good sort of girl. I cannot say that I regret my comparative insignificance. Importance may sometimes be purchased too dearly. Kitty and Lydia took your defection much more to heart than did I. At the time, they were young in the ways of the world and were not yet open to the mortifying conviction that handsome young men must have something to live on, as well as do the plain ones."

Wickham countered, "Lydia is still ignorant in the world's ways."

"My sister is but eighteen. I am four years Lydia's senior; you married a child barely sixteen and then complained of her lack of maturity. Instead of seeing Mrs. Wickham's youthful exuberance as an anchor about your neck, *gently* teach Lydia what you require of her." Elizabeth resumed her seat beside the man. "In America, you will be introduced to Mr. Buckley, a man with an eye on the American marketplace. Learn from the man and carve out your own destiny."

"And what of Lydia?" he asked dejectedly.

Elizabeth sympathetically instructed, "As you apprentice with Mr. Buckley, permit Lydia to renew her acquaintance with Mrs. Buckley. You will recall Mr. Bingley's sister Caroline from your time in Meryton. Miss Bingley became Mrs. Buckley last December." Thinking of the debacle of the woman's sorted elopement, Elizabeth smiled with some satisfaction. She should not have taken such great pleasure in the former Miss Bingley's shame, but such remained her one great sin. She could forgive Lieutenant Wickham his many perfidious acts, but Elizabeth could never quite muster a welcoming thought for Caroline Buckley. "Mrs. Buckley possesses a fine figure and is rather handsome, and she comes from a very respectable family in the North of England. The lady received her education in one of the first private seminaries in London. Mrs.

Buckley could exercise a great influence over Lydia. You could have the Society wife you have always desired," she said pointedly.

"Yet, Lydia is not you." Wickham reached for Elizabeth's hand, and she snatched it away.

She was on her feet and pacing before him on the graveled path. "Why is it that men always want what they cannot have?" She growled in frustration. "Admittedly, while you were in Meryton, we developed a camaraderie, but did you not hear me say not ten minutes prior that my attraction to Mr. Darcy overruled my good sense through much of that time? Fortunately, I recognized the draw between Mr. Darcy and myself before I committed myself to another. What misery would I know to marry elsewhere while loving Fitzwilliam? I am persuaded that the obstinacy in your speech lies in your need to best Mr. Darcy. As Elizabeth Darcy, I am no longer the prize you seek."

"Perhaps," Wickham said softly. "Or perhaps not. I shall never convince you otherwise, so my tongue will offer no further protest. I pray, Mrs. Darcy, that you have not designed a punishment that will bring your sister more sorrow."

Elizabeth could not hide her anguish. "Promise me that you shall accept Lydia's childlike qualities and treat her with a placid hand."

"I will practice the utmost patience with my wife," he said contritely. "Mayhap Mrs. Wickham and I will one day return to England richer than Croesus."

Without allowing herself time for consideration, Elizabeth said, "If a fortune would permit you to know happiness, I shall pray daily for such an outcome."

* * *

"And it is your contention, Mr. Darcy, that Lord Wotherspoon was unaware of his mother's actions?"

Darcy had not expected the courts to question him regarding Domhnall MacBethan's state of mind. "As Lord Wotherspoon was in England throughout the time these crimes occurred, I do not see how he would have had knowledge of Lady Wotherspoon's actions. Nor, from what I know of the man, would I believe that he would have approved of these heinous crimes. As my cousin and I discovered, Wotherspoon had made efforts to nurse the prisoners to health and to offer restitution for Dolina MacBethan's misdeeds."

The court official asked, "Why, in your opinion, would Lord Wotherspoon leave behind a woman that he initially protected?"

Darcy settled his eyes on the defiant figure of Dolina MacBethan. She sat proud and disdainful, daring anyone to judge her— although judge her the courts would. "When confronted by her eldest son, Lady Wotherspoon admitted that she had delivered a fatal dose of poison that killed Lord Wotherspoon's former wife and his heir. Domhnall MacBethan expressed the fear that his mother would attempt a similar assault on the current Lady Wotherspoon. I assume from his actions and words that he no longer felt an allegiance to a woman who would betray his heart. As the newly minted Lady Wotherspoon is with child, the Earl removed his wife from his mother's influence."

"The child not be a MacBethan," Dolina MacBethan declared. "I saw an end to Coll MacBethan's line. "

"I be a MacBethan," a man that Darcy did not recognize said emphatically.

"As am I," Munro said flatly. "Ye tainted the name, but ye did not destroy the line. It survived Sawney Bean's madness, and it will survive McCullough's influence."

Lady Wotherspoon shot to her feet as the judge tried to restore order. "Coll died slowly as I took me great delight in describing the shame I practiced on the family name," she shouted above the melee.

"Be quiet!" The man Darcy recognized as the lady's brother, Oliver McCullough, warned. The village butcher's voice had silenced the turmoil. The man faced charges of complicity in the court action.

Dolina turned on the man. "Do not shush me, Oliver," she hissed. "Ye know what Coll did to me. How he thought himself superior to anyone Lars McCullough sired."

"It not be that way, gel," McCullough murmured.

The woman extended her bound hands in supplication. "How be it, then?" she pleaded.

Before anyone could respond, a youth in dark clothing rose to his feet. "You killed my father." The soft coldness of the young man's words stilled the courtroom.

Then Darcy saw the gun in the youth's hand. "No!" he shouted, but he was too late. The room filled with the pungent odor of gunpowder as Dolina MacBethan stood tall for one beat of the heart before she crumbled onto the courtroom floor.

Darcy saw the major general wrestle the gun from the youth as onlookers scattered toward the exit. He sprang from where he had given his statement to reach the MacBethan matron. Turning the woman over gently, he knew immediately that Dolina MacBethan had breathed her last. As he cradled her in his arms, Oliver McCullough broke away from his jailers and fought his way to the lady's side.

"Speak to me, gel," he pleaded as he pressed his large hand to the gaping hole in the woman's chest. "Ye kinnae leave me, Dolina."

"She is gone, McCullough," Darcy said softly.

McCullough's eyes remained on the bloodied gown. Fresh blood seeped between his fingers as the Scot continued his useless ministration. "How will the sun rise tomorrow?" he asked the silent room. "From the first moment I laid eyes upon her, she has owned me heart."

The way the man grieved aloud spoke of something more intimate than what Darcy knew of Dolina MacBethan's relationship with her brother. Unable to control his curiosity, Darcy asked, "What was your true connection to Lady Wotherspoon?"

McCullough's eyes finally met his. "I suppose there be no reason for others not to know." After a long pause, the Scot added, "Dolina be me daughter. I be but fourteen when Lars McCullough's whore invited me into her bed. My stepfather never knew the truth." Tears misted the man's eyes, and he turned his head to hide his shame. "Lars claimed her, but Dolina be mine. Me daughter. Me sister. Me..."

"Your what?" Darcy encouraged.

The Scot glanced to where Islav MacBethan held his younger brother in a tight grip. Dolina's favorite son fought to be by his mother's side. "Mam!" he cried repeatedly. McCullough shook his head in disapproval, and Aulay ceased his struggle.

Darcy carefully watched the exchange before he asked, "Your lover?"

"She be everything. Beautiful. Magnificently defiant. Dolina refused to speak the more cultured tongue of her husband's family because she known it wud irritate Coll. At first, she be tryin' to be what the man wanted, but MacBethan tired of her before Domhnall be born. Then Coll, he drives me away. Although her husband placed many a woman in her stead, he wud not be denied 'is husbandly rights. Yet, Dolina be havin' the final revenge. She saw Coll to ' is deathbed. Me gel cleverly ground glass into the smallest fragments and added them to her husband's meals—to 'is sauces, to 'is sausage, to 'is meat pies. Slowly, she cut out 'is heart from the inside—one small nick at a time."

Darcy lowered the woman to the floor. One of the jailers had joined them to retrieve McCullough, and the court attendant opened a large handkerchief to cover Lady Wotherspoon's wound. Darcy handed his own linen to McCullough for the man's bloody hands.

"He hit her, you see," McCullough continued. "Coll MacBethan often used his hand to discipline Dolina for her boldness, but he cudnae break her. In fact, me gel broke 'im. She destroyed the one thing Coll placed above all others: she exacerbated the scars on 'is family name. It be Dolina who delivered the final blow. She finds a means to bring scandal to Domhnall's front door. She loved her eldest son, but she hated him, both at the same time. Domhnall had escaped to England, ye see. Lars be placin' her in Coll's bed because he be wantin' the connection to the neighborhood's largest family. Lars wud have sold his own mother for the right price, and Domhnall be the result of Dolina's lying with Coll MacBethan. Her eldest be proof that she cud never escape Coll MacBethan's influence in this world." He glanced at the quiet figure lying at his feet. "Perhaps she be knowin' peace in the next."

Darcy doubted that Dolina MacBethan's soul would ever know peace—more likely the hell fires of which the Fundamentalist ministers preached. "How could a woman hate so deeply as to destroy her own children to spite a man?" Darcy asked incredulously.

McCullough shrugged his shoulders in defeat. "When Dolina decided on a path, she rarely veered. Aulay comes by the tendency honestly."

"The youngest MacBethan will never call you *father*, but he is yours, nonetheless." Darcy's voice spoke of his uncertainty.

McCullough said softly, "The boy must never know. Promise me that no one will tell Aulay the truth."

Darcy glanced at the court official who remained by his side. The man nodded his agreement. "Only those who must know the truth will be apprised," Darcy assured. "Now, you should go with this gentleman." He gestured toward the bailiff. McCullough stood slowly and offered his hands in surrender. The court attendant led the butcher away.

Darcy looked up to see Edward advising the attorneys regarding the youth who had killed Dolina MacBethan. Exhausted by the exertion, he staggered to his feet. This journey had taken its toll on his sense of right and wrong. "Pray tell me Edinburgh will not prosecute the youth," he said with great effort.

Edward nodded to where the jailers escorted the young man through the door leading to the cells. "At least, they have listened to my plea in the youth's behalf. We will see to his reform. I have warranted a position at Alpin for the him and his mother if the authorities agree to release him into Mr. Jacks's care. Losing their father has plunged the family into penury. The government has sent his brothers and sisters to two separate homes."

"I despise this system of punishing those who are already suffering with the worst that society can bring them. How is it justice to sentence a man whose family is starving to transportation when he steals a loaf of bread for his children? There must be a better way."

Edward shook his head in disbelief. "Will this madness upon which we have stumbled never end? Too much grief. Too many deaths. No resolution."

"Despite your desire to create a memorable beginning for your joining, I fear the details of this case will forever cloud our thoughts of Galloway," Darcy observed.

"If I am to assume the duties of the Countess's familial inheritance, I would imagine there will be multiple instances when the outside world intrudes on my marital bliss. Our seeing through the twists and turns of this most unfortunate excursion into the Scottish Uplands will be a good test of my wife's mettle," Edward rejoined.

Darcy said grimly, "Yet, life should never presume precedence over the time you and my sister share. Promise me that Georgiana and your children will always take prominence."

There was a quiet dignity about his cousin. Darcy had always recognized Edward Fitzwilliam's integrity, but this convoluted race across southern Scotland to save Georgiana had proved the man's real worth. His cousin would never compromise his beliefs.

"I promise to cherish Georgiana above all others. Your sister and the child she carries remain my priority."

"Then you will do well, Cousin. Everything else will either fall in line or fall to the wayside." The sound of heavy footfalls drew their attention. "Let us finish this. I am suddenly in great need of holding my wife and child. A man can never know when God will call him to his heavenly home. Therefore, he must cling to each moment of earthly joy."

"I, personally, have tempted Fate for the last time." Edward averted his face, and Darcy suspected his cousin fought his personal grief. "Give me the contented life of the landed gentry."

Epilogue

HE AND ELIZABETH, along with the Reverend Mr. and Mrs. Winkler, waited on Pemberley's main steps for Georgiana's traveling coach to appear. It had been seven weeks since he had held his sister in his arms and bade her farewell at Alpin Hall. On that day, his wife had played light with him because he had embraced Georgiana three times before finally settling in his coach to travel to Newton Stewart.

"From a man many consider too staunch to bend," Elizabeth had teased, "that was an exceptional display of your emotions, Mr. Darcy."

He had ignored the taunt because he had observed how she had fought to keep her tears in check. She disliked leaving Georgiana behind as much as he.

They had returned to Pemberley a month prior, after he and Mr. Joseph had concluded their business in Scotland. With Bingley's multiple connections in trade, they had quickly secured the railway rights and had fostered negotiations with businesses to supply the building of the line and to maintain it afterwards. Parnell had objected to Darcy's adamant refusal to seek a monopoly. "Competitive markets will increase the line's growth potential," he had insisted when Parnell had made an unexpected call on Pemberley.

Matthew Joseph had recovered from his wounds, and he and Mary had found a house on Newcastle's outskirts where Mrs. Joseph could enjoy her garden. Their most recent letter had indicated that a law apprentice had taken an interest in Ruth Joseph. The young man called on the girl several times per week, and Mary had entertained Elizabeth with delightful missives describing the couple's awkwardness.

Bingley and Jane had returned to Marwood Manor a week prior to this time. Mrs. Bennet's retreat to Hertfordshire had presaged a safe return to the Bingleys' home estate. Elizabeth's father had escorted his wife to Longbourn. The good lady had grieved greatly at the loss of her youngest child to the "wilds of that dratful country." Mr. Bennet had assured Elizabeth of her mother's resiliency, but privately he had informed Darcy that he was uncertain when his wife might recover. "I pray Mr. Grange does right by Mary and gives Mrs. Bennet a new source of pride by presenting my wife with a grandchild upon whom she can dote. As that does not appear to be part of the couple's foreseeable plans, I shall know no quiet." Upon receiving the letter, Darcy had immediately issued an invitation to Elizabeth's parents to rejoin them at Christmastide.

They had heard nothing from Munro MacBethan, but Edward had personally escorted Mr. Wickham to Stranraer, where Mac-Bethan had met them with Mrs. Wickham in tow. The Major General had booked passage on a ferry to Northern Ireland. From there, the trio would depart for America. Edward had written of Mrs. Wickham's subdued nature. "The lady has, at last, assumed the mantle of a demure genteel lady. I have, likewise, lectured Mr. Wickham regarding the opportunity presented him, but the man remains inscrutable," Edward had written.

"Munro MacBethan was an appropriate choice to shepherd the couple. I discovered from the former lieutenant that he had encountered MacBethan previously and possessed a healthy respect for the Scot's lethal intensity. As for MacBethan, he presented his typical granite resolve, but he betrayed a bit of anxiety by constantly palming a colorful glass disc. I found the contrast quite amusing."

If Darcy had known of Mr. Wickham's connection to Mac-Bethan, he might have had second thoughts about hiring the Scot for the journey, but he trusted Edward's evaluation of the situation. Darcy had other things on his mind regarding his former foe. Something odd had occurred in Scotland. Elizabeth had yet to share the events with him, but on more than one occasion, he had overheard his wife offering God the following prayer: "Dear Lord, please permit Mr. Wickham and Lydia to return safely to the bosom of their family, and allow them to arrive in England richer than Croesus."

"She is here," Kitty Winkler announced as Georgiana's coach rolled into view.

Elizabeth murmured, "Thank God," and Darcy silently seconded her sentiment.

And then the coach came to a halt not twenty feet before them. Jasper scrambled to lower the steps before the Major General unfolded his large form and reached into the coach for his wife's hand.

Darcy's heart lurched with the familiarity of the moment, but he had not expected the woman heavily laden with child who emerged from the coach's darkness. She possessed the countenance of an angel—the same countenance that had welcomed his return to Pemberley over the years—but there was a difference, something in her eyes that proclaimed that she no longer belonged to him. His sister's heart had changed allegiance; she treasured the man who competently lifted her to the ground more than she did her elder brother. He was now second in her heart, just as she had become second to Elizabeth. It was a sobering realization for the Master of Pemberley.

Next to the moment he had first laid eyes on Elizabeth Bennet, it was the most poignant moment of his life. From the instant he had held Georgiana in his awkward twelve-year-old arms, he had cherished the swaddled infant as Pemberley's most impressive treasure.

He had taught her his values: independence, freedom of choice, honesty, and integrity. He had given Georgiana the gifts of music and art and the finest education that Pemberley's wealth could afford. He had offered his sister his unconditional love and the confidence to be her own person. Yet, even with all those things, he...

"You have not lost her," Elizabeth interrupted his thoughts. "Georgiana will never disappear from your life. Our sister esteems you above all others," she whispered softly.

"How can I be certain?" He had not questioned his wife's ability to read his thoughts.

"Watch," she said with amusement.

As soon as the Major General placed Georgiana's feet on solid ground, she turned her head to him. Immediately, she rushed into his waiting arms. Darcy lifted her to him. Despite her increased girth, his sister still fit perfectly into his embrace. He inhaled instinctively to savor her essence—to fill his senses with her.

"I have missed you terribly," she murmured as he kissed Georgiana's temple.

"As I have you," Darcy whispered. "More than words may express."

Tears misted her eyes, so he permitted his sister to escape his embrace to rush into Elizabeth's welcoming one. He thanked God daily for bringing Elizabeth Bennet into his and Georgiana's lives. If his mother truly had served as the Darcy family's guardian angel, he was certain that Lady Anne Darcy had had a hand in leading his steps to the Bennet's door. He smiled genuinely as the two women in his life spoke over one another—each communicating as well with a nod, a tut, or a groan of delight.

"Welcome, Cousin." Darcy extended his hand to Edward. "I pray your journey was uneventful." If he must lose Georgiana to someone, Darcy was thankful it was to Edward Fitzwilliam.

"Your sister has fidgeted in her seat for the last hour—so anxious to return to her home," Edward said as he gave Darcy a back-slapping male hug.

"Mrs. Darcy has worn a groove in the hardwood of her favorite drawing room. She has glanced out the window every few minutes," Darcy declared.

"Were you not looking over the lady's shoulder?" Edward asked good-naturedly.

"I admit to no such anxiousness," Darcy responded.

From where she patiently waited for her turn to greet Georgiana, Kitty declared, "Well, I wholeheartedly confess to the act. We have counted the days until Georgiana's return."

Edward bowed to the waiting couple. "I am pleased to find you among our welcoming party, Mrs. Winkler. It has been too long since we have been in your company. I hope married life brings you as much happiness as it has me." He brought Kitty's hand to his lips for an air kiss.

Elizabeth, with her arm encircling Georgiana's waist, joined their group. "You have not heard, Edward. Mr. Winkler is to be knighted for his efforts in educating the Lambton children. He and Kitty shall travel to St. James next week. That Kitty is to receive the title of Lady Winkler has bolstered my mother's spirits after Mrs. Wickham's departure."

"I am gratified by your success, Mr. Winkler, and for your wife's newest distinction. The honor is well earned." Darcy noted that Edward winked at Kitty as if they shared a delicious secret, and his wife's sister blushed prettily. Darcy had not thought that his cousin shared any intimacies with Elizabeth's sister, but something had certainly passed between them.

Kitty and Georgiana exchanged exuberant welcoming embraces. "You are a pleasant sight," Georgiana said through happy tears. "I am dreadfully sorry to have missed your wedding."

"It is of little significance," Kitty assured. "What matters is that you are once more at Pemberley."

Darcy placed Georgiana on his arm and turned toward the still-open doorway. "Yes. What is important is that my sister will rest under Pemberley's roof this evening, and that wherever she may place her roots, the road from there will lead to Pemberley."

Historical Notes

NAME HISTORY

In *The Disappearance of Georgiana Darcy*, I have taken the liberty of giving Fitzwilliam Darcy a possible connection to the real Fitz William family. However, a fictional character cannot be *actually* related to that renowned family, and I do not purport that Jane Austen named her character after the Hall clan, or those who found their roots at Greatford Hall in Lincolnshire, the direct descendants of Wentworth, Earl of Fitz William.

By 1340, the Halls had migrated first to Cheshire and then northward to Scotland. Having accepted the invitation of Earl David of Huntingdon (later King David II of Scotland), they settled in Berwickshire, specifically the lands of Glenryg in the barony of Lesmahagow.

MOUNT TAMBORA

Mount Tambora is an active stratovolcano in the Indonesian archipelago, which erupted in April 1815. With an estimated volume of 160 cubic kilometers, Tambora's 1815 eruption is one of the largest in history. Besides the number of deaths created by the heavy ash fallout in the neighboring islands, the Tambora eruption led to the phenomenon referred to as the "volcanic winter." In North America and Europe, 1816 became the "Year Without a Summer." Widespread agricultural famine and the loss of livestock met many of those living in the Northern Hemisphere. This was especially devastating to those in Europe and

North America, who were recovering from the demoralizing effects of both the Napoleonic War and the War of 1812.

KILMARNOCK AND TROON RAILWAY

To carry coal between the Duke's pits near Kilmarnock and the Troon Harbour on the Ayrshire coast, the Duke of Portland opened the KTR in July 1812. Authorized by an Act of Parliament in 1808, it was the only Scottish line for fourteen years and was the first to use a steam locomotive, as well as to have the first railway viaduct, which still stands. It also was the first to have fare-paying customers. It is now part of the Glasgow South Western Line.

SCOTTISH CASTLES

Those familiar with Scotland's most picturesque castles may recognize some of the features I have given to Normanna Hall as being a mixture of Terringzean Castle in East Ayrshire (circa 1696 and built by the Campbells of Loudoun), Auchinleck Castle in Monikie, Angus, Scotland (on record in 1501), and Doune Castle in Doune, Stirling, Scotland (circa 1400 and built by Robert Stewart, Duke of Albany), and a typical English estate. The MacBethan family had roots in both countries so the mix was necessary.

THE MURDER HOLE

A round pool near Loch Neldricken, a loch in Galloway to the southeast of Merrick, took on legendary qualities as "The Murder Hole" in Samuel Rutherford Crockett's *The Raiders*. The novel is a romantic, loosely historical adventure story released in the 1890s. The legend has it that weary travelers and strangers to the Merrick Moor were caught, murdered, and dumped into the "Murder Hole." Strangely, reeds reportedly grow around the hole's perimeter but none grow within it. It is also rumored that even in the coldest winters, the water's center never freezes. For excellent photos of this desolate area, visit Walkhighlands and read the article "The Old Grey Man, A Murder Hole, and the Merrick" (www.walkhighlands.co.uk).

Sawney Bean

Alexander Sawney Bean was reportedly the head of a cannibalistic family residing along Scotland's Ayrshire/Galloway coast during the 14th Century. According to the legend, Sawney was born in a small East Lothian village, approximately ten miles from Edinburgh. Unable to hold a job, he soon left home and took up with a woman who thought nothing of using devious methods to gain what she wanted.

With no legal means of supporting themselves, the Beans chose to live in a sea cave in Galloway. They maintained their family by robbing and murdering travelers and locals foolish enough to be caught on the roads at night.

Living incestuously, the Bean family grew to a total of six and forty. Over a twenty-five-year period, one thousand people are said to have lost their lives to the family. The Beans would cast the unwanted limbs of their victims in the sea to be washed up on the local beaches.

Unfortunately, the authorities of the time had few crime investigation skills available to them. In a time when people still believed in witches and vampires, many innocent people stood accused of Sawney's crimes and lost their lives. As missing travelers were traced to the inns in which they had taken shelter, local innkeepers were often charged with the crimes. Needless to say, travelers began to shun the area.

As it grew in number, the Bean family attacked larger groups of travelers. Their cave was designed to hide their presence in the area, so they were able to attack and then retreat to the cave, which went almost a mile into the cliffs. In addition, the tide filled the opening so people never suspected the cave as a possible hideout.

The Beans were discovered when they attacked a couple returning from a local fayre. The man was able to plough his way through the band that attacked him, but the female cannibals had managed to pull his wife from her horse. According to the legend, the Beans ripped out the woman's entrails and feasted on her along the road. When other revelers from the fayre appeared, the Beans retreated to their cave home. The revelers escorted the distraught husband to the authorities in Glasgow. Eventually, King James IV personally took charge of the case. With four hundred men, and bloodhounds in tow, the hunt for the culprits began in earnest.

From the bloody scene, the bloodhounds caught the scent and soon hit on the Beans' location. Entering the cave, the searchers found dried human parts being cured like other meats, pickled limbs in barrels, and piles of valuables stolen over the years. The Beans were brought to Edinburgh in chains. They were incarcerated in the Tollbooth and taken the next day to Leith. Because of the severity of their crimes, the Beans were barbarically executed. The crowds cut off the men's hands and feet and left the criminals to bleed to death. The Bean women were burned at the stake.

Many "experts" believe the story to be an eighteenth century fabrication, one found in the popular chapbooks and broadsheets of the time. In 1843, John Nicholson included the legend in lurid details in his *Historical and Traditional Tales Connected with the South of Scotland*. However, several local psychics claim the ghosts of Sawney Bean's family haunt the area. The legend has become part of the Tourism and Heritage Trail. The cave is on the coast at Bennane Head between Lendalfoot and Ballantrae. There is a reconstruction of the cave at the Edinburgh Dungeon on Market Street, near the Waverly Bridge.

The "meat" of Sawney's tale inspired Wes Craven's "The Hills Have Eyes." In 1994, a British film group attempted to finance a film based on the legend, but their efforts fell through. Snakefinger's "The Ballad of Sawney Bean" was a part of Ralph Records "Potatoes" collection. For more fabulous tales of the macabre, visit Mysterious Britain and Ireland (www.mysterious britain.co.uk).

Other Ulysses Press Books

Darcy's Passions: Pride and Prejudice Retold Through His Eyes
Regina Jeffers, $14.95
This novel captures the style and humor of Jane Austen's novel while turning the entire story on its head. Darcy's duty to his family and estate demand he choose a woman of high social standing. But after rejecting Elizabeth as being unworthy, he soon discovers he's in love with her. When she rejects his marriage proposal, he must search his soul and transform himself into the man she can love and respect.

Christmas at Pemberley: A Pride and Prejudice Christmas Sequel
Regina Jeffers, $14.95
It's Christmastime at Pemberley and the Darcys and Bennets have gathered to celebrate. Bitter feuds, old jealousies, and intimate secrets surface. En route home from a business trip, Darcy and Elizabeth are delayed by a blizzard and take shelter in an inn. As the Darcys comfort a young woman through a difficult labor, they're reminded of the love, family spirit, and generosity that lie at the heart of Christmas.

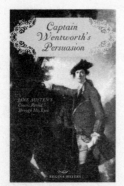

Captain Wentworth's Persuasion: Jane Austen's Classic Retold Through His Eyes
Regina Jeffers, $14.95
Insightful and dramatic, this novel re-creates the original style, themes, and sardonic humor of Jane Austen's novel while turning the entire tale on its head in a most engaging fashion. Readers hear Captain Wentworth's side of this tangled story in the revelation of his thoughts and emotions.

The Phantom of Pemberley: A Pride and Prejudice Murder Mystery

Regina Jeffers, $14.95

Happily married, Darcy and Elizabeth can't imagine anything interrupting their bliss-filled days. Then an intense snowstorm strands a group of travelers at Pemberley, and mysterious deaths begin to plague the manor. Everyone seems convinced that it is the work of a phantom who is haunting the estate. But Darcy and Elizabeth believe that someone is trying to murder them. Unraveling the mystery of the murderer's identity forces the newlyweds to trust each other's strengths and work together.

Vampire Darcy's Desire: A Pride and Prejudice Adaptation

Regina Jeffers, $14.95

Tormented by a 200-year-old curse and his fate as a half-human/half-vampire dhampir, Mr. Darcy vows to live forever alone rather than inflict the horrors of life as a vampire on an innocent wife. But when he comes to Netherfield Park, he meets the captivating Elizabeth Bennet. As a man, Darcy yearns for Elizabeth, but as a vampire, he is also driven to possess her. Uncontrollably drawn to each other, they are forced to confront a "pride and prejudice" never before imagined—while wrestling with the seductive power of forbidden love.

About the Author

REGINA JEFFERS, an English teacher for thirty-nine years, considers herself a Jane Austen enthusiast. She is the author of several novels, including *Christmas at Pemberley*, *The Phantom of Pemberley*, *Darcy's Passsions*, *Darcy's Temptation*, and *Captain Wentworth's Persuasion*. A Time Warner Star Teacher and Martha Holden Jennings Scholar, Jeffers often serves as a consultant in language arts and media literacy. Currently living outside Charlotte, North Carolina, she spends her time with her writing.